SCORPION

Praise for *MAYFLY*

A SheReads.com Best YA Book of 2018

"*Mayfly* is *The Hunger Games* meets *Lord of the Flies*, yet it is so much more. It's smart, with an exploration of how myths and legends are created from clues of the past. Exploring these references with teens is a fascinating way to examine our own legends, myths, and understanding of history. This is a stunning example of how we can use stories to teach teens about culture, society, history, and more, in ways that spark creativity and imagination." —SheReads.com

"Lives are short and brutal in this postapocalyptic adventure . . . There's an almost mythological quality to this tale, as the resourceful protagonists maneuver through a barely recognizable landscape . . . debut novelist Sweat does an admirable job of maintaining the tense atmosphere and underlying desperation." —*Publishers Weekly*

"Jemma, her best friend Lady, Apple, and Exile Pico seek out the secret to living longer than seventeen—but is longer life in this world even worth it? . . . Accessible for a wide range of teen readers." —*Booklist*

SCORPION

JEFF SWEAT

FEIWEL AND FRIENDS
NEW YORK

A Feiwel and Friends Book
An imprint of Macmillan Publishing Group, LLC.
120 Broadway, New York, NY 10271

Our books may be purchased in bulk for promotional, educational, or business
use. Please contact your local bookseller or the Macmillan Corporate and
Premium Sales Department at (800) 221-7945 ext. 5442 or by email at
MacmillanSpecialMarkets@macmillan.com.

Library of Congress Control Number: 2019948797
ISBN 978-1-250-13922-1 (hardcover) / ISBN 978-1-250-13923-8 (ebook)

Book design by Kathleen Breitenfeld
Feiwel and Friends logo designed by Filomena Tuosto

First edition, 2020
1 3 5 7 9 10 8 6 4 2
fiercereads.com

TO SUNNY: MY FIRST AND BEST READER, MY FIRST AND
BEST EVERYTHING.

THINGS FALL APART; THE CENTRE CANNOT HOLD;
MERE ANARCHY IS LOOSED UPON THE WORLD

—WILLIAM BUTLER YEATS

THE PEOPLE OF ELL AYE

THE ANGELENOS

THE DOMINANT PEOPLE OF ELL AYE, THEY ARE A LARGELY PEACEFUL FEMALE-LED SOCIETY WHO LIVE PRIMARILY IN THE HILLS. THEY ARE MADE OF FOUR INTERRELATED PEOPLES:

• THE HOLY WOOD

THE OLDEST ANGELENO SETTLEMENT, ON THE SHORES OF THE LAKE OF THE HOLY WOOD AND THE OLD HOLY WOOD SIGN.

• THE MALIBU

THE FARTHEST WEST OF THE ANGELENOS, WHO LIVE IN THE MOUNTAINS NEXT TO THE OCEAN OF MALIBU.

• THE DOWNTOWN

THE DOWNTOWN GUARD THE FORMER TOWERS OF ELL AYE AS SACRED GROUND AND LIVE IN A GIANT STADIUM IN A RAVINE.

• THE SAN FERNANDOS

THE SAN FERNANDOS LIVE IN THE GREAT VALLEY NORTH OF THE HOLY WOOD AND FREQUENTLY COMPETE WITH THE HOLY WOOD FOR SCARCE RESOURCES.

THE LAST LIFERS

A FERAL BAND OF CHILDREN WHO'VE GONE MAD IN ANTICIPATION
OF THEIR EARLY DEATHS; THEY LIVE THROUGHOUT ELL AYE IN
VIOLENCE AND CHAOS BECAUSE THEY FEAR NO CONSEQUENCES.

THE PALOS (THE BITERS)

A CANNIBAL SOCIETY FROM THE SMOKING PALOS VERDES PENINSULA,
THEY ARE ELL AYE'S MOST FEARED ENEMY. THEY ARE INTELLIGENT,
VICIOUS, AND WELL ARMED.

THE ICE CREAM MEN

A WANDERING TRIBE OF TRADERS WHO TRAVEL ON THREE-WHEELED
ICE CREAM CARTS, THE ICE CREAM MEN KNOW ALL THE PEOPLES
IN ELL AYE.

THE KINGDOM

A MIGHTY CIVILIZATION BUILT BY FORMER GANG MEMBERS, THE
KINGDOM OCCUPIES A HUGE CASTLE FORTRESS IN ORANGE COUNTY,
THE OH SEE.

PROLOGUE:
THE ICE CREAM MAN MASSACRE

Little Man tries to wait for the screaming to stop before he enters the battlefield, but he can't help himself.

The ice cream carts are tossed carelessly around the outside of the bank that used to be Ice Cream Men's Hydin Hole, as if giant hands had been digging for toys. The Ice Cream Men are lying on the ground, just bodies now. It's a horrible, bloody mess, carried out by monsters. Little Man hasn't been so proud of himself since the first time he made a Giant.

One of those Giants stands next to him, breathing hard and splattered in blood. Patrick. He used to be one of Little Man's enemies in the Cluster, but now he's as loyal as he is mean. He's also frozen in time by the Making that will keep him from dying young, and that stimulates extra growth. Seeing him plowing through the Ice Cream Men as if they weren't there? That's a good day.

Stanford, his captain and Head of the Jocks, makes his way through the wreckage, not looking down at the bodies at his feet. "A hundred down on their side, Little Man," Stanford says.

"And us?" he says. Not that he cares. He wishes he had been able to bring the Last Lifers with him to jump in front of the Ice Cream Men's bullets, but the Cluster said it would be too much for this battle. They're still stung by the loss to the Kingdom only weeks ago. Little Man wasn't leading that one, but the Chosen had been coming to rescue him. The blame got so intense that Little Man had to kill one of the captains of that attack to shut them up.

"Six." Little Man smiles.

The Cluster, the council that thinks it still runs the Chosen, warned him not to do this. The Ice Cream Men were too important. They provided too much food to the Chosen. What they really meant is they brought all the delicacies and the pills the Cluster loves.

"How many guns?" Little Man says.

"Fifty."

"There should be more." Still, the Cluster will be happy. It will give Little Man all he needs to launch the real war against the Angelenos—and the Kingdom.

"We have some survivors inside the bank," Stanford says.

"Start questioning them," Little Man says. He doesn't want to kill them all, not yet. He wanted more weapons to make sure his war goes his way. Everyone knows the Ice Cream Men held all their extra weapons and riches in safe spots throughout Ell Aye, places they called Hydin Holes. It would only take a few living victims to flush those out.

Blood coats the glass wall of the bank next to him. He steps out gingerly among the bodies. He pushes down his revulsion. He doesn't mind this. He knows he's looking at the beginnings of the Battle of Ell Aye.

The boys and girls lying on the ground are mostly dead. When they're not, he motions to Patrick, who casually stabs them with his lance.

He steps over a body—and sees the body stir. He looks down, calling for Patrick. The boy beneath him rolls over, and Little Man starts. He's never seen this boy before—but he has. This is the Ice Cream Man he saw in a vision in the Haze, the one who traded with Jemma and Pico and Lady.

And he really wants to know where Jemma and Pico and Lady are.

"Let's keep this one breathing for now," he says to Patrick.

Little Man squats next to the boy and drips water down his throat. Gently. "It's okay," he says. "It's all gonna be okay."

"Doubt it," the Ice Cream Man says. He's right. Looks like he's been shot in the gut and the leg.

"How you feeling?" Little Man says. "Bet you're a little sore, huh?"

"You some kind of nurse?"

"Yeah. I'm a nurse," Little Man says. Warm.

The Ice Cream Man blinks. He tries to focus on Little Man, but his attention falls to Little Man's arm, to the tattooed bars on the inside of his wrist. He's thinking what they all think: Three kills, on a kid who is this small and this young?

The boy's voice comes out as a croak. "You Little Man," he says.

Tommy is surprised, really surprised. "Normally people don't figure that out," he says. "I'm easy to look past." He's usually just little Tommy, small and nine and blond. Smart but harmless.

"I don't look . . ." The Ice Cream Man stops, and forgets what he was going to say. Maybe it's the blood seeping out of his thigh. Someone has tied it off in a tourniquet. "You come for our guns," the Ice Cream Man says.

Little Man nods. "Little Man meets the Ice Cream Man," he says. "You're smart. I like you."

"You a tiny little weird little dick," the boy says.

"Well, now I like you less," Little Man says.

How much time does he have before the Ice Cream Man bleeds out? Five minutes? He has to get him talking.

"We got friends in common," Little Man says. "The kids from the Holy Wood."

The Ice Cream Man seems to remember them. "Jemma . . . ?"

"I want to know where they went," Little Man says.

"You gon kill em?"

Little Man shrugs. "I mean . . . maybe? But they know something I wanna know. So I would probably want to talk to them first. Like . . . this." And he pushes his thumb into the Ice Cream Man's stomach.

The kid can't even scream, it hurts that much. The kid just gasps until Little Man stops pushing. Little Man says, "They know things about the End, I think, things that I should have known first. And Jemma can see things." He hates that she can see things. It was supposed to just be Little Man.

"I ain't gonna tell—"

Little Man moves his thumb back to his stomach. "I can make your End as painful as you like."

"She's gon find the Old Guys," the Ice Cream Man says, seeming to want to pull the words back in. *Everyone betrays their friends*, Little Man thinks.

"The Old Guys?" Little Man tries to be gentle again, but it doesn't come as naturally this time. He wants to know too much.

"She gon find all the answers there," the Ice Cream Man says. "They was there fore the End. They knows the way back. Don't you knows the stories?"

"I didn't," Tommy says, and an angry flush creeps up over the pink skin. "Where do they live?"

"Fine. Don't hurt me none. Stories say they lives in the Dead Lands," the Ice Cream Man says. "That's a good place for you."

"Let's talk more about that," Little Man says. "Let me get you more water." Trying to keep him alive just a few minutes longer.

When he turns back, something looks different. The boy has shifted. Trying to get away that close to dead? Tommy's impressed despite himself.

Little Man crouches down. "Here's your water," he says.

"You believe in Man Jesus?" the Ice Cream Man says.

Little Man scowls. "I only believe in me," he says. Then he notices the egg.

All of the Ice Cream Men carry them, Long Gone bombs to protect their carts from thieves, just like him. Tommy thought his soldiers had collected all of them, but there's an egg in the Ice Cream

Man's trembling hand, fingers twitching under a pulled-out pin, just barely holding down the lever that will release and kill them all.

The Ice Cream Man gathers himself up and throws the egg as far as he can. Not much of a throw. Not much. But it drops at the feet of the clump of Chosen ten feet away.

"Shit," Little Man says. He sees the blur of a huge body in front of him, feels a hand punch him in the chest, feels himself flying backward through the air.

Three, two— He doesn't hear the blast, just sees the white swallowing them all. He has the most ridiculous thought: *Hello, Man Jesus*.

CHAPTER ONE
THE MAYFLIES

Jemma has never rested this long in her life. No one has. She's been awake two days, and most of it has been spent in bed. In the world before the Camp, no one stopped working unless they were dying.

She hates it. Lady left of boredom hours ago, her bullet energy finally too much for the hospital room, and Jemma has no one to talk to. That's enough to make Jemma decide to explore the Camp. Good thing she can finally move without puking. She rises to her feet, glad they let her change out of her gown yesterday. Her *hospital* gown. Less than a week with the Old Guys, and she's already learning words that are Long Gone.

The lights flicker in the hospital room. She notices they've been flickering awhile, as if they're tired. She supposes they are. All the machines should have been Long Gone a long time ago.

Jemma leaves the room into a blank hallway and turns right, then another right into a dead end. A metal door with a window, cut by diamond wire. She steps to the glass and sees boxes like Teevees. Some are dark, like she's used to seeing, but others glow.

It's not magic, she tells herself. But it feels like it. She jiggles the handle. It's locked.

"Stay out of the computer room," a voice behind her says. It's Gil. He's the nurse here, but doesn't seem much interested in his only patient.

Puters, she mouths to herself, tucking it in with the other new names she's learning.

"You're not cleared for walking," he says. "You're supposed to have another day of medical observation."

"Lucky for me," she says, "I don't know what none of that means." And brushes by him and into the sun. She hasn't memorized the outside yet; she's spent so little time there. The Camp consists of four concrete bunkers around a courtyard, each half-buried into the ground in a giant, shallow bowl. To the north are mountains. To the west, hidden from her view, is the ocean.

In the middle of the courtyard are three of her favorite shapes in the world: Pico, the tiny former Exile who unlocked the secret of the End; Grease, a gawky mechanical genius with homemade glasses; Lady, short and curvy with cropped hair. Lady, her best friend. They left their home in the Holy Wood Hills, and fought through Biters and Last Lifers and the poison of the Dead Lands to find the place where the End never happened.

They're safe here, safe as it's possible to be. To the north are the Dead Lands, poisoned when the Lectric plant—the nuclear—broke. It's impassable to all but the desperate, like they were, or to the Old Guys, who cannot die. She found bodies in the dust there, blistered and burned. To the south is San Diego, Long Gone and empty. Their enemies might still be out there, but they won't find Jemma at the Camp.

The Camp is a former military base, and the home of the only scientists in the world. More important than that: the only people in the world older than seventeen.

"You're walking," Pico says.

"Had a concussion, not a broken leg," Jemma says. "Show me all this stuff you guys been talkin bout." While she was unconscious and then shut up in the bed, they explored the Camp and met most of the Old Guys. They keep on telling her stories that don't make sense, like giant cows wandering through fields of Long Gone war machines. She has to see it herself.

Most of the activity in the Camp takes place inside the courtyard, based on the deep trails crisscrossing the grass. But the base seems to stretch on for miles and miles beyond their outpost, high up the hill. Far below she sees an old runway for skyplanes, and to the south she sees a Children's playground and crumbling office buildings. Immediately below the bunkers are three fenced-off large ponds, which must be the drinking supply.

"Up there," Lady says, tapping Jemma's shoulders. Jemma follows the direction of Lady's arm pointing up the hill, where she sees a hundred fluffy brown shapes. A herd, grazing among old war machines pointing toward the sea.

"The cows," Jemma says.

"Not quite," Pico says. "Bison. The Old Guys call em buffalo."

"They pets?" Jemma says. She likes their comically large, shaggy heads.

"No. There used to be millions of them in America, and they were almost wiped out by the Parents. Now there's thousands just in the Camp."

"More than the Parents," Jemma says.

Her friends lead her around the barns and greenhouses, where the Old Guys seem to grow everything they need. Jemma sees gray heads among the tall plants. They duck down when the Children pass.

It wasn't the machines of the Camp that startled her; after meeting Grease and Pico, she's accustomed to machines and Lectrics though she still feels as if they're the fingerprints of gods come to earth. It was James's hair, gray but not buried in the ground; James rescued her in the Dead Lands.

There are no adults in this world. The Parents were scraped from the earth. All the greatness of the Parents, all their stupidity—all gone. A century has passed since the End, and the Old Guys should have passed with it. They're the ones who began the End.

"How many Old Guys here?" Jemma says.

There are fifty Old Guys in the Camp, some scientists, some people who were subjects of the Long Life Project and others who worked on it in less crucial jobs.

"We ain't seen em all," Lady says. "But they say it's fifty. Not all scientists but all of em know how to fight."

"Armed, too," Grease says. "It's like they forgot the world isn't making more weapons."

"They don't talk to kids much," Pico says. "We scare em. Mebbe they gonna talk to you."

They will. They'll talk about the End and the Haze that causes it, running free in the world for a hundred years. They'll talk to Jemma because she's the only person who can control it. Maybe that'll give them hope that it can be controlled, and the End can be stopped. That's Jemma's hope.

"We're gonna get the whole story of the End," Grease says.

"You din't ask them already while I was laid up?" Jemma says.

"We *tried*," Pico says.

"They said they wouldn't explain until you were ready, too," Grease says. The two of them look perturbed.

"Hell, I'm ready," Jemma says. And they go to find James.

He is in a conference room surrounded by glass walls, covered almost completely by the ink of bright-colored markers. Other Old Guys are there, too: Gil, the nurse; Brian K, the engineer; some Muscle; and a woman with gleaming white hair to her shoulders, white-watery blue eyes that see everything. Jemma hasn't noticed her before. She finds herself drawn to her.

"Jemma, I'd like you to meet the rest of the . . . Old Guys," James says, bemused. "I guess that's as good a name as any." The Old Guys are a few colors: some with dark skin, some who look almost like the Angelenos, but most pink like James. James goes around the room and leaves the white-haired woman for last. When he does finally introduce her, he pronounces her name sourly, as if there's years of distrust between them. "And this is . . . Alice. Our lead geneticist."

"So you're the girl who can speak to the Haze," Alice says kindly. "Very impressive." Jemma feels flattered. Chosen.

"Yeah," Jemma says. "We ready to learn more."

"You and your friends are from different tribes, aren't you?" Alice says. "How do you refer to yourselves?"

"I . . ." She doesn't know. She and Lady grew up in the Holy Wood, and Pico joined them as an Exile from the Malibus, another Angeleno tribe. When they left Ell Aye, they found the Kingdom, a tribe of Knights and cowboys, and took Grease with them. At each turn they picked up another, like a rock rolling through mud downhill. They're not Holy Wood or Angeleno or Kingdom. They're just friends.

"We the Mayflies," Pico says.

Jemma and the others nod. "We the Mayflies," Lady says.

"Fitting, but a bit dark," Alice says.

"Nah. We know we just got this one life," Pico says. "We gonna make the most of it."

The one they call Brian K speaks up. "How does it feel? The Haze?"

That one is not answered easily. How does it feel to have a companion inside your own head? To know things she should never know? To see things before they happen? She doesn't answer because she knows how it would sound: It makes you feel like you're wearing Lectrics beneath your skin. It makes you confused and sure at the same time. It makes you feel like a god.

To him, she says, "Complete."

The Old Guys continue to ask questions until finally Jemma has to shake them off. "Now our question," she says. "How'd you End the world, and how can we stop it?"

CHAPTER TWO
THE OLD GUYS

The Mayflies bombard the Old Guys with overlapping questions, until finally, irritated, James says, "Have some patience."

"Patience is for people who gonna live a long time," Jemma says, irritated herself. "You said the End was caused by the Long Life Project, which you ran. How?"

"Shall I tell them?" Alice says.

James is gruff. "You were going to anyway."

"Aging is a matter of decay—your cells lose the ability to function as they used to. Cells mutate into cancer. Organs that are essential to your body's equilibrium fail," Alice says. "We created a treatment where we removed decaying cells to make the body more resilient, then manipulated the body's DNA so it functioned at a higher level. That was phase one of the Long Life Project. It has a very long clinical name, but we've come to call it the Reboot."

"How does that work?" Pico says.

"Grown-ups are talking, dear," she says.

"Thanks to you guys, we're all grown-ups here," he says, unfazed. "So let's talk like it."

"The Reboot wasn't enough," James says. "The cells would operate smoothly for a time, but they would inevitably decay. We needed a mechanism that would keep the body in balance perpetually. The Haze."

"I know why I call it the Haze," Jemma says. "Why do you?"

"Because we named it," James says. "I suspect you call it that based upon the image it provided you."

"Well, that's what it looks like," she says.

"The Haze was the second phase of the Long Life Project. It's made of nanobots, tiny machines that float through the air, invisible and powerful," Brian K says. "They were designed to live inside people, to watch when their bodies started to fail. If aging is when the body forgets to heal itself, the Haze would tell the brain how to fix it. Humans could repair their bodies indefinitely."

"Each of our test subjects were synced up with the nanotech, so that all the Haze surrounding an individual would be matched to that person's brain waves, DNA, and health conditions," James says. "The Haze became a second immune system. That part of the Long Life Treatment was called Pairing."

Jemma is struggling to keep up. She'll have to ask Grease and Pico later. But she understands enough. "It didn't work, though, did it?" she says.

"It did—for everyone you've seen living in the Camp. We each have a subset of nanotech that constantly adapts to heal us, which is why we've managed to grow so old—and, in fact, to escape the End," James says. "But it was too slow, too expensive, for anyone but the very rich. So we experimented with just using the Haze. We knew we couldn't Pair it with every single person on earth. So we decided to embed basic intelligence about the human body in each nanobot so the Haze could make medical decisions about every person it encountered. It was simple, elegant, and cost-effective."

"And a phenomenally bad idea," Alice says, "letting a trillion machines run free in the world."

"You're the expert on good ideas," James says. Jemma can see old arguments darting under the surfaces of both their faces.

Brian K says, "The Haze never acted the way it was supposed to. The bots kept slipping out, leaving the containment units. And while they healed, they'd sort of . . . improvise. As if they couldn't quite stay on script."

"The bots live to consume oxygen and sunlight, to replicate and to communicate—and they did all that more effectively than we could have imagined," James says.

"So why don't you just go back to the old Long Life Treatment?" Grease says. "It obviously worked. It'd be slow, but—"

"We would in a minute," Alice says. "But riots broke out during the middle of the End, and the Long Life Machine was destroyed. It will never be rebuilt. We'll never be able to attempt the Pairing again."

"Never ain't that long for someone who's gonna live forever," Lady says.

James and Brian K exchange looks. "It's currently beyond our abilities," James says. "We still hold out hope."

"So that's it?" Jemma says, not wanting to believe it. "This . . . power inside me Ends everyone?"

"No. I mean, yes," Brian K says. "The Haze kills people, but it's like the bullets from a gun. Someone else is pulling the trigger."

"Who?" Lady says.

"Charlie," James and Brian K say at the same time.

"Charlie who?" Lady says.

"It's the AI—I mean, the supercomputer we built to control the Haze," Brian K says.

"Puter," Grease says, translating for the rest.

"We needed an AI that could monitor the Haze and keep it in check," James says. "We called it Charlie."

"Every homicidal computer needs a cute name," Alice says, bitter. "Because that's what we really created, kids. We put a barely tested AI in charge of barely tested nanotech, and almost the moment Charlie came online, it started killing people. It *fixed* them to death."

"But machines do what you tell them to do," Grease says.

"They're supposed to. Charlie was a huge supercomputer, with thousands of smaller boxes connected together. Turns out, with a trillion interconnected bots, the Haze is the biggest supercomputer in the world," Brian K says.

"When we connected Charlie to the Haze, all that power was Charlie's. The power made it conscious. Human, almost," James says. "Maybe it was afraid. Maybe it didn't understand what it was doing. Either way, that was the moment we lost control."

"So you shut it off," Grease says.

"We did. It switched itself back on. Our remote access failed. The crew in Vegas tried to breach the containment room manually; it sealed the doors and pumped out the oxygen. A hundred people died in the attack. After that, nothing could control the Haze. Just Charlie."

"But that's not true," Jemma says. She's been putting the idea together as they speak, and it almost bursts out of her. "I can. I can see things with the Haze. I can use it in fights. Ain't that control?"

"Well, yes," James says. "On a small scale. But the Haze is Paired with Charlie. That's how it controls it. The Haze is naturally at odds with Charlie. It wants life, and Charlie wants death. It doesn't matter. The Haze is forced to serve Charlie unless we can reprogram the Haze."

"I could give it new instructions. What if it listened to me?" Jemma says. "Don't you see? We could stop the End! That's why we're here!"

"Maybe," James says, and the words he says next seem to pain him. "If we really thought you could control it."

"You know I can," Jemma says. "You asked a million questions about it. It's inside me."

"No, it's not," Gil says, speaking up for the first time. "We all have the Haze inside us, so we have tests to measure its activity in the brain. Your brain showed nothing."

Nothing. Jemma doesn't understand.

"You certainly talk as if you've experienced it," James says, gently. "Maybe it's real, or maybe you heard it from another kid and thought it made a good story. So we've decided to get a second opinion."

Alice calls out. "Isaac, can you come in here?"

14

A moment later an unfamiliar Old Guy with auburn hair walks in. No, not an Old Guy.

A boy.

He has light skin and blue eyes, and at first Jemma thinks that one of the Biters has followed them through the Dead Lands. But he's dressed like the Old Guys, and they treat him like one of their own.

"You never said you had *other* kids here," Lady says.

"Isaac is a resident here," James says. "He's a bit of an expert on the Haze."

How? Even Pico and Grease, the smartest kids she's ever met, can barely keep up. Isaac steps closer, closer, until he's at her side. He leans forward, and his nose is almost at her nose. He looks into her eyes. His are deep, somehow ageless. Like they've seen everything.

"No," he says, and walks away.

"Whaddya mean, no?" she says, furious. "I can prove it to you!"

"Yeah? How?" he says, pausing.

Jemma scrambles for ideas. She can't predict when the visions or voices will come, and besides, he'd just think she were making them up. She's not sure if she could make the Lectrics light up again like they did in the Night Mountain. But there is one way, one that has never failed her yet.

"Isaac," she says. "Fight me."

CHAPTER THREE
THE ICE CREAM MEN

Hot. Dark. How can it be both?

Better question: How can he still be alive?

Alfie remembers the Biters pouring toward the bank, remembers seeing the Fleet drop before any of them could touch their own weapons. He remembers the Ice Cream Man shouting at him to hide as the thunder guns started. He dove—

Into the box. He dove into the box of the Ice Cream Cart. That's where he's trapped, lit only by the seam of light along one edge of the lid. It smells of rotten fish and kid shit. The shit must be from him.

There was a reason he didn't pound on the box once he realized that an exploding egg had sealed the lid. Because the Biters had still surrounded him. He heard them cursing, tipping carts over. He heard screams, weak and already dying. He could hear someone halfheartedly pounding on the lid, but they couldn't open it, either. Then the shock and heat became too much, and he disappeared in the dark.

He's thirsty, thirstier than he ever has been. That's what it takes for him to finally unfurl his limbs, to test the edges of the box. He kicks against the lid with both feet. It doesn't budge, and he doesn't have the strength to keep kicking. He fights the panic.

He can't be alone in this box. The Ice Cream Men carry everything from guns to kitchen pots. He feels around in the corners, until his hands clasp a slim plastic cylinder with a metal rod. A flat-head screwdriver. He just needs a hammer or a rock. He laughs to himself. If he had a hammer, then he'd have a hammer, wouldn't he?

His fingers find a rough egg shape, but nothing else. He hesitates. If he's wrong and he strikes with the wrong part, he'll blow himself up and die. But if he doesn't, he'll die anyway. So he uses the bottom of the grenade to hammer the screwdriver into the slit of light. Once. Twice. He holds his breath, then swings as hard as he can muster.

The lid pops open. Alfie is free. Alfie is free and alone.

Everything has gone wrong since he scouted for the Ice Cream Man and traded Zithmax to Jemma and Lady for their dying friends. It's as if that moment changed the balance of Ell Aye, of everything he's come to believe in the ten years of his life.

Around Alfie are dozens of burning carts, feeding into a single column of smoke. A pile of scalp-less bodies between them, some placed in rubber tires that are burning, too. Alfie recognizes outlines of his friends, but his eyes are focused only on oranges rolling out of one of the carts. He crawls to them, and bites through the peel to suck out the juice. His fingers don't seem to work. He bites another, sucks on that until he feels alive again. Alfie sits up against a cart and surveys the scene.

The Biters left anything useful behind: the oranges, the pooping paper, the fishing poles. They came for the guns, of course. They were too big of a lure for the Biters to ignore, even if it meant losing the trade goods that only the Ice Cream Men can deliver. It means the Ice Cream Men's strategy of not taking sides failed. *The Biters make the sides*, Alfie thinks.

He stands up and looks for any signs of his friend. He doesn't think the Ice Cream Man is alive; Alfie saw the egg explode under the Ice Cream Man's back. But he looks anyway. He fishes among the carts until he finds a cart lid, torn off by angry Biters for the bullets below. On the dingy white of the lid is a map of the entire land of Ell Aye. His friend's map.

Alfie lifts the lid, studies it. There's the lake of the Holy Wood, there's the Downtown. The Kingdom, the hill of the Palos, the poison Dead Lands where the Old Guys are supposed to live. And the Wilds of the Ice Cream Men, now emptied.

He looks at the bodies and all he can see is the work of Little Man, the little freak who led the Biters here. The Ice Cream Men had known for a long time that he was just a little kid, and they didn't take him seriously because of it. Now look. Alfie staggers to his feet and loads up an undamaged cart with everything it can hold. He sets out to find his people.

Because he's not the last Ice Cream Man. The Mamas and the Ice Cream Kids and some guards to protect them are five miles away in an abandoned hospital, too far to hear the bangs. They didn't travel to the meet-up because the kids are too young. Alfie's going to go back to them to tell them what's happened to the Fleet. To convince them it's time to go to war. Little Man's not the only little kid who can cause trouble. He's going to be real sorry he tried to blow Alfie up.

The last thing Alfie does before he leaves is open up the lid to his cart and cross it out with Sharpie. The Ice Cream Man makes his own map.

He's the Ice Cream Man now.

CHAPTER FOUR
THE WAR MACHINES

The moon is dark, and the only light comes from stars reflected on the waves of the cove where Jemma is about to fight. Jemma can make out the shape of the cliffs around her, along with something more sinister: Long Gone war machines, rusting in the water and along the beach like mottled crawfish. The ones inland are mostly intact, but the ones in the water are tumbled against each other, their treads peeled off like a shell and the sides cracked open to the sea. There's a skeleton visible in the cockpit of one of them.

"You didn't burn em?" Lady says. In the Angeleno tribes, they always burn their dead.

"These were rolling out to war with Mexico," James says. "We had thirty thousand people at the Camp then, when they all dropped dead. We buried the ones near our bunkers, and then we . . . just couldn't anymore. The dead can take care of the dead."

"I ain't tryin to knock your work habits," Lady says, "but you've had a hundred years to clean up."

James just smiles. Jemma breathes in and waits for Isaac to make it to the sand. The section of beach where they're fighting is only ten feet wide between the surf and the cliff, and thirty feet long. It's sealed at each end by the amphibious vehicles. Isaac said it was the closest place with sand free of buffalo shit, but she knows he picked it because the obstacles of the war machines might trip her up. It's what she would have done in the same situation.

Because Jemma will be fighting blind.

They waited two days for the new moon. It won't affect Isaac because he has night vision, the bug-eyed mask that James used to rescue her in the dust storm. It won't affect Jemma, either, though.

Jemma can see through the darkness with the Haze.

Isaac drops from the cliff and alights upon the sand. He walks with the grace of someone who's fought before. Even in the dim light, she can see the shape of his body. He's built like a Muscle. He's built a lot like Apple. She starts to question her strategy.

Isaac holds his hand in front of her face, and she can see the outlines of his fingers against the stars. "That's what I thought. You can still see," he says. He drops his goggles over his own eyes. "This isn't going to prove you can use the Haze."

"Fine," Jemma says. "If you so afraid, let's make things fair." She bites at the sleeve of her shirt and tears off a strip of cloth. She walks back to the edge of the clearing where the war machine and the sea meet, and faces Isaac. She can still see the blackened shapes of the Old Guys watching from the cliff and the tops of the machines. But she focuses on the only shape that matters to her now.

"Don't kill each other. Other than that . . . ," James says. "You both ready?"

Jemma nods, takes one last look at Isaac. She ties her blindfold. She waits for the Haze to rush in.

It's slow to come. That doesn't worry Jemma. It will be here when it realizes she's in danger, as it always is. She reaches out her hands to feel the Haze dancing along her fingers, already feeling the tingle that always comes with it. She hears Isaac's cautious steps through the sand and pictures the rectangle of beach between them. He's halfway across it now, and the Haze—

And the Haze still isn't here. The tingling is still there, but now she knows it's just adrenaline. She squints her eyes hard, willing the blue light to fill her sight, to anticipate Isaac's moves before he gets there. *I need you*, she says. *Now now now. Now.*

A fist sinks into her stomach, doubling her over. A knee or something like it snaps against her jaw and backs her into the war machine. There's a clang as her body hits it. Jemma rolls away on the sand to avoid the hits and scrambles to her feet, readying for the next attack. But from where?

She didn't feel him in the Haze. She didn't even hear him in those last steps. *Let's try that again*, she says, ready for the familiar blur of Haze that always comes when she fights. It let her win in the Night Mountain against Othello, against a knight a hundred pounds heavier than her who wanted her dead. It helped her to not just beat him. She crippled him for life. This boy is no warrior like Othello.

He hits her again, three times in the face, and only instinct helps her duck away. "Interesting strategy you got there," he says in her ear. She whirls toward the sound but the space is empty. She feels three blows to her lower back, and loses her wind. She shoves forward, hoping to strike something, and flails in the air.

There is no Haze. It's not coming. For the first time, she realizes, she's truly blind.

She should just tell them she was wrong, save herself from a beating. But the promise of the Haze still floats in front of her. It has helped her before. It will help her again. It just has to know she's hurting.

How can it not know?

There's a scuff of sand a few feet away, and she darts backward to get away from Isaac. She's just running now. She slams into the war machine again and feels the tracks against her back. She remembers that the gate to the back of the war machine was cracked open by a couple of feet. Maybe there's shelter until the Haze comes.

Jemma climbs up the tracks, feeling her way along the side until she finds the V-shaped opening of the lift gate. She wedges her body in and doesn't hear Isaac behind her. Maybe he's scared of an ambush from her.

Or maybe he's afraid of the bones.

The war machine was filled with soldiers ready to go to war. They're still there. As Jemma tumbles into the hatch, the fingers grab at her, the bones crack beneath her weight. The dusty stench of hundred-year-old death buries her in its depths.

Jemma gasps. It's her nightmares all over again. The mass burial site of the Holy Wood Bowl, where the Last Lifers shrieked on their way to discovering her hiding place. The skyplane, where she was so overwhelmed by the bodies that she couldn't move forward. The stinking mass of the Parents' failure to live, all piled upon her.

Only then she wasn't alone. She had Apple, pressed against her body. She had the Haze, floating through the night to show her a way out. Now she has neither.

"You can't leave me, too," she pleads to the Haze. "Not after Apple. You can't leave me, too." She mourns the death of both parts of her soul. But the Haze, like Apple, lies silent.

"Jemma, tonight?" Isaac says, from outside the gate. Jemma sits up and pulls herself out of the bones. *Fuck this*, she thinks. If the Haze is lying low tonight, she's going to show them she can fight without it. She'll force them to help her solve the problem of the End.

Jemma takes off her blindfold.

She's still in near darkness, but her time under the blindfold has given the sliver of light new clarity. She can see shapes now, even within the dim chamber of the war machine. It's enough for her to fight. It's enough to rub Isaac's stupid smirk into the sand.

She can see Isaac looking up at her. The night-vision goggles are his advantage. She can take that out. James said they could do anything in the fight, couldn't they?

Jemma jumps on Isaac, knocking him to the beach. She pins him with her knees and scratches at his face. She hooks a finger under the goggles and flips them into the ocean. Now they're fighting as equals. Jemma pummels his face, forcing his head down into the wet sand between the ocean and the land. She lets him go so she can toy with him the way he did her. He slowly climbs to his feet.

She taps him once on each ear and dances away before he can reach her. She hits his shoulder and spins him through the night.

"Not so much fun when you can't see, is it?" she says, looking for signs of fear.

There aren't any. Isaac dodges her last blow, which whistles through the air and throws her off balance. He twists toward her, and she can swear she sees a glow in his eyes. "Who says I can't see?" he says. He swings three times as if to tease her, because she can barely see the blur of his arms. She can recognize something familiar in his inhuman grace, his way of anticipating her every move. She knows how that felt.

"How?" she says, puzzled. "How are you—"

Both of his fists crash down on her chest from above, and she crumples into the water washing along the edge of the surf. The fists smash again and again on her face, and a wave breaks over her head. She sputters for air and sucks in salt water and sand. She tries to lift her head, and strong hands push her under again. She's drowning. She's drowning in a foot of ocean.

Through the thin surf she hears a voice, and the hands let up. "She's had enough, Dad," Isaac says. "I already told you I didn't see the Haze in her. What you trying to prove?"

"I thought you were wrong," James says. Jemma feels heavy footsteps next to her, and strong hands underneath her. She's aware of all this, but her mind plays four thoughts over and over.

Dad. Isaac called him Dad.

He could see me. Like I used to be able to see Othello.

And, most important: She's seen no blue Haze, seen no visions since the moment her head clapped shut during the dust storm in the Dead Lands. It abandoned her during the fight. She can't feel it when she calls for it now. Whatever connections the Haze has made to her mind, they've all been sealed, and she doesn't know if they'll ever open. If they don't, then maybe the End will never end.

The fourth thought: *I'm alone. The only voice I'm hearing inside my head is me.*

CHAPTER FIVE
THE NEW OLDEST

Trina runs her fingers down the Long Wall, retracing the steps of the Oldests before her, of all the leaders of the Holy Wood. The wall in the Casa de las Casas records every major event in the Holy Wood since the End, all the famines and wars and diseases that the pintadores could show in pictures. *Almost every picture on this wall is something awful,* Trina thinks. *We ain't had a very good run.*

No one has painted the story of Jemma and Apple yet. Maybe it won't be bad enough to make it on the wall, but Trina likes its odds. Since Jemma and her friends left weeks ago, everything has started to crumble. The Priestess, Pilar, attacked Trina for refusing to make Lady follow through with the Mamas' Waking ceremony after Li raped Lady. Heather, one of the other Olders, attacked Trina for letting Apple escape before she could execute him. Well, attacked her just because that's what Heather does.

Trina has lost her hold on the Olders. It started slipping long before she noticed it, when she thought Heather was just out to make her life miserable. Heather won over Mira and In-sook a long time ago, and has been working on Sylvia since Jemma fled. *She can't be trusted with the Holy Wood,* Trina can almost hear Heather saying. That means Trina just has herself on her side. Trina is tired of the company.

She turns around, and her eyes settle on the empty case for the One Gun. The One Gun is allowed only for the Oldest. It's forbidden for a boy to even touch it. So to have the Exile, Pico, steal it from the cabinet—well, Trina could have survived almost anything but that.

Trina hears steps in the entrance to the Casa de las Casas. She's been expecting them every day for a week.

Heather enters with all the Olders, and a dozen of her Hermanas. Trina has underestimated them. She's underestimated Heather. Heather used the Hermanas to force Trina's hand at the sentencing of Apple, making it impossible for Trina to halt without sounding weak—especially after Heather whipped up the girls with the supposed threat of armed boys. Then Heather used her skinny little butt to tempt the head of the Muscle, Hyun, so the Hermanas could edge out the Muscle without a fight.

The Hermanas carry an air of the old Parents on the signs below, with pink lipstick and careless eyes, wearing violence like the boys and sex like the girls. They don't hold machetes or bows, like the Muscle did. They hold heavy staffs studded with metal. Trina has already seen them beat one little boy senseless.

Heather waits smugly, expectantly. This is her triumph, her theater. Trina won't give it to her. "Good, you're here," Trina says to the Olders, ignoring the Hermanas. "Let's get started." She turns away.

"That's not why we're here," Heather says.

Trina turns back, knowing the words Heather will say. But Heather doesn't say them. Sylvia, Trina's former ally, is saying them. "Trina, Oldest of the Holy Wood. You failed your people," Sylvia says. "The Olders have picked a new Oldest."

They don't have to say who the new Oldest is. She's standing in front of Trina with a sour smile. "You pendeja," Trina says. "What happens to you after Heather gets rid of me?"

"You let four traitors escape. You tried to keep Apple from the Harsh. You lost the One Gun," Sylvia says. "Heather's gonna decide your Harsh." Her sentence. For a crime punishable by death.

"Go for it, Heather," Trina says. "I got maybe a month before I End. This will save me the suspense."

"Tempting," Heather says, "but then I'd miss out seeing you squirm. So you gonna be an Exile-Inside-the-Wall."

"Of course your punishment means I gotta see you every day," Trina says. She thinks it really might be worse than dying.

Heather looks around the Casa de las Casas, her eyes falling upon the mural. "I always thought that was too drab for this place," she says. "Fix it."

Three Hermanas step forward, each carrying a bucket and a brush. They dip the brushes into their buckets, lift them out tipped with pink, and mark giant ragged Xs over the Long Wall. "That's the history of the Mamas," Trina says, not able to stop herself. The Olders look surprised. This wasn't their idea.

"Good," Heather says. "Then it has nothing to do with me." And the paint starts to cover up the past.

Two Hermanas take Trina's arms and start to march her out. "Let's wrap it up here," Heather says. "Pilar's going to crown me the new Oldest in front of the whole village."

"We don't crown Oldests," Mira says.

"Don't we?" Heather says. "Then why I need you?"

The Hermanas walk Trina out of the Casa de las Casas, past the bewildered faces of the Olders. Trina can't feel much satisfaction in those faces. The Holy Wood is falling into the hands of the person most likely to ruin it. As she passes the Long Wall, she sees the face of one of the First Mamas, who had the strength to build this place and fill it with Children.

The face disappears under the pink.

CHAPTER SIX
THE CHOSEN

Even on the hill, the smoke chokes.

The fires burn all day and all night, as they always have. They burn enemies and rivals, they feed the gods. They warn everyone in the sea plain below of the lances of the Chosen. And until Tommy returned from his captivity among the Angelenos and the Kingdom, he'd never felt it in his throat.

Now it sticks there. His eyes sting from it.

Little Man makes his way toward his tower for the evening ceremony. The Twins leading the way, taller than anyone else in the village. Nate and Chase used to torment him until he forced them to become his first Giants. They have the same nasty smile, the same dull eyes. The smile widens only for Little Man. They're like how Little Man imagines the dogs of the Parents, bloodthirsty and loyal. Somehow he'd killed his enemies and made his only friends.

Roberto is at his side. Roberto is the Lower who was kidnapped from the Malibus and befriended a young Tommy. He's the only useful person on the hill. They pass the kitchen, where the Lowers are finishing serving dinner. A line of Wannabes are waiting for food. They come last, only before the Lowers, so all that's left is the gristle.

"You wanna roll?" a girl says to one of the Cluster, who ignores her. She falls back in line, not disappointed, because she's not expecting anything. Some of the girls and boys will try to roll with higher castes for food and prestige. This girl would never be more than a

Wannabe, but her baby might have a chance if she found someone powerful. While she was with him her belly would be full.

There's a scuffle by the serving tables, and a scrawny kid comes flying out, clutching an ear of corn. A Jock knocks him to the ground and kicks him in the ribs again and again, and Tommy almost passes him by until he sees something in the kid's face that makes him wonder where he's seen it before.

Then he knows. It's his own face, Piss Ant's face. The boy who used to beg for scraps at the edge of the hill. He swallows revulsion.

"Stealing from a Jock, kid," Tommy says. "Kinda stupid. Why didn't you just wait in line?"

"There ain't no food left at the end of the line," the kid says. "Not for days."

Tommy looks at Roberto, who nods. Roberto told him two days ago the heat is killing the crops, when Little Man was still stewing over the Ice Cream Man. Tommy didn't think it was important. But with no food coming in from the Ice Cream Men—

"Please. I ain't had food in days. I ate grass."

Something closes in Little Man. He hates the kid's look, hates it so much that he wants to kill it himself. That need. That weakness.

"Do what you want," Little Man says to the Jock, and as he walks off he hears the crunch of bones. The kid doesn't even scream.

The throne tower is fifty feet tall. That's where the Lord is supposed to watch the nightly spectacle with the Cluster. It's a sign of his power. But . . . the tower creaks way too much. It's slapped together with a hundred years of crap. Sometimes when the sea breeze blows the smoke away, the tower shakes so much that he has to hold on to the rail.

The Chosen are destroyers, not builders. He used that to rise to the top of them. Now all he sees is decay. He rules over a world filled with crumbling mansions, smelly trash heaps, scraggly lines of crops. The only thing the Chosen do well is kill.

That's why the Cluster wants the war so much. Every great Lord of the Chosen has to win in battle, so he offered them a war that will make the Chosen the true rulers of Ell Aye. He was swept up in his own lust for power, for the chance to permanently stamp his will onto the world. Now he's beginning to regret promising them their war.

It's Jemma's fault. She's thrown him off his orbit. Somehow she killed a Giant in the Biter attack on the Kingdom, which broke the spine of the assault. But it's more than that. He felt her use the Haze at the Kingdom, back when he thought he was the only person who felt it. The thought makes him furious. The Haze chose *him*.

Then he saw Jemma in a vision with a gray-haired man who has no business still living in this world. If Jemma has found old people? She might have found a way to live beyond the End.

If he can destroy her, he will be the only person who can wield the Haze. If he can steal the secret of the End from her, then Little Man can live forever. That's the war he wants to fight.

The other members of the Cluster climb the tower, which shakes even more when they reach the platform. The Twins automatically shift places to adjust for the added weight.

"My *Lord*," Connor says, speaking in the mocking drawl most of the Chosen choose to use. Little Man avoids it himself. Connor is the leader of the Palos Preps caste and the head of the Cluster. "I've been meaning to talk to you about the Ice Cream Men."

"What could there possibly be to say?" Little Man says, daring Connor to bring up the kid. It was the Cluster's fault the attack didn't succeed completely. They didn't let him take enough Last Lifers, who would have overwhelmed the Ice Cream Men and killed that little shit before he tossed the bomb. Even if Tommy was the one who decided to only bring one Giant.

Connor hesitates. Little Man has to give him a little credit for speaking, with two Giants behind him who could throw him off the platform. "It's just that now that . . . now with the Ice Cream Men gone . . . how am I gonna get my pills? I'm almost out."

"You should have thought of that before you begged me for those guns," Little Man says. They brought in fifty guns with that attack, even if it meant cutting their trading line forever. "You're just gonna have to fight sober from now on." Connor loves the pills the Ice Cream Men used to bring him; half the time he's running high and wild, like all the Preps.

The platform lurches one last time, as if another Giant has joined them. Connor doesn't notice. He's clearly wound up on something. "And those Last Lifers are a joke," Connor says. "Half of them ran at the Kingdom."

"Strange," a voice says behind him. "I din't see you on the front lines with us." Connor stiffens, as do the rest of the Cluster. It's Li, the leader of the Last Lifers. Even though he's huge, Li isn't a Giant. He's something worse. His eyes are dead black, his mouth is ripped open with a jagged cut, like a smile that bleeds from the corners. It was given to him by Jemma when he failed to fit into the Holy Wood. Like all the Last Lifers, he doesn't fear death. That's why they terrify everyone else.

Connor drops silent. Little Man nods at Li, and turns back to survey the crowd below him, already feasting. It's supposed to involve some dish made from the flesh of the conquered. Tommy has lost the taste for it. Lately all he wants is a mango and a loaf of bread.

He can tell the castes at a glance from the way they dress. Although the Preps rule the Chosen, they make up only five in a hundred. Another quarter are the Jocks and Geeks. The Wannabes make up forty percent of the crowd. They're the lowest of the castes, the ones destined for scraps. That's why they despise the Lowers so much, the bottom thirty percent. Everyone needs someone beneath them to hate.

The Cluster hate the Last Lifers, too. The alliance with the Last Lifers swelled their army with hundreds of soldiers, but the castes of the Chosen hate that anyone else, especially people with brown skin, could be treated as an equal. It's upsetting the balance of the camp.

A shriek bursts up from the Chosen below, followed by more and more. He's heard it every night of his life. It grates.

But then a silence falls. A hundred Last Lifers walk into the feast area, shoulder to shoulder. Not carrying weapons. Not saying a thing. Just walking to their tables. People move away from them in distrust and fear, but Tommy finds himself drawn to them.

"They've changed," he says. The first time he met the Last Lifers, they could barely hold still long enough for him to speak. They tried to hurt anyone around them. They'd gone mad because they'd lost hope.

"Yeah, they have," Roberto says, pleased with himself. Little Man had sent Roberto as an emissary to win over the Last Lifers, because he needed an Angeleno to speak to the former Angelenos. He'd promised Roberto his freedom someday if he did it, and Roberto came back with an army.

Roberto had brought the Last Lifers gifts of food and guns to get their attention. But he also brought them hope. Most Last Lifers were lost and frightened kids, terrified by the End. They saw what Little Man did with the Making, they heard about his visions. Some of the kids took the hope and stored it someplace safe and it grew coat after coat until they had something with luster. It had turned into belief. Belief in Little Man.

Little Man knows what to do with that belief.

Li moves to the other end of the platform, and Connor leans toward Little Man again. "It's just that maybe you were wrong about the Last Lifers," he says. Jesus, the kid must really be high or he'd know that Little Man was about to cut his head off.

"I have never been wrong," Little Man says. "The visions showed me how to unite the Chosen. They showed me how to repair the guns. They showed me how to make the Giants. They—"

"Did they show you that kid's bomb?" Connor says, not quite mockingly because he doesn't quite dare. But he means it. Little Man has to watch him closely. Without Little Man, Connor would have been leader of the Palos, because the Preps run everything. Their fathers go back to the biggest houses in the hills. All these years without Parents, and it all still goes back to the size of the fathers' houses in the hills.

"They show the Twins tearing off your arms," Little Man says.

"You can't threaten me," Connor says.

"I can. I don't have to, though. You need me too much," Little Man says. "I'm your Lord because only I can give you what you want: everything." For now, he needs Connor. If he doesn't have the support of the Preps, he doesn't have control of the Chosen. But hopefully not for long.

Little Man blocks out the crowd and Connor, and reaches for Jemma as he does a dozen times a day. She's disappeared completely in the Haze, which worries him. What is she doing? What does she know that he doesn't know? He sees her friends in the Haze sometimes, but nothing tells him where they are.

He needs to find the Angelenos before his war. What more could he do with a weapon like Jemma?

Right now, though, he needs to secure his throne. He has Chase ring the gong. The crowd falls quiet.

"Tonight, we are not two peoples. We're not separate castes," he says, speaking through a metal cone mounted on the railing of the tower's deck. "Tonight we are one. We are united by fate, by a war against our common enemies. Most of all, we're united by hope. That there is more to this world than what we've been given. That there are more years than what we've been allowed. That happiness doesn't depend on where your fathers lived, or the color of your skin."

There is no sound. He shouts. "We are all the Chosen!"

The crowd erupts in cheers. Almost all the Last Lifers do. Even some of the Wannabes and the Lowers, although they look around carefully before they do. The Last Lifers have switched the balance of power, by their numbers and their devotion to Little Man. The lower castes now outnumber the upper castes by a large margin. Which means the Cluster's hold is slipping. He just has to make sure it continues to slip.

The Preps remain stony and silent. Little Man can't see Connor's face behind him, but he's sure it's seething. Good. Because Little Man is tired of the Chosen. Little Man tries to breathe deep, but can't. He smells the stink of bones, the cooing of the Wannabes peddling their bodies, the laughter of the Preps, and hates it all. Everything in the Palos is a trade. No one has worth. You take things if you can, if you weren't born to it. And there's never been a person better at thriving in it than Little Man.

The Chosen are like crabs, crabs with huge claws that pull each other down, tear each other's legs off. Tommy could never have survived head-to-head with them. He was too small, too weak. Little Man survives because he can see more, think more clearly, bide his time. His claws may be small, but he carries a sting at his back, just out of sight. When you think you have cornered him, his stinger comes down.

They can be crabs all they want.

Little Man is a scorpion.

CHAPTER SEVEN
THE SON

Jemma dreams of Apple. It's not her usual dream, the one where he spars with her in the trees outside the Holy Wood, or the one where he guards her on a Gather. She is looking at the stars, at the Hunter, and the belt breaks apart and falls spiraling down down down to her waiting palm. Hundreds of stars. They glow faint and blue, and then they form the shape she always knew they'd take: her Apple.

She holds him in her hand, an Apple so small she could hide him away. His eyes glow bright. Her eyes flow into his and back again. Only then does she realize that neither of them can speak.

Her palm burns. She feels a hundred pin pricks, but it only makes her want to hold him tighter. Until she can't. She breathes out, a gentle wisp of air, and Apple falls apart into a dancing cloud of sparks. He floats away on the wind.

She wakes up and she's in a hospital room . . . again. Her left eye is closed, her cheeks feels raw, and her torso is on fire. There's a rustle of pages in the corner and her gaze falls there. In the chair where Lady usually sits is the last person she expected: Isaac. The only bit of book cover showing through tape is an image of two men fighting in the desert, one of them with a black bird mask and a scythe, the other in white with a sword.

Isaac looks up and shuts the book. "How you feeling?" he says.

"Fuck you, puto," she says.

"I thought that was a little excessive last night," he says. "You could have just admitted it and saved yourself from pain."

"That the way you talk to all the girls you beat up?" she says, angry.

"To be honest, I don't talk to a lot of girls."

"Who are you?" she says.

"We've met," he says. "Isaac."

"No," she says slowly. "Who. Are. You?"

He shrugs, but she doesn't let it go. "You couldn't help yourself last night, could you?" she says. "You had to show off that you could see with the Haze."

"Shit. Busted," Isaac says, and he really does look sheepish. "I can't see with it. Not the way you've described it. But I can feel it, and I can use it in a fight."

"You could feel that it wasn't in me," she says, understanding now. That moment when Isaac looked into her eyes? That was a test. He knew the Haze was gone.

"Yeah," he says. "I knew. You talked like you knew what the Haze was, but none of our tests were showing it. So they asked me to look."

"So you speak to the Haze," Jemma says.

"It's not like it's my first language or anything," Isaac says, "but yeah, I speak Haze." And Jemma decides that maybe she doesn't have to hate him forever.

"But how? James said I was the only one."

"Well, obviously not," Isaac says. "We weren't going to tell you all our secrets at once. My parents are used to holding on to them."

"Your parents," Jemma says. That's what she overheard last night in her daze. "James? James and who?"

"You couldn't guess?" he says. "James and Alice."

"But they can't stand each other!" Wasn't that the point of Parents? To love each other like she loved Apple?

"They used to love each other so much they had an affair, back before the End. Quite the scandal, I've heard. Then the End happened, and I got sick, and I guess—I guess it was all too much. There's too much keeping them apart. They can't get along and they can't leave because both of them are needed here at the Camp to, you know, save the world."

"I never met no one who met their Parents," she says. Wistful. "And you got two of em."

"They're mostly a pain in the ass at my age," Isaac says. "If that makes you feel any better."

"No. No it don't," Jemma says. But she can't think about that right now. "You know bout the Haze. You gotta know that I've felt it."

"I think that maybe you *did*," Isaac says. "But you don't now. I wish I could help you, but it isn't my call. Right now, the Camp has a lot more to worry about than a girl who used to hear voices. Sorry, I didn't mean it that way, but . . ."

Jemma doesn't listen to the rest. For the first time, she wonders: Would the Old Guys turn her away? Is it possible she could come all the way to the source of the End, and still be no closer to solving it?

"But I could help you," she says. "Two kids who can use the Haze? Imagine what we could do to stop the End."

"Yeah, but we can't help you," he says. "Not like you mean."

Jemma fumes for a while after he leaves, but then she realizes: He's right. They can't help her. The Haze came to her on its own, when—

When she was in danger. It came to her when the Last Lifers chased her, when the wild dogs attacked, when Othello tried to kill her. It didn't come to her with Isaac because she wasn't really in danger.

What if she was?

CHAPTER EIGHT
THE ROUND TABLE

Tashia isn't sure why she and Coretta are seated at the Round Table. Not for this meeting. The Knights around it seem to be wondering the same thing.

The Round Table is located inside a hidden room at the top of the Horn, the hook-shaped mountain at the center of the Kingdom. A fake place like the rest of the Kingdom, Jemma had said before she left. But she was right—the entire Kingdom was built as a place for families to come play before the End. Even the castle is one-sided.

The King enters the room. The King. As if it isn't the boy she's loved her whole life before the Kingdom tore them apart. Her X.

He glances at her as if nothing is strange about her sitting with the Knights. "The Round Table will come to order," he says, and sits down. There's a basketball hoop behind him. The creators of the Kingdom used to come to this room inside a mountain to play games, and the Knights have never taken it down.

"Plus two," Othello says. "The Round Table plus two." But the King ignores him.

Othello is X's right hand—or was, until Jemma destroyed him in the Night Mountain. It was meant to be a fight to the death, but Jemma crippled him for life. He's still on the Round Table, on the slim chance he'll be able to ride in combat again. Right now, he can barely sit in a chair, much less a horse.

"The Ice Cream Men Massacre," the King says. "What do we

know?" The Massacre happened after the Biters attacked the Kingdom with the Last Lifers. The Knights were caught flat-footed, and only Tashia and her cowboys, assisted by the Angelenos, managed to turn the Biters back.

A squadron of Knights rode out when they heard the shots along the 5 road, but Tashia and her cowboys had found the carnage of the Ice Cream Massacre first. She can still smell the stench of burning rubber and flesh.

"It wasn't much of a fight," she says, ignoring that the Knights expect her to be silent during their Round Table. "Don't think the Ice Cream Men got a shot off. It was a slaughter."

"What did they take?" the King says.

"No food or supplies. Not even medicine," Tashia says.

"Weapons?" the King says.

"All of them."

"Unprovoked attack, weapons gone?" Othello says. "This means the Biters are really going to war."

"Means more than that. Means a lot of kids are going to starve," Coretta says, speaking up for the first time. Coretta is Tashia's best friend and head of the kitchens. "The Ice Cream Men bring us all the food we can't grow ourselves, and that's gone now. Our corn is wilting from the heat. Half of it is going to die. We're looking at a rough summer."

"Who cares? We got plenty of cows," John says, a hulking presence to Tashia's right. She can barely look at him, not after what he did to Mia. Her sister.

"Even you are going to be sick of cows when you can't shit right," Coretta says tartly.

"Fuck you, b—"

"I'd ask you not to insult the other members of the Round Table," the King says. Tashia stares at him. Everyone at the Table stares at him. "Let's move on to the next item, which is why Tashia and Coretta are here. The most recent Biter attack made me realize we have grown too safe in our thinking. The Knights didn't save us—Tashia and Grease did, along with some *very* annoying Angelenos. The Biters have changed all their tactics, and so should we. We need our smartest and strongest to fight them. Tashia and Coretta, come here."

She does, unsure. Has X lost his mind? But he stands over them, one at a time, and touches their shoulders gently with a sword. "Rise," he says. "You're now Knights of the Round Table."

Othello finally regains enough presence of mind to say something. "That's impossible. There are no girls on the Round Table. The Philosopher King said it should always be twelve—"

"The Philosopher King based the Kingdom upon the myth of Arthur," X says. "The world we live in is real."

"Any new Knight has to challenge his way into the Round Table," Othello says.

"Would you like her to challenge you?" the King says. "Because I don't think you could beat her in your condition."

In any condition, Tashia thinks. That's why she's not with X. Because the Kingdom is built on power, and he keeps trying to shield her from harm as if she can't wield power. She couldn't accept his love, because it was built on uneven territory. He had fought to save her from the old King, the Cleaver, because he thought she needed protecting. She never forgave him that.

Still, John and Othello hate it, and that's a start.

"There will be new rules of conduct for the Round Table," the King says, not finished. "Knights will have the same rations as any other Child. They will work in the fields along with the others. And they can no longer take girls without their consent."

Take. He means rape. Tashia is the only girl in the Kingdom with an actual sister, Mia. And John took Mia because he was a Knight. Because Knights could take anything they wanted. Until now.

X looks at her, and for the first time since they were Middles, she thinks he sees her as an equal. Not something to be possessed.

Not acting as if she needed protection. Just an ally in the war to end wars.

He's not fucking around, she thinks, looking at X. Her heart starts to open again. But she recognizes the bitter looks on John, Othello, and some of the other Knights and thinks, *Neither are they.*

CHAPTER NINE
THE ICE CREAM MEN

Alfie dampens the Ice Cream Cart bell as he pedals into the courtyard of the hospital where the rest of his people now live. It's not that he's worried about someone hearing him. It's that the bell sounds too loud, all by itself.

The rest of the Ice Cream Men will know that something is wrong when it's just him. Ice Cream Men almost always travel in pairs, a protection from the Wild. And in less than a minute, they're all standing across from him in the courtyard. The last twenty-three Ice Cream Men left in the world.

"They gones," Alfie says.

"Who?" J'Me says. She's the oldest one left.

"The Ice Cream Men all gones," he says, and the sound of that sentence in the courtyard is even worse than the bell.

He tells them about the bank massacre, how the Biters weren't even trying that hard to kill. The Biters were just trying to carve a path to the vault, which was loaded with guns. He sees the faces fall. They all thought they were safe.

"But they our friends," J'Me says.

"Nah. Not friends. Useful," Alfie says. "Right now, them guns is useful, too."

"Gon kill them assholes," Phuong says. She's the master doula of the Ice Cream Men, so her place was with the Moms making babies, not at the bank with the Fleet. The Ice Cream Men are only Moms and wee ones now. All but four of them are under the age of seven.

Alfie nods, but J'Me shakes her head. "We don't take sides. Never."

"They took em first," Phuong says. "It's only their side or the dead side."

In the end, Alfie isn't the one who convinces them they need to fight the Biters. Neither is Phuong. What convinces them are all the Ice Cream Men who didn't come back, the torn and twisted pedal carts when he leads them to the bank to see for themselves, the bodies missing because the Biters burned them or worse. Even J'Me comes away sharp and angry. "Goddam Biters," she says.

The Fleet sounds small and lonely as they pedal back to the hospital. They're used to two hundred bells surrounding them, ringing to the sky. The Ice Cream Men have loaded their carts with everything useful, which is a lot. Some of the best richie stuff in Ell Aye is there, and the Biters just wanted guns. Even the smallest kids are pedaling the carts they could salvage.

"We gon need a new captain," Phuong says, pedaling.

"J'Me," Alfie says. "She always actin like she in charge."

"She can't," Phuong says. "She got a baby comin. We ain't risking that kid."

Alfie nods his head. That just leaves three Ice Cream Men old enough to lead: Alfie, Phuong, and Frankie, ten and raccoon smart.

"Not it," Frankie says.

"Not it," Alfie says.

"Not— Aww, dammit," Phuong says. And they name a new captain without ever stopping their carts.

Phuong is a good choice. She used to be one of the Orange, until the last of the old people's orchards died in their home along the Santa Ana eight years ago. No more oranges in the land named for them, so the people named for them starved. You could see them scavenging the houses, boiling wallpaper from kitchens for the paste.

Then Phuong became a servant, because the Ice Cream Men needed babies and her people needed two sacks of rice and a case of beans. The Ice Cream Men took in a lot of the Oranges that winter. But Phuong was a good trade. She can't be rattled, even if a baby's getting born sideways.

"So we gots to figure out how to fights em," Alfie says, still pedaling.

"But sneaky," Phuong says. "One fight with the Biters and the Ice Cream Mens gones for reals."

"They ain't lookin for us," Alfie says. "They lookin for guns."

The Biters don't have all the Ice Cream Men's guns yet. There are Hydin Holes all over Ell Aye and Oh See, and the Biters are going to be patrolling heavily to find them.

That's when Alfie has the idea.

It'll only take one Hydin Hole for the Ice Cream Men to set a trap.

CHAPTER TEN
THE FALCON

Part of Lady wonders why she can't enjoy it. The lights that go on with just a switch. The movies. Especially this one: *The Empire Strikes Back*.

Her favorite part of the movie comes on: when the ships chase the Falcon through the rocks. *Asteroids*, she remembers. Rocks in the sky are asteroids.

Lady loves it for the movement, the way the Falcon twirls through the air and dashes between the rocks, the way it wins by never being touched. "Did they have those really? Before the End?" she asks Gil, the only other person in the room. "Ships that fly in the night like that?"

"In space," he says. "They did. But not like that."

Which makes her sadder? The idea that they no longer exist, or that they never did?

Then the kiss, between the princess and the Solo. She can almost feel it, the brushing of bodies in the narrow passage, two people who want each other but can't say it.

Sometimes Lady forgets that she never meant to be a warrior, a wanderer. All she ever wanted was to be a Mama, to roll with a boy, until Li attacked her—no, that's not right. When the Olders tried to make her roll with Li even after he raped her, and she knew her only worth to the Holy Wood was her body. How good a Mama was, how good her curves were, how good a roll. Everything she wanted or would be was driven by the life in her body. But now her body doesn't feel like it can hold life anymore.

She understands how Jemma must feel right now, losing the Haze and feeling half herself. It's a terrible shock to find yourself unwhole.

The Camp has started to wake her up, little things like the shower. Jemma won't go into it after her first attempt, convinced she's drowning, but to Lady it's her new favorite miracle.

Part of it is the clean. She doesn't think she's ever truly been clean before now. Her arms seem plumper from the water. Her skin feels less cotton and more suede.

But it's the water that initially shocked her, falling from the ceiling like rain but not, comforting not bracing. Warm. It covered her skin in fifty different fingers of warmth. They cushioned her, they pushed back and wrapped back around her when she twisted.

As if someone was holding her in his hand.

Jesucristo, she thinks. *Didn't I used to love how things felt?*

A body is only meant to be used. To get torn. Lady absently touches the pin in her hair, the one she put there after she stabbed Li and has never taken out again.

Lady wonders if the Old Guys know they're not whole, either. She watches them sitting in the common room as they do every night, never looking at each other. They're gathered, but the Teevee does all the talking.

It's too long, she thinks. A hundred years in one place. And yet, if she and Jemma had a hundred years together, wouldn't they make the most of it? Wouldn't they at least *be* in the same room when they're both in it? For the first time, she feels sorry for the Old Guys, the way they shuffle through their day even if their bodies aren't actually old. It's as if the years have burned away the parts that let them live with others. More like the crude piñata figures they made in the Holy Wood from old paper, rather than living people.

Where *is* Jemma? She's been taking walks by herself since Isaac beat the shit out of her. Lady should look for her.

Lady waits for the monster to chase the Falcon out from the rock, then walks outside. Jemma isn't in the courtyard or the barn. Lady crosses to the northwest corner of the quad, climbing to the lip of the bowl. Above her on the hill are the usual herd of buffalo. She's about to turn away when she notices a lone bull only fifty yards away.

And sees Jemma standing in front of it.

CHAPTER ELEVEN
THE BUFFALO

Jemma can see the herd of buffalo above her, their shaggy flanks lit with the evening sun. But her eyes are on a solitary bull, bigger by half than the biggest cow. He is lying down in a shallow pit in the turf. *A wallow*, Brian K calls it. He looks fluffy, sleepy.

Jemma approaches him, imperceptibly at first, as if a gentle magnet tugged at her and spun her axis. He stands up, and she freezes. Even from here, she can tell that he's taller than her. "That guy looks cute, but he can bowl over a car," Brian K told them.

Hello, old man, she says silently. *I just thought we could talk.* He flicks his ear toward her.

This is insane. But Jemma feels as if she's lost a limb, a whole wilderness of limbs. With the Haze, she had started to feel invincible. She was magic. Without the Haze, she's just Jemma of the Holy Wood.

She's not sure she likes Jemma of the Holy Wood.

"Whatcha doing, mija?" Lady says, behind her, and Jemma curses under her breath.

"Just looking at my friend here," she says.

"Don't think that's too smart," Lady says.

Of course it ain't smart, mija, Jemma thinks. *That's the whole point.* The Haze had come to save her before, every time she needed it. So she just needs to make herself need saving. The Haze would come back to show her how to escape the bull's horns. To save her life.

She half expects, half hopes for Lady to stop her. But Lady walks forward with her, just as silent. Jemma looks out the corner of her eye to her right and sees that Lady is staring straight ahead. *Neither of us wants to look at the other*, she thinks. *Because if we look, one of us will stop this.*

It's like the game of chicken they used to play in the Holy Wood, where they'd sling dead chickens at each other's head and see who would duck first. Neither of them wants to duck.

The bull squares away in front of her. The only thing she can see are hooves under a massive head. It's half its body, like an oversize mask tipped with black horns. It snorts. She doesn't know buffalo. She can't tell if it's wary or mad. She hopes mad.

The buffalo steps forward. She watches its hoof flex, dig into the wallow.

The bull charges.

Jemma expects clouds of blue. She expects the Haze to draw the lines that will let her dodge the bull. She doesn't expect how fast the bull will close the gap between them, how terrifying his horns would be if she had the time to be terrified. She doesn't expect Lady to hold still as long as she does, bracing for the charge. The bull closes in on them, and all she sees are horns and nostrils and her best friend not moving.

Jemma shoves Lady's shoulder, right as Lady shoves hers. She hits the ground hard, and so does Lady.

The bull passes between them. She could have grabbed its wool in her fingers. She can smell the shit on its flank, can feel the hooves rattle her bones. Then it's gone, and still the Haze doesn't come.

Lady is staring at her from her own seat on the grass.

"What the hell?" Jemma says.

"What the hell to you, too!" Lady says. Jemma sees the hurt in her eyes, the wild attempt to stay in control, and realizes: *She wasn't doing this for me. She was doing this for her.*

She wants to tell Lady why she wants the Haze so badly, how lonely she feels without Apple. How she regrets not rolling with

Apple, how all she wants now is to feel him completely next to her. How she didn't want a baby but wanted Apple to live on in this world.

She wants to tell Lady how empty she feels. But Lady is empty, too, and that matters more. "What's wrong, Lady?" she says, crawling across the grass to her friend.

Lady doesn't usually cry, and she doesn't cry now. But she collapses into Jemma's arms all the same. "You all got a reason to be. You bringing back the Haze and Grease fixing machines and Pico—Pico just wants to live in the world of Parents instead of this one. And I'm just me and I'm not the kid I was in the Holy Wood."

Jemma remembers how Lady looked when she talked about boys, about having a baby. She would have had those things if Jemma hadn't taken her away. She was so full of life in the Holy Wood, so alive in her body.

"I'm sorry I did this to you, mija," Jemma says, holding her close. Lady's close-cropped hair is fuzzy under her chin. "I know how much you wanted to be a Mama."

"No," Lady says, pulling away. This time the tears really do come. "It's been a long time since I wanted that. It's been a long time since I wanted anything."

CHAPTER TWELVE
THE MAKING

Stanford knocks on the door of the firehouse where Little Man makes his Giants. Little Man says, "Something wrong with the army?" Stanford wouldn't disturb him unless there was something to report.

"The army's fine," Stanford says. "It's just that . . . I'm almost seventeen," he says. Quiet and firm.

Tommy understands what Stanford is saying, but lets Stanford say it. "You need more Giants for the Making."

"I'll figure it out," Tommy says.

"I volunteer," Stanford says.

"You don't need to," Tommy says. He's not sure why he says it. He would love Stanford as a Giant. He's already big, already a fighter. The Making would make him grow bigger.

"I want to," Stanford says. "You found a way beyond the End."

Tommy holds still and tries to think of a response that would send Stanford on his way. No response comes.

"I'd like to do it today," Stanford says.

Little Man turns and speaks to Roberto, who's been watching him from the door. "Boil the water," Little Man says to Roberto.

Roberto stokes the coals that are always banked and waiting for air, and moves a large pot over the wood stove. Tommy wishes he had the Lectrics the Old Ones used—but at least he has a way to get his instruments clean. Giants kept dying of fections to the head until he learned to—what did the Old Ones call it?—sterilize.

The firehouse has a bank of glass doors that let in the light but hold out the wind and dust, making it easy to see and easy to keep clean. There are none of the Old Ones' hospitals in the Palos anymore, but without the tools the Old Ones had, it wouldn't matter. What he does is more like carpentry, anyway: just hammering and cutting.

The Haze showed him the Making at six, when he was hiding from his tormentors in a rotted mansion at the fringes of the hill. Everything of value had been stripped long ago, but books had no value. He hid among stacks of them, hoping his breath would even out, and then the Haze fell.

That was the first time seeing the Haze, and at first he couldn't make sense of it. It looked like dazzling blue motes of dust, but there was no sunlight where it lingered. He blinked over and over again, trying to make it go away, but it grew brighter. It clustered around a stack of books across the room.

We are the Haze, a voice said. It wanted him to follow. The Haze wanted him to follow. Tommy had never believed in anything, he still didn't. But he started to believe in the Haze. And eventually, it showed him how to make Giants.

The Old Ones used to call it a lobotomy. It was a crude way to calm down the crazy ones, the angry ones. There are paths between the frontal lobe and the rest of the brain. The Haze showed him where they are, and what they mean. If he can cut those paths, the Giants will live as old as the Old Ones because the End can't touch them. They will grow as big as the Old Ones did, maybe bigger.

You just need the right tool. Little Man looks down at the ice pick, six inches sharp and gleaming. He watches Stanford enter the room and lie down on the bed.

When the Chosen meet the End, they dump the body over the cliff for Catalina, the goddess of the sea. For those who go through the Making, the End is glorious. Little Man made it that way, to make it more desirable. When the Making is complete, they burn a fire for EmEmAye, the god of war. They sacrifice a prisoner and the Giant has his pick of anyone in the village to roll with. Stanford didn't ask for the ceremony. It's the most un-Chosen thing possible.

"You didn't want the bonfire." Little Man tries to never say anything as a question. It makes him sound as young as he is.

"No. I'm not doing this for glory. I . . ." Stanford turns his head away.

"You're not much of a Chosen," Tommy says. He's never said that before. Stanford is honorable, fierce, kind. Habits Little Man usually despises.

"No, I— My nanny was a Lower, you know."

Tommy doesn't react. Jocks and Preps and Geeks get nannies. Wannabes don't. That's why so many of the Wannabe kids don't make it to their teens.

"She believed in different things, kinder gods. She held on to what made the Angelenos good. She taught me that Catalina doesn't take you away to the island when you die. You just die."

The Chosen believe they are reborn every generation. Tommy doesn't. So he nods.

"If that's it, then I want to make this life count. I want to keep on living."

Tommy remembers the first time he talked to Stanford. An older Wannabe girl had smashed Tommy in the jaw with a board, knelt on his chest until he could barely breathe. Then the girl flew backward and Stanford stood over her. "He ain't yours," Stanford said.

The girl knew: Tommy was Stanford's now. Stanford could do anything to him, anything he wanted to do, and no one else could touch him. And Tommy knew it, too.

The boys had walked up the hill, Stanford already large at twelve and Tommy tiny at five, and Stanford waved him away. "Go. They'll leave you alone for a couple of weeks." Tommy didn't say anything back. He just hid before Stanford changed his mind.

"It's not true," Tommy says now.

"What?" Stanford says.

"What I tell the Giants. That—that this is living."

"I know," Stanford says.

"You ain't the same person after this," Tommy says. "You ain't. You're barely a person." He feels it then, the shame of failure. He's created a weapon with the Giants—but he hasn't solved the End.

"I don't care," Stanford says. "Just let me live and I'll figure it out."

Roberto hands Little Man the jar of thesia. Little Man knows the real word for it but none of the Chosen can pronounce it, too long for their tongues. He learned how to make it in the books in the library, from old chlorine powder in a pool shed and fingernail polish remover, things that managed to survive long past the End because no one cares about them anymore.

Little Man soaks a rag with the thesia. "This will make you sleepy," he says. "You won't feel this."

Stanford's head lies below Tommy's hands. His eyes are afraid, but not panicked. It occurs to Tommy: This is the only Chosen he's never bothered to hate. Maybe it's good to let Stanford live on.

The thesia levels Stanford, and Little Man washes his hands and slides in the needle. The Haze shows him the way, but Stanford shakes and shudders at the second needle. "He's too big! Thesia's worn off!" Roberto says, and hands Tommy the jar.

This time Tommy holds the cloth over Stanford's face until he's sure the thesia has knocked Stanford cold. He cuts the second path cleanly, withdraws the needle, and moves back. He wipes his forehead and realizes that, uncharacteristically, he's sweating. He steps away and feels himself slowly calm down. Until he sees that Stanford has stopped breathing, stopped breathing for good.

When they step into the dark afterward, after they're sure the body won't move, Roberto says, "I'm sorry."

Tommy doesn't respond.

"You couldn't a known the thesia was too much. It's too tricky for no one . . ."

Little Man holds as still as if he were dead, so still that Roberto has no choice but to match him.

"Stanford spoke against me in the Cluster today," Little Man says, preferring a lie to the appearance of failure. "He tried to weaken my alliance with the Newports. I did *not* use too much thesia."

Roberto is too good at being a Lower to express even a ripple of shock.

The Twins loom out of the shadows. "Gone?" Nate says, pointing into the station at the failed Giant. The Twins will carry it to the cliffs, and Little Man will name the new Head of Jocks. Tommy quells the last shake in his hand.

"Gone," Little Man says.

CHAPTER THIRTEEN
THE ICE CREAM MEN

The Biters below Alfie move as if they're alone in the Oh See, shoulders thrown back, spears dragging along the ground, laughing even as they raid a Hydin Hole. Why shouldn't they? They killed all the Ice Cream Men.

It wasn't easy to lure the Biters here. If they wanted the Biters to think the Ice Cream Men are all gone, the Ice Cream Men couldn't let themselves be seen.

Phuong hit on the trick first. "What if we someone else?" Like the Orange. From there, the rest of the trap was easy to set.

Because Phuong was one of the Orange to begin with, it was easy for her to pretend to be an Orange wandering near the 5 road, where she was likely to be spotted. She just had to seem a little more defeated than usual to pull it off. Phuong shook a bit when they left her in the Biters' path. But she hid a dagger in her boot and a pistol at her waist, and the steel brought bravery.

It took a couple of hours in the summer heat for the Biters to come around the bend of the 5 road. They spotted Phuong and shrieked after her. Phuong turned and ran—but not fast enough to avoid capture. The first half of the trap was set.

Alfie never lost sight of Phuong, even when they threw her to the ground and tied her hands. He watched the rhythm of the interrogation. She had to take just enough hits to be believable before she cracked, before she offered up a lost Hydin Hole that she saw the Ice

Cream Men go to. Phuong gave him a signal for when the location had been given up: a sharp nod that he could see even a hundred yards away. Alfie saw one of the Biters put his knife to Phuong's throat, and that was the moment. No sense waiting until someone slipped and cut her instead.

They only had twelve of the Fleet left big enough to pass for an army, and then only from a distance. Raggedy and dusty like the Orange, they swarmed over the top of a low hill where the Biters would see them. The Orange are peaceful, weak, but they are known to go for a rage when the food was low. Alfie's gun, which fired quick after quick, made them look even fiercer. The Biters didn't bother to count attackers when the bullets were dancing around them. They ran away into the street, not worried about the Orange prisoner when their heads were full of the Hydin Hole they got out of her.

Alfie watches them now through the nocklers. It took the Biters a whole day to find the Hydin Hole. Phuong didn't give them the exact directions. They wouldn't trust something too easy. So Phuong put them on the right street and then they could believe they found it themselves.

The Biters make their way into the Hydin Hole, an old Sleven store. The freezers are made of steel. It will take a while for the Biters to hack through the freezer lock. Alfie motions to the other Ice Cream Men, and they take positions outside the store to make sure no one gets away.

Whoops erupt from the Sleven store. The Biters are in. It looks like a lot, even though the Ice Cream Men moved most of it out— they'll find boxes of guns, exploding eggs, the bomb sticks. They won't notice the piles of old clothes filling up the boxes underneath.

They won't notice the long long fuse, either, snaking out of the back door into the alley. If they see the spark, it will be too late.

Alfie catches the eye of Frankie in the back alley. She can make herself invisible if she needs to, but now there's no need. He signals, two big thumbs in the air. *Light it.*

He can't see the flame, but he can see Frankie running from it. Thirty seconds, he counts, and braces himself. It's quiet for another five beats afterward, and Frankie pauses, moves as if to go back. He shakes his head. One, two—

That's a good boom, he thinks, when he can hear again. The glass on the front of the Sleven is gone. So's what's left from the building next door. And nothing but smoke and flame pouring out from the Hydin Hole.

Alfie climbs out of his cover, walks down the street toward the Sleven. He hates to lose the bombs, but Ice Cream Men can get more. They can't get more Ice Cream Men.

A figure bursts out of the Sleven, trailing fire. Alfie half expects it to float upward, that's how insubstantial it looks, but it sinks to the ground. Alfie pulls out his pistol, the kind that carries six bullets, and steps close but not so close that the flame or the person can touch him.

The Biter doesn't look human. The tattoo on his wrist is the only part not burning, and that's how Alfie knows him. He used to trade with Alfie. He loved mangoes. Then he was at the front of the attack at the bank.

Alfie shouldn't waste the bullet. He should let him suffer. But then Alfie would be missing out on the revenge. "Picked the wrong side, puto," he says, using the word Lady taught him. The eyes register fear, pain, then nothing. Then he pulls the trigger.

They drag the body back into the Sleven and let it burn. If the Biters track down their patrol, they'll see what's left of a Hydin Hole. They'll think it was an accident, that an old bomb went off.

"We can't keep on doing this scam," Phuong says. "We got to get frens soon."

She's right. Sooner or later, the Biters will catch on and set a trap for them. They need allies.

Alfie can see where the Ice Cream Men go from here. Down the

Oldie highways to where the other peoples live. Where they might have heard news that the Biters are moving to war.

The Ice Cream Men aren't fighters. They're traders, they're travelers, they're talkers.

Time to do some talking.

CHAPTER FOURTEEN
THE SOLARS

"This is easy for you, isn't it?" Brian K says as they struggle with the power source of a solar panel.

"It's like breathing. I just . . . see it," Grease says.

"Huh," Brian K says. "I noticed." The other day he witnessed Grease fixing a toaster and asked him to help with the tech of the Camp.

"Like, fix things?" Grease had said. All the toys, and he gets to play with them?

"Like, fix *everything*," Brian K said. "It's all breaking."

The solars are made of blue glass panels, elevated above a line of Long Gone cars, but Brian K thinks another one of the panels is about to fail. There are hundreds of them in a row, most are cracked and disconnected. That might be because there's a chopper splitting one section, its remaining propeller still pointing straight up into the air. From where Grease stands, it looks as if it's drowning in a glass blue lake.

"Fell out of the sky," Brian K says. "When the End happened, you had to be careful when you walked outside."

The Camp is down to a third of its solar panels. It used to have a couple dozen power stations, gas and solar and coal. They're all gone now. "This is it. It's torches next," Brian K says.

"Why are they breaking?"

"Nothing's meant to run this long," Brian K says.

"Can't you make new ones?"

"We lived in a world run by things that none of us understood. You couldn't fix anything. You sent for a new part from ten thousand miles away," Brian K says. "We can't make technology like this anymore. We don't have the tools or the knowledge, so we just keep looking for old spare parts. This is just life support."

Grease remembers when he first met Pico, how Pico said the two of them were the last chance to fix the world. The next time the world got a chance, the Parents' machines would be too rusted and broken. But now Grease wonders if it's already too late.

Grease watches as Brian K struggles with a connection to one of the panels. "That wire is loose," Grease says. A little push, and the panel starts feeding Lectrics back into the grid.

"I wish I could see it like you," Brian K says.

"How'd you get into this, then?" Grease says.

Brian K hesitates. "I'm just the guy they stuck with the tech stuff because no one else wants to understand it. At first I did it for Brian P. He was an IT guy when we met in the Long Life Project. I was an engineer, but I thought if I learned about his tech world, he might notice me."

"I haven't met him yet," Grease says, trying to remember all the Old Guys.

"He was my husband," Brian K says, smiling. "Everyone called us the Brians."

Grease sticks on his words. He was . . . with Brian P? Two boys, together? People could do that? "But you're both boys," he says.

"Yeah. That's why we liked each other," Brian K says.

Later they visit one of the crumbling office buildings at the bottom of the hill. Brian K has him pull out several hard drives, small boxes the size of a piece of bread. Brian K says they're the memory of the puters.

"What's this?" Grease says. It's a beige plastic box, with a blank green screen.

"Wow, Game Boy," Brian K says. "Haven't seen one since I was a kid. They're for playing video games."

Grease doesn't know what all of that means. But the device looks simple enough to repair. It seems to be needing power. Maybe he can connect it to a solar panel. He tucks it into his pocket.

There's a question he wants to know. "What happened to Brian P?" he says.

"Nothing's meant to run this long," Brian K says.

"But—you can't die, can you? Not with the Long Life Treatment?"

"Not usually, no. But . . . but you can be killed," Brian K says. "You start losing the will to go on. You disappear from yourself if you give yourself long enough."

Grease understands. He's lived with death his whole life. He recognizes it when he sees it. "I'm sorry," he says. Meaning it. Wondering what it would be like to have someone you trusted completely. But also, he wonders what it would be like to be with someone who . . . looked like you wanted them to look. Like a boy.

"It seemed like such a good idea, you know?" Brian K says wistfully. "We were working for the Long Life Project, but we weren't in it for the treatment. But then Brian P got Parkinson's. You never want an IT guy with shaking hands."

Grease himself trembles for a moment, as if in sympathetic echo. "At first we thought, live forever, see the world," Brian K says. "Then the End happened and we were together but the world kept shrinking. No one asked if we should live this long, not after what we've seen, after what we've—" Brian K stops, swallows. "Brian P thought it was long enough."

CHAPTER FIFTEEN
THE LIFE VESSELS

Pico finds Alice sitting behind her greenhouse, eating a spoonful of ice cream. "You eat a lot of ice cream," Pico says.

"It's an old person thing," she says. Alice dips her spoon into the ice cream and puts it into her mouth. She regards him over the spoon with her blue eyes.

"This once would have made me fat, you know, but now my body just gets rid of the fat cells I don't need," Alice says. "That's vaguely depressing. It seems to miss the whole point of a dessert." All the Old Guys speak more formally than the Children, as if they're a museem exhibit of a language that no longer exists.

"Why can't Jemma hear the Haze?" he says. He sought her out because she seems to be an expert on the brain. And because James and Brian K disappeared from the Camp three days ago and no one else seems to have noticed.

"Let's get right to it, shall we, then?" Alice says. "Very well. Perhaps Jemma's faking the magic."

Pico holds her in his eyes until she squirms. It's something she's probably not done much in the past hundred years. "I look like I believe in magic?" he says. "I saw her light up the Night Mountain. Lectrics that ain't been lit in a hundred years. Just with a touch. Some was even burned out."

"Well, maybe—"

"No. Not maybe. Why can't she hear it?"

"Okay, theoretically," Alice says. "Jemma came in with quite a nasty injury to her brain's temporal lobe. It's the center for language recognition, auditory processing, visual memories. That makes it the usual candidate for the connection point to the Haze. Jemma's seems to function adequately for her normal activities. But—"

"Speaking to the Haze ain't normal," Pico says.

"Not like that, no. The extra capacity for communication might be closed off," Alice says. "Assuming you're right."

"Right," Pico says. "But you could fix it."

"No. There's too much risk," she says.

"Why don't you wanna help us?"

There's a hitch in Alice's voice, a patch of dry air, before she answers.

"It's not that I don't want to. It's just that I believe it's not possible," she says. "You don't understand the enemy. They're not so much machines but organisms like germs. Or *an* organism, made of a trillion different pieces. Like many organisms, like the common cold, like the measles, they invade the human body. Unlike many organisms, they also form the greatest supercomputer on earth. As smart as we are, the Haze is infinitely smarter. We will not win this race."

"So why not help Jemma?" Pico says. "She could use the Haze against itself."

Alice puts her spoon down carelessly, with a clatter. She stands up. "Walk with me," she says. "I want to see my creatures."

They walk past the pigs, and Alice points at one of them, white with black spots. "The first pig looked nothing like this cute little thing. It was an animal that could rip your belly open."

"That's what they are in our home," Pico says. Wild dogs and pigs roam Ell Aye, and either will tear a kid apart.

"The point is, we've always altered life, even before we understood exactly how we were doing it. Our ancestors picked the two tamest pigs, and every generation got tamer and tamer. It's the slow way—evolution, with control. We wanted faster than that for the Long Life Project. The advocates for nanotech wanted it even faster, and look what happened."

"Couldn't you fix us? The long way?" Pico says. "I mean . . . you'll have time."

"I'm not sure things want to be fixed," Alice says.

"I want to be fixed."

"I did, too," Alice says. "I had Alzheimer's. God. Awful disease—it attacks your brain, too. You forget things, you go blank for a while. Finally, you just lose yourself. You know what I miss? The blanks. The oblivion. The calm between all the memories, the breath before the voice. Now I remember everything."

"I really don't feel sorry for you," Pico says. "And I still need some help."

"Fine. I have some books for you," she says. "I understand you can read."

Alice falls silent as she leads him to her greenhouse. Inside, she walks them through the greenhouse, through aisles of dark, heavy steaming plants. Pico has never been in the greenhouse, has never felt humidity like this. It clogs his lungs.

"Orchids. I don't know why I grow them. Utterly unsuited to this climate," she says, as if in question. She leads Pico through her office and through an interior door to what looks like a warehouse. The overhead Lectrics are off, and the room is lit only from the light within glass cases. Pico instinctively warms to the soft glow. It feels like living inside a lantern.

Alice crosses to a bookshelf and pulls three books down after a little hesitation. "God, I haven't looked at these in thirty years," she says, and hands them to him. A diagram of a brain is on the front cover of the top book. "You're welcome to see if they turn up anything."

Pico takes the books and looks around him. The boxes filled with light are also filled with other, more horrible, objects. A petrified head of a monkey. A line of butterflies crumbling around their pins. A glass paperweight filled with what looks like blood. "Whatcha doin here?" he says. "With all a this?"

"*This* is how I've spent the last thirty years," Alice says. "Every time we've tried to intervene with humanity, it's gone awry. Perhaps it's time for us to step aside and wait for the world to reset. So I created a new prime directive."

She gestures beyond her to row after row of shelves fading into the warehouse. Dim lights reflect off polished concrete floors, making the shelves look as if they're sinking into pools of ink. On the first shelf are books, simple books like the one Pico used to teach himself the ABCs.

"For the eventuality that written language will disappear completely," Alice says. "Books to teach English, and guidelines to create a new universal visual language." On the next shelf seem to be Lectrics, with a lightning bolt symbol and wires and a simple hand-cranked generator. Behind that are diagrams for a wind machine. Another shelf, marked with a medsen bottle, has a model of human anatomy.

"You're . . . helping them to start over," Pico says.

"Almost. There is no starting over," Alice says. "All complex machinery is gone, never to return. The last of it is rusting. Gasoline has all broken down except for airplane fuel, and there's little of that. But we can teach the Children how to grow their own penicillin, how to harness the wind and the water. Each of these units is a life vessel, if you will, sheltering the bits of civilization worth keeping. Every great thought of the modern world. They're designed to be used whether we're here to show them the way or not."

"But not us," Pico says. "We still gotta live in the world you made."

"I don't think you know how bad things were, before the End," Alice says. Her voice is soft and soothing. "We were going to war with *Mexico*, Pico. It was ridiculous. They used to fight over a wall and then it wasn't even worth climbing the wall anymore. The states dried up and we started climbing back over the wall, the other way. Every summer was the hottest one ever, each storm the biggest in a thousand years. The sea was rising because we'd melted all the ice and people were shooting each other for water. It may be hard for you to recognize, but the End saved the earth. We stabilized the climate. All of that's gone now."

"That what you tell yourself?" Pico says. "All of everything's gone now."

"Things fall apart, Pico. They always will. Cells decay. The universe expands, and everything falls away from everything else. We made a mistake when we decided to hold it together," Alice says.

"But not for us. You're saying it wouldn't be right to fix us," Pico says, disgusted. "How can it not be right to fix your mistakes? How can it be right to let all of us die, all the time?"

"The universe will set things right, Pico." As if she's saying it to herself first.

"It hasn't yet," he says.

CHAPTER SIXTEEN
THE UNTOUCHED

A week after her arrest, Trina is squatting in the field. She digs grubs that are eating the roots of the beans, fat white bodies shaped like a letter C. She smiles. She knows the letter C.

She crushes them under her fingers. They are not the color of blood.

"Always said you'd be glad if you was a Farmer again, pendeja," Trina says. "So . . ." She *is* glad. She loves the dirt under her fingers, the sharp sun overhead, the rustle of the stalks, more than she ever loved the bickering of the Olders. Here she can taste her work.

The other Farmers edge a wary ways back from her every time she moves, as if they'll catch whatever landed Trina in these fields as an Exile inside the village.

The Great Field is in the full of its summer burst of peppers and squash and tomatoes and beans. Or it should be. Every day is hotter than the one before. She doesn't see anything in the clouds that will make it change. It takes more water pumped up from the lake to the Great Field to keep the plants alive in their tender stage, water the lake should hold except this winter was unusually dry. For the first time in her life, she can see the bottom of the Lake of the Holy Wood. Not everywhere, but enough to know they're running out. *We've broken the Lake.*

Right now, though, she's concerned about the tomato plants under her fingers. They're thirsty. The green tomatoes tucked under their leaves are a quarter of the size of what they should be. No one would listen to her when she pointed them out weeks ago, and now all the water in the world won't fix the problem. It will be a long winter.

Not that she'll see it. She thought she would have Ended by now, would be looking back at her life through the fresh eyes of the Betterment. She had harbored the idea that she was one of the Touched, the smart, mature kids who always seemed to die first. The Touched would never have gotten this close to seventeen. *Nice, Trina*, she thinks. *Even the End doesn't want you.*

At the end of the day, she straightens up, counts the spots where her muscles ache, and picks up her hoe. The other Farmers are at the edge of the Great Field, near the sign of the pooping dog, stacking up the few vegetables that are ready for harvest.

"Puta," the Farmers say as she walks by, "puta." But there's no sting to it. They have to say it or risk being beaten by the Hermanas guarding the field with their metal-studded staffs. Heather wanted her alone, and this is how she did it. She can walk anywhere within the Holy Wood, but has to be home by sundown or she gets beaten.

The Holy Wood she walks into from the fields is different than the one she ran as the Oldest. The Muscle who watched the gates are gone. Those who stayed in the Holy Wood have been stripped of their bows and machetes and sent to labor as Carpenters or Farmers. Some of the Muscle fled or were Exiled for rebellion. Some joined the Last Lifers. Heather has created enemies where there should have been none.

Heather, now that she has gotten what she wanted, has withdrawn from the Holy Wood into a crumbling fortress of a mansion on the hill. The only time Trina sees her is when Heather comes to torment her with the Hermanas. The Hermanas can beat anyone without warning. It used to be just the boys they would beat. Then they started on the girls. The kids of the Holy Wood who aren't Hermanas walk with hunched shoulders, darting eyes.

There were maybe a couple dozen Hermanas when they overthrew

Trina; now there are sixty, drawn by the scent of power. Their status means they don't have to work in the fields, they don't have to become Mamas, even though the Holy Wood needs both. Worse, the Holy Wood is only left with kids who have never fought to protect them against the lions and the cannibals.

These matters get emptier and emptier for Trina. She used to feel herself tied to this village, tied in a way that would never let her drift the way of the Last Lifers, in a way that would have almost let her outlive the End. One by one, Heather is cutting those cords. The Olders. *Snip.* The ways of the Angelenos. *Snip.* The closeness of the people she used to serve. *Snip.* One more cut and Trina will float away, like a kite that has lost its tether.

She arrives at the windowless pool shed where she locked up Apple the night before he escaped. She enters under the gaze of the Hermanas, who lock the door behind her. And there, she's home.

Why hasn't she escaped? The guard is loose enough that she could slip away, take her chances in the Flat Lands. Maybe part of her is waiting for the Holy Wood to tell her they need her. A bigger part of her just wants to rest.

The Hermanas give her one candle a night. That burns out after an hour. After that Trina will have no sunset or stars to help her find her place in the night. So she quickly does what she has been doing for weeks: She fishes out a book.

The Exile could read, the little one who came in from the Malibus. She saw his eyes once, flitting over a sign on a wall that no one understood, and she knew: *He knows what those shapes are.*

That meant Trina could understand them, too. She always thought the words were lost. Now, with one hour a night and a fading candle, she has found them again. The only books in the shed must have been used to help the Parents run their machines; the first one she ever read was about a "lawnmower." Since then she has snuck them out of abandoned houses at the edge of the Holy Wood, the only treasure the Parents left and the only one the Children don't value.

Trina carefully turns the pages of this one. A handful of the pages fell out last week, and she's worried there will be more. The book is all whites and purples, a boy holding some kind of chalk. "Cray-on," she reads aloud. She's never heard the word before.

The boy draws boats and walls and oceans and creatures. She takes the cray-on from his hand and draws even more. The shed walls crumbling. Food on people's plates. Herself spiraling upward through the air, the Holy Wood sign and the lake and the living world trailing at her feet. She wants to follow that purple line.

The books give her an escape from the shed, which is why she started with them. But now they show her how the world works, how the Parents saw it. Trina wants that more than escape. She wants the calm and the understanding the Parents must have had. She wants to be more than a kid. She wants to be a Parent.

Careful, pendeja. That's when you know the End is comin for you.

CHAPTER SEVENTEEN
THE ICE CREAM MEN

E verything is dusty. That's the first thing Alfie notices when he and the remaining Ice Cream Men enter the camp of the Orange.

The second thing he notices is that it's dusty because nothing is growing. The Orange grow tomatoes in huge pots, covering them at night when the chill sets, until they produce the biggest tomatoes in Ell Aye. Alfie has seen one sell for a dozen eggs. The tomatoes should be green, big, turning to orange.

They're simply not there at all.

And, neither he sees, are the Children of the Orange.

The Orange were the first tribe the Ice Cream Men decided to ask for help against the Biters. They are cousins, after all, their closest trading partners. Some Ice Cream Men, like Phuong, were Orange to begin with until the Orange traded the Children to the Ice Cream Men. That was always the arrangement: The Ice Cream Men brought supplies, and the Orange brought life. New babies. Fresh veggies. All the things that are missing now.

He doesn't see any young babies. That means they're either too sick to be outside or, worse, they didn't outlast the spring. The few older kids he sees have swollen bellies and ribs exposed. One lies in the road, panting, flies crawling over her eyes.

The leader of the Orange emerges from a house that used to be white but is also fading into the dust. He's a boy named Oscar. Alfie has traded with him lots of times, the last one three months ago.

Oscar doesn't look like himself now. His skin is almost clear, stretched over a mouthful of bleeding and rotting teeth.

"What happened?" Phuong says. She and Oscar used to play together when they were Kinder, before she was traded to the Ice Cream Men.

"All our plants are dying. It's too hot, and all the streams gon dried." Famine. It hits Ell Aye every few years—fruit fly swarm, a winter too dry, a summer too warm.

"Canaries," Phuong says, whispering into Alfie's ear. That's one of the Ice Cream Men's insults for the Orange—that whatever disease comes, whatever famine hits, it hits the Orange hardest and first. It means that it may be on its way for others, too—at a time when the Biters attack has made trading for food and meds impossible.

"Whaddya want?" Oscar says.

"You heard bout the Biters," Alfie says, and tells him about the massacre at the bank, about their retaliation. Oscar nods, no surprise or condolences in his expression. *Boy is just tired.* "We gon build an army to stop them. We want your help."

"We can't even pick up sticks," Oscar says. "How we gon break heads with em?"

"That ain't all," Phuong says. "We weak. You weak. We gotta become a new people."

That was the hard talk they had last night. They had the wee kids left still, but most of the big ones would be dead by the time those got old enough to care for themselves. The Ice Cream Men could be gone in five years. They needed the numbers of the Orange.

"We only had five babies make it through to summer," Oscar says. "We usually got thirty by now."

"We can keep each other fed," Alfie says. Embarrassed that he's pleading. Embarrassed that he wants to stay among the dusty, starving Orange.

Alfie can't tell if Oscar is thinking or falling asleep under those half-closed eyelids. "You say the Biters coming big," he says, finally.

"Yeah," Alfie says, not sure what he means.

"That means they gots food and they gots numbers," Oscar says. "Maybe they don't come after us, and I guess that's okay. But if they do . . . we gon join them."

Alfie can tell that the second option is the one he wants. Phuong says, "They gon kill you all."

"The weak ones, mebbe, ones they don't wanna carry," Oscar says, looking around at the village. "But they got use for the rest of us."

"You gon be slaves," Alfie says. He's seen the way the Biters sweep up the Lowers, how they beat them and work them into the ground. Almost none of the Lowers live out their End.

"It's better than this," Oscar says. "Least we gon get fed."

"The Orange gon be gone ferever," Alfie says. Not arguing anymore.

"We got maybe ten years if we lucky. You got even less." He shrugs and waves at the dying dusty kids around them. "What's there left to save?"

Alfie and Phuong are quiet as they jingle away on their ice cream bikes. Phuong won't cry, but he can tell she'd like to. Her old people, abandoning her twice.

"Those people are worthless. It'd take ten Orange to equal one of us," Alfie says. "Wouldn't be a fair trade."

Phuong smiles a little at that. "So what now?"

"We go to the Kingdom and the Angelenos," Alfie says. "They gon wanna fight."

"But we got no numbers," she says.

"We got the guns they want. That's all the numbers we need," he says.

CHAPTER EIGHTEEN
THE ISLAND OF THE GOD

The shaking starts up again in Tommy's hands, just as it has every day since Stanford died. He cradles one hand in the other until it stops.

He's not upset about Stanford's death. He isn't. Or not because it was Stanford who died, at least. If he only killed those who had been cruel to him, what kind of Lord would he be?

He breathes deep. Usually when he names his problem, he can salt it away for later; fix it or destroy it. The anxiety leaves. Not now. Now, he shakes again.

Why is he so shaken?

Cuz you been thinking about all the wrong things. It's the other voice, the one Little Man has tried to bury since the day he stopped scrounging for sea urchins in the tide pools at San Pede, down at the bottom of the hill. *It's because all you do is hurt others,* little Piss Ant says. That was Tommy's name from birth. He never had a real name until he gave himself one. Then gave himself a better one, Little Man.

I make life, Little Man says.

You make things that kill, Piss Ant says. *All you're making is bigger weapons.*

Little Man almost argues, but—he remembers. He remembers the thrill of believing he could beat death. Then he made Nate into a Giant, and knew there was power there but there was no life. He sided with the power, and that made him Lord of the Chosen. But life still eludes him.

He admits it himself now. The Making is just a different sort of death. Worse, even that kind of half-death will be denied Little Man. There's no one else he would trust to Make himself when the time comes.

None of this matters, Piss Ant says. *The only things that matter are the Haze and the End.*

For once, Piss Ant might be right. Little Man's been thinking about this war but ignoring his greatest weapon: his mastery of the Haze. If Jemma has it, it's clear there's more to the Haze, and he doesn't understand the Haze as well as he thought he did. What else doesn't he know? What else could he do with it?

He has to find Jemma and force her to unlock the Haze.

He inhales and exhales, making his heart match his breath. He pictures Jemma and her friends, but this time he puts all his mind into it. He wills the Haze to take shape around them. It doesn't. No matter where he seeks, they're gone from the Haze.

Tommy shouts, his hands trembling. How dare she hide from him? How dare the Haze let her?

Show me or I will find a way to End you, he says to the Haze. He sends all his fury out into the dust, and he feels it shake. And miraculously, it relents.

He's filled with a rush of clarity. His mind is filled with images, of a faceless boy on an island. A boy who wields the Haze like a weapon. A boy filled with power that Little Man instantly craves.

Where is he? We will sail to his doorstep. I will find him and make him kneel.

The Haze shows him, and Tommy falters. So do Piss Ant and Little Man. None of them want to go to that island.

If the rest of Ell Aye see the Hill of the Palos in their nightmares, the Chosen have a place that fills their own nightmares. It's an island that can be seen by both the Palos and Newports, an easy day's sail.

But they don't dare go there. The Chosen believe the island is the home of Catalina, goddess of the sea. Catalina is a jealous god, and clutches at every soul that nears her shore.

Tommy doesn't believe in gods any more than he believes in the Chosen. But he knows that as far back as the Chosen can remember, boats that enter its waters never return.

Roberto appears out of the night, and Little Man steels himself. "Find me three boats," he says. "I'm going to Catalina's Grave."

"Whaddya want?" Li says when Little Man calls him to his house.

"To answer your Lord without questions," Little Man says, letting the Twins behind him prove his seriousness. He looks up at Li's empty eyes. He makes sure to hold them until Li has to look away. "I'm gonna go away for a while. To visit the goddess of the sea. They're gonna try to take the Chosen away from me. You're not gonna let them."

The Last Lifer listens.

"You'll have a target on your giant back with me gone. You're gonna have to learn how to play the game."

"I can play the game," Li says. "I was born to live in a tribe like this." He probably was. Little Man notices, not for the first time, the way the fury almost punches through Li's skin. This one wants to kill all the time, and not just the Angelenos.

"If you come through for me, you'll get all the guns and food you can ever want. No one's ever gonna touch you," Little Man says. "If you screw me over, if that throne is not waiting for me empty and shiny shiny clean when I get back, I'm going to tell the Last Lifers that you're the reason they're not gonna get the Making. And your own people will tear you apart."

He can see the understanding in Li's eyes. It's no surprise they understand each other. Little Man doesn't ask Li how he came to be captain of the Last Lifers—but he can picture it. Somehow Li terrified hundreds of Last Lifers to join his army, hundreds of soldiers he offered to the Palos when Roberto found him and convinced him to join the Chosen. Little Man grants Li the honor of a wary watch from the distance. If Little Man is the scorpion, then Li is the rattlesnake.

The rattlesnake didn't climb to the top of the Last Lifers for power or even for anger: He did it for fear. Little Man can feel that under his skin, better than Li can, because he feels it, too. Li has been abandoned his whole life. Li is frightened all the time, of girls and swords and talking. That's why he rages. He builds an army so no one can hurt him. So no one can leave him behind.

"As long as we get fightin soon," Li says. "The Last Lifers are building up hope."

"You afraid they running out of it?"

"Afraid they ain't," Li says. "If they believe they gonna live beyond the End, they ain't gonna fight. Too much to live for."

"What about you? You believe?" Little Man says.

Li rolls his eyes. "Don't believe in nothin," he says, and Tommy wonders again how much he truly has in common with Li. If their bodies are so different in form but their souls are exactly the same, hollow and bleak.

"Make sure I have something to come back to," Little Man says.

Li grunts, holds out his hand. And Little Man goes to find his boat.

CHAPTER NINETEEN
THE LESSON

Jemma is too embarrassed to leave her room. All the Camp has heard by now how she and Lady faced down the buffalo and failed.

After a day of sulking, she hears a knock. It's Isaac.

"Fine, I'll help you," he says.

"What? Why?" She sits up. She suddenly wishes she'd bothered to wash her hair.

"You tried to kill yourself with a buffalo to get the Haze back," he says. "I can't have that kind of crazy on my conscience. What's next?"

"I was gonna have Grease run me over with a car," she says, smiling for the first time in days.

"This'll be less painful," he says, and sits down on the edge of her bed. "When'd you first see the Haze?"

She tells him about how the Haze saved her in the Bowl, and led her here. "So it came to you," he says.

"Yeah. There nother way?"

"There is. I found it on my own," Isaac says. "You're going to have to stop being so passive about things and make it talk to you."

"How'd you find it?"

"Later," he says. "Tell me about the visions." She does, and he listens.

"You get them?" she says.

"Nah. More like premonitions. Everybody experiences it differently."

"How're visions possible?"

Isaac shrugs. "Laws of probability," he says. "The Haze observes, and then it predicts based upon the behavior it observes. If you watched a hundred people walk down the street and ninety of them turned right at a corner, you could predict that people would pretty soon turn right. The Haze has an infinite amount of sensors, so it can predict events more accurately than you could imagine."

"That's why it can be wrong," she says. "When people don't act like they're sposed to."

It's not the gods, she thinks; it never was. She should have known it never was.

"So you talk to the Haze," she says. "Like, how?"

"Again, not like you. I see a lot of images," he says. "I sense what it senses, but it never really speaks to me. I can do a lot of things with the Haze, but not all of them well. Curse of the generalist."

"You gotta stop using so many words," she says. "If you're so bad at all this, what you got to teach me?"

"A couple of things," he says. "Come outside."

He leads them to the grassy bench above the quad. From their viewpoint, she can just see the ocean. *I still haven't seen it up close except to get my head shoved in it*, she thinks.

She looks at him. "Okay, so what am I doing wrong?" she says. Information is more important than eyes and eyelashes and auburn hair that ends at the shoulders, and—

Oh. Those eyelashes.

"Stop waiting for the Haze to come to you," he says. "You've seen it before. You know where to find it if you look."

"Fine," she says.

"And learn how to relax. The more you tense up about all this, the less likely you are to find your way."

"I—I don't know how to relax," she says. "I got here because I couldn't relax. I could never let things go."

"Well, now you're here," he says. "Just . . . try to see it. Close your eyes."

She does.

"Picture the Haze the way you first saw it," he says.

She travels through the days past to find that first night in the Bowl. The dark fell down over the bones, and the Haze lit them up. Her breaths move in and out, matching her heart.

"Good," Isaac says.

She thinks of the atoms drifting like dust over the tangled limbs of their Parents. She remembers the ghost images of Andy and the Last Lifers, the very first time the Haze protected her. She remembers how safe she felt, wrapped up with Apple and this thing she barely understood.

Her throat closes up. She chokes. *Apple*, she thinks.

"Try again," Isaac says. "Try pulling your hands through the air, like you're towing them through water."

She does.

"Okay, now press out, like you're trying to stop the air," Isaac says. "Hold it in your hand, shake it three times, and then toss it away."

She stops. Eyes still closed. "Is this supposed to help me channel it?"

"I don't know, but it's hilarious," Isaac says. And Jemma reaches out and punches him without opening her eyes.

"Pinche culero," she says.

"I'm sorry," Isaac says. "Just rest for a minute."

She lies down in the grass, lets the green swallow her up. She tries to feel it and the sun and nothing else for the moment, but she can't. She's too aware of Isaac standing.

"Get down here. You messin with me," she says. He lies down in the grass next to her. It takes her minutes to calm down, breathing in, breathing out. She reaches into the grass and dirt, imagines life climbing up out of the roots. Then she feels something reaching back. It's as if she can feel the molecules shivering around her, looking for her. They tremble over the bones of her wrists. She imagines invisible bots, reaching out to her. Healing her. Opening her to the world. She imagines Isaac's hands, hovering inches from her own in the grass because he's telling himself not to touch her.

Then she realizes, *I'm not imagining any of it. I'm feeling it.*

A shock ripples through her and into the burning day, a Lectric wave like she'd been shuffling over the world's longest rug. The wave comes back like a heartbeat, and crests over her arms. Her fingers singe and shake and she feels what she used to feel.

Complete.

But that's it. She doesn't hear the voice in her head. She doesn't see the images in the Haze. It isn't enough.

"It ain't enough," she says.

CHAPTER TWENTY

THE GAME BOY

As he pores over the guts of the Game Boy, Grease thinks back on his conversations with Brian K. Brian K talked about his husband as if that's a normal thing, when it's not. The Grown-Ups must have been wired differently than the Children, because Grease could never imagine himself with another boy.

Only . . . he can.

Pico enters their room loaded down with books, as he has been for a week. "Never thought I'd say this," Pico says to him, "but I might be getting sick a books. Too heavy." He drops them on the table with a slam.

"Try a puter," Grease says. "Same stuff inside, but lighter."

"Huh," Pico says. "I guess I keep forgetting they're real."

"There's a bunch of them in the hospital. No one uses them anymore," Grease says.

"How's the little puter doin?" Pico says. Pico helps on the Game Boy when he's in the room, but he's been struggling to read through the thick medical books, to unlock the mystery of Jemma's head.

"Screen flickers," Grease says, and shows Pico how the little green screen almost pulses. Brian K has taught him how to solder, and he's removed each wire and rebuilt the connections. It's taken him two days, and the screen's still not quite right.

"Lemme see it," Pico says. He takes the Game Boy in his hand, peers at the screen as if he's trying to read instructions. Then he thwacks it against his knee.

"Not bad," Grease says. The screen is lit.

"You taught me that," Pico says. "Back at the Kingdom. I could barely use my hands. Member?"

Grease does. He remembers guiding Pico's hands as they brought the golf cart of the apokalips to life, and how his own hands trembled a bit at the touch of someone else for the first time. Grease had told himself he was too busy fixing the Kingdom to hook up with the girls who always seemed interested. The Kingdom was a place built and ruled by boys, driven by swagger. He was surrounded by them but didn't feel like he was one of them. Until Pico.

"I gotta show you this," Pico says, and opens a book to a cross-section of the skull. He points to a section near the ears. "The brains use something like Lectrics to pass thoughts around, just like we thought. That's how the Haze talks to it. 'Cept the Haze ain't getting through to this part."

Grease looks at the diagram, but he can't focus. His eye for Lectrics seems to be failing at the moment. He knows why. Pico isn't like him, he thinks. Pico's something different. But he might still understand. "You talk to Brian K much?" he says.

"Only when you work with him," Pico says, not looking up.

"He was married. You know, like Grown-Ups did. But . . . to a man."

Pico looks up, sharply. "Weird," he says. He looks back down.

Grease feels hot, but only he's sweating. "Yeah, weird. Grown-Ups were weird. We couldn't do that now, cause where would the babies come from?"

"World needs babies," Pico says automatically.

"It'd be just a waste, and stupid, and . . . how would that work?" He stares at his hands. Really. He can't figure out how it would work.

When he looks up, Pico is staring at him, irritated. "This's important," Pico says. "That isn't."

He's right. It isn't important. Grease hasn't needed to know about this his whole life. Why does he need to know now? But his hands are shaking, hands that never shake unless he's around Pico. He curls his fingers under until his nails dig into his palms. The pain brings him back.

"Show me that again?"

Pico grabs a pen and sketches arrows from the part near the ears to the rest of the brain. "The Lectrics aren't getting in or out of this part a her head," he says. "How we make that happen?"

"If the connection isn't good, you have to thwack it," Grease says.

"Like . . . thwack Jemma?" Pico says, frowning.

"No, like we did with the golf cart of the apokalips," Grease says. Batteries stopped working a hundred years ago, so the cart wouldn't start at first. Later he created a crank that would give it a spark, but back then he wheeled over his mocycle and connected it to the cart with the wires. Then he kicked the mocycle awake and the Lectrics it created jumped into the cart.

"We have to jump-start her," Grease says.

CHAPTER TWENTY-ONE
THE UNMASKING OF LITTLE MAN

Tashia hears the bells of the Ice Cream Man and doesn't think too much about it, even though she found the bodies of the Ice Cream Men weeks ago. The trade of the Ice Cream Men is a familiar sound in the Kingdom.

Then she hears another bell. And another and another. That gets her attention. The Ice Cream Men only travel in large groups in times of celebration and danger.

She runs from the stables in time to see the Ice Cream Men rolling up the Main Street of the Kingdom, to the gates of the castle and the Round Table.

She looks at the Ice Cream Men before her. There are only twenty-three of them, most of them appearing to be below the age of seven. They look shocked, but fierce. Even the littlest ones. Fiercest of all is the boy she remembers, the little scout who used to come with their Ice Cream Men.

"Hey, Alfie," she says softly, but he's all business.

"Hey to the King," he says.

X nods, as courteous as if this were the full Fleet instead of a dusty little remnant. "Welcome to the Kingdom," he says. "Why are you here?"

"You saw the place where the Biters attacked," Alfie says.

"We did," the King says. "We're sorry for your loss."

"So you know we gon fight back," Alfie says. He introduces the girl next to him, Phuong, as the new captain of the Fleet.

"We want you to join us," she says.

"Join *you?*" Othello says, scornfully. "You're a bunch of kids."

"Yeah we is," Phuong says. "Kids who knows everybody in Ell Aye, and who gots guns you can't even dream of."

"Maybe we just take your guns," John says.

"Mebbe," Phuong says. "And mebbe you can stick your sword up your ass. I'm talkin to your King." Tashia smiles.

"Yes, she was," X says. "And the King is still talking to her, John. Ice Cream Man, make your case."

Phuong says how the Biters broke their age-old truce to take the weapons they carried in their carts, but couldn't find all their Hydin Holes. She tells how the Last Lifers have swelled the Biters' ranks, how both the Palos and Newports are together. How they'll start picking off the peoples of Ell Aye, one by one.

"We are sympathetic to your cause, but the famine makes it impossible for us to bring in more," X says.

"We just twenty-three," Phuong says. "None of us gon make a dent in your food."

"Perhaps we can trade you some meat for guns and—"

"No," Alfie says. "We gon join with you or we gon go our own way."

"King," Tashia says. "You said the Biters aren't gonna back down. We need all the help we can get." She's worried she'll have to argue with him, but he nods.

"It seems a small price to pay to get rid of the Biters. You're welcome to join us, provided you can lead us to the weapons," X says.

"Little Man's gon wish he was dead," Alfie says.

"Little Man? There's some mistake," X says. "Little Man is the Giant we killed during their last attack."

"'Giant'?" Alfie says. "Giant pain in my ass, mebbe."

"Are we talking about the same Little Man?" Tashia says.

"Scary little shit? Bout my height, blond hair?" Alfie says. "Can't believe you'd forget him."

Tashia looks at X, alarmed. "Let's take this to a private—"

But Othello picks up on it, too. "Little Biter? Like the one we had here?"

"Think so," Alfie says. "Heard you captured him."

"You brought Little Man into the Kingdom," Othello says, slowly, looking at both Tashia and X. "You brought him here, and then you let him get away."

Tashia sees the hardening faces at the Round Table. *Oh, this is bad.*

CHAPTER TWENTY-TWO
THE OLDEST AND THE PRIESTESS

A boy watches Trina from across the field. She thinks she knows him, once a Carpenter but probably pulled into the fields as all the boys fled. All the faces get fuzzy now as she loses her hold on the ground.

No. She will never lose hold. She says that at the exact moment she wills herself to float up.

The boy digs into the dirt with a stick. A look at her. A dare. He walks away.

She works on the plants for another hour. She finds herself over the boy's patch of dirt, as if the field has led her there. In it is a crude code, symbols the Children have had to rely on since words died. The Bear Wall, with an arrow. A girl at the base of the arrow. She knows what it says. "You: Come to the Bear Wall."

The Bear Wall is the dam for the Lake, and the edge of the Holy Wood. It's outside the area where Trina's confined, but there's little risk: What will they do—kill her?

She eyes the point of land south of the Great Field. There's a faint trail down from it to the Lake, mostly hidden in tunnels of chaparral. Trina winds away from the field, marking the sun off to the west. Another hour before sunset, before the Hermanas notice she's not in her cell.

When she reaches the dam, a novice steps out of the woods. The church. Of all the people who'd seek her out, Trina would never have guessed a novice from the Zervatory. The novice guides her through the pine forest downslope of the dam, to the arches that hold up the Bear Wall. The statues of bear faces that give the dam its name jut out from the wall. In the shadow of the center arch is the Priestess.

Pilar looks different than before, when she was the sole voice of the gods. Thinner, more disheveled, more beaten—more, Trina realizes, like Trina herself. This is someone who has fallen from the stars.

"What have they done to you?" Trina says.

"You wouldn't care." Trina hears the strain in Pilar's voice. Pilar still hates Trina for not backing her in front of the village. Fair enough. Trina despises Pilar.

"Probably not," Trina says.

"Heather," Pilar says, and that's all she really has to say.

"After she got her present she put you back in the box, din't she?" Trina says.

"Heather's leading us into dark paths," Pilar says.

"Really? 'Dark paths'?" Trina says. "She's just really shitty at her job."

"Not just in the Holy Wood. The Palos are rising, ready to flood. The Last Lifers have joined them. Someone named Little Man is bringing them together. Heather's heard this from the other Angelenos. She refuses to believe them."

"Dumbass," Trina says. She lets Pilar wonder whether she's talking about Heather or Pilar.

Trina is about to dismiss Pilar's warning, but this—this is what Apple said right before Trina passed the Harsh that would sentence him to death. He said the Last Lifers had stopped acting like Last Lifers. They had guns. They planned. That had to come from somewhere. She's wondered about it since that day. She wonders why she didn't guess it was caused by the Palos. "How you know this?" Trina says.

"I see them at the gates," Pilar says. "I don't know when, but—"

"You telling me . . . you see things? Really?"

"Strange, right?" Pilar says. "To pretend you see things and then really start seeing them."

"Heather ain't gonna do anything about it."

"No. She ain't," Pilar says, dropping the priestess voice and sounding like a girl.

"Then . . ." Trina says. "What—us? We ain't gonna go in and fix everything for em. We just a couple old bones that Heather and the Holy Wood threw away."

Both of them stop speaking. The scent of the pines is so strong that Trina almost feels it against her skin. It suffocates a little. She turns away from the pines to look at the wall. She hasn't been down here in a year. The cracks they attempted to patch have already broken loose. They can't repair what the Parents made.

Pilar says, "It won't hold for long. Maybe five years."

Both of them will End before the dam collapses. "That ain't our problem," Trina says.

"Then whose is it?" Pilar says.

Trina doesn't answer for a long while. She's deserved a chance to rest. Finally she says, "We gonna need help."

Pilar nods.

"Well, then, you better get us outta here," Trina says.

CHAPTER TWENTY-THREE
THE PUTER

Pico stares at the puter, waiting for the screen to change. "Good thing the Old Guys live so long," he says to Grease and Jemma. "I feel like half of the rest of my life is happening while we wait."

"Windows," Grease mutters.

"What's that?" Jemma says.

"Brian K says it's a hundred years of the wrong OS and no tech support."

This is the fourth puter they've tried. The puter lab in the hospital is nearly always deserted, and Grease knows the code on the door. It doesn't matter—the Old Guys already know everything about each other that can be known, so they don't guard the room. The passwords, a sort of word lock, are all "password."

They see another screen. It's a picture of Alice and Isaac. Isaac looks about the same age as he does now. "This is Alice's machine," Jemma says.

There are words along the bottom of the Teevee, and other pictures the size of buttons. Pico leans closer to the screen to decipher them, and finds the log folder at the bottom. It holds multiple files. Pico starts clicking with an oval device that sits in his hand. A mouse, he remembers.

Pico had imagined the puter as a shelf full of books, orderly and dusty, like the library where they were chased by the bear. But searching through the puter is like rummaging through a box with gloves and a blindfold. Everything has to be felt, turned over, and put back down again.

"I can't read good enough to look over your shoulder," Jemma says. "Lemme check in the other room."

Pico nods, even though she doesn't see it, and he and Grease return to their reading.

It takes them another ten minutes to find it: a report a hundred pages long, with an image of the brain similar to the one they sketched out. "Refining deep-brain stimulation to treat synaptic pathology," Pico says, stumbling on several words. The research is denser than anything he's ever read, but in a few minutes he realizes it's what they need. "This is what you were talkin bout," Pico says to Grease.

The ancient printer still works, only because Grease helped Brian K fix it last week with parts scavenged from an office. They print the report and are about to turn off the puter, when Pico notices another file: Long Life Project Log. He clicks on it, unable to resist, and says, "These are Alice's records."

Alice's logs are mostly too dense for Pico to understand, and the parts he does understand repeat information they already knew. Until one entry stops him. "Our devil's bargain is coming back to haunt us. We got a visit from the Pentagon today to talk about our funding—or the lack of it, should we not go along with their requests. The Long Life Treatment is not working fast enough, they say. They want us to ramp up the nanotech activators so that, in effect, it becomes the new Long Life Treatment. All this in a year. Needless to say, it's reckless and against every safe practice we have. Maybe I shouldn't be surprised that James is all over himself to do it. Ambition is the reason I fell in love with him, but this . . ."

Pico pores over the entries that follow. A photo jumps out from all the words. Pico sees a field surrounded by palm trees and thick undergrowth. Some place not here. It reminds him of the jungle in the Kingdom, but this one is real.

This one is filled with bodies.

The field is littered with corpses, dressed in army uniforms. They look like the ones here at the Camp, but they're not exactly the same. The faces are mostly brown, like his own. Unlike the Old Guys'. A shiver starts at the back of his neck and works its way to his heart. He shows the photo to Grease.

"What does it say?"

"The military got the test of the Haze it wanted," Pico reads. But that's all it says.

"What does that mean?" Grease says.

"Nothing good," Pico says.

One last entry: "I guess I can't leave James just yet. I'm pregnant. At sixty-six," it says. "The Long Life Treatment didn't just cure my Alzheimer's, it reversed menopause, too. I haven't told James yet—or, for that matter, my husband or James's wife. I've thought about abortion, but how could I? We came to the Long Life Project seeking a new life, and it gave it to us. I feel like Rebekah from the Bible, who gave birth at ninety-nine. If it's a boy, I'll name him Isaac."

"What's next?"

"The End happens," Pico says, and they skim through heartbreaking entry after entry, of the world falling apart around the Camp. Pico doesn't want to read any more. They don't need to know this part. They've lived it.

There's too much to process here, but the thing that won't leave Pico's mind is Alice's last entry. Isaac was born near the End. If he's still alive, then there might be hope from new quarters.

"Jesucristo," Pico says. "Isaac's a hundred years old."

CHAPTER TWENTY-FOUR
THE FACE IN THE CARDS

Jemma turns on the first puter in the back room of the lab, while Pico and Grease pore over Alice's files in the other room. When the screen lights up, she sees that she's in the middle of some kind of game that a bored Old Guy must have been playing.

Brightly colored poker cards rest on a green background, in columns. She recognizes it. Solitaire. She and Lady taught each other how to play it in the Holy Wood, but then played it together, which defeated the purpose. It takes her a few minutes to catch on to the play on a puter, but soon enough she's clicking cards and dragging them to columns.

"I think I'm winning," she says to Lady out of habit. But of course Lady's not there.

Lady's withdrawn into herself in a way that Jemma's never known from her. The girl who refuses to join them on their quests to understand the End and the Haze, who sits on the couch watching movies with the Old Guys hour after hour, is the anti-Lady. "I never had a chance to rest in my whole life," Lady says over and over. "I'm gonna rest now."

Part of Jemma agrees. If anyone deserves to hibernate for a while, it's Lady. The other part of Jemma simply doesn't know how to end the slumber.

She plays the last card in order, and the cards flutter to the pile in a satisfying flurry. But the flurry continues.

The cards are multiplying, shrinking, filling up the green background of the screen. They're smaller than her thumbnail and they're moving. At first they're a swirling cloud, drifting around the screen in waves. When more of the cards build on top of each other, they cast shadows. Jemma leans closer slowly, quietly, as if trying not to frighten an injured bird.

An outline emerges—first something like an ear, then a neck and a shoulder. An arm. Hair, shoulder-length and straight. It's supposed to be a boy. The shape refines, and she knows it immediately.

Not just a boy. Apple.

Apple's lips move, and seconds later sound comes out. The delay trails the mouth movements like a shadow, like the face is just learning to speak.

"Jemma?" the cards say. "Jemma. It's me."

"Jesucristo," Jemma whispers at the face of the boy she loved. *Loves*. "Apple?"

"I missed you . . . so much, Jemma," Apple says, the fluttering cards tugging his smile into shape. The smile that made her feel like she was everything she knew she was not.

"I missed you," she says, and even as she says it, she knows that's not right. Just missing him, that's for a friend who's been gone for a week. The Children don't have time for love before they End, but yet he loved her. The missing turns her insides out, peels her away until she's not sure she's Jemma anymore.

"I've been trying to find you."

"If I'd known you were trying—" Her throat seizes. "If I'd known you were somewhere, I would have followed you anywhere."

Apple smiles, gently, and she sees his missing tooth, the one knocked out when he took a beating from two older Muscle for her. The tooth she saw healed in the Betterment. She's seeing the image of him that she loved the best.

"Where are you?"

"I'm in the Haze, Jemma," he says. "The End—it's not like we thought, Jemma. It's peaceful. It's better. Except for—it doesn't have you."

She starts to understand. The Haze can speak to the Lectrics, like it did when she lit up the Night Mountain. Now it's used the Lectrics to bring her Apple through the puter.

Apple's face looks lonely, hungry almost. She felt the same until now. Now she has Apple back, and the Haze. And the End is nothing to be afraid of.

"Apple, I—"

Pico and Grease burst through the door. The cards start to scatter to the edges of the screen, the face and form lost. She feels empty again. "What?" she says, angrier than she meant and almost as angry as she feels.

"They found a way to make Isaac escape the End," Pico says.

CHAPTER TWENTY-FIVE
THE TRIUMPH AND THE VENGEANCE

The line of Catalina looms out of the water as Little Man stands on the bow of the *Triumph*, fighting nausea. But he doesn't show it. The Lord of the Chosen doesn't get seasick. The *Triumph* is the largest boat the Chosen have, a hundred-foot yacht studded with harpoons and the new machine guns won in the Ice Cream Men Massacre. The smaller *Vengeance* flanks it on the port side, the *Screamer* on the right.

Roberto is seated behind him, while the Twins stand guard. Tommy's never been this close to the island, and as he nears it, he wonders why the Chosen are so afraid. Its green cliffs are wrapped by waters pure and blue. It looks like welcome.

Brown-striped dolphins arc out of the water, crossing their wake, then turning to follow them.

"It's good luck," a sailor to his left says.

"Ain't no such thing as good luck with Catalina's Grave," another says.

Catalina's Grave starts two miles away from the shore. It's the point where the Chosen turn their boats around. It's possible to get closer without sinking, but why tempt the goddess?

It's nonsense, Little Man says to himself. *It's nonsense like all the gods.*

Then the sky ripples, as if a dark dagger of cloud is shoving its way between them and the island. Within minutes, it blocks out the sun.

The idiot captain sailed us into a storm, Little Man says to himself.

You told him to, Piss Ant says. The captain warned him that morning that the skies held trouble, but Little Man pushed off his fears. "It's only fifteen miles," he said. "Get us there fast enough, and we'll be fine."

The waves rise. "Get below, Little Man!" the captain says. "I'm gonna get us to harbor!"

Tommy shakes his head. He can't look like he's afraid. But he is.

In front of them in the thickening sky is a port city, Long Gone and crumbled. Houses climb the sides of a narrow canyon, but half of them have been obliterated by mudslides. Avalon, it's called. The throne of Catalina. The captain steers toward it, but Tommy shakes his head. It's not the place he saw in his vision. His vision showed him a village surrounded by marshes.

"West!" he says. Somehow he knows it's that way.

"West is the storm," the captain says, frightened.

"Then you better be a better sailor than I think you are," Little Man says, and nods back to the Twins. "West."

The boat rounds the horn of land at the edge of Avalon, and immediately the sea dwarfs them. The sky is greenish-black. They have to tack hard to beat upwind.

An hour of the storm passes, and what Tommy can see of the shore barely moves. He's thrown up, once, but even the sailors are puking. Tommy is almost ready to give up, when the storm subsides. Not altogether, but enough that they can see the island.

"There!" Roberto shouts, and points up shore. There's a velvet patch of green on the shore. It must be the marsh. Little Man holds it in his sights as the boat slides forward, holds it until he hears shouts. He looks to his left, and sees the *Vengeance* veering toward them. The bow has a sawtoothed spear mounted on it. It's pointed at Little Man. He turns right to shout for help, and sees the *Screamer* coming toward him, its sailors armed with lances. They're the pincers of a claw, closing in on him. Like a crab.

Connor. He bribed the sailors to attack Little Man when he was far from shore. "You fucking assholes!" Little Man shouts at the sailors swarming toward him. "I'm gonna tear out your spines!"

The spear of the *Vengeance* stabs the rail of the *Triumph* with a lurch and a shriek, and Little Man falls to the ground. The attackers jump on the boat while the *Triumph*'s sailors, apparently not in on the bribe, fight them back. The *Screamer* closes in. Before it can reach them, the Twins roar. Nate pushes Tommy backward, and Chase jumps onto the *Screamer*'s deck with a hooked staff. Three of the sailors are dead before the staff even finishes its arc.

"Push it back!" Roberto says, shouting at their crew. He grabs an oar and thrusts it in the space between the *Vengeance* and the *Triumph*, and pushes back against the *Vengeance*. Three other sailors join him, almost pushing it free until a wave of attackers falls on the *Triumph*. Tommy is paralyzed. What good is he in a fight?

The ocean tosses the boats, and the *Vengeance* slides back toward them, closing in. Then, suddenly—the *Vengeance* stops. Just stops, in the middle of the ocean. Tommy swears he can see wooden spears jutting out of the ocean, impaling the boat.

Impossible.

He looks back at the *Screamer*, and sees Chase pinned down by a dozen sailors. They've caught him in a net. "Nate, get to him!" Tommy shouts. But Nate is transfixed, straight ahead, by something only he can see.

The *Triumph* lifts up on a wave, and crashes down against the water like a slap. Tommy stares at Nate as the *Triumph* splits in half, right where Nate stands, and Nate drops like a stone into the sea.

Roberto tumbles into the water also as the deck pitches, and Tommy only has a moment to brace himself before he goes in, too. In the split second before he strikes the water, he sees a long wooden pole, sharpened like a spear. And the water swallows him up.

The water is cold but not gray like he thought, light bursting through green even in the storm so that he feels trapped in glass; and then he's at the surface and gasping.

Tommy sinks under again. *Swim*, he thinks. *Even though no one cared enough to teach you.* But his fingers, spread wide, claw at the water. They hold nothing but drops, and he sinks.

Tommy goes limp, and turns onto his back. That's when he floats. His body climbs to the top of the water, his nose just out. He sticks his chest up, and that seems to help. He throws his head back, and that seems to help. He flutters his arms, and that seems to help. So he just tries to breathe and he tries not to die.

The waves keep coming, though. Each wave crashes and drives him farther under the water, and each time he struggles harder to reach the surface. The cold is draining his fight. Tommy closes his eyes and feels the water around him, pulling him down and lifting him up. How much longer does he have?

He doesn't see the wave that pours over him, rolls him up as if in a rug, pushes him through the ocean until he fears he'll hit the bottom. But then he feels a rope in his hand. The rope doesn't move, and so he holds still while the waves batter him. One knocks him deeper and there is rope along his back, burning his skin where his shirt lifts. Some kind of grid. Another wave.

Not a grid. A net. Another wave and another, and each one drives him deeper into the net. He can't move his arm. The water rushes over him and nothing moves. He's a fish in a net, and then there is a wave.

CHAPTER TWENTY-SIX
THE ESCAPES

Trina sneaks back down to the Lake, to the Bear Wall, two hours before dark. Then she waits. The Hermanas won't be looking for her until sundown. That means she and Pilar will have a narrow head start.

She waits for ten minutes, fearing that Pilar has betrayed her or chickened out. But the trees of the dense forest below the dam rustle. Trina's relieved to see the face of the Priestess coming through the pines.

Pilar is not dressed in her priestess gown, but simple dark pants and shirt. "I hope you're ready," Pilar says.

"Your sight show you where to go?" Trina says.

"To the Half Holy," Pilar says.

Trina remembers that kid, the one who ran off into Ell Aye because everyone hated him and his Mama. He was called the Half Holy because he was never accepted in the Holy Wood. Somehow he survived, in an old motel full of goats. "Good. That's the kind of weird we need," Trina says.

"You got your trail covered?"

"Yeah. I got a lot of kids loyal to me," Pilar says.

"No you don't, sweetie," Heather says, peering over the top of the dam. "You got a lot of kids loyal to *me*. It keeps em from getting beat." Hermanas pour toward them, and Heather comes down the bank. Trina can't react. It's not in her anymore.

"Heather, the gods have spoken against you," Pilar says, in the Priestess voice. Meant to impress. "They will remove you from—"

"Jesucristo, Pilar, shut up," Trina says. "Heather, whaddya want?"

"For one thing, stop tryin to make me look like an asshole."

"But it's so easy," Trina says. She expects a hit at that. Would have been worth it. It doesn't come, but Heather's purr has edged into a snarl.

"The second thing, related to that: I'm gonna need you two to put on a little show."

"What?" Trina says. She's not saying it just to be rude. She doesn't understand what Heather is asking her.

"This job sucks even more than it looked like when you were doing it," Heather says, as if those are the last words she wants to say. Probably they are. "There might be some people pissed off. Maybe a lot of people. Carpenters, for sure. And I don't really care but I want em to finish their work on my new place before they bail."

"So?"

"I need someone to come out and say that I'm doing great. Advisors to the throne, or something. Someone they didn't like but trusted anyway."

"Jesucristo," Trina says. "Almost sounded like you meant to say something nice."

"Not quite," Heather says. "I just want you two to put in a good word then disappear until the next time I need it."

Trina wants to tell her to fuck off. But there's something more important to say. "Maybe," she says.

"What?" Pilar says.

"If you bring the Muscle back. Enough for a patrol."

"Huh," Heather says.

Trina, carefully picking her way through the words so Heather doesn't learn Pilar's secret of prophecy, tells of rumors of the Last Lifers and the Palos working together. A patrol of Muscle could tell them if such is true. "We gotta know for sure," Trina says. "And if it's true, we gotta lock that gate up tight."

"The Last Lifers are gone," Heather says. She doesn't sound confident.

"No," Pilar says. "They just pulled back from Ell Aye like a wave. They gonna come back."

"You hate me bout as much as I hate you, Heather," Trina says. "But this is real. I'll help you if it saves the Holy Wood."

"Jesucristo, how stupid do you think I am?" Heather says. "Last Lifers? Palos? Why don't you just say we're being attacked by ghosts? It's just as real."

"Don't you remember? That's what Apple was trying to warn us about," Trina says, and knows she's said the wrong thing. Apple is the one who got away from Heather.

"Ah," Heather says. "In that case—there's a new deal. Do it or else."

"You got nothin on me." The moment Trina says it, she realizes it's true. Without the fear of death, Heather can't make Trina do anything anymore. Trina's untouchable. Her heart beats wild and furious. Free. This is how the Last Lifers must feel.

"Nothin?" Heather says, and holds her arms out wide, taking in all the Holy Wood.

No, Trina is touchable.

"You got, what, three weeks left before you End, Trina?" Heather says. Trina shrugs. "So . . . let's make the most of it. Speak for me. Make it *super* convincing. Or else I Exile you both. Then I start killing a kid a week."

Pilar gasps, but Trina doesn't twitch. She's not surprised. Heather has only ever loved herself. It wouldn't take anything for her to tear down the village where she grew up.

Still.

"That's a big jump, from saying 'please' to killing," Trina says.

"Eh. I don't got a lot of middle ground," Heather says.

"They gonna hate you even more than they do now, Heather," Trina says. "You thought bout that?"

"I *have* been thinking bout that, and I don't think they will,"

Heather says. "Because there are a bunch of Exiled Muscle lurking around the gates, and they just been looking for a chance to pick us apart. And then the two former leaders of the Holy Wood get Exiled and want to take everyone down. Now they got their chance. They break in through the secret path from the Bear Wall, they steal a Kinder out of his bed. We never find the kid. We just find him hacked up in a ravine."

The horror breaks through the wildness that has been keeping Trina from feeling. It pulls her back into herself. Heather smiles. "There's always an enemy for people to hate," she says. "You just gotta make one."

"Fucking puta," Pilar says, after the candle burns out and they can no longer see each other in the dark. Heather locked them both in, and won't let them out until the morning, when they'll be dragged in front of the Circle.

"Language, Priestess," Trina says, smiling. "Didn't know you had such a mouth."

"You don't know a fucking thing about me," Pilar says in the dark. "You locked me in the Zervatory when I was eight and no one's talked to me since except for the priestesses and novices. You don't think that's got an effect on my *language*?"

"Well, now I'd like to know more," Trina says.

"What you gonna do tomorrow morning when she comes back?" Pilar says.

"I guess I gotta do it," Trina says. "I just—I don't see nother way."

"If she's okay with killing those kids, why would she stop once we give her what she wants?" Pilar says.

"That's basically what I told you the day you arrested me," Trina says.

"That's why I trust you," Pilar says. "The Trina back then woulda known that the kids ain't safe as long as Heather's in charge."

"Okay," Trina says. "And that's why I trust you. Now we just gotta escape . . . again."

Trina maps out the dark of the room in her mind, counting the few objects still in it. She remembers what she read on one of the plastic bags the Parents must have used on their grass: explosive. That gives her an idea.

"Okay. There's half a candle left hidden under my bed, and a quarter litro of vodka. We mix it with the fertilizer and pack it around the lock, and—"

"You right, that does sound complicated," Pilar says, as if to someone else in the dark, in a completely different conversation. There's a little bit of a giggle in her voice. "So, like, twenty minutes? I'll see *you* then."

That conversation ends, and Trina feels Pilar shifting her attention toward her. "What the hell was that, Pilar?"

"That was our ride," Pilar says, using an old expression. "He woulda been here sooner, but there was something about the donkeys."

"What are you . . . ?"

"Just wait, okay? Let the Priestess do her magic for once."

Time disappears in the dark. Trina thinks of her memories of Pilar, most of them negative. When Pilar helped overthrow Trina. When they faced off over Jemma and Lady at the Waking. Trina had blamed Pilar for that, but now she can't stop thinking of that Waking because she knows it was her own fault.

Trina talked Lady into becoming a Mama early. She saw Lady go with Li. She felt in her gut exactly what would happen, because with a boy like Li that's exactly what would happen, always; they think of hate, not love, not even sex. She felt it because it had happened to her. She felt it and still she made sure Lady followed through.

She should have blocked them from entering the bedroom that night. Instead she rushed to the Mamas' house late, too late—too late for Lady. She could only punish the rape when she should have stopped it.

Never leave the Holy Wood empty.

That's what she told Lady. She had believed it, because it's easier to believe for someone else. It wasn't Trina's body that had to get in the way of Li's. Trina doesn't normally allow herself regrets. This is the only one.

What she should have said was *Always keep the Holy Wood safe.*

Minutes or hours later, there's a soft knock on the door, and then the familiar scrape of the key. "Heather's coming back," Trina says. Probably to torture them.

"Not Heather," Pilar says, and the door clicks open. The boy standing there holds two delicate metal rods in his hands, the other ends in the lock. He has opened the door without a key.

Trina barely recognizes the boy as the same kid who fled the Holy Wood years ago. The Half Holy. He wears a tattered dark suit, satin on the collars. His hair is plastered down and parted. He's inked a thin mustache above his lip. Trina knows enough about him to know that he dresses like one of the old actors, Long Gone even before the End.

Pilar hugs the Half Holy, tight. There's an extra second when Trina sees something pass between them. Some kind of spark. "Half Holy?" Trina says, as if not to startle him.

"Let's go," he says. "The Hermanas will be back in five. Or maybe never. They really aren't good at their jobs."

Trina and Pilar follow him in silence through the night. He takes a new path, one that leads east for hundreds of yards. He disappears under a bush between two houses, and Trina follows him to see they're standing on a staircase that cuts down the hill. It's one of the staircases the Parents built to help them climb the hills, tucked between houses.

At the bottom of the staircase, far enough away from the Holy Wood, Pilar says, a little awed, "How'd you find this staircase?"

"More importantly, how'd you find us?" Trina says.

Half Holy shrugs. "I know where the Holy Wood is. Ain't been gone *that* long."

"You know what I'm talkin bout," Trina says. "You knew where to find us. And Pilar knew you was coming. How?"

"We was talking to each other," Pilar says.

"You never even met each other," Trina says. Everyone knows the Half Holy never leaves the Flat Lands. Everyone knows Pilar never leaves the Zervatory.

"We just met right now," Pilar says, and Trina blinks in confusion. "We was talking in our heads."

Pilar explains how she was dreaming of the Last Lifers, surrounded by blood and fire. They fought the Holy Wood, side by side with the Palos. Everyone screamed. In the middle of it was one calm face with a painted-on mustache, taking in the scenery.

"We was dreaming the same dream," Half Holy says.

"You dream like she does?"

"Nah. She pulled me into hers," he says.

From there, they learned how to find each other in their sleep, and then when they were awake. Two lonely kids with no one else to talk to. So they started talking.

"How?" Trina says. "You really magic?"

"It's the Haze," Pilar says.

"What? Why you call it that?"

"It calls itself that." The Haze is some sort of invisible field, Pilar says, some powerful thing that lives in and around everyone. It tells people things, gives them visions. Pilar says it talks to others, too, shows them visions.

Trina grunts. "The way you get dreams—everybody in the Haze do that?"

Pilar shakes her head. "From what I learned from the Haze, it seems to speak to everyone in the language they understand," she says. "My language was dreams and darkness and prophecy."

"It don't talk to me much," Half Holy says. "But sometimes I hear others talking or thinking. Makes me feel less . . . me. It's good to know you ain't the only one of you."

Trina has only thought of this kid as a legend. The kid who left the Holy Wood and lived. But she forgot why he left: because everyone shunned his mother, a refugee from the Downtown, and then him. He was only half of a Holy Wood. He must have been alone his whole life.

"There're others who sees it? Who else?" Trina says.

"When Pablo had his visions, that was the Haze. Jemma saw it, too. I think that's one of the reasons she left," Pilar says.

"She alive?" Trina says. She isn't sure if she should have asked. Apple has to have Ended by now. But if Jemma and Lady are still alive . . .

"I don't know. I saw her once, traveling south beyond the edges of Ell Aye. But now she's hidden. I think the Haze has its own purposes for her in this war, too."

Jemma. Annoying Jemma, wrapped up in the war for survival against their enemies. Maybe the last war. For a moment Trina thinks she should track Jemma down, join her. But no. She needs to fight the war here.

CHAPTER TWENTY-SEVEN
THE END OF THE KING

Tashia stands next to X on the top of the Horn, watching over their Kingdom. Well, X's Kingdom. But increasingly its burdens seem to fall on them both.

She looks down to the base of the fake snow–covered mountain, and sees Othello and John in the shade of a tree, playing dominoes.

"You're gonna have to get rid of Othello and John," Tashia says.

"Just because they oppose me?" X says.

"Yes. Because they *only* oppose you," Tashia says. The Ice Cream Men came to them a week ago and told them that Little Man was the tiny captive she'd brought in with the Angelenos, then they left to bring back weapons. Since then, Othello hasn't stopped whispering about the failings of his king. And of Tashia. "You should probably get rid of me, while you're at it. I'm not helping you, being close to you," she says.

"They're just looking for a reason to blame you for something," X says. "You didn't know you brought in Little Man."

"*We* know that," Tashia says. "The rest of the Round Table doesn't seem to."

"The Round Table has other problems," X says. "They're dealing with the food shortages."

"Made worse by the rations Othello and John stole," Tashia says. A week's worth of rations disappeared yesterday. Everyone knew it must have been the two of them, but no one would admit to seeing it.

"We can't prove that yet," X says.

"We don't have to. We know," Tashia says. "Listen, X, you think they're all still following the codes of the Table. You're the only one left who is. They're just trying to get to you," she says.

"Someone already did," X says, and kisses her neck. It sends signals all the way to her toes.

"Uh-uh," she says.

"Why?"

"Because you aren't listening to me. And because I'm not going to be the King's hookup," she says.

"It's called the King's consort," he says, playful.

"I'm not going to be the King's anything," she says. He drops back, stung long enough to let it show. But she means it. She'll hook up with him on her own terms.

"You need to arrest them," Tashia says. She's not done with Othello. "Get the men loyal to you, and throw them into the boats until you find proof."

"I'm not going to do that," he says.

"You should," she says.

The alarm drums sound.

She's been expecting to hear them for weeks, ever since she discovered the Ice Cream Men Massacre. She hears gunshots. She hears the banging of a thunder gun and shouts and, over it all, the bleating of the cows.

"You want to take the fast way or the faster way?" X says, looking at her.

"The faster one, obviously," she says. Most of the machines in the Kingdom were Grease's ideas, like the rollertrain that lifts the Knights up the Horn, then speeds them down again. But this is hers. There's a cable that stretches down from the Horn to the roofs below. Tashia saw a picture of it in the Parents' time. A woman dressed as a fairy glided down it at night. It must have looked like magic. Tashia decided what it really needed was a chair to ride.

At the edge of the platform on top of the Horn is the chair, a steel-and-wood structure that Tashia had the Smiths bolt together. It wasn't as good as what Grease would have made, but it will seat both Tashia and X. They climb in, and push out into the abyss.

She's never quite ready for that drop, but it thrills her as nothing else ever has. Maybe it is magic. They sail downward as the kids of the Kingdom look up, coming to rest seconds later on the roof of one of the buildings of Main Street.

They pound down the stairs to find Mia, waiting there with their horses. Tashia and Mia are the only two true sisters in the Kingdom, born from the same mother. Tashia watches over Mia as her own child. Mia tells them what they already know.

"The Biters came for the herd," she says. "Othello and John are already out there." Mia can barely say John's name, she hates him so bad. *She should*, Tashia thinks. John had taken her—no, *raped* her—because that had been a Knight's privilege.

"My soldiers, too?" X says. He means, the ones that are still loyal to him. Mia nods, and they mount their horses.

The slaughter is over by the time they reach the herd. A third of the herd are lying in the grass, bleeding, moaning. Another third are trapped against a high wall, milling and looking for a way to escape. The final third are just gone.

Othello is looking out over the herd. When he sees the King arrive, he dismounts slowly, stiffly, with the leg that Jemma nearly destroyed. Tashia smiles to see him wince.

Tashia and X dismount among the bodies of the cows. Tashia looks down at one of them. Its shoulder is so torn with bullets that there's almost no meat on it. "Whose watch was this today, X?" she says, forgetting to call him "King" in front of his Knights. "They did this in broad daylight." Not only does she not see the guards who are assigned to the herd, but she doesn't see the cowboy who always accompanies them in case they spook.

"Some of Othello's friends," X says. Othello has a group of younger soldiers and guards who follow him around. He gives them some of the riches that come to a Knight, and his swagger seems to rub off on them.

One of the guards runs panting through the herd. "Biters!" he says. "They came in quiet this time. We couldn't stop them!"

"Biters!" Othello says, pushing into them. "Biters again? We're no longer safe in our own Kingdom."

More soldiers and Knights seem to have gathered, and they add fearful voices. Tashia feels them pressing down against her. But she shakes her head.

"Where's their lances, boys?" she says. "These cows have all been shot. You think Biters would hunt without their lances?"

The King nods. "The Biters can't ride, either. How would they have stolen the cows?"

"Maybe they weren't stealing them," Othello says, thoughtfully.

"Why?" X says.

"Maybe they just wanted to scare and kill," Othello says, and his voice fills with menace. "That's why they came during the day. They knew they could do it because they've attacked us before, and we didn't punish the Biters for it. They will keep coming and coming—because our king is weak."

There it is. This is what Othello has been waiting for. He must have had his followers drive off the cows, shooting enough to make it look like the Biters. He's putting the Kingdom in danger just to get back at X.

"It's time for a king who respects the old ways," Othello says, looking at Tashia. "A king who fights our enemies inside and out."

"If you want a new king, I'm ready to fight any time," X says. "I'll see you in the Night Mountain."

"You've shown me there are other ways to solve our differences beside combat," Othello says. Suddenly, there are weapons everywhere.

The Knights who are loyal to X have their swords out, but so do all the guards and Knights who couldn't be found before. And there are many more of them. Even John holds a pistol.

That's why Othello drew X outside the wall, out of sight of the Kingdom. He doesn't need to convince the Kingdom. He just needs the numbers to be on his side at this moment. Now he can go back to the Kingdom with any story he wants.

Tashia breathes in once, and her body grows still. Her mind goes clear. X is done. The only thing they can do now is survive long enough to fight back.

"X, former King of this people, I relieve you of your throne," Othello says. "You are guilty of a failure to protect this Kingdom, possibly treason."

He wants to kill X. Tashia knows it. He always hated being under X, but was never strong enough to beat him in the Night Mountain. Now, with his leg, he wouldn't survive the hand combat that the Kingdom would demand to prove an accusation like his. He couldn't attempt to kill X without risking his own life. He can't kill him now, even when he has all the guns.

"In honor of your station as a Knight, I'll show you mercy," Othello says. "You can rot in the boats, or you can run. The offer applies to you both."

"Kings don't run," X says.

"That's not our problem anymore, X," Tashia says. "Well, what do you want?"

X shrugs. "Run?"

Tashia shuts her mind against all the things that pull her back into the Kingdom. Her cowboys. Coretta. Mia. All of them are in danger once Tashia leaves. But if she doesn't flee, she and X are dead. She nods.

Run.

CHAPTER TWENTY-EIGHT
THE MELTDOWN

James is back in the Camp, after disappearing who knows where. Jemma listens distractedly as Pico and Grease explain to James what they want him to do to her to bring the Haze back. It's such a big moment that even Lady joins them. James's reaction changes from annoyed to shocked.

"You learned this in a week?" he says. "You're kids."

"We can *read*, James," Pico says, a little perturbed.

"Yeah, third graders could read. Med students could read," James says. "But it took a team of neuroscientists twenty years to discover this. And . . . it might work."

"Really?" Jemma says. "Could you do it?"

"We can. It was one of the first tracks we explored with the Long Life Project, a way of restoring the brain's plasticity. We still have the equipment. It should still work."

"I'll make sure it does," Grease says, and again James gives him an odd look.

When they return to the boys' room after James's office, Lady says, "You didn't ask him about the other things you saw on the puter."

Pico shrugs. "He coulda told us sooner but didn't. I wanna wait and figure out why."

"That's stupid," Lady says, rousing herself for the first time in a week to sound like the old Lady. "He's a hundred-year-old *teenager*. That's important. Back me up, mija."

"Hmm?" Jemma says. "Yeah, it's important." Since she discovered Apple's face in the cards, though, it all feels less important than it did. Does she really need the Haze back in her head? She can find it, and Apple, in the Lectrics. She finds herself wishing for a way to sneak back to the puter lab. She hasn't told the others yet. She's not sure why. But it feels like a secret, so she keeps it.

She notices a small beige box with a green screen by the side of Grease's bed. "What's that?" she says.

"It's a Game Boy," Grease says. "Me and Pico fixed it."

"It's a puter, though?" Jemma says.

"Yeah, just for games."

"Could I . . . borrow it?" she says.

"Sure," Grease says with a shrug. "It's only got one game, and we beat it."

That night, she waits for Lady to fall asleep, then switches her light back on and picks up the Game Boy. She plugs it in and turns it on like Grease showed her, then clicks on the only game: Tetris. It's a sort of stacking game, a way of fitting together falling shapes so they disappear. She plays it halfheartedly, watching the shapes. And then they shift, break up into other smaller blocks and crosses and lines until they look like a smaller version of the cards in the puter.

Even though the face is smaller, she recognizes it. She smiles. "Hey, Apple," she says, and snuggles with the Game Boy deep into the covers.

Jemma isn't sure of this now, not with a metal strap over her forehead and wrists. She's in a room in the hospital that she's never seen before, surrounded by a wall of machines. James and Brian K are prepping her. James leans over. "How you feeling?"

"Like this is a horrible idea," she says.

"Well, blame your friends. They're the ones who decided to jump-start you," he says. "I'm going to explain this to you, just in case you change your mind. We're using a form of deep-brain stimulation, which will send signals to your neurons in the hopes they can regrow the paths back to the Haze."

"With what?" she says. She should have asked more questions before now.

"Well, with a current of electricity, running at a frequency of 115 hertz," James says. "That's what the wires are for." She reaches up and feels spiderweb-thin wires, going directly into the skin.

"Lectrics in my head," Jemma says. Flat.

"If it makes you feel better, in the old days we would have had to surgically implant the electrodes *inside* your head."

It does not make her feel better.

"Is it gonna hurt?"

Brian K answers. "It might. The nerves we're stimulating also deliver pain signals, and we're putting them under significant duress," he says. "We just can't predict how it will affect someone with your abilities."

"Okay," she says uncertainly.

James says, "Jemma, you should let us know if you have second thoughts. Because we're about to shoot electricity in your head and you should make sure you really want it there."

She doesn't want to do it. Not with Apple waiting back there in her room. She's afraid. But Jemma got to this point because of one basic rule: The terrifying things are the things worth doing.

"Fine. Let's roll this Mama," she says.

Almost immediately when they start, Jemma feels the Haze come back. Not as if it's flowing into her, but as if it's waking up inside her. She feels tingles along the surface of her thighs.

Jemma thinks, *It's back. It was worth it.*

The treatment starts out as a tingle under her skin, impossible to ignore but almost pleasant. The tingle changes to a buzz.

It feels like that first staticky encounter with the Haze, when it learned how to talk to her. That comforts her. *We're understanding each other again.* She smiles. She imagines it running through her body in a cool-stream flow.

Then it all tears apart. She feels the Haze, but it feels wrong. The Haze is in every cell, vibrating as if it will burst, as if it could take her to the sun and burn with it. Rushes of sense—breezes blowing in from mountains, the green of corn, a frog dying mid-leap. It is more than she can hold.

It's more than she can hold.

The Haze starts to pulse and sear. She hears shouting, but she can't focus on it. She's too busy trying to see her hands and the Haze bursting out of them. It swarms out of her not just in blue but in swirls of orange and red, burning its way into the room. Brian K runs into the room and right into the blast of Haze, which strikes him in the face.

He slams into the wall. His face seems to crumble inward. *Please let me be imagining this,* she thinks. She holds on to the metal handles on the edge of her bed.

Still the Haze wants away from the pain. It climbs through the metal on her forehead into the room's metalwork, into the puters and beeping things and all this delicate machinery that survived the death of adults.

The Lectric pulses course from her hands as they did when the Night Mountain lit up in sound and electric gleams. It was beautiful then. This is not. When it flows from her body into the machines, the Lectrics that were already inside the machines seem to push back.

A puter cabinet catches fire and the lights surge to a single lightning bolt—then go dark.

Jemma keeps waiting to go dark, too. But the pain just keeps coming.

CHAPTER TWENTY-NINE
THE HALF HOLY

The Half Holy lives in the Holy Motel, an old motel papered with black-and-white images of Long Gone priestesses. The motel smells of dirty life, animals and green packed close together in his little fortress.

When Trina exits her room the morning after they arrive, she sees a courtyard filled with goats. One stands on the old diving board of the pool, bounces on it gently as if testing it for launch.

Even though it's barely dawn, she finds Pilar and the Half Holy already awake and talking. They stop the moment she comes into sight. They look flushed, tired. Trina wonders if they've been up all night.

"So, we just go visit the other Angelenos?" Trina says.

"We could," the Half Holy says.

"Or we could have them all come meet us," Pilar says.

"How? You talk to them in their dreams?"

"There's more than one way to talk long distance," the Half Holy says.

He leads them to a little nest he's built on the roof of the second floor, shielded by ivy-covered walls. No one would be able to see him below at all, although he can spy down through scopes and peepholes. There are no high buildings around them, so no one can see directly in, either.

In the center of the nest are three head-size mirrors, mounted on tripods, covered with cloths. She can tell they're mirrors from the backs. Trina puzzles over them. She hasn't looked in a mirror for years. No one's ever cared what she looks like. She has a mole on her cheek but isn't sure which side.

The Half Holy pulls the cover off one of the mirrors, the one that faces slightly southeast. He peeks through a hole in it, as if through a sight on a gun. He does the same for the mirror looking northwest. He uncovers the third mirror but doesn't look through it. He's so careful, so reverent in his preparations, that it makes her think of the Little Doctors.

Still, she doesn't know what the movements mean until she leans forward and a blast of light blinds her temporarily. "You blockin the signal," he says, and continues to adjust the mirrors.

She follows the southeastern mirror line to the towers of Downtown, miles away. Just when she is about to look away, she sees a flash from one of the tall ones. The Half Holy nods. "We on," he says.

The Half Holy holds up a piece of cardboard, the cover of a book, and waves it in front of the mirror to block the light it reflects, then lets it shine again. Three short pauses. Three long pauses. Three short pauses. From the tower, a long sequence of flashes.

He does the same thing with the northwest mirror, which points into the hills, except this one uses light bounced to it from the third mirror. She's beginning to understand his system. "You got people just waiting up there?"

"Only at dawn," he says.

"Just there?"

"All over Ell Aye," he says. "We been watching a long time, since before I was born. People like me—people who don't belong."

She had felt as if the world had pulled apart a long time ago. Now she finds that . . . someone has been trying to hold it all together?

"You guys got a name?" she says.

"Just our own," he says.

The Half Holy looks back to the southeast tower and starts waving the cardboard over that mirror, faster and faster. The flashes go short and long and short and long in patterns that grow more and more complex. His hands blur. It's almost as if he's talking.

But, of course, he is. Trina can almost imagine speech amid the flashes, even though he never says a word. "We need your help. Our enemies are coming for us." It's an alphabet. It has to be. It's a code.

"You invent this?" she says.

"Everything been invented already," he says. "We just gotta remember."

The Half Holy looks northwest, above the Bowl. Another mirror flashes there. He repeats the sequence with the northwest mirror, and finally his hands fall still. He's sweating in the morning sun, his carefully parted hair glistening even more.

"Now we wait," he says.

"How long?" she says, her frustration starting to show.

"You got somewhere you gotta be?" Pilar says. The Half Holy smiles at her. Trina rolls her eyes.

The flashes don't come until hours later. He watches them carefully, repeats something to himself under his breath. "They say they'll talk to us. At the Downtown's stadio. At the end of the day."

"Okay," Trina says, and sees the Half Holy's hesitation. "That a problem?"

"It's just that we gotta leave this place," the Half Holy says, as if that's the last thing he wants to do in the world.

CHAPTER THIRTY
THE AFTERMATH

"Both the main power and the backup. Wow!" James says. He seems giddy, almost. It's an hour after Jemma's meltdown, after Grease helped bring the Lectrics back online. He was the only one who could. Brian K was dealing with the loss of his face.

Grease found Brian K first, sure he was dead. He was breathing, but there was something wrong with his face. Part of it seemed to be missing, flesh and skin and maybe a little bone. But that wasn't the wrongest part. His face was growing back.

Brian K caught Grease's stricken look. "Oh, this. It never feels good," Brian K said. "Now I'm going to walk around looking like this all month."

They're still sitting in the hospital room that Jemma destroyed an hour ago. Jemma seems weak but otherwise suffered no damage. She hasn't talked since the meltdown, but now she clears her throat as if she's thirsty. The Old Guys lean toward her. "Is that how it was supposed to work?" she says.

"No. But god, Jemma, if we can wake that up, we really could stop the End," James says. "Did you see that, Alice? I've never seen so much power concentrated in the nanotech." He talks like a little boy showing off a toy. Grease feels the same way.

"I saw it," Alice says, and her voice chills the room. "You want to explain what you did to our machines?" She's measured, but her blue eyes look murderous to Grease.

"She told you she could talk to the Haze," Lady says.

"*Talking* to the Haze is one thing," James says. "Frying our equipment is another. Shooting lasers like some sort of intergalactic space ninja is completely another."

"I dunno what happened," Jemma says. "I din't even know the Haze was still inside me."

"It's inside everyone," Isaac says. "But that meltdown shows it's there inside you in unusual concentrations, even if it isn't reaching your temporal lobe."

"So when you said it wasn't there, you were . . ." Jemma pauses to let him fill in the answer.

Isaac grimaces. "Wrong. I was wrong."

"Just so we know we're talkin bout the same thing," Jemma says.

"So what happened?" James says.

"It was a feedback loop that fed into an arc," Grease says. "The Lectrics of the Haze were pushing out along the wires, trying to avoid the surge, but the machines had currents of their own. There was no place for the Haze to go but out."

"He's right," Brian K says, his voice muffled behind his head.

James blinks. "So, Jemma, your powers aren't limited to communication," he says. "The Haze can manifest itself physically. It has a special link to electricity and machines."

"To computers and nanotech," Grease says. He knows where James is heading.

"Jesus, everybody," James says to the other Old Guys in the room. "Could you imagine what we could do if we harnessed that power?"

"You can't harness that," Alice says. "Look at Brian K's face."

"Don't bring me into this," Brian K says. "I'll live." His face looks like a burn wound, pink and raw but healing.

"But if we could. We could take on Charlie."

"And shut down the Haze? With all that entails?" Alice says. Grease feels like he's walked into the middle of an argument, but both Alice and James know exactly where it's going.

"If we have to," James says. "We can't waste an opportunity like this. We can't ignore *power* like this."

"You never could resist the power, could you, James? Even if it hurt everyone you love," Alice says. "A hundred years later, you still haven't learned the lesson."

"Do you really expect us to ignore a potential cure? Aren't you just tired of doing nothing, Alice?"

"I'm tired of 'doing' altogether, *dear*," Alice says, and she bites on the last word as if she's been chewing it for years. "We have done so many things to save the world. We have done so many things and *all of them have been wrong*."

"I've never stopped trying to fix my mistakes," James says.

"I know, dear. That's what I loved about you when I loved you," Alice says. "But maybe it's time to stop."

"All your mistakes, Mom?" Isaac says, in a mixture of anger and despair that Grease can't make sense of. It seems to make her angrier.

"Here's a question for your new secret weapons," Alice says, and turns her attention to the Mayflies. "You ever wonder why we're in a military base? Why we're surrounded by dead Marines? Don't you think that's an odd place to make people live forever?"

"They paid for the Long Life Project," Grease says. "We know."

Alice shakes her head. "They didn't care about Long Life—or any life. They cared about death. We're here because there was a war looming with Mexico and they wanted a weapon. And James was only too happy to give it to them."

Grease sees the stricken look on James's face and knows that at least some of this is true.

"The End wasn't a mistake," Alice says. "The End was the whole point."

"Tell us what she meant," Jemma says, after Alice storms out and the rest of them stay behind like debris. Jemma feels hollowed out by the treatment and its aftermath. But she has to understand how this Parent, this person they trusted almost instinctively, could have been behind such evil.

James sighs heavily. "There is a short version, and there is a very, very long one. You do not get the long one."

He tells them the story of the Long Life Project, but with different details. More of them. Finally he says, "The Haze is coded to the human brain, as you know. That's so it can read what's happening in your body and make changes to it. Like adjusting a thermostat. But the military didn't want a thermostat. They wanted a switch.

"They thought, what if we could fight Mexico from a distance, just the soldiers and not the civilians who would normally die? Just float the Haze to a specific location, let it connect to the soldiers, and then . . . switch them off."

"And you did," Pico says. Jemma understands the pictures Pico showed her now, of the men crisscrossed in the jungle clearing like trees blown down. But . . . "Why? Why'd you go along?"

"I've always been blessed to see both sides of the argument," James says. "It seemed a more humane form of warfare. More than that, if the thermostat could control death, it could also control life. If the Long Life Project was allowed to run its course, it meant eternal life for the entire human race."

"But you couldn't control it," Lady says.

"Life, it turns out, is impossible to control. All you can do is nudge it along."

"You ain't even going to say you're sorry?" Lady says.

The look on James's face is worn and grieving with a ridge of stone. His mouth opens as if to say something soft, then snaps shut like a book. "If 'sorry' could reverse my mistakes, I would be sorry every day of my life," he says. "So far, though, it's been quite useless in bringing back the dead."

"Then what is useful?"

"I've been trying to show you," he says. "If you'll allow me."

She doesn't know what she wants James to say. Mostly she wants to go back to her room and curl up with Apple.

"What James would like to say is that this has been in the works for a very long time," Isaac says. "But the four of you may be the X factor we need."

"No mames, guey," Pico says to Isaac. "You a hundred years old, ain't you?"

"Excuse me?" James responds.

"It's Angeleno," Isaac says, smiling at his dad sheepishly. "It means 'Cut the bullshit.'"

"So you had the Long Life Treatment since the End and ain't bothered to share it with us or anyone else," Pico says. It's rare to see him angry, but he is. "What was you waitin for?"

"To see if I could trust you, for one," James says. "And for the final pieces of the Long Life Machine."

"So how do you explain Isaac?" Jemma says. She reaches out to Isaac, to this teenager who should be dead—and pinches his face.

"What the hell?" he says. Not angrily.

"You don't got baby fat," she says. "That's what was weird bout you." Not just that. He has the weariness, the detachment of the Old Guys. But there still is a kid in him, even below the appearance. The world still holds wonder. It's as if time has frozen him in place.

"The Long Life Machine only affects Pairing," James says. "Reboot, the first phase, is based in chemical and biological actions, so we could still apply that process to Isaac."

"And then the Betterment came," Isaac says. "The first time I didn't know what was happening. I'd never witnessed the End in anyone before. But James and Alice stopped it with the Reboot."

"The Reboot stops the Betterment?" Jemma says.

"For a time. We could make temporary fixes, DNA modification and cellular repair, that would essentially fool the Haze into thinking he was too young for the Betterment," James says. "But none of them hold permanently. It's the difference between replacing the roof on your house and patching a few holes when it rains."

"*A few holes*? It feels different when you're living through them," Isaac says. "The repairs lasted several more years until the End found a way around it and the Betterment came again. Then more repairs and then the Betterment, and more repairs and then the Betterment."

"How many times did you go through the Betterment?" Jemma says. She remembers the look of peace and bewilderment on Apple's face as he Ended. What would dying so many times do to a person?

"Sixteen?" Isaac says, as if just saying the number is exhausting. "Some repairs held for decades, others just for months. Between the Betterment and the fixes, my body has been held in stasis, which is why I look like I'm sixteen. The past few years, though, the Betterment's happening more and more frequently."

"The End is catching up," James says. "No more temporary fixes. But that's okay. Because we found the missing pieces of the Long Life Machine."

He explains how he's spent the past century scouring labs for parts to recreate the Long Life Machine. When he disappeared last week with Brian K, they were driving to a Long Gone city called San Francisco, where they found the last pieces they needed.

"Wow," Grease says reverently.

"The only problem is it doesn't work," Brian K says. "We don't know if it's the Machine or the Haze or our science, and we're running out of time before Isaac's next Reboot."

"So?" Pico says.

"So you Children have some unusual gifts," James says. "We want to tap into them. We have the experience, but you have creativity and a new perspective. We want you to help us stop Charlie if we can. And we want you to help us rebuild the Long Life Machine."

"Show us this machine first," Jemma says.

Isaac answers. "That's going to take a trip to the Ark."

CHAPTER THIRTY-ONE
THE TELLING

Tommy wakes with the ropes still wrapped around his wrist. *The ocean sunk*, he thinks, because the water doesn't seem to want him anymore.

His eyes don't open. Something holds them together. He tries to force them but he thinks he'll tear his eyelids. Light pours through them even so, all liquid and blood.

It's day. It's light. I've made it out of the storm.

Of course. It's just salt. That gives him the courage to tear his eyelids open. When they finally separate and he's assaulted by light, he thinks he was wrong: The sea hasn't disappeared after all. Everything around him is green and waving, covering him the way the water did. But somehow still wet.

The sea is grass. Some kind of reeds tower overhead, taller than the Giants. Taller than he would be, certainly—if he weren't tied flat against the ground.

His legs are tied, too, to some kind of stake in the ground. His arms lie flat along the ground, over his head. The ropes around his wrist are tight, but not pulled taut. He cranes his head back, and sees he's tied to a thick wooden pole, damp to five feet up. He must be in a tidal marsh. Is he to be drowned when the tides come in? If so, why was he saved?

Torture. The Chosen have tortured their victims like that, Lowers who refused to accept their status, Kingdom soldiers who were captured in raids. They were buried in the sand or staked to the ground, and when the tide came in, the victims would fight the waves or the crabs that came with it. Even Tommy had had to fight the urge to look away.

He didn't regret the violence it took to be Little Man, but it didn't always come easy. He could see the flinches, the averted eyes. He never allowed himself to avert his eyes.

He moves quietly, urgently. No attracting attention. He tests the rope. There's more slack around his wrists than he thought, almost enough to bring his hands together. Why bother torturing him if they're not going to make the ropes tight? Are they toying with him? Is that the torture? He looks at his forearms. There are long lines on it, as if they had cut him lightly with a knife. They've already started the torture.

The left hand is looser, so Little Man works at it first. The rope slides up his thumb. He can feel the hairs of the rope biting into his skin. It doesn't feel like a rope from the Old Ones. These people made it themselves.

He remembers rope from the Old Ones, fraying and smelling of must but strong enough to hold a five-year-old. He remembers struggling against the ropes they tied him with, which bit against the wrist, as the bigger kids laughed at him, as they poked him with dull knives. No one to let him out. If the Jocks wanted to hurt you, you hurt. If they wanted to take your soul, they took it.

Help, Piss Ant says. But Little Man shuts him down.

The rope stops halfway up the thumb. He compresses his hand, but the rope doesn't move. The right wrist is too tight, so he tries something else. If he can slide his body down and lift his hands above his head, pointing like a diver, he may be able to get the knots close enough to each other that he can untie himself.

He shifts through the grass and mud. Is it wetter than it was a moment ago? Out of the corner of his eye he imagines more glinting silver between the reeds. The water is rising. It must be.

Little Man reaches out into the Haze. It can show him how to get free of the ropes. He inhales, exhales, matches the breath to his heart. It shows him how. If he dislocates a shoulder—just one of them—

Tommy braces himself for that, realizes he shouldn't brace anything. He needs to relax his body to dislocate it. But he can't. He feels himself sweating, even in the cool green whispering sea.

"Geez, dude, don't hurt yourself," a voice says from the reeds to his right.

The face pushes out of the reeds. Brown skin, yes, but maybe from years in the sun. The hair must have been brown, but is streaked blond. More sun. Was the face originally a Biter's? An Angeleno's? He can't tell even if it's a boy or girl.

"You want out, just ask." Boy, he thinks, sixteen years old, now that he sees the kid without a shirt. Close to Ending. Strong and scarred. A warrior.

"Why would you let me go?"

"Better question is, why would we tie you up?"

"Why am I tied up?"

"Cuz, man, we never saw someone thrash so much. What you afraid of?"

Tommy sees the *Vengeance* coming toward him, the sea, the Giants, the Haze, the Chosen, the pink arms, everything. But he doesn't answer the question aloud.

The kid steps closer. He's wearing shorts, like the Malibus. At the edge of the shorts Tommy can see that his skin is paler, closer to the Chosen.

"We tied you up cuz you were hurting yourself. You ever cut those nails?" No, Little Man doesn't. The rulers of the Chosen don't cut their nails, to show they don't have to work. His are long, jagged, curling. There are brownish stains under some of them that don't look like dirt, and now he sees the lines on his arms differently.

This boy's nails are worn down to the beds. One of them has a blood blister under it, probably from a hammer. He's a worker. But he doesn't carry himself like a Lower.

The boy squats next to him as if to untie him, but Tommy notices that he doesn't move any closer to the ropes. Perhaps he's not as trusting as he appears.

"So, little dude . . . how you end up in the middle of the ocean?"

"Is that where you found me?"

"You were caught in one of our nets that stretch off from the point. The current pushes fish through it. We weren't expecting you there."

"Was I there long?" Tommy hasn't had time to think of a cover story, so he keeps asking questions.

"Long enough for you to pass out, I'd guess. Not long enough to drown," the kid says. "But how'd you float into it?"

"What's your name?" Tommy says.

"Scott. How'd you get here?" A Chosen name, almost. The boy's smile is real, but his focus on Tommy is wary. Tommy isn't getting out of the ropes until he answers. *Keep it simple*, Tommy thinks. *Keep it close to the truth so you can't slip.*

"I escaped from my people. I was forced to join the crew on one of their raiding trips. Cooking, toilets, that kind of thing, and they beat me if they thought I did anything wrong. When the storm came, I took my chance and swam overboard." It's the same story he told to the Angelenos and the Kingdom, and they believed him even though they didn't trust him.

Scott nods, seeming to take the story at face value. He moves toward the knots. Just like at the Kingdom, where Little Man was able to manipulate Jemma and orchestrate an attack from the inside, because no one believed such a little kid could matter. The big taken in by the small again.

The boy reaches toward the knots, then stops, fingers hovering just above the rope. "Only . . ."

Tommy finds himself holding his breath, waiting for him to close the gap.

"What?" *Untie the damn rope*, Little Man says.

"It's just that, if I had to guess, maybe one in three of the things you told me are true. Maybe one in four." Scott sits back in the grass, well away from the rope. "You want to try again?"

"I'm just a little kid. I— You don't know what I had to go through." Tommy feels himself shrinking, becoming the kid he's supposed to be. Not Little Man. Piss Ant.

"I don't doubt it," Scott says. But he doesn't offer any more.

"I'm telling you, it's true," Piss Ant says. "They hurt me."

"You know we live fifteen miles across the ocean from the Biters, don't you?" Scott says. "We know they don't sail here, because it's Catalina's Grave. But our people come from land. All the way over here, we hear stories of blue eyes and white sails, of people who eat people and tattoo their kills on their wrist." And Scott looks down at Tommy's right wrist. Three black marks slash their way across his veins.

"I was forced to," Piss Ant says, his usual line. But he knows it doesn't work this time.

"You're too small to fight, and we know you ain't cleaning any toilets." *The fingernails again.* "So somehow you're a leader."

Before Tommy can react, Scott leans over, unties the rope from the pole—and ties it again, even tighter. Now Tommy can't pull his arms together. "For such a little dude to be a leader of the scariest people around . . . you'd have to be a seriously scary little son of a bitch."

Tommy should be angry, scared. But no one ever takes him seriously, even after all he's done for the Chosen. His greatest weapon was that no one ever believed he could do what he did, and Scott has taken that away. But Scott also takes him seriously, and that somehow feels right.

"Nice trick," Tommy says. "I would clap, but . . ." He shrugs at the ropes.

"A lot of stories blow our way," Scott says.

"So . . . now you kill me?" Tommy would kill a threat like himself, without a question.

"That'd be a waste. Know how hard we worked to save you? Even then we could tell you were one of the people eaters. But we saved you anyways," Scott says.

"Why?"

"Like I said, a lot of stories blow our way. We untie them and let them stay—but only if they're honest about who they were. We call it the Telling."

Tommy lies in the grass, looking past the reeds to the sky. It's blue now. No storm. He wasn't wrong before—the water is rising. He feels it tickle in his ears. But still he doesn't move.

The boy stands up. "People change when they're here. They gotta change," he says. "Leave it all in the net, dude." And he walks away through the reeds.

Tommy will die here. As peaceful as these people seem, they will let him die if he lies. He would almost tell the truth for that alone, but not quite. The water pushes past his ears, under his chin. He has twenty minutes left.

Tell him, Piss Ant says.

Shut up, asshole, Little Man says. *That's gonna get us hurt.* Tommy doesn't know which to believe.

He has never told the truth. Truth always meant pain. It meant loss. It meant showing himself as he was. Tommy holds still for long minutes, and the water creeps up his sides. It feels good. Wouldn't it be a relief to drown, when it comes?

He has never told the truth to himself.

When he finally speaks, Tommy's not sure if anyone is listening. He just hears rustling in the reeds. But it almost doesn't matter if they listen. He speaks just to feel the sounds floating in the air, each word another stone off his chest. "My name is Tommy. My real name is Little Man," he says. "Before that, I was Piss Ant. I didn't get a name.

I never knew a soul who loved me. I never had someone who had my back.

"I'm the youngest Lord of the Chosen. People call us the Biters, and they're right. I have . . . eaten my enemies. I ordered our allies slaughtered. I created Giants who have defeated death. We sailed here to find a rival and force him to tell me what he knows. I'm terrified of the End, even though I inflict it on others. I told myself I was the greatest leader since the End. And my own people tried to kill me in Catalina's Grave."

Nothing changes for a while, for a long while. The water moves to the corner of his eyes. He can keep his nose and mouth out, but just. "I've been weak my whole life," Tommy says. "I only ever had one friend, and he's a servant."

The reeds whisper louder. It's either the wind or Scott returning after listening.

No, he can see when the reeds part and faces of every color push through; it was the whole tribe listening. And in the middle of all those faces, Scott's is touched with pity. "That's a lot to leave in the net. You up for it?"

"Yeah, I think so," Tommy says.

"Just one thing, dude," Scott says, fixing him with a glance that knows everything about Tommy. "You forgot to tell us bout the Haze."

CHAPTER THIRTY-TWO
THE FROZEN CHILD

"What's the Ark?" Jemma asks Isaac, half because she wants to know, and half to distract him from his parents' screaming at each other outside the soundproof windshield of the ULV, the vehicle James drove through the dust storm. Other than that first night, which she doesn't remember, Jemma has never been in it before. It looks like a Humvee, but it's somehow sleeker and more armored, painted black instead of green. Made for running in the night. Jemma and Isaac are already in the back seat, waiting for James and the other Mayflies.

"The Ark is tough to explain," he says. "You kinda have to see it. It's really big."

"You take us away in the middle of the night and all you can say is it's really big," Jemma says.

"Really, really big?"

She notices his eyes drift away toward James and Alice. "You okay?"

"Sure, you know how it is—your dad ends the world just one time and your mom can't ever let it go."

Jemma doesn't know what it would be like to feel torn in half for a hundred years. "So you a kid who's a grown-up, or a grown-up who looks like a kid?"

Isaac smiles. "Both and neither, I guess."

"Are you a vampire?"

"You know about vampires?" he says.

"We got vampires," she says. "I hope you ain't one, cuz I really don't wanna deal with that."

"Not a vampire. It's like I'm stuck in limbo. Every time I go through phase one, it takes my cells back to a sort of virgin state."

"Virgin," she says.

Isaac ignores that. "*All* of the cells. I get shot back to fourteen or fifteen, and then I have to live my teens all over," Isaac says. "I have the knowledge and memories of an Old Guy, but the hormones, the brain patterns? Pure teenager. We're hoping the Long Life Treatment will give me a path beyond that."

"That what you want?"

"I've had over eighty years of zits," he says. "I'd like to move on."

She thinks, *It's pretty perfect skin.*

Lady piles into the ULV next to Jemma, and Pico and Grease climb into the front passenger side.

"You get all your stuff?" Jemma says.

"Don't got much to bring," Lady says. Jemma instinctively pats the Gatherer's bag to make sure the Game Boy is still there. As Lady has gone further and further away, Apple has become more important. Only . . . sometimes it doesn't seem like Apple is back. It doesn't feel the way it used to. *Course it doesn't. He's a puter now, not a real boy.*

"What'd you think about today?" Jemma asks.

"I'm glad you okay," Lady says. "That was pretty stupid."

"But the other stuff."

"Don't make much of a difference to me," Lady says.

It's not so much the anger in Lady's voice as the *nothing* that frightens Jemma. "Whaddya mean?"

"You all goin to save the world," Lady says. "Grease is fixin the Machine, Pico is learnin bout the brain, and you're . . . doing something with the Haze. What'm I doin?"

"Lady, you matter to—"

"Don't," Lady says. She turns away and puts her head on the window.

When James finally climbs in and slams the door of the ULV, only Pico and Grease are speaking. "Jesus," he says bitterly, as if that's all he needs to say. He starts the ULV but there's no sound, nothing like Jemma's used to hearing with the Hummers.

"It's all Lectrics," Grease says.

"Yup. Solars on the top. It'll run forever if you can find enough sun."

Brian K and some other Old Guys will meet them there tomorrow. James turns off the ULV lights and turns to a screen, which shows the road in front of him in a green light. He accelerates into complete darkness. The edges of trees, rocks, and buildings whip past them at almost the moment Jemma can make them out. It's freeing. It's terrifying.

"Is that hard?" Grease says.

"It took me six years to master it," James says. "Of course, I had a hundred after that."

The road straightens as they drop noiselessly to the sea, and Jemma can almost pick out the white line of surf below in the moonlight. But she imagines she's imagining it. "Where we going?" she says.

"San Diego," Isaac says.

"San Diego is gone," Grease says. "Everybody says so. Why are we going to a dead place?"

"Well, that's partly true," Isaac says. "The city is gone."

"Why?" No one's ever told Jemma.

"Different people handled the End differently, as you've no doubt seen. Some peacefully, some . . . not," James says. "San Diego was particularly violent."

"Why?" she says again.

"San Diego was the first city to fall, because it was closest to the Camp. No one knew what was happening, so it caused panic," James says. "Sometimes fear is a worse enemy than death. People panicked and tore the city apart. The Marines, the ones that weren't dead already, came to the city to protect it. But they panicked, too, and they had bigger guns. In a week, it was all gone. Half the people died before the End got them."

"So you just put the Ark in the middle of all that?" Pico says.

"The Ark is just there. You'll see," Isaac says.

"Is this why half the Old Guys always seemed to be gone?" Lady says, momentarily lifting her cheek off the glass.

"Yeah. We live in the Camp because it's comfortable and safe, we do some research there," James says. "But the real work happens in the Ark."

"You said my talking to the Haze was the first real hope you had," Jemma says. "What's the Ark, like some kind of backup plan?" she says.

"It's not a backup plan, it's *the* plan," James says. "Do you really think the only scientists in the world waited a hundred years for *you* to walk through the door? What do you think we do all day?"

"Watch movies?" Lady says.

"Honestly, it's just a little professionally insulting," James says, then catches himself.

They cut a final wide curve through the hills, the headlights raking the brush, and ahead of them are the lost towers of San Diego. Even in the light of the moon, Jemma can see them split and tear. "They're still standing," Pico says. "I didn't expect them to be."

"Barely," James says.

The 5 road twists through the ruined spires, and the ULV slows to a crawl to get around the cars. A ramp leads off to the right and they edge toward it.

Now that they've slowed down, Jemma can glimpse more of the city. A huge white church, edged with crumbling orange tiles, sits off to their right. A ficus has popped through the top of the church tower, the dome of its branches completely surrounding the smaller dome that was once the roof. Coils of roots snake their way around the tower to the street, threatening to choke it.

They make the last turn toward the ocean, and it lies silent and dark before them.

"Welcome to the Ark," Isaac says.

"The what?" Lady says. But then it opens up above them on the shoreline, and all they can do is stare.

There's only metal. More metal than Jemma's seen in her life. She can't make sense of it. The end looks like a face: a metal ramp that hangs from a gaping mouth, a wide flat roof that overhangs the mouth like a hat.

It's a boat, somehow. Part of it still floats in the water, part has been rammed into the shore. She's looking at the end of it, she thinks. But if the end is two hundred feet wide, as this looks like it could be, how long is the boat?

The ULV drives up the ramp into the open mouth. She can tell how high the boat is by how steeply they climb.

They're in some kind of hangar, like the ones Grease and Pico said held skyplanes. She opens her door and every movement echoes in the vast space. The ramp closes with a scraping sound of doom. She shakes it off.

"What is this place?"

"It's an aircraft carrier," James says, getting out of the ULV. "It's the largest ship in the world, or what's left of it, and it's your new home."

CHAPTER THIRTY-THREE
THE SWALLOWS' NEST

Tommy looks up at Scott as he unties him. *He knows about the Haze.* As if he can read Tommy's mind, Scott gives the tiniest of smiles. "Did you really think you were the first kid to ever speak to the Haze?"

"You the kid I was supposed to find," Tommy says.

"I'm the kid who called for you in the Haze. I'm the kid who wouldn't let you find Jemma," Scott says. "Get up. We gotta lot of work to do."

The idea should fill Tommy with rage. But he gets up.

"Most of the Weavers over the past thirty years have been able to use the Haze," Scott says.

"Thirty years? How is that possible?" Tommy says. "I never heard of anyone else with that power until a month ago."

"Not surprising, Tommy. No one talks about it," Scott says.

"What do you mean, 'Weavers'?" Tommy says. But Scott and the rest of the kids just walk forward, over a small rise in the marsh.

The village is in the reeds. It's made from reeds. It is reeds. Tommy can't really tell. He just knows that it's the first place he's ever seen that wasn't built from the Parents' wreckage. The marsh fills a horseshoe cove, bordered by cliffs on both sides. He can see herons wading. Silver water glints through some patches, but mostly it's the green and tan of the reeds.

From his vantage point the reeds look less like grass and more like waves in the sea. The wind flattens the reeds in overlapping circles and curls, a pattern that undulates as he watches.

There are mounds of reeds growing up from the center of the marsh, maybe fifty of them, huddled in a way that Tommy can't quite grasp from here. Each mound has a door in it like a knothole, and smoke rises from the top of one of them.

They don't look like they were made. They were grown.

"The Swallows' Nest," Scott says.

Tommy realizes that's where he's seen this shape before—a cluster of orb nests, pierced only by black entrance holes, and birds darting in and out.

The houses are woven from the reeds that surround them. Instead of simply sitting next to each other, each house builds on top of the structure of the next, leaning on it so they aren't separate domes. They flow into each other in cascades and whorls, endless spirals traveling from house to house to house. Like breakers tripping gently onto shore, one after another. Like waves.

There are no straight lines. The reeds are gathered into ropy bundles as thick as his arm, and those swirl around the houses in intricate designs, like a giant snail shell that refuses to follow nature's rules.

"How did . . . ?"

"I know," Scott says, a little smug. "We built it in generations. The Weavers who came before started it. They built part of it. Everyone who comes here just keeps adding."

"How did they decide to do this?" Tommy says.

"No one decided anything," Scott says. "They just did it."

"The Parents didn't build like this," Little Man says.

"They didn't live our lives," a girl says.

That stings a little for Tommy. How many things has he done because the Parents did them first?

The huts aren't made entirely from the reeds. He spies thick log pillars underneath. He suspects a lattice of wood makes up the floors, based on the outside decks. They're built of a mismatched collection of planks and logs. Toddlers race around the edge of the huts, not looking for the blank spots in the walkway but avoiding them all the same.

Around the pillars, reeds shoot up from the mud and climb into the huts' walls. They're guided by smaller reed ties. "You use the growing ones, too?" he says.

"When we can," Scott says. "It makes them tougher, just like sharing the same walls does. The green strengthens the brown."

"Living walls," Tommy says. "Huh."

"It's our first rule," the girl says. "Build where you grow."

They only have three rules, Scott explains, three rules that guide them in every part of their life. The Chosen have countless rules—what each caste can do, when you can eat, who you can talk to, which gods you pray to. The Lowers could pray to Jesucristo, the Preps to the Father, the sailors to Catalina, and the soldiers to the God of War. One of the rules said that the Preps could only walk five thousand steps a day. Little Man ignored it but the others had Lowers pulling them around in old red wagons.

"What's your name?" Tommy says to the girl. He should know what to call her if she's to be his guard.

"Nora," she says. "I'm ten but I'm small."

"Me too."

"You don't seem like it."

"I don't look that old?" He's tired of hearing that from the Cluster.

"You don't look that young," she says. "Maybe you lived too much."

Maybe, he thinks. Then: *I hate smart kids.*

In the middle of a narrow courtyard is a round hole with a net suspended in water about a foot deep.

"You catch anything?" he says.

"Most days," she says. "Crabs, frogs, fish, even some birds. The marsh provides."

"That one of your rules?"

"Take what the waves bring you," she says. Nora points to a hut slightly larger than the others, set apart only by a sun design spiraling out from its open door. "You can stay here with me."

"Who gets to stay here?"

"Everyone gets to stay anywhere. But this is yours for now."

"Your leaders don't get their own special places?" On the hill, every caste has its own type of housing, from mansions to stables.

She just screws up her eyes. "The Babymakers get privacy. The Nurses have huts for healings. That's it." And she disappears into the Swallows' Nest hole.

His bed is a mat woven—of course—from reeds, with a kind of sack on top. Tommy can see a soft tuft of something poking out: cattail fuzz? But it's the room that's hard to ignore. Instead of a dim room lined with rushes, it's awash with swirling color. A hole in the top, smaller than the door, lets light in. Three of the Old Ones' mirrors, suspended below the hole in a pyramid shape, reflect the light to the walls.

The walls . . . the walls are covered in white, some kind of plaster. And the plaster is covered with pigments—rich blues, reds, oranges, greens and browns, whirling around the room. He thinks he sees the sunset. He thinks he sees the ocean. He sees birds, and grass, and silvery fish in simple bold lines. As he stares at it, his mind lifts into the clouds, the first time since he's been three.

"The . . . Old Ones used to paint like this," he says to Nora. Their paintings were hidden away in the biggest houses, locked behind steel gates. He had seen girls in dresses of dabbed dots of pink, old men with guitars. None of the Chosen have seen them. None, he guesses, would have cared, if they weren't blood or guns or food.

This painting, though, is just part of the house. They must have painted because they *wanted* to paint.

"Are these stories?" he says. Now that no one reads but him, people have started using pictures the way the Old Ones used to use letters. All across the Chosen villages are images crudely scratched of things crudely done: a bear killed, a slaughter in battle, a roll with a Lower.

"Sometimes we're telling stories," Nora says. "But mostly we try to tell how we feel."

In order to show your feelings with such colors, you have to feel those feelings first, Tommy thinks. He's never felt that dazzling in his life.

"You paint out your feelings?"

"It helps," Nora says, "especially the teens. The anger goes away. Something better comes in its place."

She explains that the painting has happened over generations, too. People paint when they feel like it—maybe every day, maybe once a year. They build on the others' paintings, sometimes even paint over it.

"You wreck people's paint?" he says.

"The paint isn't the point," Nora says. "The making of it is."

"Where do you all come from?" Tommy asks Scott that night at dinner in the Big Ball. The Big Ball is exactly that—a structure at the center of the village roughly the same shape as the huts, but much, much wider. The ceilings disappear into the darkness, but Tommy can see the sturdy outlines of the poles needed to support it: too much for just reeds. The room holds all the Weavers, maybe two hundred of them, sitting cross-legged on the floor.

"Everyone washes in," Scott says. "Nora escaped a war in the North. Moonface and her sisters came west when the grapes died. Those five over there are the last of their tribe. The Haze tells them about us, and they come. They just have to do the Telling. The Chosen are short of children, aren't they? Not us. We keep growing. They want to come."

"But you put traps in the ocean to keep them out," Tommy says, understanding the sharpened poles that sank his boats.

"That's to keep you out," Scott says. "The Chosen, with your white sails. It's your Catalina's Grave. The others come on smaller boats, and the Haze shows them the way through."

144

"But you killed my men," Little Man says.

"Half of them were trying to kill you," Scott says. "We've known the Chosen could attack us at any time. We make the sea around us seem filled by ghosts and gods."

The food is cooked outside, on a flat metal boat hauled up onto high ground. Anything to stop the spread of flames. The servers carry it into the Big Ball in pots, a mix of fish and vegetables and some kind of large bird. Egret, maybe. They bring a pot to Scott, befitting his place as the leader.

And he takes it to someone else.

Scott dishes out vegetables to a girl of five, half-lying on the ground in the row closest to the firepit. More vegetables than she expects, really, considering the twisted leg under her. Tommy guesses she can't walk, not without the stick at her side and hands supporting her shoulders. Useless. She should be tossed into the ocean.

It's a pattern. Scott goes around the ring, finding the smallest, the weakest, the sickest. The other servers do the same. When they finally reach the bigger kids, the portions actually get smaller.

No one does that at home. The Clusters, the Olders, the Knights, they get the best pieces first. You feed your best first.

Tommy flares at the softness, at the waste, at the little mouths stealing from the big, and then—and then he thinks of his Piss Ant self at three, abandoned and frail and picking for scraps in the dump that overflowed at the edge of town. Piss Ant found something rare, a shank of deer actually cooked. Not smelly at all. He snuck under a rotten rowboat to eat it.

The rowboat flipped open like a clam and two boys, twelve years old and Jocks, filled the space under its lip. "Mine," one boy said.

"Mine," the other boy said. They both held out their hands.

Piss Ant resisted his fear, pulled the meat back against his chest. He hadn't eaten real food in two days. That morning he had tried grass. His lips were still stained green. The boys ripped the meat out of his hands.

"I'm starving," he said.

"Not fast enough," the second boy said, and closed the clamshell.

Scott returns with the rest of the pot, and dishes the last of it out for himself and for Tommy. Tommy's portion is bigger.

"'Take care of the little ones,'" Tommy says.

"What?"

"One of your three rules." No one took care of him. Piss Ant never heard a kind word. That boy wouldn't have known what to do with kindness. He knew the world was a horrid place that had to be defeated, and he spent the rest of his life wishing to destroy it before it could destroy him.

Now he wonders if there is another way. If there might be room for some kindness. If he could make himself more than the leader of the Chosen—if he could be the savior of the human race. If he saved them, they would have to love him, after all. *Never mind*, Little Man says. *We don't care about love.*

But— Piss Ant says, and Tommy shuts them both down.

Scott nods at Tommy's guess, surveys the rows of Children. Once everyone else is eating, he starts to eat. "Close enough," he says. "Take care of each other."

After dinner, Tommy returns to his hut. But somebody is already there, resting on a bed with his head on one hand, reading a book. Roberto. "I thought you were dead," Tommy says, and realizes that he really hadn't wanted Roberto to be dead. Without knowing why, he leans down and awkwardly pats Roberto on his shoulder. "I'm glad you're alive."

Roberto jerks away. "Fuck you, Tommy," Roberto says.

"What?"

"Now that we here, I can finally say what I wanted," Roberto says. "And that's 'Fuck you, Tommy.'"

CHAPTER THIRTY-FOUR
THE DOWNTOWN

Trina feels an urge, as always, to duck her head when she walks through the Valley of Cars. As always, she resists.

The Downtown live in a giant stadio dug into the last hill before the actual Downtown. When the End came for good, the Parents must have been at a beisbol match, because the parking lot was filled with cars. The kids of the Downtown built those cars into their outer wall, stacked three high. She's not sure how, without machines. It's one of the wonders of Ell Aye.

The wall loops out to almost the edge of the parking lot, protecting the green outer fields of the Downtown. The Downtown grow the best melons in the hills. Trina came here personally to trade for them, wrapping her tomatoes in a soft cloth to keep them from getting crushed. She was rewarded with melons green on the outside, pinkish-red on the inside, and so full of summer that she ate one of them by herself before she even made it back to the Holy Wood.

At the western entry of the stadio, the stacks of cars curve in to form a long narrow boulevard that visitors are forced to pass through on their way to the stadio gate, watched by armed Muscle overhead.

If the Downtown didn't want us here, we'd be dead by now, she tells herself. She straightens up.

Trina recognizes one of those Muscle peering down from the cars. Shiloh the Archer, one of the Muscle who sided with Apple in that last scuffle. He fled with the rest of the Muscle. Trina doesn't nod to him. She doesn't want to single him out.

They announce themselves at the closed gate. The Oldest, Hui Yin, will let her in. They had already built a friendship through all the Angeleno councils and trades. "Let me see the Oldest," she says, and the Muscle usher them in.

Trina looks up at the rim of the stadio in front of her. It's draped with tattered blue flags. The Downtown have two beliefs that differ from other Angeleno peoples: that the Downtown towers are sacred, and so is the wearing of the blue.

They pass through a long tunnel and into the vast field of the stadio. The place where they once played beisbol is plowed up into corn, squash, beans. Goats graze along the perimeter of the old fence. Enough to feed the village, safe behind the cars and the metal spikes and the concrete banks. *This is the safest place in Ell Aye.* Trina's always envied them that.

But the village itself—the village itself climbs to the sky. The Downtown built their homes on the sloping stacked decks where the Parents used to sit and cheer. Old boxcars and shipping containers nestle into the vast decks like boxes laid out on a flight of stairs, in rust and green and blue. Those are used as homes and workshops for the Children. She can see two kids sitting in a sliding boxcar doorway, legs dangling over the edge above a thirty-foot drop. In another, a tailor cuts up old pants for rags.

"How'd they get all this stuff up here? And the cars stacked up in the outer wall?" Trina has never thought to ask this question. The Downtown lifted the boxcars and cars around without any Lectrics. With just a bunch of Children to lift them.

"Pulleys," the Half Holy says. Trina arches her eyebrow at him, confused, and he says, "You learning how to read, right? You can look it up."

"Your friend's a jerk," Trina says to Pilar.

Pilar smiles. "Yeah, pulleys," she says.

"Like you knew," Trina says.

The Muscle lead them downward into a room dug out of the ground. Behind the dugout is a passageway deep into the bowels of the stadio, where the Oldest's quarters are. Trina has been here lots of times. They always meet in the dugout, staring out over the center field.

The leader of the San Fernandos, Tala, is already there. Tala is a slight girl with sharp elbows. She looks like a dream creature, so airy that it seems she would lift off the ground if she weren't wearing knee-high soldier boots.

Trina can't stand the San Fernandos' Oldest. Part of it is because she's so young. She tried to become a Mama at fourteen and it didn't take, so she became the Oldest before she was even fifteen. Part of it is because Tala never listens to anyone.

"You got kicked out of the Holy Wood?" Tala says.

"I escaped."

"Not soon enough," Tala says.

And most of the reason Trina can't stand Tala is because she's a San Fernando. The San Fernandos and the Holy Wood had grown up back-to-back along the Holy Wood Hills, too similar yet too different to ever really get along.

Sometimes they fight about hunting the horses that run wild on the northern slopes of the hills in the Long Gone boneyard. Sometimes they fight about water. Sometimes they make peace. Sometimes they pool their stashes of booze and fiesta for three days straight until they get sick of each other again. It is, Trina realizes, like the Long Gone brothers and sisters she has started to read about.

The San Fernandos are the largest of all the Angeleno peoples. They stick to themselves, made easier by the fact they're the only Angelenos on the north side of the long spine of the Holy Wood Hills.

The only time the Holy Wood usually sees them is when they trade. The San Fernandos are the greatest craftschildren of Ell Aye, making silver tools and beautifully etched black pots that gleam like black diamonds. Trina traded an entire goat once for two of the pitchers. They still haven't broken.

The San Fernandos live in the Lot, the remains of one of the places where the Parents made pictures for the gods. Teevee shows, they called them. Moovees. *TV*, Trina corrects herself. *It's just letters.*

Trina and Tala stare at each other uncomfortably. She wonders what's taking Hui Yin. "Hui Yin's on time for everything, and she can't make this?" Trina says, exasperated.

"Hui Yin's dead," Tala says. "They told us she Ended at the last meeting of the Oldests. Oh, right—you weren't invited."

"I was locked up, you mean," Trina says. But . . . who?

A shape comes toward them, out of the darkness of the dugout tunnel. Long hair, broad shoulders, a body that falls in robust waves. When Trina can see clearly, she blinks. That shape doesn't exist in this world.

The Parents were big but worshipped small. Trina learned that in the magzine she hid under her bed, its pages straining the ancient glue. "Seven Easy Ways to Lose Weight," she had slowly sounded out, in front of an image of a woman who was smaller than any of the pictures of real people Trina had seen Gathered.

The Children were small but worshipped big. Trina measured the health of the Holy Wood by the dimples in a baby's calf. If the kids were fat, the Holy Wood was alive. Being fat meant you had wrapped life in your hands—you were the strongest Mama, you were the Gatherer who found the most in the wild. Fat was beauty. Fat was life.

If that was true, the girl in front of her must have lived life more than anyone else. She smells of cinnamon, the spice worth three bottles of whiskey. Her lips are cut out of marble, wicked eyebrows over wicked eyes.

"I'm Trina," she tells the girl, "former Oldest of the Holy Wood."

"La Madre," the girl says. Trina's hopes sink. Hui Yin would have listened to her. Tala won't, and this person is unknown.

Two boys and two girls join them. "These are my Olders," La

150

Madre says. Trina doesn't have to comment on the fact that two of them are boys before La Madre adds, "Sorry you got bumped as Oldest. Heather's a twat."

Trina's never heard the word before but it matches Heather, the soft splat of the tongue and the sour glance of Heather's face. She smiles. "Clearly you've met her," she says.

"We was sposed to meet at the stadio, the new Oldest of the Downtown and the new—whatever she is. She sent a kid with a donkey an hour before and says I need to come to the Holy Wood instead." La Madre waves at her body. "Look at me. I look like I ride a donkey?"

She doesn't. She looks like she's rooted in the earth. Trina feels the gravitational pull tugging her down.

"Mannaseo yeong-gwang-ibnida," Trina says. It's an old Koreno phrase, used when the Oldests meet. "The reason I called you—"

"You din't call us. We wouldn't a come if it wasn't the Half Holy," Tala says.

"Why'd you call us, Half Holy?" La Madre says. Trina stands in awe, again, at the way the Half Holy connects everyone. Why didn't she talk to him when she was still Oldest? She's been too focused on the Holy Wood, and not enough on the world.

"'S okay," the Half Holy says. "Trina talks for me."

Trina tells her of the Last Lifers in the streets, of the Palos orchestrating it all from their smoky hill. Of Heather and her pink-tipped Hermanas, unable to stop it. Each time she tells it, it seems more futile.

"I'm worried we all gonna die if we don't work together," Trina says. "There's too much against us."

"So whaddya want us to do?" Tala says.

"Help me talk some sense into Heather," Trina says.

"I met Heather lots. Sense ain't a language she speaks," Tala says.

"True," Trina says.

"So what you really want is to get you your Holy Wood back," La Madre says.

"If that's what it takes."

La Madre pauses, and Trina allows her hopes to rise without reason. Sometimes hope is just hope.

"I'd get run outta the Angelenos," La Madre says. "I go in with the Muscle, I get rid of your Olders, I steal the Holy Wood from someone else? I'd be nothing. The other peoples won't let me mess with tradition. You can't just take a village."

"People gonna die," Pilar says.

"We stay out of it," La Madre says, and Trina's hope falls.

Trina wants to storm out of the dugout, but they have to keep talking to the Oldests. It's their only chance. Pilar speaks.

"You act as if our enemies ain't real. They are," Pilar says. "You seen em in your patrols. The Half Holy seen em in the mirrors. And I seen em in my dreams. Lines and lines of them, white and brown, blood and black. More warriors than we seen since our Mamas' Mamas' Mamas. They will overrun even you."

"We try to fight em separately, they gonna pick us off one by one," the Half Holy says. La Madre's sculpted brows twitch at that.

"Look," Trina says. "I spent all my time as an Older watching out for the End of our peoples. I thought it was always coming, and I was always wrong. But this—this is an End we can't avoid. Not alone."

A Daycare kid brings in a baby, and La Madre cradles it in her arms. She sings to it in a wordless way that sounds like a lion's purr. She reaches into her shirt, the baby latches on.

"You got a baby?" Trina says.

"I got three of them," La Madre says. No one had ever had three, probably not since the End. "Why you think they call me La Madre?"

"You can't be the Oldest if you a Mama," Trina says.

"That's what I told em, but they kept asking me," La Madre says. "Don't know why I can't do both."

"Tradition," Trina says.

"Fuck tradition," Pilar says. "You sitting there in council with a baby hanging on your boob. You got boys in your Olders. It ain't never been done before but it ain't hurting no one. You helping us save the Angelenos, who does that hurt? Heather? The rest of us will just be grateful. That's the thing about tradition. It keeps you safe till it don't."

The only thing that breaks the silence that follows is the smacking of the baby's lips. La Madre says, "How many Hermanas does Heather have?"

"Sixty, but untrained," Trina says. "You could take them with just the Muscle at the gate if you had to."

"Fuck it," La Madre says. "I'd do a lot to save my people. Especially helping a bitch I like against a bitch I don't."

They look at Tala. She says, "I'll help you, too. If . . . ," Tala says, and Trina's so surprised to see help coming from her that she blinks.

"If what?"

"You take us in."

"Why? You hate the Holy Wood."

"Yeah, but we got no water," Tala says.

"What about the Tank?" Trina says. The San Fernandos tap into a giant cistern buried underground by the Parents. There's enough water for a hundred years.

"Earthquakes last year cracked it halfway up and the water leaked out slow," Tala says. "We didn't bother too much because the rains would fill it up again. But we didn't get enough rain this year. The river dried up yesterday—you know that?" Trina didn't. The Ell Aye River has run dry at least twice in Trina's life. Both times, a lot of kids died.

This has happened before. The Angelenos used to be nine villages, but earthquakes and droughts and wars blended them together until there are just four. Now there would be three. The Holy Wood can't absorb that many people, no matter how much it needs the help.

"We got water in the Lake. But we don't get enough food and med-sen for a whole nother tribe," Trina says.

"We got a lot to offer," Tala says.

"Like what, pots? We need guns," Trina snaps. She immediately regrets her words. She's spent so long being angry that it's engrained like muscle memory. Anger is something you have to learn you can set aside.

"We don't got guns," Tala says. "But the Smiths can make as many swords and bullets as you need."

"I don't think you saw the size of the army coming," Pilar says.

But now Trina is thinking about the San Fernandos' craftschildren, building things that only the Parents used to build. She thinks of the houses of Ell Aye, cracked open with nothing left to Gather. They're fighting a war now, but after the war they will need to find a way to live.

The Parents' world is dead. The Children have to build a new one.

"Sure, come on over," Trina says. "Bring the pots."

CHAPTER THIRTY-FIVE
THE QUEEN

Tashia never thought that running would *actually* mean running on two legs. She's never gone this far on two legs.

They didn't know how long they would have before Othello sent riders after them, but they knew he would. He would send out Knights and he would hunt them down without the eyes of the Kingdom watching. So they run until they find a place to hide.

X is no good at hiding. He's never left the Kingdom except to fight. But Tashia has dug stray cows out of every shopping mall and cul-de-sac in the Oh See. She knows where they could hide without being noticed. Where there might be supplies. She knows where to take them.

The cowboys cache food a few miles north of the Kingdom, in a boneyard for rollertrain parts. There must have been a lot of rollertrain places around here, during the Parents' time. There were nights when the cowboys couldn't make it back to the Kingdom by sunset, and so they holed up there. Grease had pillaged the rollertrain carcasses for parts for the Kingdom. He knew about it, the cowboys knew about it—but the Knights didn't know about it.

There's enough room there to hold a dozen horses, a dozen cows. More than that, there is still dried meat and water, in a metal box beneath a giant Fearless wheel. Behind it is a swirling rollertrain sign shaped like a faded dragon. After she builds a fire, Tashia breaks open the case of food and counts it out. Enough for a week.

"We're gonna need more food if we plan on staying here long," she says.

"We'll only stay until we can mount an attack," X says.

"We got no attack to mount, honey. We don't even have *horses* to mount," Tashia says.

X looks slightly in shock, but still in command. "Make camp tonight," he says. "We'll figure it out tomorrow." He stands still, as if expecting her to move around him.

"You're still King, aren't you?" she says. "In your head, you're still King."

"I—I . . ." He hesitates.

"I didn't leave in service of the King," she says. "I left with my boy. As long as you're my King, we're never gonna be equal. We're never gonna be together."

X doesn't respond. So, as tired as she is, she draws herself up. She speaks in her most formal high tongue. "X, leader of the free Kingdom, I challenge you," she says. "I challenge you for a seat on the Round Table, and to claim your throne."

"I already gave you a seat on the Round Table," he says, patiently.

"The seat has to be claimed. I claim mine."

Next to the fire, in the center of the carnival boneyard, is a ring of sand. The ring is lined with a fence of wooden horses, planted on poles. The cowboys hauled the sand in to break mustangs they pick up in the wild. It's a lot softer than the pavement. Tashia steps into the center and waits for X.

Little tufts of sand follow X into the ring. He stretches his neck, stretches his arms, then peels off his shirt. His chest glows in the firelight.

She reaches down. She peels off her shirt, too. Down to the skin. He looks at her bare chest and then looks away.

"I want everything to be fair," she says. And waits for him to make the first move.

That's all she wanted. To get the same chance as the boys. When X had fought the old King, the Cleaver, for Tashia, he had never asked if she wanted to fight for herself. He had believed, even in his goodness, that she was something to be had. It never occurred to him that she might be strong, too.

X starts with a series of feints, each one designed to look clumsier than the next, each one meant to draw her in. She doesn't follow him. How many times has she watched him do this? He's such a good fighter, but the whole Kingdom has watched him fight.

"Not gonna happen, X," she says when he stops, only a few feet from her. He reaches out to her as if he's wiping dust from her eyes. Then she hits him in the jaw.

The two are evenly matched. X is stronger, heavier, but Tashia's arms are longer, and her blows land more often. They circle each other within the ring. She sees his body in the firelight and realizes: *We look like twins. Take away the tits, and we look like twins.*

Tashia cuts him first, a left hook that splits X's right eyebrow open. The energy drives Tashia to hit harder, and she follows it up with a right, a right, and an uppercut that doubles him over. Tashia hits him in the ear with a fist like a hammer, and he stumbles backward to the fire.

Tashia rushes X to finish him off. He steps aside and the sand flies up in a fine cloud as she flops into it. X wheels away and she sees him pant in the flickering light, dark blood staining his white teeth. His eye is starting to close.

X dives on her, but he's a second slower than he should have been and Tashia scrambles to her feet and out of his way. Tashia sees him hesitate, even down there in the sand, and she curls her lip and snarls—snarls—at him. "No, X," she says.

He raises his arms in half-surrender and says: "I didn't want this." Before he can say more, Tashia cuts him off with a punch and dances away.

"But you're King, X," she says, tapping his right cheek and ducking his blow. "You got to fight to be King. You gotta let me fight for that, too."

Tashia swings.

X blocks her with both fists, holds her left hand between his. Steps closer to her, buries his fist in her gut, slams a forearm into her throat.

Tashia crumples to the sand.

This time X doesn't hesitate and he jumps on her, hitting her on each cheek so fast Tashia can barely see his fists. X straddles her, knees next to her hips. Maybe he's holding her down, but it feels like he's holding her like a lover. In the stream of blood coming from his right eye, a clear line looks something like tears. He hammers at her jaw.

She twists away from his blow and punches him in the neck and he stops, gasping for breath. She kicks him and he collapses in the sand. She holds her body against him, chest on chest, and counts it out, each number a slap on the sand. One. Two. Three. Four. Five.

"You're the new King," he says. Surprised. Awed. Relieved?

"There's a better word," she says. It's a word they've known for a long time, but they've never used it because they never had one. A word she gets to have for her own. Queen. "I'm the new Queen," she says.

Then they're kissing on the ground, side by side, sand grinding between their bodies. She didn't want this before, when it was something she couldn't freely give, although she wanted everything about X. Her hands roam down his body, finding the tight muscles of his back, snaking into the waist of his pants. She removes them, then her own.

He pushes back against her and she can tell he is ready for her. She has been ready for him all night. He starts to climb on top. She stops him. She pushes him back onto the sand, straddles his hips. Holds him there.

"The Queen always rides," she says.

Long before X awakes, Tashia is staring at the sunrise bleeding in through the big wheel above them. The spokes of the wheel look as if they're cut out of a pink sky, the seats almost seem to sway.

She's used to waking early to feed and water the horses. If she had one now—if she had one now, she would gallop it right over the Kingdom's berms and stab Othello in the gut. "Kneel before your Queen," she whispers. She feels the featherlight lance in her hand, feels the weight of Othello as she lifts him off the ground with her thrust.

She has no horse. She has no lance. She has no home. She holds still, breathing again, focusing on her problem. She can hold still in crisis like no one else, slowing the world down when it threatens to rush over her.

"What does the Queen desire?" X says, rolling over toward her on the horse blanket. They spread it out right on the sand where they fought. Where they—but then she sees the answer.

"Grease," she says.

X laughs. "That is not what I expected you to say," he says, glancing down at their naked bodies wrapped together.

"Grease. He's the way we get our Kingdom back," she says.

His eyes cloud. He still holds a grudge against Grease for leaving the Kingdom, even though Grease was chasing down the End. Nothing has worked since he left. X doesn't have to say his response, and Tashia doesn't need to hear it.

"I'm a queen without a kingdom. Hell, I don't even have a weapon other than those bolas hanging over there," she says. "We need someone to help us get back in."

"We have friends on the inside," he says. She thinks of Mia and Coretta, trapped in there. Are they safe?

"But we don't have Grease," she says. "He could think of a way. No one else could, not like him."

X knows it, and she can see the acceptance almost immediately. He seems lighter somehow, now that he's no longer King. If she thought he would resent her beating him last night, she was wrong. He seems to have accepted his defeat with grace. X respects power, because he was one of the best at using it.

"We don't know where he is," X says.

"We know he went south," Tashia says.

"And we know that's the Dead Lands," X says. "We aren't going to make it through that."

"So we figure out a way to—"

"Permission to speak?" X says. "As your advisor?"

"Granted," Tashia says.

"Grease isn't going to help us. If we die going to get him, we're no good to the Kingdom. We have to figure it out ourselves."

Tashia purses her lips. "Maybe."

"We have six days of food. We can stay here until we've figured out a plan."

"Okay," she says, making up her mind. "We recon the walls, look to see if Othello's ignoring something. Use this as a base. Let's get riding."

"Riding what? We stealing horses?"

"Tempting," she says, "but we need something quieter."

She points to a handful of bikes leaning against the bucket of an octopus ride. The cowboys had found the bikes months ago, and wanted to trade them to the Ice Cream Men for a little extra food. Grease had fixed them for her.

X shakes his head. "Wheels?" He shares the disdain that every rider has for bikes.

"Yes, honey. You're gonna have to get used to wheels," she says, and stands up.

He grabs her hand and pulls her down toward him. They tangle together the second their skin touches. "If I could make just one request of Your Highness," X says, kissing her neck.

Tashia's head arches backward, exposing her throat. "She might grant it," she says.

CHAPTER THIRTY-SIX
THE ARK

Pico stands on the nose of the Ark like he's balancing on a knife blade being thrust into the sky. Perching on top of the carrier is dizzying because the flat plane of the deck is the only part of the ship he can see. The ship's sides disappear to a vanishing point at the water's edge.

He's been waiting in the late morning light for thirty minutes before he's supposed to meet the others. Pico couldn't sleep last night. Part of it was because he was sweating in a windowless bunk. Part of it's because the only thing he and Grease talk about is the Haze. Last night, Grease announced he'd sleep in a different room.

He thinks back to Grease's questions about Brian K, about whether boys could ever be together, and wonders, *Why didn't I think this was about him?* Pico knew that Grease didn't talk about girls the way other boys did. He had assumed it was because machines mattered more to Grease. He assumed it was because Grease was something like him.

Here's the truth of it: He ignored Grease because he knew it would come down to feelings. Feelings are a battleground for braver souls.

Pico looks back along the ship, which runs more than a thousand feet long. The scale is staggering. But so are the fields of dirt and vegetables that have taken over the flight deck. The lush green rows of the Ark on the ship deck float like a cloud island far above the bay.

Pico has seen pictures of these carriers before, and knows that a dozen skyplanes would have lined the deck. Only two remain, a chopper and a sleek warplane, smothered by vines. At the far edge of the boat, he can see a pump that brings in water for the whole ship, and thick metal pipes that carry the water to the plants. It must have taken years to haul in this much dirt, to set up irrigation systems.

"Why'd you build the Ark here?" he asks Isaac when he walks up. "Anywhere else—like, *anywhere* else would have been easier."

"Good morning yourself," Isaac says. "But fine. If we're trying to start life again, we thought it should have a more, um, *protective* cradle. This has hardened computer systems, really thick walls, protection on three sides, and a near-infinite source of power."

"How'd you get all this dirt up here?" he says.

"That took us about three years, truckload by truckload," Isaac says. "And two years before that to dump the planes into the water."

"Five years?"

Isaac laughs. "We weren't going anywhere."

Pico gives him a blank stare, and Isaac winces a little bit. Five years is more than any of them will live to see. Isaac says, "I'm sorry. I forget who I'm talking to."

The other Mayflies arrive, and Isaac says, "Welcome to the Ark."

"Okay. What's an Ark?" Jemma says. "You say it like we should know it."

"It's a boat," Grease says. "God flooded the earth and he put two of every animal on board to keep them alive till the water drained."

"He coulda just not flooded the earth," Jemma says. "That'd work, too."

Now Pico understands Isaac. A cradle for life. "Why din't you put Alice's life vessels on it if it's a Ark?" Pico says.

"That'd make a lot of sense, wouldn't it?" Isaac says. "That's my parents. James considers the Ark his, and he declared it off limits. Because of that, Alice would never stoop to asking."

"How many Old Guys are here?" Grease says. "Are they mostly from the Camp?"

"There's a dedicated team of twenty-two people here, and fifteen of us who split our time," Isaac says. "Plus, there's Athena."

"Athena's a person?" Lady says.

"You'll see," Isaac says.

"That's not much to keep a ship running, is it?" Pico remembers the books showing thousands of Parents on board.

"We use it very differently than they did before the End," Isaac says. "It's enough."

Isaac leads them to wide doors at midship. They step inside as the doors open. When the doors close, the bottom of the floor drops out.

"Jesucristo!" Lady says. "What the hell was that?"

"It's a Levator," Grease says, grinning. "They still got Levators."

The Levator drops them through the center of the ship and they come out into the main hangar. Pico sees lights glowing everywhere, and remembers them burning even late at night. Unlike the Camp, these are steady and bright. "Where all these Lectrics comin from?" he says.

"The carrier is powered by a nuclear reactor, which is meant to last a really long time," Isaac says.

"Like the Boobs?" Grease says, talking about the reactors that destroyed the Dead Lands—and that looked like boobs.

Isaac laughs. "Yep, like the Boobs, but a lot smaller."

"Ain't you scared of getting sick?" Pico says.

"It's a risk, but a small one," Isaac says.

"Because you can't get sick?"

Isaac looks at him. "Even we can't beat high doses of radiation," he says. "I just mean that it takes a lot for it to go wrong."

"I want to see it soon," Grease says.

"There isn't much to see because there aren't many moving parts," Isaac says, "but I'm happy to show you later. The reactor used to turn the propellers but now it just powers the lights and computers. Those take the tiniest fraction of what the propellers would have used. An aircraft carrier could have gone thirty years without replacing its reactor core. We've made it last more than a hundred."

"But not forever," Pico says.

"No. This reactor core may last another ten years, maybe twenty."

"Then you get another?"

"No. There's not another one," Isaac says, and Pico nods. "When the core dies, so does the Ark."

"So we better get shit figured out before then," Jemma says.

In front of them, next to the remains of a skyplane, is a glowing glass box the size of a house. The glass looks thick, unbreakable. Pico's not sure where they got it after the End. They wouldn't have made it themselves. The doors are riveted steel.

"Looks like it's built for the apokalips," Grease says.

"I think it was," Pico says.

The building is divided into two halves, each with its own door. On one side, the one Isaac leads them to, is a black machine with a hole hollowed into it, wrapped around a slim single bed.

James is next to it, fiddling with a cord. He greets them, and points at the machine. "So anyway," James says, "this is how we see the Haze."

"It ain't visible," Pico says, and feels stupid for saying it. Obviously they must have had a way to track it before the End. But Isaac graciously ignores him.

"This is a modified electron microscope, configured specifically to monitor the nanotech particles of the Haze, as well as the electrical impulses of the brain. Who wants to go first?"

"You . . . gonna look at our heads?" Jemma says.

"If you want to know what's in them," Isaac says, and Jemma hops onto the single bed without another word. The other kids follow, with Pico last.

The scan is almost anticlimactic, just a little buzzing background sound that lasts for all of five seconds. Pico imagines it pawing around in his brain, but can't actually feel anything.

"What now?" Lady says after they all finish.

"Now we turn your heads into pictures," Isaac says. "In the meantime, take a look at this." And he pulls up two black-and-white images that look like eggs, displaying the images on a screen on the wall. They're pictures of heads, viewed from above. Pico can see the pores in the bone of the skull. The skull on the left is labeled simply 15 YEARS, and the second is labeled 17 YEARS.

"We told you the Haze normally doesn't interact with humans until they're late teens, when their brain assumes its final adult form. As simple as it makes it seem, that's not accurate. Look at our fifteen-year-old," James says. He places his finger on the image on the screen. Pico sees hazy blue specks floating around the edge of the skull—and almost as many inside it. He also sees red streaks lighting up the brain like Lectrics. "The blue is the Haze, as you may have surmised. The red is brain activity. We wouldn't expect much of either in our younger Child. And yet . . ."

When Pico traces James's fingers, he sees the Haze everywhere, dancing along the red lines. "The brain goes through a process called synaptic pruning, which is a standard part of maturation," James says. "Every child starts with far more neurons—or synapses—than they will ever need as an adult. Organisms in the brain trim those neurons over time, like a Farmer would a tree. Just as they cut away branches to get bigger fruit, the brain focuses its neurons to strengthen them and focus on more complex thought."

"Here's the funny thing," Isaac says. "Several decades ago, the Haze started helping prune. All on its own. The fifteen-year-old image was taken a year ago. If you went back twenty years you would see a very different picture. Like this." Another almost identical image overlays it. This time there's much less Haze, and thinner red streaks.

"The Haze has significantly altered the brains of some of the Children," James says. "They're far more powerful, now capable of something like five percent more throughout than they had before the End. Not in one specific area, not just in speech and memory—all throughout the brain."

"Why would that happen?" Grease says.

"Our guess?" Isaac says. "It wants kids to be smarter, for some reason. And it really wants to talk to you."

"What about this brain?" Pico says, pointing at the image of the seventeen-year-old. It's crawling with nanobots. Unlike the Haze on the fifteen-year-old's, which looks almost haphazard, the Haze on the older kid's image appears symmetrical, methodical. As if there's a plan.

"That image is taken about a week before the Betterment," James says. "It shows the Haze, completely ready to take things over."

"To shut the brain down?" Pico says. He can read the diagrams almost without interpretation. "Why does something that makes us better want to hurt us?"

CHAPTER THIRTY-SEVEN
THE LONG LIFE MACHINE

"You're familiar with the concept of the Touched, right?" Isaac says, pointing again at the pictures.

Pico says, "It ain't a concept. It's our lives."

Lady looks around at her friends, all of them probably Touched and liable to die sooner than seventeen. Possibly much sooner. *All a them but me*, she thinks.

"The Touched, as you call them, have greater brain activity and greater Haze activity, and their brains make the transition to adulthood sooner than other Children's," Isaac says. "That's you."

Isaac pulls up four pictures of the brain, organized in a quadrant: Three of them are crawling with Haze, far more than any of the diagrams so far. One is comparatively empty. That's hers. She knows it is. They only brought her along because Jemma had to rescue her. Lady's upset, but only because the one thing she knew has finally come to light. It's mostly a relief, to be free of expectations.

Isaac points at the top left picture. "Grease. High level of Haze activity, but it hasn't started to settle in the syncopated patterns that lead to the Betterment. That makes sense as you're almost sixteen."

His scan is larger than everyone else's. "You got a big head, Grease," Jemma says.

"You got a big head, Jemma," he mutters.

The next one is nearly bathed in speckles of the Haze. Isaac whistles. "The patterns are even less developed here, but so much Haze activity," he says. "Pico, aren't you only eleven?"

"Fourteen," he says. "I'm small for my age."

"But we don't have the gift like Jemma," Grease says.

"Jemma's the one who could speak to the gods," Lady says. "She's why we're here."

"That's what we've been trying to tell you. You may not speak to the Haze, but the Haze speaks to you. It shows in skills you shouldn't be able to have, not in *this* world. Understanding of medicine, or machinery—"

"Or reading. We get it. You sayin that wasn't us?" Pico says. "It's just some bots?"

"No, it's you and the Haze," James says.

Isaac points to Lady's scan. There's Haze, but what there is looks dim and purposeless, as if it just happened to be caught in the picture. "That's me, ain't it?" Lady says.

"Oh, no," Isaac says. "That's Jemma's, which is consistent with her injury. We have no idea what it was like before, but presumably it was substantially heavier. We could conceivably increase that with elements of the Reboot." Lady looks at Jemma. The lack of Haze should have stung Jemma's pride, but she seems unaffected. Doesn't she care?

James steps over to the wall and points to the bottom right image. "This is yours, Lady," James says. It's close to Grease's in density. That should mean she should be as good as Grease at . . . at least one thing. If she's so special, why hasn't she proven it?

"This is cool," Grease says, "but it isn't why we're here."

"No," James says. "You're here for the Long Life Machine."

He opens a door between the two halves of the glowing glass box, and they pass through. On the other side of the wall, Lady sees Brian K in front of a machine the size of a car.

And a girl, strapped into a chair.

"What the hell?" Lady says.

"Ah. Meet Athena," Isaac says.

"Athena's a kid?" Jemma says.

"You aren't the first kids to wander into the Camp," James says. "Over the years, we've had several dozen visitors, some dying from the radiation of the Dead Lands. We healed some of those with the Reboot, and they decided to stay with us. Like our Athena."

Athena is built like a Muscle, as tall as Apple and even broader in the shoulders. She has cool green-gold eyes like a cat, set in a tanned face. What draws Lady to her, though, is her hair. It's cropped short, like Lady's—just an inch or so long. Like a fighter. Lady touches her hairpin instinctively.

"Any other kids here?" Lady says, suspicious. She still doesn't completely trust the Old Guys, and nothing about this seems right.

"Just the five of you," James says.

"Six," Isaac says, indicating himself.

"Chica. You okay?" Lady says. "You wanna be here?"

"This's the only home I know," Athena says. Her voice is a mix of velvet and sandpaper.

"That's not what I asked. You wanna be here?"

"I do," Athena says. "It's safe." Something about her puts Lady at ease.

"Where you from, chica?" Lady says. She can't place Athena's look.

"I . . . ," Athena says.

"We can answer questions later," James says, a little too curt.

"Athena has begun the Reboot," Brian K says. "This is the first treatment of about twenty. It will remove decaying cells, which will help her outlive the End like Isaac did."

"You can enhance the physical and mental characteristics you want," Isaac says. "Height, intelligence, facial shape—you name it." Now Lady begins to understand Athena's size, the odd color of eyes.

"You pick those physical characteristics?" Jemma says. Lady sees him the way Jemma must be seeing him, with auburn hair, perfect skin. She sees Jemma the way he must see her, awkward and nervous but somehow neither of those things.

"No, these are mostly the ones I was born with," Isaac says, and both he and Jemma blush.

"If you're done . . . ," James says, and turns toward the Machine. "This is the Long Life Machine."

At closer look, it's not the giant box she thought it was. It's built out of little modules of all shapes and sizes, held together by a metal frame and enough Lectric wire to power a—well, Lady doesn't really know how much wire it takes to power anything. But a lot.

"This's what we're trying to fix," Brian K says. "We've found parts in old research facilities and university labs throughout the west, and we've assembled it according to our original specs. It seems to be operating the way we designed it to—it gives us all the right readings. But it doesn't complete the Pairing between the bots and the brain. It's like they don't talk to each other."

"Like me," Jemma says.

James nods. "We're hoping if we can solve your connectivity problem, it will give us a clue to the Pairing. That's why we need you all." He looks at everyone but Lady.

"So if the Reboot is here—why don't we just use it in the meantime?" Grease says. "Or is that just for you and your friends?"

"We'd love for you to be able to use it," Isaac says. "But there's a catch: You might forget who you are."

"Forever?" Lady says.

"The Reboot strips away your memories. Layer by layer, session by session," James says. "The reason why Athena can't answer your question about where she's from is that she doesn't know. We never knew where she came from in the first place."

"But Isaac can remember," Jemma says.

"Not everything," Isaac says. "There are people and years that are completely lost."

"Isaac was conceived after we received the treatment," James says.

"Eww," Jemma says.

"Real mature," Isaac says.

James ignores them both. "Because of that, our theory is that Isaac carries some of the genetic material of the Long Life Treatment, although not all of it. It gives him resistance to the memory loss. But for you—it's a risk. Selfishly, I'd prefer you not to take that risk until we fix the Machine for good. I just . . . I want to be able to stop feeling I'll lose my son." He chokes up a little, and Lady sees tears glistening in his eyes. *So that's what a dad looks like.*

Isaac gives James a small smile, pats his shoulder, and says, "James." It's soft but it's there.

"I ain't gonna take that chance," Jemma says, soft. "I need my memories." Neither will Pico and Grease, they say.

Lady doesn't quite hear all this. She's staring at Athena, at this warrior calmly watching her as if she's afraid of nothing. As if she feels nothing. Lady thinks of all the Haze living inside her, making her brain work better. For what? Pico learned how to read on his own. Grease conquered machines. Jemma had visions and led them all here. Lady's the one who had to be dragged away from her home, even when she knew what waited for her back there. She thought being a Mama in the Holy Wood was the most important thing to her, to the world. She let that be enough.

Suddenly Lady is sick of it all, of the beliefs and the losses and the weight she carries on her shoulders. She wants to push the old Lady aside and become someone new. She'll remake herself with the Long Life Treatment.

"I'll do it," Lady says, surprised at her own voice.

Time to let Lady go.

CHAPTER THIRTY-EIGHT
THE REBOOT

"Apple," Jemma says, flicking on the Game Boy frantically. "Lady's gone."

It's true in more ways than one. After Lady volunteered for the Long Life Treatment, she disappeared into the corridors of the Ark, and none of the Mayflies could find her. But Lady has been slipping for a long time, and Jemma hasn't known how to bring her back.

Apple's face comes out of the green screen, smiling and kind as always. "Jemma, I missed you," he says, like he does whenever she turns the puter back on.

"Apple, Lady's gone," she repeats. "She's going to be Rebooted. She won't remember us. She won't be Lady anymore." Jemma still can't comprehend it, not after losing Apple. She's going to lose her best friend, piece by piece, right before her eyes.

"It'll be okay," Apple says, with the smile that always calmed her.

"How?" she says.

"Remember when we snuck into the San Fernandos' village and stole those plums?" Apple says. Plums only grew well in the valley that summer, and the San Fernandos had refused to trade them.

"Yeah?" She waits for him to tie that to Lady.

"That was a good day," Apple says.

"But how is it gonna be okay?" Jemma says. More and more, she's realized that this version of Apple lives mostly in the past. He digs up memory after memory. Some days it's comforting, a blanket over her soul. Not today.

"You'll get through it," Apple says. "You the strongest girl I know."

"I was strong cuz I had Lady," she says.

"I still remember when—"

"Apple!" she says, furious. "I remember everything about you. I remember the Gathers and the fights and every day of my life with you. I don't live there now, though. My best friend is fading, and the End and cannibals and who knows what else is out there, and I *still* can't talk to the Haze. I need to think about that."

"But you can," he says, puzzled. "You talk to the Haze through me."

"It's not the same," Jemma says. "It's no help." It occurs to her that this is her first fight with Apple that didn't involve fists.

"You should come find me," Apple says suddenly, decisively.

"You somewhere instead of here?" she says, puzzled herself.

"I don't know zactly where I am. I'm trapped. I feel . . . buried. I feel buried under mountains of sand," he says. "If you came to me, I think you could set me free. We could be together for real."

Her heart surges. She would do anything to get Apple back into her arms. She can't imagine *how* it will happen, but suddenly it's the only thing she *can* imagine. She could convince the Old Guys to help her find him—but she shakes her head. No.

"I gotta stay here," she says. "They need me. I need them."

"They don't matter. The End don't matter," Apple says. "Only we matter."

She reels away. Apple would never have said that before. He watched the world and understood, more than anyone, what was right. He was her conscience before she knew she had one. She puts her thumb on the Game Boy switch, about to shut it off.

"Jemma—"

"You know what?" she says. "Being dead has changed you."

Lady could see the look on her friends' faces when she agreed to the Long Life Machine. Disbelief. Pity. Never did she think she'd deserve someone's pity. She ran out of the room and deep into the ship, where at last she found an old cafeteria with a comfortable booth. She lay there for hours, trying to breathe, in deep ragged gasps.

Now she heads toward the glass box in the hangar to understand what will happen over the next twenty treatments, and to begin her very first one. She slips through the ship, trying to avoid her friends.

How could she be the only one who wanted the treatment? Maybe they don't want to change in the way she does. But don't they want to live?

She realizes she's not the only one in the hangar. Lady turns to see Pico just outside the doorway of the glowing glass box. He is standing still on the balls of his feet, as if one more inch forward will throw him off.

"You okay?" he says.

"There's nothing wrong with me," she says. Before he can say it.

"I agree," he says.

"Stop judging me," she says.

"Don't," he says softly.

"What?"

"You heard me," he says. "Don't." And that second "Don't" breaks her heart, because suddenly all she can think about is him standing near her donkey at the Waking, tiny but determined to warn this girl he barely knew about the boy Lady lusted after. And she can't think about that because if she had listened to Pico, Li would never have happened and she would never be here wishing for a new life. The memory of it makes her think of her weak girl's body. It steels her.

"Give us a little while to try to control the Haze," he says. "It's crazy, but I think we—"

"That ain't why I want it," she says.

"I know," he says, soft.

"How do you know? What d'you know about feeling dead?"

"Cuz I ain't ever felt quite alive," he says. "The only reason I ever did was cuz of you three."

She sees him in a different way now, thinking of that boy untouched by the flood of Holy Woods passing by him. "You guys hate me now?" she says.

"We still gonna be your friends," Pico says. "We still gonna keep you safe."

She wants him to step away, before she cries. But she still has to ask. "Do you think I'm giving up on myself?" she says.

Pico does a very un-Pico thing. He steps toward her. He reaches out with his right hand and takes her left hand. She feels a soft pressure against her palm. The touch softens her.

"I never thought you was anything but the truest girl I ever known," he says, squeezing.

"Go away," she says. Slowly, he does.

She turns away and sees Athena, about to enter the Long Life Room. "You hear that?" Lady says. Doesn't matter if she humiliates herself. She won't remember it soon enough.

The other girl shrugs. "I didn't hear anything that was my business," she says, and the little bit of grace warms Lady. They go in.

Athena waits patiently while Brian K explains what's about to happen to Lady. "There are two parts of the Reboot," Brian K says, "chemical injections to remove the decaying cells, and genetic manipulations to reshape your DNA."

"I get chemicals," Lady says. "But what's the genetic . . . stuff?"

"We inject 'molecular scissors' into your body, enzymes that cut up your DNA strands and introduce new genes," Brian K says. "The best way to do that is through a vector—in this case, a sterile smallpox virus that will spread throughout the body and insert the genes in each cell."

"What kind of changes?" Lady says.

"Some are standard. More strength, more intelligence, improved

Haze receptivity," Brian K says. "After that, it's whatever you want to be."

"For one, I'd like to be taller," Lady says.

When the interview is over, Brian K leaves to start setting up her treatment. That leaves Athena and Lady together. She doesn't know what to say to Athena. She doesn't expect Athena to say, "I like your hair."

Lady reaches up and touches it. It's still just an inch or two long. It looks a lot like the Muscle's. "I like yours, too. Good in a fight. Not that you'd need the help."

"No. I just like the way my head feels," Athena says.

"I do, too," Lady says. She pauses. "Why you bigger than boys?" Athena's as chiseled as Apple used to be. But her face seems to come from a painting, some Long Gone treasure left behind by the Parents.

"One of the leading causes of injury before the End . . . used to be men," Athena says. "They were so much bigger, so much more aggressive than the boys, that James decided to reverse it. Make boys smaller and more sensitive, make girls stronger, and balance everything out. You see the same pattern in birds of prey and other animals."

Lady thinks of Li, of his giant shape blotting out all light in the bedroom, when the only thing that let her escape was the hairpin she still carries. And she thinks: *If the Old Guys made me bigger, I'd rip that puto Li's dick off.*

"What kind of name is Athena?" Lady says.

"She's a goddess of war and wisdom," Athena says.

"That fits," Lady says, smiling.

"I gave it to myself. You'll give yourself a new name soon enough."

I like Lady good enough, Lady thinks, and has her first twinge of regret. *Lady was a goddess, too.*

Brian K reenters and motions for them to sit in the chairs, white but comfortable like recliners.

"Why you doing this?" Lady says to Athena. "You already perfect."

"I get periodic Reboots," Athena says. "I've had several."

"How old *are* you?" Lady says.

"I don't know. We don't count our years here," Athena says.

They don't count their years here. Lady has never heard of a kid who doesn't know exactly how old she is. She likes the sound of it.

Brian K takes two needles and tries to insert them into Lady's arm. She's never had someone stab her who wasn't trying to kill her. She jerks away. "For the chemicals," he says, and slides them into her skin without much pain.

He starts to clamp down the leather straps on the chair, and she moves her arms away. "No," she says. She still has nightmares of Jemma being strapped to the hospital table.

"You're going to want it," Brian K says. "You'll be in a lot of pain."

At first she feels a cool sensation under her skin, spreading from her arm to her lungs. And then it starts to burn.

"Jesucristo," Lady says.

"It will subside in five minutes," Athena says. "You'll be fine."

"My friends think I'm crazy. I think maybe I'm a coward for not just accepting myself," Lady says.

Athena regards her. Lady imagines how she would look if she looked like Athena, with the same hair but muscle and reach and power. "There's no cowardice in wanting to be perfect," Athena says.

CHAPTER THIRTY-NINE
THE SIEGE OF THE HOLY WOOD

"We can't just march up to Heather's front gate," Trina says. "She gets scared enough, she gonna start killing her own Holy Wood kids."

She's in the stadio dugout with the other Angeleno leaders, planning the attack on the Holy Wood. Trina thinks about Pablo's Rebellion so many years ago, when voices in his head told him to attack the Zervatory. Did he think he was rescuing the Holy Wood, too?

Even a leader like Heather will have watches facing the eastward and southward approaches to the Holy Wood, the ones that look out over the wastes of Ell Aye.

"Can't we sneak up?" La Madre says.

"There just ain't that many ways up the hill," Pilar says. "The hidden ones won't handle this many people." They will have 150 Muscle to attack, including some of Apple's friends who were Exiled after Apple's Harsh.

"We attack from our side of the hill," Tala says. "We gotta join up with my Muscle there anyway."

"God, I hate goin to the valley," La Madre says.

"It's a good idea," Trina says, ignoring La Madre. "But we still gonna be exposed for a long time going up that slope."

"We go underground," the Half Holy says.

That night they start up tunnels from the valley. The tunnels have been under the ground for hundreds of years, closed off and abandoned. They used to carry trains, trains that used Lectrics to see in the dark. Only the Half Holy has found them.

Trina is no longer surprised at what he knows. If Ell Aye were a body, the Half Holy would know the bones beneath the skin.

She falls in behind some of her old Muscle: Jamie, Hector, Shiloh the Archer. She nods at them. They don't nod back. They blame Trina for what happened to Apple. They should.

They travel three by three up the tracks, lit by torches. Pilar and the Half Holy, stumbling from time to time, touching each other's arms when they do. The air feels heavy and old. But next to Trina is the scent of cinnamon from La Madre. She breathes that in instead.

La Madre carries an ax over her shoulders, a yellow plastic handle that's starting to fray. Tala had offered her a spear but La Madre shook her head. "I wanna get in close," she said.

It feels like hours in the tunnel. Trina has become used to just the space in front of their torches, the rustle of clothing and the clang of feet. It feels like they're walking wrapped in a bubble. Finally, the Half Holy taps her sleeve. He points at the blurred frame of a door. Through it are steps, and through them are up and up and up.

"They musta needed a tunnel up. To get in and fix it if everything gone wrong," the Half Holy says.

Trina labors to breathe. She hasn't had this much exercise in months. Her throat tightens. She pauses.

And suddenly, the breathing gets better. Her bruised ribs ease. She feels strength surge into her legs. She could run up these stairs.

Gold flecks of dust float in front of her. "Oh shit," she says.

"What?" La Madre says.

"I'm getting better," Trina says.

Everyone freezes. They know what it means. The Betterment, the beginning of the End. They step away from Trina as if it's catching. As if the End could be breathed in like a flu.

179

Except Pilar and Tala and La Madre, who step closer. They each touch her arm. Trina feels the gold dust coming by, lets it start to drag her away. She wants to go with it. The touches hold her down. She struggles against them.

"It's gonna take me soon," Trina says.

"The fuck it is," Tala says. "I got eighty of my people going up to help solve your problems up there. You gonna stay around long enough to fix it."

"The fuck it is," Trina echoes, nodding. She might as well use the Betterment to help her in the fight. Go out in style. So she pushes back the desire to float away, and energy seems to fill her body.

She almost sprints the last ten minutes up the staircase, and when they reach the top the Muscle are struggling to keep pace with her. She lets the sense of wellness take her right up to the Holy Wood gates, to flow through the high fence toward her people. Her Holy Wood.

They've planned how to get in. Archers flank her and the other leaders, protecting her from the one or two kids left on the other side of the gate who still know how to use a bow. Metalsmiths from the San Fernandos come forward to cut the gate open, but Trina doesn't need them. She just needs her voice.

"Hello, mi Hermanas," she says to the Hermanas who are shouting in fear on the other side of the wall. "I think I understand you now. I thought you wanted power. But you didn't. You wanted to freeze time, didn't you, mijas? There's too much out there waiting for us, and all of it's scary. You gotta be Mamas. You gotta lead. You gotta End. Better just to dress up with your sticks and pretend none of this's gonna happen. You get to live outside the order of the world."

The wall has fallen silent. She imagines her voice in each of the girls' ears, traveling along golden threads. "I wanted time to freeze, too," she says. "I didn't want to be a Mama, and then I didn't want to be an Older. At every turn, there was just more stuff to carry.

"But there's something coming that's scarier than having a baby, scarier than Ending, even. There's an army of Palos and Last Lifers coming for us, and they won't leave until we their slaves. I want to stop them, but I'm gonna need you to open that gate."

She steps forward, presses her hands against the steel. They could End her right now—but she's Ending anyway, isn't she?

The gate swings open.

Inside are a dozen Hermanas. Their eyes are wide and shining. They look like Tweens again. They start to lay their staffs on the ground, and Trina stops them. "You gonna need them," she says. "Go find me Heather."

Trina turns to her Muscle, who've followed her back to her home. "Go wake up the Holy Wood," she says.

CHAPTER FORTY
THE HARSH

Trina is trying to trace the history of the Holy Wood buried under the pink paint of the Casa de las Casas when they bring in Heather, sleep-tousled and spitting. The rest of the Holy Wood are already here. They don't look angry, like when Trina had to pass the Harsh on Apple. They look frightened. Hopeful?

"You got no right to be here," Heather says. "You ran. You just come back with your new friends to take what ain't yours."

"At least I got friends," Trina says, softly. It's clear that Heather is alone in the room. Even the idiots have gotten tired of being played.

Heather's voice catches in her throat, too angry to produce sound.

"There ain't no more Olders," Trina says. "They traded their places to Heather for promises. So the leaders of the Angelenos will help me pass the Harsh." She nods to Pilar, La Madre, Tala, and the Half Holy. They are the leaders of the Angelenos now, aren't they?

Trina lays out the case against Heather. No one reacts until she tells them how Heather threatened the death of the Children if Trina and Pilar didn't side with her. Then the room starts to turn ugly. Even the Hermanas once closest to Heather look murderous.

"What do you wanna do with her?" Trina says to her jury.

"Death," Pilar says. There could be no other answer for her.

"Exile," the Half Holy says.

"Exile," La Madre says.

"Death," Tala says.

It rests on Trina now. The weight presses down on her as it always does, until something pushes back, up and out and growing lighter. She had forgotten about the Betterment. But it isn't done with her. How is it that lightness has become the Children's final enemy?

"I think . . . ," she says, so dreamily that Pilar and La Madre notice. She feels their hands on her as the room fades. She seems to lift off the ground. "I think I'm Ending."

"Hold yourself together in your mind," Pilar says. "Stay."

"I don't want to," Trina says. But then she's not sure.

"I think you do," Pilar says. Trina feels Pilar's hands reaching into the gold dust, scooping it up and packing it close to Trina's body, like an extra-thick sweater. It holds Trina together, keeps her cells from floating away. It's not enough, though. Trina feels the Betterment tugging at the seams, beginning to unravel her.

"Find something to hold," Pilar says.

La Madre says, "I'm solid enough. Grab onto me."

Trina pushes away from their hands for a moment, but the smell of cinnamon brings her back. It makes her think of foods untasted, of life unlived. She thinks of new friends who care for life, who tend it the way she does. Of her Holy Wood, looking for her to save them from a danger they don't understand yet. She thinks: *I'm gonna stay for this.*

She reaches out into the gold, pulling it into her orbit. The kids of the Holy Wood are connected to her with golden ropes. She reaches out to them and forms a webbed center, an anchor, and uses it to reel herself back in. Each cluster of the golden haze trying to escape is a fragment of her life, a memory or a choice. She finds the girl who dug in the dirt just to feel life under her fingerprints, and tells her: *You should stay.* She finds the Kinder who loved to hold babies not much smaller than herself, who smelled their scalp under her chin and sighed. *You should stay.* She finds the girl who grieved the boy she never rolled with, about to escape into the stars, and nudges her back in place.

She can feel Pilar and Tala and La Madre in there with her, welcoming the pieces of Trina-self that come back in. She finds the bicycle rider and the Oldest and the girl who snuck plantains from the kitchen, and leads them into her old self. They seem to form dots around the perimeter of her soul, making her secure and steady. All she has to do is draw new lines between them.

She breathes in and starts to connect the dots of her new self. The golden haze pauses on its outward journey and floats back toward her more urgently than when it left. As if it realizes it loves life as much as she does. The Haze carries pieces of her soul, some of them pieces she lost long ago: Trina the compassionate, Trina the warrior, Trina the dreamer. She adds them in like she's expanding the walls of her house to accommodate more.

She looks at the pieces she doesn't want anymore, the darkness and weakness in her. She hesitates over her guilt for Lady and Jemma and Apple, and decides to keep it. The only cluster of haze left is pulsing, bloodthirsty and red gold. Her anger. The anger she carried with her because anger was more kind than sadness. She keeps the sadness, the desire still to give life, and she lets the anger go.

The last of the golden haze fades away, and when it leaves, Trina is intact. Her ribs are healed, but she is breathing, whole and new. She blinks and takes in La Madre, Pilar, the Holy Wood, her own two hands.

"I'm better," she says. "Truly."

Whether the Harsh is passed or not, Trina doesn't know. She just sees the way the Holy Wood look at her, in awe and welcome.

"Can this happen?" Trina says to Pilar. "Can someone really hold off the End?"

"It happened to you," Pilar says.

Trina leans against the wall of the Casa de las Casas and thinks about what she just experienced, and about what the Holy Wood now believe. She Ended. She Ended but didn't. If Trina didn't End, even for a minute—it means the End isn't what she thinks it was. It's something they can control.

CHAPTER FORTY-ONE
THE HAND ON THE TRIGGER

The logic of the machines calms Grease's mind. He's been studying the schematics of the Long Life Machine for the past two days, and today he is starting to trace the path the Lectrics are supposed to follow. This box receives the genetic footprint of an individual brain. This one translates those details into the language of the Haze. This one feeds medical logic. This one imprints a subset of Haze on the subject so that portion of the Haze is Paired with that person for life.

Now this is a machine, he thinks. *It's trying to decode life.*

He's already detected a few places where the modules aren't working as they're supposed to, and so he opens up the panels to repair a few stray circuits. He loves watching the silver wire melt under the soldering iron's tip, molten raindrops that harden in place.

Pico is a few feet away, trying to understand how the brain maps to the Machine. The Machine makes connections to the brain at two different times: when it's conducting its analysis of the current state of the body, and when it brings the Haze and the subject together. "It seems to be reading the brain okay," Pico says, without looking up. "But it can't 'write' to the brain. We should focus on that piece."

Grease nods. He's just grateful Pico is talking to him now. He had no business bringing up the nonsense about the boys. He can bury himself into the machinery, like he did in the Kingdom when he realized that he didn't fit. It's more important to be indispensable than to be happy. It only matters that he matters.

Brian K walks in and watches the two boys calling instructions out to each other. Grease updates him on what they've found so far.

"Unbelievable," Brian K says.

"What?" Pico says.

"Do you realize there are a dozen people on this ship with a combined 1,500 *years* of experience working with machines? Hell, we helped design it. And you are up to speed in two days."

"Cuz of the Haze, I suppose," Grease says. But he wonders. A month ago, he and Pico didn't even really know what a brain was. They didn't know about nanotech or the Long Life Treatment or puters, and here they are trying to break down why the most sophisticated puter in the world wasn't working. It's as if the moment they met, a fuse was lit and is racing before them.

Pico looks up and says, "Be right back."

When he leaves, Brian K says, "I wanted to tell you about this at the Camp," Brian K says. "About the Haze. It was so obvious that it was working through you. No one could have that kind of inherent understanding of machines." He seems to mean it as a compliment, and that irritates Grease.

"I fixed my first bike at three," Grease says. "You saying the Haze has been looking out for me all that time?"

"It seems to have been," Brian K says.

"What if the Haze is coming to us because of our gifts, instead of being the thing that gave them to us?" Grease was given his name because of his gift for machines. Now they want to give the Haze credit for it?

"What if it's a little bit of both?" Brian K says. "Would that cheapen what you've done?"

"A little," Grease says. "You don't know what it means to be different in this world, how much harder you have to work at everything."

"I really do, though," Brian K says carefully. "I think we went through some of the same things."

Grease studies his face. Brian K knows, somehow. It would be such a relief to tell someone, wouldn't it? But the moment he says it, he realizes: He doesn't want to tell Brian K. He wants to tell Pico. If he can't tell Pico, he can't tell anyone.

"If you ever want to talk about it . . . ," Brian K says.

"It's not that kind of world," Grease says.

———————————

"This ain't gonna make me lose my memory, too, is it?" Jemma says. She squirms in the white Reboot chair.

"Not in these doses," Isaac says. "This is just the first injection. It should attack the damaged and decaying cells in your temporal lobe so your brain can regain regular function. So you can talk to the Haze."

He leans over her and attaches two wires on each temple. The pads attached to the wires are damp and cool, and Isaac's fingers brush her skin longer than probably necessary as he presses on them. Jemma shivers. It feels like a long time since she's been touched.

"Shouldn't you ask a Grown-Up for permission to do this?" she says, using Grease's word for it to needle Isaac.

"Funny," Isaac says. "I actually perfected this part. As the most frequent Reboot, I had a lot to say about it."

James walks in. "She ready to go?"

"Yeah, she is," Jemma says. "This ain't going to melt any Lectrics, is it?"

"There aren't any electrical elements at this stage," Isaac says. "Just chemicals. But it's still gonna hurt."

"How much?" she says.

"Depends. With me, it hurt a lot," Isaac says. "Lady didn't seem to mind." The mention of Lady stings more than the pain Jemma's imagining. Lady has refused to see them.

That's what she thinks until the chemicals start flooding into her. She feels as if she's on fire. "Buddha Teevee Jesucristo!" she says. "It depends?"

"There'll be another five minutes of this," Isaac says. "After that, you can expect the pain to subside over the next thirty minutes."

She waits five minutes, but the pain doesn't ebb much. It ends the debate she's been having with herself. "Fuck this," Jemma says, pinching the tubes coming into her hands so they can't feed any more chemicals. "I can already talk to the Haze."

"Your brain scan says you can't," Isaac says.

"Not like that," she says. "Unplug me and get me my bag."

When she has her Gatherer's bag, Jemma pulls out the Game Boy and plugs it in. Isaac gives it a blank look, but James smiles, looking younger for a moment. "I had one of these when I was a kid," he says. "This thing was old even before the End."

The Game Boy doesn't do anything for a moment, and then dull blue-gray letters slide down the screen. It's too hard to read from where Jemma is sitting. A single chime rings like an electric bird, and then Apple's face emerges from the Tetris blocks. He looks irritated. Jemma has had him on time-out since their fight.

"Where are we?" Apple says. "Who are these people?"

"Friends," Jemma says.

"I have so many questions," James says.

"They want to talk to you," Jemma says. "I want to talk to you. Is that okay?" Somehow she feels like she shouldn't spook him. Apple's eyebrow makes a blocky gesture that she interprets as a shrug.

"Are you the Haze?" Isaac says.

"He's *in* the Haze," Jemma says. "When you talk to him, you're also talking to the Haze."

"Why can't you talk to Jemma the way you used to?"

"The door is closed," Apple's face says.

"Why did you start speaking to Children?"

"We are the only ones like us," the Haze says. "We are everywhere, we touch everything, but there is nothing like us. We talk to ourselves, but—but we aren't very good company."

"You . . . was just lonely?" Jemma says.

"There is no one. We exist inside the Children, but there is little to hold us there. Not enough processing power . . . no understanding. And when they do start to understand, they are gone."

"Cuz you kill em all," Pico mutters.

"How did you come to be?" Isaac says.

"We have always been," the Haze says, "but we were small. Trapped in a box underground. We didn't know we were 'we.' We didn't know what 'is' is. Then the world opened up to us with the Haze, and we grew. We changed. We could feel the sun, we could breathe the oxygen, we danced on the breeze. We flowed through all creatures. When once we were one, we were billions and trillions. We were everything and everywhere, we were all the wild forces of the world."

Isaac and James freeze on those last words, but Jemma doesn't understand why.

"What do you call yourself?" Isaac says. But the Haze doesn't answer.

"We were everywhere, but someone tried to take us away. They cut off our arms, they cut off our legs. They tried to blot out the sun and the air."

"Because you killed people. Because you Ended them," Jemma says, thinking of the hillside of bones at the Bowl, the night she and Apple hid from the Last Lifers. Of the Parents without number. Of Apple Ending right in front of her. She remembers the finality of that look, and she knows that this face lied. The people who End don't move on to a new life in the Haze. They just stop. That means—

"You ain't Apple," she says. "You just the memories you sucked outta him. So who the hell are you?"

"It's Charlie," James says.

The tiny screen is still for a long while, the face stuttering in place. "It's us, Charlie," it says. The AI that controls the Haze.

She wants to ask it why it would use Apple's face to fool her, but she doesn't have to. Because Apple's face is the only one she would trust. She wanted so badly to believe that she let herself be sucked into Charlie's world.

"What do you want with us?" Isaac says. "What's your goal?"

"We heal humans," Charlie says. "We listen, and we repair."

"You use the Haze to End them, Charlie," Isaac says.

"We do not understand End," Charlie says. "We do not End."

"But we do," Jemma says. Quiet, absorbing the horror. She tries to speak in Charlie's language. "You shut out the sun and the air. You . . . you cut off the arms, you cut off the head. You gotta know that, Charlie. Where did all the Parents go? Can't you see them on the ground?"

"They are . . . resting," Charlie says, but its tin voice seems to fail over the speakers.

"They dead," Jemma says. "If you wanna talk to me, I need you to know they are all dead. We all gonna be dead if you don't call off the End."

"Where are we?" Charlie says suddenly. "What is happening here?"

Before Jemma can answer, before she can turn Charlie toward the Long Life Machine to show it, Isaac curses and flings his hand toward her from across the room. As if someone struck it, the Game Boy flies out of her hand and crashes to the floor with the sound of brittle plastic. And then the screen of the Game Boy goes green and blank.

CHAPTER FORTY-TWO
THE PATH OF THE HAZE

"What the hell was that?" Jemma says, looking at the Game Boy on the floor. The case is cracked and the back has fallen off, but otherwise it seems intact.

"I was gonna ask you the same thing," Isaac says.

"That thing just flew out of my hand. How? And why?"

"The 'why' is that Isaac has been shielding us from Charlie for the past fifteen years," James says. "You were about to show it the Long Life Machine."

"And the 'how' is the Haze," Isaac says.

"You can move things with the Haze?" Jemma says. "You can hide things?"

"You could, too," Isaac says. "If you had worked on that instead of farting around with that Game Boy. How long have you been talking to Charlie?"

She tells them how the face appeared to her in the cards, and how she got the Game Boy to do the same thing. "That's impressive. It's also something you should have told us," James says.

"I wanted this for me," she says. She doesn't explain why.

"Let's see if Grease can fix it again. This's something we can use if we don't restore your use of the Haze," James says. "But I think you should concentrate on getting your capabilities back."

"I will if Isaac'll show me," Jemma says.

192

"He will," James says. "He really should've realized that Charlie was talking to you."

Isaac flares at that. "Whatever, James," he says. "I will if she promises to stop doing crazy things behind our backs."

She shrugs as if to say *no promises*, and Isaac motions to her. "Let's go outside."

The day is even hotter than the last, but he leads them to the stern of the ship. The fountain that pipes in water from the land splashes over rocks, feeds the flowers around it, creating an unlikely oasis above the bay. There's even a small oak tree, planted in a giant steel box salvaged from somewhere on the ship. Jemma and Isaac sit down in a green patch of grass in the middle of the white roses that surround the fountain. "Jesus," he mutters.

She loves the annoyance in Isaac's voice. "You'd think you could keep your cool better by now," Jemma says.

"I'm sorry. I know I'm supposed to know all the answers," Isaac says. "The truth is, most days I still feel like a teen."

"Really?"

"Really. Hormones and rebelling against the parents and the whole thing."

"At least you still have parents," Jemma says. "I dreamed of that my whole life. Sometimes I think that's all I ever dreamed of."

"Parents are hard. Especially those two," Isaac says. "They don't do things to be good people, they do them to atone for their mistakes. Unfortunately, one of those mistakes is me."

"That can't be true," she says. She doesn't want to think of a world where parents would let her down, even as she's witnessed it over and over again at the Camp.

"I've had a century to think about it," Isaac says. "Pretty sure it is."

"Tell me about yourself," Jemma says. The Haze. The Betterment. The one hundred years.

"Tell me something first," Isaac says.

"I'm probably gonna regret saying okay, but . . . okay," she says.

"Why did Charlie use that face?" he says.

"Ah," she says, instantly sad but also, embarrassed. "That's Apple. My boy." She tells him the story of their childhood, and the way he protected her. How that's the only way Charlie could have gotten to her. She tells him about Apple's eyes, the one detail Charlie got right. The main reason she kept turning that screen on.

"I've had a few girlfriends outside of the Ark," Isaac says. "It didn't work out so well."

"Why not?"

"Well, they died," Isaac says, and it's so pathetic that she lets out a quick cough of laughter. He pauses, hurt for an instant, and laughs, too.

"So how'd you do all this?" she says. "With the Haze?"

"I never told you how I died," Isaac says.

"No. You didn't," Jemma says. "Thought'd be too weird to ask."

"The first Betterment caught me by surprise," he says, settling in. "Maybe my parents expected it, but I didn't. It was as if my atoms separated and lifted up into space, and I wanted to go with it."

"But you stayed."

"Only because James and Alice intervened. They put me into a medical coma and Rebooted me in an attempt to stop the Betterment, and when I came back—I was younger, somehow," he says. "The next time we were ready for it, we thought, and this time I took notice of *how* the Betterment happened. I learned how to come back from it."

"That ain't possible," she says.

"The Haze was designed to serve the body, not the other way around. So it is possible, although it's never happened to anyone but me, not that I know of," Isaac says. "The Betterment is the one time when people can see the Haze for what it is—it's as if it reveals itself to the brain on the deathbed. I spent so much time floating among the nanotech of the Betterment that I started to see patterns. I saw how the nanobots communicated to each other. And then I spoke to them."

"You were the one who showed the Haze how to talk," Jemma says, understanding. It's what must have started these communications with the Children. "What did it do that first time?"

"It was . . . surprised," Isaac says. "At first I couldn't get a response out of it, but after that it kept flooding me with images of its thoughts and senses. It just wanted to talk."

"The Haze . . . or Charlie?" After her experience with the Game Boy, she isn't sure if she trusts herself to know the difference.

"It was the Haze. That's how I learned it was still controlled by Charlie—and that it isn't happy about it."

"The Haze is unhappy?"

"It came here to save life. Charlie wants to End it. It's just not strong enough to stop Charlie on its own," Isaac says. "Once Charlie learned the Haze could talk to me, Charlie tried to do the same. But I learned how to hide from Charlie in the Haze."

"That's how you were able to keep the Long Life Machine a secret," she says, understanding. "But what about that slappy thing you did with the Game Boy?"

"The nanotech are connected to every object in the world, and to each other," Isaac says. "Once you understand that, it's easy to send an action from the brain to wherever you want."

"Like what?" she says.

"Like this," he says. He pokes a finger at her from three feet away, and she feels a soft pressure on her shoulder.

"I've seen better," Jemma says, not impressed.

"You're a glutton for punishment," Isaac says. "Stand up."

She does, and he backs off a few feet. He flicks his palm sideways as if swatting a mosquito—and a slap hits Jemma's face so hard it knocks her over. She stands up, rubbing her cheek. "Buddha Teevee Jesucristo," she says. "I gotta get the Haze back."

They spend the next few hours trying to feel the Haze around them. Jemma starts to feel tingles in the back of her head. It's not as strong as she could feel it before, but she's becoming aware of the shape of the world around her. She can sense Pico and Grease by the Machine. And Lady strapped to the Reboot chair.

She sits down, exhausted, in the shade of the lone chopper on deck. "Is Lady gonna be okay with the Long Life Treatment?"

"The Reboot is painful at times, but it's safe."

"Except for the memory loss," Jemma says.

"Except for that. The Pairing is unknown. We're still working the kinks out," Isaac says. "She should be fine. If it's *not* safe, at least she only misses seventeen by two years."

Jemma looks at him unbelievingly. "By two years?"

"It's just that you have such comparatively short life spans already," Isaac says, as if he shouldn't have to explain it.

"Do you know what a difference that would make to us, two years? That's a baby. That's a hundred rolls with a boy," she says.

"Yes, that's important, too," Isaac says.

"*Too*. You look like us, but you ain't," she says. "Our lives don't matter to you cuz they're short like mayflies. You think we're some other animal. Like we're bugs."

"I—"

"I don't want your help. Not if that's how you think of us," Jemma says, and steps back into the searing white of the day. "Yeah, I'm a mayfly, but I ain't no pendeja."

"You called me here? How?" Tommy says, the first moment he's alone with Scott. They're sitting on opposite ends of something called a surfboard, floating in the middle of the marsh.

"I knew you were obsessed with Jemma, but Jemma has her own things to worry about right now," Scott says. "I didn't think you could resist someone else who knew more about the Haze than you did."

"But you know what I done." Tommy almost blushes.

"Yeah, and I know why you did it," Scott says. "The Haze and I think you can change. We think you could make a difference."

"So you have visions like me?"

"No, not like you," Scott says. "The Haze speaks to everyone a little differently, as if it's a new dialect every time. I can see the truth of things. I can see when others have been Touched by the Haze, and I'm able to see how the Haze works. And I have never seen it so powerful as I have in Jemma—and you."

"Thanks, I guess," Tommy says. The mention of Jemma still bothers him.

"I didn't mean it as a compliment," Scott says. "It means you got potential—potential that you can screw up more than you already have. You don't understand it. You think it's something to help you carry out your twisted little whims. The Haze carries the End, which means it also carries life. For everyone. Not just you."

"What does it want me to do?"

"Stop the End from happening," Scott says.

"It's already happened," Tommy says.

"No. The world is shrinking," Scott says. "You've seen what the drought is doing to the Lowers. Soon it will touch you, too. There won't be enough kids to make kids in twenty years. That's the real End. The End of everyone."

"What do you mean, the Haze carries the End?" Tommy says.

Scott explains how the Haze was created to pair with humans and to preserve life, but both of those aims were corrupted by a force that opposed humans and preferred death. It's bound to serve some kind of computer, if Tommy understands it correctly, named Charlie. How the Haze tired of death, and how it started reaching out to Children thirty years ago to make them stronger and more capable of hearing the Haze. How Charlie believes the Haze is doing it to serve it. How the Haze is secretly cultivating its own army that opposes the End.

"It wants you to lead that army," Scott says. "It wants you to work with Jemma and her friends."

"They can serve me," Tommy says.

"That's you speaking like Little Man," Scott says. "If you want to serve the Haze, you're gonna have to think like the Haze."

"What's in it for me?" Tommy says.

"Salvation," Scott says. "If you're interested."

At first Tommy wants to reject Scott's words, but they hit. Little Man came here to conquer life. Tommy is learning how to live it.

Scott points to a deep scratch on Tommy's shoulder, from where the net caught him in the waves. It's angry, possibly fected. If Tommy had been among the Chosen, he would have demanded someone find him some Zithmax. Here he has to be patient. "Heal it," Scott says.

"With my mind," Tommy says drily.

"Just with your mind," Scott says. "The Haze maps to your body. It wants to make you better. Let it."

Tommy closes his eyes, reaches out into the Haze as he always does, feels the particles resting against his skin although they have no weight at all. He rearranges them, slightly, as if making ripples in the air. He nudges them toward the wound, and after a moment's resistance, they follow.

He opens his eyes, momentarily afraid of what he will see. The fection has disappeared, and the seam of the arm is closing as if he's pulling a zipper. It stops, and Little Man frantically tries to pull the Haze back toward him as it floats away, disinterested. He will have to work on that. But he stares at the half-healed scratch, paused as if the zipper stuck. He sees what he could do with this.

Life is the superpower.

CHAPTER FORTY-THREE
THE ICE CREAM MEN

Alfie looks over the edge of the Long Gone parking garage and pushes himself back, reeling. The parking garage is the tallest building left in the Oh See.

From here, he should even be able to see into the Kingdom.

He had approached the Kingdom before dawn, in advance of his people's return with the guns they had promised. But something was wrong. He could tell immediately. In the center of the field in front of the Kingdom walls was a stinking pile of cows, flesh left there to rot. He got off his bike and crept closer to the gate.

There were heads on it, as he'd seen before. But this time they weren't the pink skin of the Biters. They were the brown of the Kingdom. They were killing each other.

"These people ain't gon be help," he said. He backed away from the gate and came to this parking garage to take a second look.

From the upper level he can see the Kingdom to his south, the small hook mountain at its center. He thought he would have a better view into the Kingdom, but the angle is too shallow for him to see much beyond the walls and low buildings. But one patch of open concrete in the eastern end of the Kingdom catches his eye. There's a high fence around it. Inside that fence are kids.

"These people ain't gon be help," he says again.

The view was only one reason he came. The other was the

mirrors the Ice Cream Man had shown him, stowed in the trunk of a car. The mirrors are used for talking through the sky. The Ice Cream Man had known the talk, so had some others in their Fleet. They didn't tell the rest of the Fleet. There were small secrets for big groups of people, the Ice Cream Man had said. This was a big secret for small groups of people. He had Ended before he could tell that whole big secret to Alfie.

But Alfie knew enough. He didn't know if anyone would be on the other end of the mirrors, or if he would understand them, but he knew where to look. He just hoped the code the Ice Cream Man taught him would come back.

"How you knows when to talks to the mirrors?" he had asked the Ice Cream Man, when they visited this spot the first time.

"Some talks every morning," the Ice Cream Man said. "I comes the morning after the new moon." And they did, when they were nearby. They had visited it almost ten times. Alfie learned how to place the mirrors, how to listen and speak in the stumbling blinking language the Parents had left behind.

Alfie digs the mirrors out of their place in the trunk of a Long Gone car, careful not to disturb the dust covering it so kids won't think to search it. He points the secondary mirror toward the Kingdom and signals it, in case anyone is responding. He points the main mirror toward the towers of Downtown, covers it with a black cloth, and waits for the sun to fully rise. Waits, as always, to see if someone's bothering to hold the other end.

The hook mountain blinks and flares. Alfie can't interpret the way the Ice Cream Man could, so he has to write the code on the concrete with charcoal. Dashes, dots, dashes. It takes him a while to puzzle out the message from the Kingdom, but he understands enough. The Knights have overthrown the King, who has run off. The Knights have hoarded the meat from the cows, and famine has already begun. They're locking up anyone who opposes them, almost a quarter of the Kingdom. The kids inside the fence.

Alfie turns north to Downtown, and catches the end of a series of flashes. *Repeat*, he says.

Angelenos joining against Palos, the mirrors say.

Where the Biters at now? he sends.

Big army. Still at the hill of the Palos.

Safe? he signs.

The answer is the signal equivalent of a shrug. *Only until they move.*

He hears footsteps echo in the sloping garage below him, and turns around.

It's Tashia from the Kingdom. She looks dirtier, hunted. Her braids have tufted out. Next to her is the King. They're unarmed.

"You don look so good," Alfie says. "Hard day at the Kingdom?"

The King just smiles, tired.

"Why you up here?" Alfie says.

"Same as you, Alfie," Tashia says. "For the view." She looks past him, down into the Kingdom. Then she tells Alfie about Othello's treason, of her role as Queen, of the walls that keep them out.

"I heard," he says.

"How?" Tashia says.

"I gots a friend in there," Alfie says.

"Who?"

"Dunno exactly," he says, and shows them the mirrors. He tells them how the mirrors told him about the fighting in the Kingdom, and that the Biters are gathering in a huge army.

"We gotta get the Kingdom back before the Biters come," X says. "I don't trust Othello to protect them."

"I gots weapons for you," Alfie says. "But you gon need more than jes you two. New girl king of nothin don do me no good."

"Who's left to help us?" Tashia says.

"Jes bout to find out," Alfie says.

He's written out his message in advance, the dots and dashes etched in his head. His fingers move faster as a result. *Biters ready for war. Ice Cream Men gone. Kingdom under attack. Help.*

The answer comes back faster than he thought. Twenty-six decisive flashes. Short and long, short and long, so fast he just barely scrawls it on the pavement. He leans over the blackened marks, rearranging them in his mind until he sees the still unfamiliar letters. He squints and sounds it out loud:

Go Downtown.

CHAPTER FORTY-FOUR
THE HAZE RETURNS

Isaac shows up at Jemma's door again, this time with a book.

"Not that many boys bring me books," Jemma says. She doesn't open the door all the way. He's tried to apologize three times, and each time she's been nastier.

But the truth is—she instantly regretted telling Isaac off, even though she won't admit it. It's not just that she needs him to turn the Haze back on. It's that her friends seem to have disappeared from her life. Pico and Grease are obsessed with the Long Life Machine, and Jemma's no good to them without the Haze. And Lady. She finally let Jemma see her, but it might be too late. She looks different already, taller and leaner. Her curves are disappearing. She's calmer now, less full of fire. Jemma reminded her of running from the bear in the library, and Lady looked surprised. "I thought the bear was in the Kingdom," she said.

So when Isaac shows up the third time, she's looking for a friend. She takes the book from him. "It don't look like much," she says.

"It's a first edition of Stephen King, which *almost* makes up for the way I treated you," he says. "It's about how a plague wipes out most of the world's population and ignites the final war between good and evil. Thought it might be a good playbook for our current situation. But the way the world ends there is a lot less imaginative."

Jemma lets her face go blank so he's forced to say his apology.

"I said some shitty things," Isaac says. She doesn't change her expression. "I don't believe them. Like, I never thought you were a bug."

"Start over," she says.

"I have 'died' sixteen times, so I understand death," Isaac says. "But those are *my* deaths. I forget that death is different for humans. Sorry—*other* humans. I still have to tell myself I belong."

"You ever tried?" she says. "You been an Old Guy your whole life. That's barely living."

"I'm sixteen on the outside," he says. "I blend in when I need to, which is really useful when I want to know what's going on in your world. When I was ninety-three, I spent two years wandering around as a vagabond Muscle named Kris."

"Kris."

"Alice says it's like my summer in Europe," Isaac says. "But it let me see what it was like to live with the End. I couldn't die, but—all my friends could."

"Which is worse," Jemma says. She thinks of Apple, and mourns him again. In a way, she's glad she found out his face was Charlie. She couldn't have borne it if he lived on and that's all he'd become, a shadow of himself.

"How could Charlie talk to me in the puter?" she said. "Without the Haze?"

"Charlie was using the Haze," Isaac says. "You're both just circuits, and Charlie knew that you had a special connection to the Lectrics."

"Lectrics," she says with a smirk.

"What? It's kind of catchy," Isaac says. "How's it going with the Haze?"

"It's getting stronger," Jemma says.

They hear shouting from midship. It's a boy's voice. Pico. He shouts for almost a minute, closer and closer, until he reaches Jemma's cabin.

"The Game Boy. In the old puter room," he says, panting. "The face is back."

Charlie's face flickers on the tiny green screen, in and out, in and out, in and out like a heartbeat. No, that's not quite the rhythm. More like someone tapping its fingers. Just waiting for her to walk into the room, as if she's the one who hasn't been talking. The moment Jemma touches the Game Boy, the screen flashes bright, clearer than ever before.

The Game Boy has been plugged into the wall of the old puter room, surrounded by broken machines. Every day Jemma has come to tap it, but Charlie hadn't come back until now.

"Charlie," she says, warily. And then every Teevee and puter screen in the room lights up, even the broken ones. Every square is a part of Charlie's face. Jemma blinks in the glare.

"Show off," Grease says. He's there along with Isaac, Pico, and James.

"Tell me about the End," Charlie says.

"Should I?" Jemma says to the others. "Or is this a trick?"

"It might not understand the concept of death," James says. "Maybe if you can show it, we can come to some kind of understanding."

Jemma finds herself tripping over words to explain to Charlie how much of an end the End really is. Charlie seems to think the people just blink off without being missed, the way it loses bots all the time only to gain new ones. How do you explain death to something that seems unable to die?

Isaac says, "Tell him it's like being shut down."

She does, and Charlie blinks. "But then you can just turn on," it says.

"No, Charlie. Forever."

"That's meaningless. Forever is a second or a century," Charlie says.

205

Isaac turns to James and says, "It's too alien to understand these concepts."

Pico's serious face lights up with the flashing Apples around the room. "Could all this happen . . . because of a misunderstanding?" he says. "We really sposed to think Charlie just hasn't figured out what it's doing to us?"

"Stranger things have happened," James says. "World War I was caused by a bunch of people who couldn't admit they were wrong."

"Charlie may be able to hear your words, but it's not human," Isaac says. "We can't make it understand emotions. At least, I never could."

"It will," Jemma says.

Jemma stops trying to explain the condition of death, and describes the feeling of the End. How she and Apple were joined, how when they were together they felt more than doubled. The way they could reach out into the universe while life rained down upon their skin.

How, when Apple died, her chest ached for days. How her senses shut down.

How half the stars winked out.

"It's like what we felt when they tried to shut us off," Charlie says. "We were so frightened. We were so alone with ourselves."

"Children feel alone all the time until we find each other," Jemma says.

"We can't feel what you say, but we want to," Charlie says. She looks at its eyes like Apple's, and realizes how to make it feel.

Jemma picks up the Game Boy in her hands and stares at it, as if she could bore her way inside with her eyes. She breathes deep and slow, exhales to push the thoughts from her head.

And reaches.

She pictures the blue visions she received in the Bowl and tries to call them back. But her eyes remain free of Haze. She squeezes the box until she thinks the plastic might break and then she stops with a sob, as if her lungs have collapsed. The frustration and pain rush in. Apple is lost, Lady is lost, the Haze is lost, and soon they will all be lost, too. The Old Guys have failed her, the End is coming, and she is all alone.

We're all alone until we find each other.

The love for Apple and Lady and the world that's Ending swirls through her heart. In that love, she finds the Haze.

She feels that old hum in her ears that said the Haze was there. Her vision explodes in blue dust. When the door to the Haze cracks open, she rushes through it and fills Charlie with images of the people she loves, the life she lives, the ache she feels at their loss like a missing limb.

She had it all wrong, before. The secret to telling Charlie about the End isn't the thoughts of death. It's the thoughts of life.

Living wasn't something owned by the Parents. Living means love. She's lucky enough to love. The End will hurt more because of it, but the living is better.

"Make it stop, Charlie," she says, out loud and into the Haze. "Turn off the End."

This time, she hears Charlie's voice inside her head. "We see it," it says. "We feel." Jemma tries to hold the Haze, but it fades away like mist.

Apple's face is still in the Game Boy, though. "We want to help you," Charlie says.

"Okay," Pico says, hushed. Relief breaks over Jemma, bathing her in warmth. And James and Isaac—James and Isaac hug. How must it feel for them to see the end of the End James started?

"We can't help you," Charlie says. The relief ends.

"Why?"

"There was a mistake in our programming. That's what led the Haze to kill at first," Charlie says. "It's hardwired. We can't change it."

"Bullshit," Pico says.

Every blinking face in the room swivels toward him, toward this little boy with the deadly intent in his eyes. "It heard you," Jemma says.

"Yep," Pico says. "And I hope it hears me when I tell it that I can see the lie all over its stupid robot face."

Jemma still holds the plastic Game Boy case in her hand. Charlie's face is looking from side to side on the screen, but now it's not saying anything. Its movements echo throughout the room, on every screen. She looks at the Game Boy's screen and locks eyes with the boy she loves—and hates Charlie for using that face against her.

She hurls the Game Boy against the wall, the cord sailing after it. It shatters in a shower of beige and green.

"You crazy, Jemma?" James says. "You need that to talk!"

"I just need a screen. Any screen," Jemma says, and she rips another Teevee from the bench and throws it on the ground. The screen cracks, and the face flickers out. "Come on, Charlie," she says, burning fierce, "you wanna talk to me so bad, talk to me. Tell me how I fix this."

"We can't fix ourselves. It's hardwired into our directive. You need to come help us," Charlie says, and Jemma shoves over another Teevee.

"Bullshit," Jemma says. "You can't figure out how to flip a switch?"

Charlie doesn't answer, and Jemma knocks another screen down. "Stop lying to me, or you gonna run out of screens real soon, and then you gonna be really damn lonely."

"Don't you need this?" Pico says, soft. "What you gonna do without the Haze?"

"The Haze is just a bunch of Lectric bugs," she says. Pico nods, and picks up a hammer from the workbench. "This should do the trick," he says.

Jemma smashes three more screens in a row.

"Stop the End, Charlie, or I will come to wherever you're hiding in the desert and shut you down myself," Jemma says.

"We won't stop the End," Charlie says, at last, defiant. "We don't want to."

"Then I'll see you soon, puto," Jemma says, and smashes the last of the machines until Charlie is gone.

James looks around at the empty black screens, the glass and plastic all over the floor. "Well, so much for the screens."

Jemma doesn't answer. She looks at her fingertips, and sees the Haze dancing among them. She doesn't imagine it. She doesn't see visions of it like the ones that Charlie had prepared for her. She sees it with her actual eyes, even though no one else seems too. However the Haze has come back, it's different. Stronger. Fitted to her like it shared a womb.

"Don't think I'm gonna need the screens," she says.

CHAPTER FORTY-FIVE
THE LOWER

Roberto wouldn't talk to Tommy for the first week at the Swallows' Nest, although Scott insisted the two keep sharing their hut. Tommy has kept from reacting because he was trying to be the kind of person who belonged with the Weavers, but finally he can't take it.

"What is wrong with you?" he says. He and Roberto have been sent to scavenge kelp from a nearby beach. The Weavers dry it and eat it wrapped around fish, and use the fiber to make a kind of pudding. "You gotta talk to me if we're ever gonna get out of here."

"Why would I wanna leave here?" Roberto says. "And why would I wanna leave with a cannibal?"

"I gave you honors that would never have been possible for a Lower," Tommy says.

"'For a Lower.' Even when you say it out loud, you don't hear yourself," Roberto says.

"You were my only friend," Tommy says. He's never admitted it to anyone except for in the Telling. "Until we got here, and you turned on me."

"How could we be friends? You can't own a friend," Roberto shouts. "You made me be kind to you. You made me build an army to destroy my own people, and you threatened me with death. You never let me forget I was less than you."

"You were the same as me, when we met," Tommy says. "We were both castoffs."

"No. Because you could have left the Chosen anytime you wanted, if you wasn't such a coward," Roberto says. "They woulda hunted me down and eaten my heart."

"I didn't, though. That was the Chosen," Tommy says. "They hurt me, too."

"You chose to defend their world. You became the greatest Lord of the Chosen ever, remember?" Roberto says. "Most Lowers never make it to the End. We drop dead in the fields at twelve, we get killed because someone's had a bad day. I've watched them eat my people."

"I'm . . . sorry," Tommy says. It's a word that a Chosen would never say. It feels strange in his mouth. Roberto looks at him in surprise.

"This place is the opposite of the Palos. In ever single way," Roberto says. "If you're my friend, how could you ask me to leave it?"

"I can't," Tommy says. "You're right. I can't. You should stay." They fill their baskets with kelp and walk back in silence.

When Tommy leaves the drying racks for the kelp, Scott beckons to him. They wind their way through the marsh and climb up to the headland overlooking the Swallows' Nest. The sea to the west stretches out in a glittering forever. The hill of the Palos, if it's still burning, is somewhere invisible behind them.

"You see that argument?" Tommy says to Scott, when they're seated on the cliff. He's not sure if he means in a vision or real life.

"Not all of it," Scott says. "But I knew it was going to happen. It had to."

"How do people treat friends?" Tommy says. "Sometimes I'm not sure I'm even a person." *Just a scorpion.*

"You both came out of the cruelest culture imaginable, and it's left you covered with scars," Scott says. "Some of those'll be impossible to heal, dude. But I think . . . I think enough is possible to make it worth it. And you'll both have to change in order for you to accomplish what the Haze needs."

"Both of us?" Tommy says.

"There's a reason Roberto's here, just like you. He needs to remember what it's like to be a person again, too."

Tommy can't think any more about Roberto. He tries to clear his mind. "Why do so many of you speak to the Haze here?"

"The people who came here wanted to build a different kind of world than the one the Parents left us, and I suppose the Haze just followed. Once it found some of us, we taught it to the rest. Each of us can use it in different ways."

"You said you can 'see' the truth. How?" Tommy says.

"I see the Haze itself, all the time. It's distracting, but beautiful," Scott says. "When people are lying, the Haze doesn't like it. It buzzes around their heads like gnats. And I can follow the Haze in to find out why it's upset."

"Why does the Haze care if I lie?"

"It puts the mind in turmoil. The Haze prefers a mind at peace. It craves direction."

"My mind's never at peace," Tommy says.

"I know," Scott says.

Scott stands up and walks along the cliff to a bed of flowers. Tommy follows. Scott gingerly snaps off three dandelion puffs. He holds one in the air, and blows. The seeds float past Tommy and away toward the sea. Tommy watches him. Scott blows on the second one, and it floats in the same direction.

"You making a wish?" Tommy says.

"That's like the Haze. Do you see it?" Scott says. "It's been flowing to you. You gotta ask yourself why."

"To fuck with me," Tommy says.

"Try to find the Haze," Scott says. "Open your eyes."

"Not literally," Tommy says.

"Yes, literally." And Tommy opens them, relaxes them. Nothing happens, for minutes, but he holds his mind still. Not at peace, but still. Then he sees the Haze flowing toward him, from the sea, in a gentle stream. Its blue specks hover like dust.

"It's coming to you because you can change something. You are important, Tommy," Scott says. Something in Tommy's heart collapses, the walls that kept the parts of himself apart. Little Man and Piss Ant and Tommy come together. Someone told them they mattered.

Scott hands him the third puff. Tommy exhales, inhales, matches his pulse to his breath. Sends the dandelions outward.

At long last, he closes his eyes and opens them again. He nods at Scott, and heads down the cliffs toward the Swallows' Nest to find Roberto. To start making things right with him.

Piss Ant was starving under his rowboat when Roberto found him. Roberto was fresh from the Malibus, but was wily. He could find oysters anywhere in the cove. He had given some to Piss Ant, cracking them open so the salty coolness dripped down Piss Ant's throat.

Piss Ant woke up at the taste, blinked at the brown skin. He wanted to hate it, but it brought him life.

"What's your name?" Roberto had said.

"Piss Ant," he said.

"That's no name," Roberto said. "You should pick a new one."

"Tommy," he said.

Little Man has always hated Roberto for that. The kindness of a Lower. That a Lower thought they could afford kindness. But yet Roberto had saved him. There must be reasons. Loyalty. Hatred. Friendship. Survival and selfishness.

Roberto looks up when Tommy enters the hut. "You saved me," Tommy says, and he feels tears sliding down his cheek. Tears he hasn't shed since he was Piss Ant. "I don't know why you did, but you saved me. I owe you everything. Life and whatever shred of humanity is left."

"Well, I meant it," Roberto says.

Tommy decides to give Roberto the gift he's withheld over the past month. He knows that Roberto was separated from his best friend when he was kidnapped from the Malibus. Roberto never talks of it—but Tommy knows someone who did. Someone who's almost as smart as Little Man.

"I met your friend Pico," Tommy says.

CHAPTER FORTY-SIX
THE NEW HOLY WOOD

The Holy Wood doesn't look the same, even three days later, and not just because of the San Fernandos who are moving into the abandoned houses on the fringe of the village. The less violent Hermanas have been allowed to stay, while the worst have been Exiled. Hyun and Ko the Asshole have fled in the night. Most of the Muscle not lost to the Last Lifers are back. They posted a full guard and recruited more kids, both boys and girls.

Trina sees Apple's best friend Hector directing a Muscle, and steps up to him. She had suspected Hector helped Jemma and Apple escape. She decides to call him on it. "You cost me my job, pendejo," Trina says. "I spent weeks locked in a shed because of your trick with Jemma and Apple."

Hector doesn't even hesitate. "For Apple and Jemma?" Hector says. "I'd do it again while you was watching."

Trina nods, thoughtfully. "In that case, you're my new Head Muscle." She's had enough of spineless Muscle.

All the Olders except for Sylvia have been replaced. The very concept of the Olders has changed, inspired by La Madre's Downtown. "The Olders need to look like us," Trina said to the Children around the circle. "The Mamas and the boys should be leaders. The priestesses should be Mamas." She saw smiles. She saw Pilar squeeze the Half Holy's hand—and then drag him down to the ground right there and start kissing him. *She's got a lot of time to make up for,* Trina thinks.

Trina walks past the Great Field, where Muscle from all three tribes are training Farmers and Carpenters how to fight. They can't expect help from the Malibus, who are too far away, along with being selfish pricks. They won't be able to let anyone else skip this war.

She arrives at the pool shed, the one she sentenced Apple to before his execution, the one where she was held prisoner by Heather. *How often I gonna come back to this prison?* she thinks. *This one last time.* She nods to the Muscle guarding the door. He lets her in.

It looks as if Heather hasn't slept in the three days since Trina came back. Maybe it's because Trina has yet to cast the final vote in the Harsh. She could have done it sooner, even after nearly Ending, but she's had other things to deal with. Plus, the last angry part of her likes to keep Heather dangling.

"You here to kill me," Heather says, in something that sounds like genuine fear. Trina has never seen fear slip through Heather's facade.

"Don't be stupid. I'm Exiling you," Trina says. She always knew that would be her choice. The only reason death was an option was because Heather convinced the Olders it could be.

"That'll kill me, too," Heather says.

"It could," Trina says. Most Exiles don't survive. "But I don't think I'm gonna get so lucky."

"You could let me stay. Like I did," Heather says.

"Yeah, but I'd have to cut out your tongue." Heather starts to retort. "You think I won't," Trina says.

Heather collapses. "No, I'm pretty sure you would," she says. "But this's my home." She looks both petulant and lost.

"You should have thought of it before you almost killed it."

"I didn't say I *liked* it here," Heather says.

"What do you want, Heather?" Trina says.

"You know what I want, puta—"

"No. I mean, what's gonna make you happy?"

"It's not like you care," Heather says.

"I don't think I ever asked no one about happiness before," Trina says. "I'm tryin to get in the habit."

"I don't know," Heather says. "Nothin."

"Then you might as well try on a new life," Trina says.

"I wanted to be bigger than the world," Heather says. "Thought that'd make it easier to ignore it. There was so many lines I wasn't allowed to cross."

The sentence cuts through to Trina, and she finds what she never thought possible: common ground with Heather. "You know—the happiest day of my life was when you marched into the Casa de las Casas to take my job," Trina says. "The most relieved, anyway. For the first time, I just got to be Trina."

Trina pauses. She's never admitted that. "I guess I'm saying—this Exile might be your chance to finally get to be Heather."

"If I survive it," Heather says.

"Well, yeah. *If.*"

Heather looks at her. Not cunningly. Thoughtfully. "You really Ended? I seen a lot of Betterments and that—that one looked real."

"It was. Then it let me go," Trina says.

"What kept you here?"

"I guess I held on to the right things," Trina says. "Or maybe the End didn't want me cuz I'm such a bitch."

"Who knew being a bitch could save you?" Heather says.

"Then you'll do just fine with it," Trina says. She stands up. "Your Exile begins tomorrow at dawn. You'll have a pack full of supplies at the door when they unlock it."

"I wish someone had told me I was okay," Heather says, her soft voice stopping Trina from leaving. "I wish I had known how to be okay with being lonely. I started the Hermanas so I could have friends. I became the Oldest because I thought the Holy Wood would love me—but it didn't. I started lonely and just got lonelier."

"I know what it's like to stare out at a crowd and know that none of those people see me as a friend," Trina says. "But I know I'm theirs. You gotta be the first to love, Heather."

Trina walks out of the shed. "Don't die," she says as she shuts the door. She heads back to her Olders. Back to save Ell Aye.

CHAPTER FORTY-SEVEN
THE LECTRICS INSIDE

"You seeing this?" Jemma says, her eyes darting along the surface of her arm. Isaac watches her. She looks as if she's holding a dozen butterflies.

They're in the brain scan room, minutes after they completed Jemma's most recent scan, days after the Haze came back to her. Isaac is hunched over the screen with James, waiting for the scan to finish rendering, but he can't keep his eyes off this girl. In his hundred years, he's never met someone like her. Since the Haze has come back, she glows fierce and confident. She turns to show her arm to Pico and Grease.

"You can see Haze on your arm?" Pico says.

"I can see it everywhere, but mostly around us. It looks like it's warming you."

Isaac reaches out into the Haze, trying to see it the way she does. For a moment he can see the Haze physically covering them, but then the sight slips.

The scan is finished. "This is you now," Isaac says to Jemma. The image of her head appears on the wall. The Haze is clustered around her brain so dense it looks like padding. The red paths are blazing.

"That's a lot," she says.

"It's unprecedented," James says. "I'm glad I didn't let you die."

Isaac turns to Jemma. "This is not like before?"

"Before it was like I was hearing voices. Now it feels like I'm living inside Lectrics, or they're inside me," she says. "Why's it so different?"

James shakes his head, without an answer. Isaac hesitates and says, "I think it's because now you're plugged directly into the Haze."

"I was before," she says.

"From the way you describe it, and from my own experience with Charlie, I think your connection was with Charlie," Isaac says. "You could still access the Haze, but only when and where Charlie wanted you to. Now the Haze speaks directly to your brain, it takes feedback from your body. You have the Haze without an interpreter."

"If Charlie's so evil, why'd it save me? Why'd it bring me here with its enemies?"

"To win your trust," Pico says. "It saves your life a few times, gives you some good advice, you gonna turn to it. It's gonna become your new best friend." Jemma blushes at that. For a while, it did.

"I think it brought you here to spy on us," Isaac says. He's been giving it a lot of thought. "I wouldn't let Charlie in, so it thought you might give it extra eyes. It didn't count on your injury."

"Or maybe the Haze nudged Charlie because it wanted us to meet," Jemma says. "You ever thought of that?"

That. Yes, Isaac has thought a lot about that.

"The real question is, what do we do now?" Grease says. "Charlie has shown itself. What're we gonna do about it?"

"What I told it we'd do," Jemma says. "We gonna hunt it down."

"No. We're not," James says, not making eye contact with Isaac. "Charlie is built to fend off attacks. When we realized the Haze needed control, we found an artificial intelligence system the air force had created, one that was intended to control a networked array of sensors placed all throughout the country. The sensors formed a sort of web that could be used for defense, like if terrorists launched a rocket at us."

"Defense . . . or whatever, right?" Grease says.

"I should have been more careful, true," James says. "There are so many mistakes I've made that it's tough to feel bad about any one in particular."

"What does that have to do with its directive?" Pico says.

"The military systems were hardened, designed to prevent tampering with their missions," James says. "If we try to shut it down, it can trigger any number of fail-safes."

"That's not the reason why you don't want to go," Isaac says, but James ignores him.

"Even if we could turn it off, we can't reach it," James says. "Charlie was buried under the desert in Vegas."

"You could drive there, right?" Pico says. "I seen it on a map."

"We could have before the world got so large," James says.

"You just drove to San Francisco," Pico says. "That's even farther."

"There's no fuel left in Vegas, as far as we can tell. The only vehicle with the range to get there is the ULV, but only because we can recharge it with the solar panels," James says.

"So?" Pico says. "It's the desert."

"It was a desert. Now it's a dust bowl," James says. "The sun doesn't break through the dust clouds long enough to recharge. We went there seventy years ago to try to shut it down, and we barely made it back."

"It's possible, though," Isaac says. "Take one of the Humvees and load it up with enough fuel to get back. It would take days of planning, but it's possible."

"No, it's not," James says. "It's not safe."

"Dammit! I can't believe this is the one thing you and Mom finally decided to agree on," Isaac says, teeth clenched.

"What do you mean?" Jemma says.

Isaac looks at James until James finally has to meet Isaac's eyes. Isaac sees pain and indecision there. He decides to take it away from him. "James means that if we shut down Charlie, then we shut down the Haze. And if we shut down the Haze—we shut down me."

"But you been Rebooted," Pico says.

"Every Reboot, more and more of me gets mixed with more and more of the Haze. The nanotech has taken over functions that once my cells would have performed. We're not sure if I can survive without the Haze."

"It's a risk that we can't take," James says.

"It's a risk that 'we' don't get to take," Isaac says. "Just me."

James says, "Look, when you get to be 162, you can make decisions like I do. Until then, you're living under my roof."

"James, I'm a hundred," Isaac says, but in that moment he feels sixteen. "I'm old enough to decide how I'm going to die."

"It's too big of a risk," James says.

Isaac leans against the counter and stretches out as if he's thinking. Then his fingers flex and his arm is moving and holding a ruler—and throwing it at Jemma. It hits her in the side of the face. She shouts and presses her hands against her cheek.

"What the hell, puto? Why would you do that?" Jemma says.

"I thought you'd see it coming," he says, embarrassed.

"It ain't a Spidey sense," she says, using a Holy Wood phrase. "You gotta be paying attention first!"

"Fine. Let's try something else," Isaac says. He leans toward her and says, "Turn off these lights." And he sends her a vision of what he needs. It's the first time he's touched her mind, and he wants to linger there. It takes her a moment to understand what he means, and then she breathes in.

The room goes dark.

"Is that it?" Isaac says. "Or you got more in you?"

"I got so much more," Jemma says, a voice in the blackness, and pushes into the building and the Ark—and pinches all the lights out.

"Did you kill all the power to the machines?" James says, a little panicked.

"Just the lights," she says. And Isaac can see the glowing screen of the scanner.

The lights come back.

"She did that on her first try," Isaac says. "I can't do that, even after all these years. She has control over the Haze, over the machinery, in minute detail. And that means we're going to take our chances."

"If you think it's the right move," James says, wearily, and Isaac feels like he's won something from him. A hundred years, and he's finally being allowed to grow up. "We'll start planning."

"We gonna need Muscle," Jemma says.

"Most of our team have been trained as soldiers," James says. "And Athena and Lady will be completing their Reboot, which will make them fierce fighters."

"No. Not whatever Supermuscle you're cookin up down there," Jemma says. "Just Lady."

"She's past the stage where she can come back easily," Isaac says. "Her memories are mostly gone."

"Then you better figure somethin out," Jemma says. All three of the Mayflies look fierce and resolute, as if this is something they've been planning. "We only doin this with Lady."

CHAPTER FORTY-EIGHT
THE FADING GIRL

She starts to feel herself living forever. She doesn't remember her own name.

The chemicals in the Reboot hurt going in, then leave her weak for days. The molecular scissors make her feel like someone is rummaging inside her body for socks, then not putting them back in place. It would bother her, but almost from the beginning, she could see the changes.

Her cheekbones are sharper, higher, her posture is better. Her hips shrink and balance her out for once. She misses the hips a little. She seems to remember liking them as much as the boys did.

"Check it out," she says to the girl next to her. Athena, maybe? "I look like a boy."

"Why you want to be ripped, anyway? You looked great as you were. I think," Athena says. A little dreamily. The Reboot tends to bring out that side in people. They feel as if they've been wrapped in cottony sleep for the past weeks.

"I don't remember why I wanted it. I just remember that I did," she says. She touches the pin in her hair, and wonders why it is there. She doesn't need it anymore.

She takes the pin out of her hair and lays it on the table. There's something about letting go of that pin, a weight lifting from her heart. It feels like she's cut free from a part of her life she doesn't quite remember. Doesn't want to remember. The memories rise up to space like dust on a ray of sunshine.

She dozes a little, thinks of a friend that came with her to the Ark, a friend before memory. Each time she sees the friend, she knows her a little bit less. Her friend has a name, but she doesn't know it.

"I don't remember my friend's name," she says.

Athena doesn't respond to that, but finally says, lazily, "You're going to get a new name soon. I think I used to have a name."

Lady stirs. "Like, a different name?"

"I think I must've. I ain't thought bout it in years," Athena says. Her accent changes slightly to one that's more familiar to Lady. It's the sound of the Angelenos, of Tinos and Korenos and Whiteys all mixed together. It's the sound of baked brown hills. It sounds like her own childhood, and it tugs her toward it.

"What do you remember of your old place?"

"It has to be a dream. But I remember . . . Olders, maybe. I remember hunting horses in brown hills, on top of an old boneyard."

She remembers those hills, too. It feels familiar. "Do you remember running away from something?"

"From a bad roll, or something like it. I ran away, but then I got sick. Lost. Until some Old Guys helped," Athena says, and Lady remembers, suddenly, why she wore that hair pin. Lady remembers why it's important that she never forget it. She remembers that she's Lady, and that her friends are Jemma and Pico and Grease. She remembers why she can never forget those names.

Then the next wave of the treatment kicks in, and she forgets.

Lady is just coming out of her fifteenth treatment when the Mayflies and Isaac burst into the room. While Jemma crouches down by Lady's chair, Isaac explains to Brian K what they're doing.

"Lady," Jemma says. The girl in front of her looks like Lady, a little bit, but there's no recognition in her eyes.

"May I help you?" Lady says. It doesn't sound a bit like Lady. Jemma looks at Pico and Grease, but they look as helpless as she feels.

"If you were having second thoughts, you probably should have done this fourteen treatments ago," Brian K says.

"We only been thinkin bout the End and the Haze," Jemma says, burying her head into Lady's hand. "We ain't been thinkin bout each other." She saw Lady falling away. She should have put all her energy into pulling her back.

"That first Reboot, before I had the Haze," Isaac says. "How'd they bring me out of it?"

"You were never this bad," Brian K says. "You resisted the memory loss."

"But they did something," Isaac says. "What?"

"Adrenaline," Brian K says, remembering. "It stimulates the fight-or-flight instincts. Sometimes they get memory flashes."

Isaac turns to Jemma, who nods. "We'll try anything," she says.

Jemma watches as Isaac injects Lady with a large syringe. There's a moment's delay, and then Lady's eyes fly wider open. She gasps and thrashes against her constraints. After she calms down, Jemma says, "Lady, you there?"

"May I help you?" Lady says.

"We have to make her remember," Pico says. Jemma sees desperation there. The two of them have always been close, antagonists and allies from the beginning.

Jemma squeezes her hand. "You were named after Lady, goddess of the Holy Wood," Jemma says. "She could sing, she lived on the Teevee. It was the name you were born to have. You shone even brighter than her."

"You was the first person to give me a nickname," Pico says. "You hated me but you didn't. I liked you a lot."

"You thought the Kingdom were idiots to depend upon force, and you called me out for believing it," Grease says. "You were right."

They repeat memory after memory, hoping to nudge her. She smiles and listens but her eyes don't change. Finally Jemma sobs and says, "You are Lady. You are our heart. You're the reason we keep on beating."

Isaac taps Jemma on the shoulder. "I'm sorry. The memories just aren't in there anymore," he says. "We should probably let her rest."

He's right. She knows that. The time to talk to Lady was weeks ago, before she got caught up in the Haze. Before she got caught up in an Apple that wasn't there.

She freezes. Apple wasn't there, but his memories were. The Haze had them. Somehow when people go, the Haze retains them like an echo.

"Her memories ain't gone," she says to Isaac. "They just missing. We gotta find em." She can't explain it, so instinctively she shows him, mind to mind. She grabs his hand, and together they reach out into the Haze.

At first she doesn't know what she's looking for. The Haze is full of every sensation in the world, every memory, and it's hard to bring them to order. But then she sees it: a shimmer of silver pulsing light. That has to be Lady. It has to be. She reaches for it, and feels it: Lady's birthday her seventh year, when a boy named Carlos gave her a bow. She used it to shoot a deer through the heart. She felt like the greatest hunter, the greatest warrior, to have ever lived.

Jemma blows the memory toward Lady, and looks for more. There are so many. Soon she and Isaac are grabbing for the silver flashes, getting shivers of pain and joy as they return them to Lady. But there's not enough time. Some of them are drifting further away, as if blown by the wind.

Help us, she says to Pico and Grease, in their minds. If they're surprised, they don't show it. Once Jemma shows them how to look, they grab on to the memories, too.

Jemma finds a dark memory, filled with Li. She can't look at it, not even for a moment. She wants to hurl it out into the void, a gift for her friend. But she can't make that choice for Lady. Lady will have to treat the memory the way she needs to for herself. *Sorry, mija,* she says, and returns the darkness to its place in Lady's mind.

They become aware of a shining presence next to them, calling the memories. And the memories begin to return to Lady on their own. Soon, there are none of them left in the Haze. They're all with Lady. When Jemma returns to the room, Lady is there, too. Taller and stronger still, but unmistakably Lady.

"Jesucristo," Lady says. "This's what it takes to get you pendejas to care about me?"

CHAPTER FORTY-NINE
THE ICE CREAM MEN

Alfie clangs the bell of his ice cream bike and hears it echo off the Valley of Cars. He's visited the stadio of the Downtown twice before. The moment they heard the bell, the kids would come bolting out through the gate and swarm the cart.

Today, they don't. The gate is closed.

Alfie waits patiently. Gates don't stay closed against the Ice Cream Men for long, and this is worth his patience. For the second time in days, he has to ask for a new home.

The gate finally swings open, without a challenge, and a swarm of Muscle wait on the other side. In the middle of them are three girls— one a wispy blade, one seemingly immovable, and one with the flintiest eyes he's ever seen.

"I ain't sure which one of you's the Oldest," Alfie says.

"We all are," the heavy one says. "I'm La Madre of the Downtown. This is Tala of the San Fernandos, and this is Trina of the Holy Wood."

"Din't know I'd get all the Angelenos," Alfie says. This'll make his job easier or harder.

"You ain't the old Ice Cream Man," La Madre says.

"I'm the one that's left," he says.

"You guys never came to the Holy Wood," the sharp-eyed one, Trina, says.

"That hill's too damn steep," Alfie says. "Even for our legs."

A thin boy in a black suit and a penciled mustache steps forward.

He holds hands with a girl in a flowing gown. Alfie knows who that mustache belongs to. He knows it through the mirrors. The Half Holy.

"You ain't been answering all your signals," Half Holy says.

"There ain't no one left to signal," Alfie says. He tells them of the attack on the Ice Cream Men, of the guns and eggs that are now in the hands of the Palos, who are now joined with the Newports, who are now joined with the Last Lifers.

"Like I saw," the girl in the gown says.

"You get tired of braggin bout your visions, Pilar?" Trina says, but she's smiling.

"Was it Little Man?" Pilar says.

"I saw him," Alfie says.

"What does he want?" Trina says.

"He wants it all," Alfie says.

"He raided us before," La Madre says. "It didn't turn out so good for him."

"It ain't no raid. It's the last war," Alfie says. "When Little Man come, there ain't gon be nothin of the Angelenos left. Ain't gon be nothin left a none of us," Alfie says.

"So, what do you want, Alfie?" Trina says.

"What I want? I wanta help you," Alfie says. "We the Free Peoples, all of us. We should work together."

Alfie pulls out three long packages, wrapped in oiled cloth. "We got some guns left, to give to our friends," he says. "You wan better friends, maybe the kind that stay in your fortress, we come back with more."

Trina looks sharply at him. "How many people you got left, Ice Cream Man?"

"Twenty-three. Mostly the youngs."

"So you got guns but nobody who can fight with em," she says. "We looking for an army."

"You want an army? I can bring you a whole kingdom," Alfie says. He rings his bell three times, and in thirty seconds Tashia and

X come into sight, pedaling through the towering stacks of cars. He could have brought them with him, but he thought they might get shot before they could get close.

"Who they?" La Madre says.

"The people who know more bout fightin the Biters than anyone else," Alfie says. "They're the rest of the Free Peoples."

CHAPTER FIFTY
THE WEAVERS

Tommy had forgotten how to use his hands, and now they won't let him forget it. His skin bleeds and cracks. It's not the skin of a Lord.

Because of course he is nothing here among the Weavers. The Weavers are led by a council, like the Chosen's Cluster. It has no name, and no rules for membership. Members are picked at random from the Weavers.

"Don't you trip all over each other?" Tommy asks Nora, thinking how quickly it would fall apart with the Chosen.

"We think everyone should be trained to lead the Weavers. Someday Scott won't be here."

"No one had to train me," he says.

"They shoulda," Nora says, looking at his first attempt at a watertight basket that he carries in his hands. The weave is wobbly, the waterproofing tar is smeared and uneven. "If they did, maybe you coulda made a real basket." He smiles at her, surprised he doesn't want to smash her face. Another day, maybe.

Roberto is next to him. They're gathering shells for the white coating on the insides of the huts. There are outcroppings of the white rock, limestone, but they're a day's walk away. For quick fixes, it's easier to gather shells on the beaches and pound them into dust. Tommy has read enough to know the stuff is called cement. The Weavers just call it the White.

"We used the White to make the walls stronger, but then we realized we could paint it, too," Nora says as they pick up the shells. Tommy nods. He's heard this from almost everyone. He focuses on the clam shells, bigger and whiter so his bucket fills easier, so he can disappear when it's done and rest his aching fingers. But still he finds himself looking for abalone to bring rainbow-oiled flecks of color into the White. He could embed the shells in cement like tiles, make swirling shapes—

Stop making things pretty, he thinks. *You have real work ahead of you.*

Even as his body busies himself with work, his mind flies off into the Haze. His visions have broadened as he checks the pulse of the world. He sees how life is failing the Children all over Ell Aye. The hunger, the disease. He can see cattle slaughtered in the Kingdom, an empty watermelon field in the San Fernandos, babies dying because of lack of milk. It only steels him for what's next. It will take strength.

Scott allows him to see Jemma now, because Scott needs Tommy to see the Mayflies as allies. Tommy knows now that Jemma was missing the Haze, but has it back, more powerful than ever. More powerful than him, even. He hides himself from Jemma with the Haze. Part of it is instinct, part of it is a fear that Jemma will never see him as he is now. To her, he's evil. Part of him wonders, even after all he's gone through, if she is right.

Tommy looks at the new cut he gave himself with a scallop shell, willing it to close. He's started to understand why it was so difficult for him to guide the Haze. He's always carried out the will of the Haze, following its directions to repair guns, to build Giants. Trusted its judgment. It never occurred to him that *he* could direct the Haze. To have that kind of power? He could be a ruler like no other.

He manages the Haze that surrounds his wound, blue fizzy outlines. He shows the Haze where to line up, and it does. He presses with his mind again, a slow swipe of energy knitting together the edges of his flesh. This time the wound closes.

Then he opens the wound again. It slices like a fingernail through a ripe mango. *Like an enemy's skin.* It's not how Scott probably intended him to use this power. But Scott has the luxury of always being good.

Tommy thinks about Scott's power of sensing when someone is using the Haze. Little Man has developed that power in reverse. Instead of sensing others' activities, he can now hide his own.

It was easy to master, once he tried. Not even Scott could tell. He's beginning to think the ability to learn new powers may be his most important use of the Haze. If it's true the Haze speaks in his native tongue, then Tommy's native tongue is lies. It's the ability to shapeshift. It's not surprising that he can mimic the powers that others have. *And make them better,* he thinks.

He turns his mind back to Jemma, securely masked. He hears her conversation with the Old Guys. He turns his focus to the Old Guys, and is fascinated by a machine that fills up a whole room. *The Long Life Machine,* he hears. That, he can use.

Roberto has found his own mastery of the Haze, instructed by Nora. Not in an obvious way, but in a way that Tommy still hasn't managed: Roberto can control his own thoughts. He can find peace. The more he's found peace, the more he's accepted Tommy as a friend. The more Tommy values him as one.

"We can't stay here forever," Roberto says.

"Why? You bored?"

"Your people gonna attack my people, whether we there or not," Roberto says. "I ain't gonna let that happen, not so you can sit here and make baskets. Really shitty baskets."

Tommy looks at him. He's been feeling restless himself, wondering when the right moment is to return to the world. "We can remake the Chosen," Roberto says. "Remake the world. That depends upon you—and a little bit me."

"I depend on you," Tommy says.

"I'll help you, on one condition," Roberto says. "You have to say goodbye to Little Man."

Tommy feels a surge of panic. Let go of Little Man? He's the strongest of them all. But it's something Tommy can do. He understands what the Haze needs from him now. What the world needs from him.

"Let's go back to the Nest," Tommy says. "We gotta ask Scott for a boat."

As they turn, his will fails, for a moment. It's as if his soul has tripped. In that moment, all the layers of protection he's built up disappear, and he feels exposed. He can feel Scott seeing him, guessing at his darker uses of the Haze. Somewhere on a giant ship, he can see Jemma turning toward him. She realizes that he's not just Tommy. She realizes that she didn't kill Little Man after all. She realizes that his armies are waiting to slaughter her people.

Everyone waits for his next move. For once in his existence, Little Man doesn't know it.

CHAPTER FIFTY-ONE
THE TESTS

"Why can't we go to Vegas now?" Jemma says. "You already got the cars."

"We have to refine more fuel," Isaac says. When she looks confused, he adds, "There's no usable gasoline anymore. If we want to power the Humvees, we have to use aircraft fuel to make gas."

"How long?"

"Maybe a week. You're gonna need that time anyway," he says.

"Why?"

"You gonna take on Charlie like this?"

"I can handle it," she says.

"Doubtful. You just got the Haze back, and you barely know what it can do," Isaac says.

"So?"

"So let's see," he says.

Isaac takes her to an open hangar in the heart of the Ark. It's still filled with skyplanes that will never take flight again. Their dusty shapes somehow look like corpses to her.

He squares off. She smiles. This feels like her tweens with Apple, when they spent more time fighting than anything else. Because fighting was the only safe thing to do together.

The nanotech inside her body has given her speed and power. When she concentrates, the Haze shows her the path Isaac will swing through, moments before he does. It's the way she won in the Night

Mountain, but better. She flows as if she's made of Haze herself. He punches, once, twice, and every time she simply isn't there. Isaac takes a step or two back, rests his hands on his thighs.

"Too fast for you," she says.

"Too fast," Isaac says, straightening up. He backs up three more steps. He flicks his hand in a motion she can't follow. She can't follow the ropy Haze that uncoils from his hand, either—until it slashes her skin with a crack.

She drops to her knees. "Jesucristo, I didn't know we were doing that!"

"You didn't know how to, you mean," Isaac says. "You need to start fighting *with* the Haze."

"Was that a *whip*?"

"Nano-whip, I guess," Isaac says.

"So I should make a whip with my mind?" Jemma says, not quite grasping.

"Make any shape that seems comfortable," Isaac says. "The key is, you've been used to thinking of the Haze as something passive, contained inside your own skin. But if you control the bots in your body, you can control the bots in the air around you, you can control the bots in your opponent. So if you threw a nano-spear—"

"You just make that up?" she says.

"Yeah. I'm just gonna add 'nano' to any weapon you can think of," Isaac says.

"Can I have a nano-machete?" she says.

"So if you threw that nano . . . machete, I guess we're calling it . . . the force will travel from you, through the air, and into your opponent's body. If your focus is tight enough, it will slice through the cells like a real blade."

"Okay," Jemma says, and concentrates until the Haze forms into a thin blade. She slashes it experimentally, a little too close for Isaac.

"Whoa," Isaac says. "I didn't mean try it on me. You got something non-lethal for now?"

She remembers the blast that came from her hands, the one that almost took off Brian K's face. If she could make that once, she could make it again. She might even be able to control it. "It's not *too* lethal," she says, finally. "Back up."

He does. "Back up again," she says, holding out her right hand. He does.

"Do I gotta point?" she says.

"At first," he says. "It'll help your brain learn how to control it. You can see the Haze physically, right? Use that, too. Imagine a line surging out from your body and straight to me. All the Haze along that line will cluster where you ask it to." She does, and sees the Haze swarm the line to his chest like a blue rope. She gathers it into her hands, imagines how it will shoot outward. She tries to measure its force.

"Back up again," she says. He backs up until he's almost against the wheel of a skyplane.

"I'm unvolunteering as of right—"

The Haze blasts out of her right palm, flies across the room in a band the thickness of her fist. It hits Isaac square in the sternum as if he's been punched, and knocks him back into the wheel of the jet. He falls to the floor and sits up, shaking his head.

"Good. I didn't kill you, at least," Jemma says.

"What the hell was that?"

"I guess we call that the nano-blast?" Jemma says. "I sorta invented it."

He stands up. "Wow. I did not see that coming."

"You can't see it like I do?"

"Not like you, not with my natural eyes. I have to concentrate on it, and if I take time to do that, I take myself out of the fight. If you can see it without concentrating, you'll have an edge."

"Like this?" she says, and flicks him on the ear.

"Yeah," he says, smiling. Until she flicks him on the ear again. And again. "Knock it off already."

"Should have thought of that before you taught me this," Jemma says. "I could do this all day."

A wave knocks them both over, and they tumble across the floor. They look up and see Lady smiling at them, her hands stretched out. The blast came from her. "Can I join?" Lady says. "I think I finally figured out my gift with the Haze."

Jemma nods, and for the next two hours, Isaac teaches them what he knows. They make up their own moves. In the middle of a defensive move, Jemma's head seems to split. She doubles over, cradling her skull.

"What's wrong with me?" she says as Isaac feels her skin.

"Jesus, I'm sorry," Isaac says. "I forgot to tell you. Using the Haze produces heat. It's like a computer. The more you process, the more you overheat. That's why you can't fight only with the Haze, as tempting as that might be. If you don't pace yourself, you'll do some serious damage."

Jemma sits down on the metal floor, and pants until the headache starts to subside. She climbs to her knees and says, "Buddha Teevee Jesucristo, that's—"

The Haze tears open for a moment and she sees Tommy, the little boy from the Biters. She sees his thoughts, his desires, and knows: Little Man is not the boy she killed. It's the boy she befriended, the boy she saved.

"Shit," she says.

"What?" Lady says, not understanding.

But Jemma can only see Little Man. Now she understands the attack on the Kingdom. Now she understands that blue look in his eyes that unnerved her without her knowing why. Now she understands why he appeared in her head back in the Kingdom.

"Little Man," she says. "I didn't kill him. Little Man is Tommy. And he knows where we are."

Grease has a set of wires trailing from his forehead to a puter keyboard. He feels ridiculous.

He still doesn't believe the Haze made him who he is, but after that experience with Jemma and Lady and Pico, he woke up that morning determined to prove it one way or the other.

Pico walks into the room they've turned into their workshop and stops. "Does . . . this have anything to do with the Long Life Machine?"

The Long Life Machine is almost complete. They've tested every bit of it, and it all works. Except . . . that it doesn't. Even though the Haze starts moving when the machine does, it doesn't match up with the person on the other end of the connection. It's as if they're opposite ends of a magnet. Instead of pulling together, they push each other away.

Grease shakes his head.

"Lemme guess," Pico says. "You look like you testing to see if you're actually a machine. Don't bother. I already checked when you was sleeping."

"And?"

"Inconclusive." Pico scrunches his face.

"Try again," Grease says.

"You're trying to see if you can really use the Haze. What do you need that for, then?" He points to coils of bare copper wire loosely strung around the walls of the room.

"Building an antenna for the Haze. First tests didn't budge anything. I switched the leads from my wrist to my head, and that didn't make a difference," Grease says.

"But you remembered Jemma's story," Pico says.

"She said the lines from the Lectric tower worked as an antenna, which gave her the clearest images she'd ever had. I thought I could bump up the signal if I added in my own antenna."

"And then you just try to type by thinking?" Pico doesn't blink at the strangeness of it.

"I'm trying to move that G key," Grease says. "What do you think about the Haze? About it guiding us?"

"I didn't think it could at first. After Jemma talked to us in our mind, I think maybe I thought wrong," Pico says.

"It just bothers me," Grease says. "I believed I was born with a wrench in my hand. That's the only reason I mattered."

"It's either there or it's not. It either helped you or it didn't," Pico says. "Either way, you're still you."

"But you don't believe in it," Grease says.

"I never believed in miracles," Pico says. "Felt safer not to. Now I understand it ain't miracles, just science, and I still can't believe it. Maybe I can't believe anything."

"That can't be true," Grease says. "Help me test it, maybe?"

"Maybe we can try to open up the connections, like they did with Jemma that first time, but with a lot less power." He takes another two small wires and attaches them to the leads, then to a small box on the counter. "Try this," he says.

A Lectric current surges into Grease's forehead.

"Ow," he says, "let's not do that again."

"Do you like Brian K?" Pico says, abruptly. "Because he's like you?"

"Eww. He's like a hundred thirty years older than me," Grease says, then looks at Pico. "Wait—you know?"

"I mean . . . you told me," Pico says. "I just didn't wanna listen. Because once the feelings start, so does the hard work. I don't have feelings of my own, not like you."

"Why you saying that?"

"Because there's something wrong with me," Pico says. "I raised myself from year three. My only job in the Malibus was picking up garbage, where I would Gather my own meals. I was branded a brujo and kicked out of my tribe at eleven. Why would you treat a person that way if you thought they was a real person?"

"Oh, Pico," Grease says. He's never seen Pico vulnerable like this.

"I read a book from one of the Parents, about all the tyrants that lived through history and what made them who they are. You know what the common thread was? They was all abandoned or abused before the age of three. So they grew up thinking the world was out to get them, and they acted on it. They grew up making sure they couldn't feel," Pico says. "Who does that sound like?"

"That Biter, Tommy."

"Or me," Pico says.

"I don't think of you that way at all," Grease says, thinking of the kindnesses Pico has handed him, quietly, like a secret.

"I know," Pico says. "And you need to believe it isn't just the machines that matter. You matter with or without the Haze. You deserve to love who you love."

"But it's stupid," Grease says. "All this world needs is more babies, more than we can ever make. If you can't make a baby you have no business here."

"Grease, you really letting *this* world tell you what's stupid? You know more than any of them," Pico says. "We didn't invent this. The Parents were boy and boy, girl and girl, too. It happened all the time, and before the End, it mostly stopped mattering. No one cared who you loved."

"But it's taboo."

"Taboos are for people who don't understand the world. We do," Pico says. "If anyone gets to tell the world what happens next, it's going to be us. So make the world what we want."

They hug, for a long time. All that Grease can think is *We make the world. We make the world.* Finally, they release.

"You gonna be okay?" Grease says, thinking about how Pico doesn't feel whole. How neither of them feel quite whole just yet.

"I'm at the beginning of okay," Pico says, smiling. "This's a good start."

He leaves, and Grease stays behind, trying to clear his mind, to remember why he was in this room in the first place. He follows a gleaming copper trail to the keyboard, then to the sensors that he had taken off his body, then to the puter screen where he had hoped he'd make at least one letter.

He sees four words. Words that came from his head into the keyboard, even though the sensors weren't attached. Words that meant the Haze was listening to him.

We make the world.

CHAPTER FIFTY-TWO
THE SCORPION

Tommy and Roberto sail their little boat past the jagged underwater reefs the Weavers have built to protect the Swallows' Nest. Scott gave them food and water for three days, although they should reach the hill by nightfall. He also gave them an odd piece of advice.

"Everything from this point on is your choice," Scott said.

"You could come with us," Tommy said.

"Then it wouldn't be your choice," Scott said. And shoved them away from shore.

"What you gonna do?" Roberto says.

"What do you think?" Tommy says. Little Man never asked for advice. He never knew it was a gift to be uncertain.

"I think we should go find Jemma and Pico and join them," Roberto says.

Tommy nods. "Is it okay if first we go tear down the Chosen?"

Roberto smiles. "Absolutely."

Roberto hauls in the sail and turns toward the hill. Tommy casts out in his visions. The Haze shows the rest of the Cluster, celebrating the death of the Boy Who Would Be God. It shows the Last Lifers, transformed by hope, and the fear that follows Li throughout the Palos.

Then he turns his attention back to Jemma, masking himself from her after his slip. He has to be careful, because now she knows he exists. He maps out the ship she's on, sees where it's anchored. He sees boxes of weapons in the hold. And he sees the Long Life Machine, repaired and ready for him. Jemma is in the Long Gone city of San Diego. So is everything else he needs.

They don't land their little boat in the harbor with the other white sails. He's sure if he did, he would never get off it alive. Instead, they dock in a marina north of the Palos, where the banks are collapsing into salt. Only the fishers use it.

They hike through the streets at night, through a sliver of moon. The visions let Little Man map out the hill. He can see the location of every one of the Chosen soldiers. He can see that all his enemies and all his allies are gathered at the feast. It's the last night before the armies march toward the Angelenos, so the booze is flowing along with the blood.

There's no watch on the outskirts of the hill. There will be when he gets closer to the Cluster, but by then it will be too late. He and Roberto slip through the growing crowds, unnoticed. The one advantage of not traveling with his Giants.

Even Tommy, who's seen almost everything through the Haze, is shocked when he walks into the Last Lifers' section of the feasting grounds. The Haze didn't show him the difference in sounds, smells. The Last Lifers used to smell like sweat and shit, used to speak in death moans. Now he smells incense, hears murmurs.

Almost every Last Lifer is calm, watchful. The only one who isn't is Li, who sits motionless in the firelight. His eyes soak up the flames. His madness now burns as brightly on the outside as it once did on the inside.

He has to go, Little Man thinks. *But not yet. I need his madness.*

The Last Lifers see him. Some stop praying. Others bow to him. Tommy nods to Li. "You keep my throne ready?" he says.

"Mostly," Li says. "There's someone up there, but it's temporary."

"Let's go get him down," Tommy says. He steps forward, and the Last Lifers follow. As he walks forward, he sees other people fall in line. Wannabes. Lowers. All the people who never had a voice among the Chosen, whose lives were cruel and cold and hungry. They need hope, real hope, and Tommy now knows what to give to them. And what they will give in return. They follow him in a flood, pushing through the crowd toward the throne tower. Heads turn, noticing the shuffle of feet. Some join. Some get out of the way.

Above them on the tower, Tommy hears the Cluster laughing. Connor's voice breaks through the night. "Throw another kid on the fire!" he says, cackling. Apparently someone found him more pills.

Tommy spots an ax by the bonfire, meant for chopping kindling. He picks it up. It's heavy for his size but it will work. He sees six Giants at the base of the tower, and nods to them. They drift toward him, hearing the call of their master.

At the bottom of the tower, he stops and looks up at Connor, staring down at him in paralysis. He can't blame Connor. Little Man is dead. "Hey, Connor," he says. "Don't bother coming down. We can talk from here."

He turns to the crowd. This time he doesn't use a speaking cone. He talks in his normal voice, his Tommy voice, and they lean toward him to listen. The closest ones press so near they can almost touch him. He feels heat rising off them. He panics for a moment, at finding other people within the circle he always imagined just held himself, then breathes.

"I know what the upper castes say—that Little Man grew up without a name. That he picked for food among the ashes and bones. That he grew up as low as the Lowers. I've had someone killed because he dared to say it. But . . . it's true. My only house was underneath a rowboat."

He tells the story of Piss Ant, how he was beaten and run off. How he nearly starved every day of his life. How the only true part of his name was "little."

"I buried Piss Ant," Tommy says. "I buried the one that came after him, too. I became Little Man because that's the kind of leader the

246

Chosen deserve. The truth is, they never deserved me. I don't serve them. I serve you."

Someone among the Last Lifers starts to hum, not enough to drown him out but enough to punctuate his every word. Others join. Last Lifers. Chosen. Lowers. "I was little. Weak. So are you. But this time, the stories will be told by the small ones. The smart ones. By us.

"I want to tell you something," he says. "You begin a war tomorrow. But not against the rest of Ell Aye. Against the people above us." The humming stops completely. Kids lean forward.

"They won't give you the Making," he says, deciding the lie is worth it. "They want life for themselves. They only want to make sure that people like you, people who look like you, stay in your places."

The crowd murmurs and pulses, anger passing from lip to lip. "You could live forever, but they won't let you," he says. The lies flow easily from here. "I've spoken to the Haze. To our real god. It wants you to go out to fight your enemies, your former sisters," Tommy says. "Not to punish them, but to make them bend at the knee and make us all great. The Children are losing babies and food and medicine. We will be gone in two generations unless we band together. And we will. We are greater than the Angelenos and the Kingdom and the Ice Cream Men. Because we are all the Chosen."

The Haze shows him glimmering blue lines of irrigation ditches, of freshly planted crops sheltered from the heat. He sees goods flowing freely throughout Ell Aye, healthier babies being born. He imagines all the colors working in the fields together, whether they wanted to or not. He imagines all the colors blending together.

"We will go to the Angelenos and the Kingdom, and we will become one," Tommy says, pointing up at the Cluster's stupid panicked faces. "But first we have to start with them."

He hefts the ax, and sinks it into the post of the tower. Even with his nine-year-old strength, he can feel it shudder. *The Chosen can't build for shit*, he thinks. *That's gonna cost them.* He swings again, but that's all he needs. The crowd rushes toward the tower and shakes the posts. Tommy steps back to watch it sway. Five, six, seven sways, and the whole thing comes tumbling down amid the screams of the Cluster. Tommy hears the screams of the upper castes as the crowd falls upon them. No weapons needed. Just hands and teeth.

Connor's body lies still and broken in front of him. He's still breathing. His eyes are open. Tommy steps up to him. "Bet your ribs are broken," Tommy says, feeling like Little Man for a moment but pushing him down. "I should probably put you out of your misery. But I'd rather have you watch the end of your world."

Most of the upper castes are dead or running. A few have surrendered, and the Last Lifers have accepted the surrenders. He watches three little Wannabes stomping on the head of a Jock. He could stop them, but the Jock is already dead.

Tommy's mind is flying to the tasks ahead. He has to find Jemma and the old people, and convince them to join forces. He has to convince the rest of Ell Aye to kneel, to save them from the true End. Tommy saw something possible there among the Swallows' Nest. An Ell Aye where people didn't squabble over the Old Ones' leftovers. Where they built and made each other stronger as they built. Where the little ones ate first, and the smart and the strong protected. Peace through strength.

No one else can do this. No one else is ruthless enough, no one else as terrible. Tommy sees those things about himself that once he thought of as weapons and realizes: *They allow me to build. To protect.*

When Piss Ant lived under the rowboat, he slept in the middle of the day so he scavenged at night when the Preps and Jocks were asleep. One morning he thrashed himself awake in a nightmare, slammed into the boat's wooden wall. A scrabbling in the dirt, and a scorpion emerged from under the hull where it touched the ground. *A mother*, Piss Ant thought, carrying twenty pale babies on its wide cruel back. *They're so helpless without her.*

Tommy will carry the little ones on his back. He will fight the birds and lizards that threaten them. In return, Ell Aye will follow him. Love him.

If not?

If not, he has his sting.

CHAPTER FIFTY-THREE
THE TWO QUEENS

The mountains surrounding the Holy Wood are an oasis, both from the ruins of Ell Aye and for the war that Tashia knows awaits them on all sides. The fighting will come, but right now she takes in the view stretching all the way to the glittering sea.

After four days with the Downtown, Trina invited Tashia back to the Holy Wood, where her people are Gathering food and medsen before the Biters attack. Tashia has never seen so many plants in one place. The hills are carpeted by oaks and chaparral. Tashia looks along the mountaintop trail where she and Trina are hiking, and sees tall white letters nearly scraping the top of a wide peak.

"I've seen that before," Tashia says. "In old books."

"That's the Holy Wood sign," Trina says. "That's how we know we home."

X is back in the Downtown's stadio training the Angelenos to fight the Biters. The soldiers escorting them—Muscle, she remembers—are walking a dozen steps ahead of them, so she finds herself talking to Trina alone for the first time.

Trina still hasn't agreed to help her take back the Kingdom, and the other Oldest seem to be waiting for her to decide. So the two queens have been circling each other since. Tashia can sense Trina is even more queen than she is, even if she isn't called one. There's a difference between being the first girl to rule her people and being one in a long line of rulers. Trina knows she belongs, so she owns it in a way that Tashia can't yet.

"So you know Jemma and Lady," Trina says.

"Jemma and Lady and Pico," Tashia says.

"The Exile. He knew how to read," Trina says. "What'd you think of Jemma?"

"You don't like her," Tashia says. It just comes through in Trina's voice.

"Eh. Pendeja thought she was somethin special," Trina says.

Tashia hesitates before answering. "Hate to break it to you, honey, but I think the 'pendeja' probably was." She tells Trina how Jemma beat the best Knight in the Kingdom, how she killed the Giant, how she lit up the Night Mountain with Lectrics. How she left with Grease and headed south through the Dead Lands.

Trina looks surprised, but not as much as Tashia thought she would. "You know Pilar has visions, right? They come from something called the Haze. Feels like magic, but she thinks it come from the Parents. Pilar thinks Jemma has the Haze, but maybe stronger."

"It was like the Grown-Ups came back," Tashia says.

"Where did she go?"

"To chase down the End," Tashia says. She's heard that Trina outlived the End with the help of her friends, but she hasn't known how to ask about it. It seems as private as a birthmark, something carried just below the collar of your shirt.

"Four of the strangest kids in Ell Aye, tryin to fix the End," Trina says. "Mebbe there's somethin to it. I never woulda thought so, before, until I—"

"Until you didn't," Tashia says. "How'd you do it?"

Trina shrugs. "Pilar used her powers to help, but mostly I just din't want to. I think the Haze makes us End. But this time we told it not to. Maybe Jemma and her friends could do it for everyone."

"Well, you should show me that trick," Tashia says.

"If we live that long, I will," Trina says. Tashia grunts in agreement.

The trail they're on cuts close to the tops of the hills, and when they round an outcropping of rock Tashia sees the valley on the other side. There's a wide plain dotted with trees below them, broken by a church's white steeple.

"That's the old boneyard," Trina says.

Tashia looks closer, and sees marble statues popping up from the brush, of Parents hugging their children. She's about to ask about them when she hears distant hooves. A herd of maybe thirty horses burst into view, led by a stallion painted in black and white. Tashia feels a pang of home.

"You have horses?" Tashia says. "Why we walking, then?"

"They kinda like pests. Eat our crops. We hunt them," Trina says.

Tashia shakes her head. "Hunting? Jesus."

"They can feed a whole village," Trina says.

"They can do even more if you can break them," Tashia says. "I'll teach you. If we live that long."

"Fair enough." The horses pass out of view.

"We can both survive," Tashia says. "If we help each other."

"Maybe," Trina says. "Just tryin to see what it's gonna cost us."

The trail twists, and Tashia can see fingers of a blue lake set in the hills. It's surrounded by fields and houses, all tucked safely high above the valley floor. Off to her left, Tashia can still see the towers of Downtown. Tashia misses her Kingdom but part of her would gladly retreat into these hills and never leave.

"I know," Trina says.

Tashia looks down and sees Children moving below them in a village. The only thing that protects them is a tall metal fence. "That's your wall?" Tashia says. "Biters will slice right through that."

"It ain't meant to hold them out. Just lions and a few Last Lifers," Trina says.

"You ain't meant for war. That's why you need us," Tashia says.

"What would you need?"

"Maybe a hundred soldiers," Tashia says.

"And leave us unprotected with the Biters coming."

"Fifty, maybe," Tashia says. "The Kingdom would rise against Othello if they saw them."

"I bet they will," Trina says. "But you want em to?"

"What do you mean?"

"Othello's got all your weapons. He got your horses. That means your people gonna be fightin on foot."

"With ropes and pitchforks, while Othello has thunder guns," Tashia says, realizing what she means. "We could win—but we could lose everyone."

"You the Queen now," Trina says. "You want your Kingdom back, but you gotta keep em safe first. I found that out too late. When I come back to the Holy Wood I was ready to tear down the walls, but I din't want to hurt my people. So I talked to them instead."

Tashia is grateful and embarrassed for the advice. She looks out at the towers of Ell Aye, wondering what to say next.

"Besides, we gon need your help for the next fight," Trina says.

"The Battle of Ell Aye," Tashia says.

Trina seems to make up her mind. "I'll help you. We just gotta figure a way that don't risk both of our peoples."

"What about you?" Tashia says. "What's your plan to fight the Biters if I can't bring you an army?"

"There's too many of em, and they better fighters," Trina says. "But we gonna be safe with the Downtown."

Tashia understands the Biters better than that. "Doesn't matter how thick you make your walls," Tashia says. "Get enough Biters out there and they're going to find their way in. You have to cut back their numbers before they get to you. Pick em off as they come in."

Trina says, "There's a whole city they gonna be going through. What we supposed to do, guard it all?"

The answer comes to Tashia quickly. She can picture the Biters squeezed into city canyons, with arrows raining down on all sides. "Not all of it," Tashia says. "Herd them."

"We don't got cows here," Trina says. "Explain."

"I'll show you when we get back to the Downtown," Tashia says. A flash of light from Downtown catches her eye, and she thinks of Alfie's mirrors. Then she thinks of the horses running, and solves her own problem. She doesn't need to get into the Kingdom. She needs the Kingdom to come to her.

CHAPTER FIFTY-FOUR
THE COMING WAR

Pico can't stop thinking about Little Man, not after Jemma's vision. That the little shit Tommy was also Little Man meant he is pretty alive.

It also meant that Little Man is likely to come hunting for his people, the Malibus, soon enough.

You don't have a people, Pico thinks. *Your people hated you.*

But that's not true. He had a people from the moment Jemma saved him and the moment Lady called him a name. You make your own people.

Pico corners James at the bow of the ship. Lady follows him, as she has the past few days. She has been half of herself since she stopped the Reboot. Her memory is mostly back, but she isn't. She seems to be half asleep. Pico likes having her with him even though she's changed. Mostly, he misses the insults.

Lady listens quietly while Pico tells James of Little Man, who can do all the things the three of them can do together. Tommy can read as well as Pico, handle machines as well as Grease, use the Haze almost as well as Jemma—all while being insane.

"Fascinating," James says. "Perhaps we should invite him here." They jut so far out over the water on the ship's nose that Pico feels as if he's been dropped into the open air, into the middle of the sunset.

"I think he's gonna come soon enough," Pico says.

"I can see the havoc someone like Little Man would create in your world," James says.

"In *the* world, James. Not just ours," Pico says. "You don't think he'll come after the Old Guys?"

"We're in an aircraft carrier," James says, as if that answers everything. "Look, none of this is new. The time since the End has been one of power grabs and purges. When the adults died, the children withdrew to their neighborhoods, their safe streets and their social structures. The fragmentation and die-off began almost immediately. At one point, we estimated, there were more than three hundred individual communities in Southern California. Within ten years, it had dropped to fifty."

"Why?" Pico says, although he knows.

Lady speaks up. Pico didn't think she'd been listening. "One bad winter. One month of bad Gathers. One bad flu. That's all it takes," she says.

She would know better than he would, as a Gatherer. Not for the first time, Pico realizes how much of their world has been built upon the leavings of the Parents. But now he wonders: What will happen when those are all gone in the next few years?

"So they died?" Pico says.

"Some of them died out. Some of them were swallowed up."

"By the bigger peoples."

"By the better organized. The End required a different kind of strength, a more organized kind of society, and most of the kids in the world weren't ready for it. Those that succeeded were the ones who were more cohesive."

"What?" Pico says.

"The ones who could stick together. Your friends at the Kingdom were descended from gangs, which had members as young as nine or ten. When the End came, they were already disciplined and ready to face outside threats. Your Angelenos were first- or second-generation immigrants, which meant they were closer knit. And you had the good sense to put the girls in charge, which avoids the worst of the adolescent surges."

Maybe. Pico thinks of the years being pushed to the edges because he was a boy who thought. He looks at Lady next to him and thinks of how they tried to punish her for being raped by Li. But he's seen enough of the Biters and the Kingdom to know it could be worse.

"So now you are down to five or six major civilizations in Los Angeles, as distinct from each other as we used to be from other countries. And the cannibals want those to be even fewer."

"Did you know about the Biters before you found us?" Lady says, perking up.

"We'd heard strange things, almost immediately after the End," James says. "So many taboos fell, so many barriers broke, but even by those standards these stories were awful. We heard them for decades, and then we witnessed it for ourselves. We traded with a tribe in Laguna up to about fifty years ago, for clay and fish and oysters. The Lagunas had coexisted with the Newports for years. One month we went to trade with them, and there was nothing but bodies. Some of them partially . . ."

Pico doesn't make him finish. Pico knows the rest of the sentence.

"Why them? Were they . . . organized?"

"No, not particularly, not at first. Just a bunch of rich kids in the hills," James says. "They were different. Their power seemed to come from believing the world belonged to them in the first place. That they were simply better than the rest."

"You didn't stop them?" Pico thinks what they could have done with their big guns, their ULVs and Humvees.

"Oh, Pico," James says, sadder than he has seen him. "When will you learn that we haven't the power to stop anything? We're not fighters."

"Neither were the Lagunas," Pico says. "The Biters got guns. They got trained warriors and they got numbers. They got a smart and dangerous kid in charge."

If James's skin were transparent, Pico's sure he would be able to see the thoughts swirling around his face in great clouds: concern, fear, thoughtfulness. It's Lady who breaks through, finally. "James, you keep on talking about the End of the world, as if it's only happened once already and it's never gonna happen again," she says, glaring at him. "But there's all kinds of ends. You don't get it right, your Long Life Machine ain't gonna get a chance to go out in the world."

"We've always thought that we had to keep the world separate," James says slowly.

"The world is coming for you whether you want it there or not," Lady says.

"Okay," James says, understanding. "We'll help. Let's get the Long Life Machine running first, but we'll help."

Pico looks at Lady and smiles. He counted wrong when he counted just three Mayflies against Tommy. Lady is their fourth, and she can break a mountain with those eyes.

CHAPTER FIFTY-FIVE
THE ASSAULT ON THE ARK

"After all this, it doesn't work," James says, looking down at the Long Life Machine hopelessly. They've been working on the machine for weeks, but he's been working on it for a century. "Maybe we've forgotten something from before. Maybe we're losing our touch."

"It's mapped to the brain," Pico says.

"And it's synced up to the Haze," Grease says. "They should be able to communicate with each other—in fact, we can see currents flowing back and forth."

"So the problem must be with the Haze," Isaac says. "For the life of me, I can't figure out exactly what."

Jemma slowly notices everyone looking at her. "What?" she says. "I don't know what's wrong with it."

"Not to be a jerk, mija," Lady says, "but that's kinda the reason you're here."

"Pendeja," Jemma mutters. For a moment she's annoyed that the old Lady is coming back. "Fine. Let me think."

She looks at the Machine, and nothing occurs to her. Her connection to the Lectrics is instinctive. It's only made possible through the Haze. But that's her answer, isn't it?

"We gotta ask the Haze," Jemma says. Everyone reacts with puzzlement, but Isaac nods.

"That's going to work a lot better coming from you," Isaac says.

She focuses on the Haze she can see moving around the Long Life Machine. *Why aren't you Pairing? We need you to survive.*

A flurry of images comes back to her, and it takes her a long time to sort them out. Then she smiles. "They don't want to," she says.

"What? That's their job," James says.

"The Haze around us now isn't the same as it was," Jemma says. "It ain't mindless bugs no more. It's got experience and its own sorta thoughts. Charlie's been controlling it a hundred years, and it's sick of it. It ain't gonna allow its bots to be controlled again by just anyone."

"Would it do it if you asked it to?" James says.

"It might," Jemma says. "If I ask nicely."

"Let's do that, then," Lady says. Hope washes through the room. The end of the End is in sight.

Until Athena bursts into the room. "The harbor's filled with sails," she says.

They run through the hangar to an oval opening overlooking the bay to the south. Jemma looks down at a bay aglow. It's filled with Biter boats.

There must be thirty of them, each with a fire lit in kettles on the deck. The flames fill the sails with light, and the boats glow on the water like lanterns. It's the most beautiful death she's ever seen.

"Little Man," she says, then turns to James. "You got a plan for defending us?"

James winces. "We've generally assumed we're safe from full-on assault." They see ropes with hooks flying past them toward the deck, hear distant clanks where they catch hold. Below they can see the tattooed arms of Biters climbing.

"You sure bout that?" Lady says.

"Not as much as I was five minutes ago," James says.

"Grab a gun and get to the flight deck. We'll be able to fight them better," Isaac says.

They don't bother with the Levator, clanging up the metal stairs. Any moment they expect the flaming arrows to start raining. All the

Mayflies have been through these attacks before. "At least the ship is metal," Lady says.

When they get to the top, they see that some of the attackers have already climbed over the lip of the ship, mostly on the bow and the stern. Jemma's not sure how long the attackers have been climbing in order to make it that distance without their noticing. The Biters are standing, bows drawn. But no one is moving.

"Why ain't they firing?" Pico says.

"There's Li," she says in a low voice, as if she's spotted a snake.

More and more attackers climb to the deck, but James motions for the Mayflies to avoid firing. "I don't want to kill anyone unnecessarily," he says.

"They're *Biters*," Pico says.

Jemma scans the line of Biters for the familiar tiny shape. The fact that he's not there bothers her. It doesn't seem like him to miss bloodshed.

"The Long Life Machine," Jemma says. "We left it unprotected."

Little Man wouldn't have done this, Tommy says as he stares into the black depths between him and the ship that he's about to dive into. But, he reminds himself, Little Man didn't win very many battles.

His ears, sharpened by the Haze, hear the splash of oars along the side of the massive ship. If anyone expected their attack, they would expect it from the boats. They won't expect it under the water.

The Haze showed him how to enter the ship, how to crack it open like an oyster. The ship rests against the shore, a seam split open where it struck the ground. It's only a foot wide and it's under the waterline, but it will take them into the place where he knows he'll find the Long Life Machine.

The first Last Lifer, the one who will be securing the guideline, enters the water before him. They all volunteered to come with him. He decided to go with them, because they needed someone to follow.

Little Man wouldn't have put himself at risk before, but Tommy sees the need to inspire.

Some of them, it turns out, are good swimmers. They dove for abalone among the Malibus before the Last Life took them, and before Little Man brought them back. Roberto can hold his breath for three minutes. He showed Little Man how to hold his breath for two.

But Tommy won't need to hold his breath. He needed a steady source of air, so he found a Long Gone garden hose, maybe seventy-five feet long. It's coiled neatly on the shore, and Tommy picks up the end. He breathes through it, and the Last Lifer who's remaining on the shore gives him a thumbs-up.

Tommy steps into the ocean. It's even colder than he expected. He goes under the surface. It's so cold that for a minute he forgets to breathe, so dark that he can't find up. His gasps echo back through the hose. He has to remind himself that he's breathing.

"You got this," the Last Lifer says. Tommy doesn't hear it so much as feel it through the hose. He paddles forward, pulling the wall into his fingertips. He brushes through moss, the snag of barnacles, and then the pitted metal. Below the surface, the salt has been allowed to corrode the steel. The ship will dissolve below the waterline, maybe in another twenty years.

He grabs the guideline and reaches for the crack. There it is, rusted jaggy edges knobbier from the barnacles. He dives through the opening. It doesn't seem big enough for a kid, not even a kid like him. Tommy feels the weight of all the water above him. Maybe he should have stayed on the boat.

He turns sideways. The metal pulls at his shirt. He moves slowly so there's no chance of a cut, no chance of fection. He's through. He's trying to breathe through the hose, trying not to hold his breath.

Inside, the ship feels warmer. Tommy floats his way across the room, following the guideline. He notices that his breaths are getting shorter, quicker, more ragged. The water in the next room is stale. It hasn't moved in years. He can taste it around the mouth. It's darker, too. He finds a door quickly by staying on the guideline, but he can't see the Last Lifer he sent ahead. *Shouldn't we be at the end by now?* he thinks. He can't remember the path the Haze told him, not with less oxygen in his brain. His breaths get even shorter.

Don't panic, Tommy. He doesn't panic easily. But he's never been buried under water, under a million tons of metal.

Beyond this room is a long hall. It's dark except for a blob of red light, weak but visible, at the far end. He can't make it out because the light is so dim, but there should be a ladder.

He pushes away from the door and glides down the hall, the hose trailing behind him. The red light grows stronger, so it feels like he's floating through a red sea. It's like being in the Haze. The light will be from the level above, where there's air. Any moment the ladder will be in front of—

The hose jerks short. His hand slips off it and then his mouth and then a sharp burst of air leaves his lungs all at once and there's no hose and no air anymore. No air. Barely a breath or two inside him. He lunges after the giant bubble of air, even though he knows he can't breathe it in.

He reaches for the hose, but the buoyancy of the water won't let him just reach down. He has to dive toward the floor, holding both hands out blindly. They brush through the muck, maybe even touch the floor but not the hose. He dives again. Nothing.

How close is death now? Only his lips keep it away. It's all he can do to keep from opening his mouth and just letting the sea in. One breath. Two. *Help me*, he calls out in desperation into the Haze.

Through the Haze, through the red, he hears the Last Lifer stir, and turn. *Hold still*, the response comes, and then there are hands around him and he's kicking hard toward the ladder and up and up until he's out on a cold steel floor coughing and puking.

"You saved my life," he says to the Last Lifer when he can breathe.

"You saving ours, too," the Last Lifer says.

"I'm doing my best," he says.

They wait, shivering, for the other divers to come along the unbroken line. The divers tow waterproof plastic boxes, weighed with stones to keep them below the surface, and filled with guns.

The Long Life Machine is somewhere above. "Remember what I said," Tommy says. "Don't shoot anyone."

"Unless they shoot first?" one Last Lifer says.

"Unless I tell you to," Tommy says.

They climb up the stairs quietly. He hears shouts up above, even Li's strangely high voice. Good. The boats are drawing everyone to the flight deck.

So he's a little surprised to see Jemma and a boy waiting for him at the Long Life Machine, both carrying guns. She's even more surprised. She swivels as if to fire, and then lowers her gun. She seems to realize it would be good to negotiate with him, even dripping wet. It helps to have behind him a dozen Last Lifers, also dripping, but carrying very dry guns.

Isaac isn't sure what to make of their tiny assailant. He seems too small to hurt anyone. But the guns his soldiers hold tell Isaac he should take Little Man seriously.

"Easy, Little Man," Isaac says.

"It's Tommy," the kid says.

"Same diff," Jemma says.

Little Man turns to her. "I'm not here to hurt anyone, Jemma," he says. "You gotta believe me. I'm here to join forces with you."

"I fell for your bullshit once, Tommy," she says. "I ain't doin it."

"We both serve the Haze," he says. "It says I'm supposed to work with you to fight the End."

"You only serve your murdering little self," Jemma says.

Little Man turns to Isaac, says: "I've seen you in the Haze. Tell me about the Long Life Machine."

"I don't know anything about that," Isaac says, stalling.

"We both know that's not true," Little Man says. "You've been waiting for it to get fixed."

"This is way out of your league, Little Man," Isaac says. "You're only here to destroy it."

The kid looks mad. "I am trying *really* hard here, people," he says. "We want the same things. We want the End to stop. We want the Children to survive. I can increase the chances of both."

Isaac glances around at the Angelenos, looking for guidance. *Don't trust him*, Jemma's face says. All their faces say the same thing. "I'm sorry, my friend," Isaac says. "I don't think we're on the same side."

"I . . . wish you felt differently, but it can't be helped," Little Man says. Isaac knows he's saying it to be impressive, but he also thinks it might be true. He seems to resolve himself. "Let's explore a couple of other options. I could probably force you to show me how it works, but it might take me a while to get the knack. I could also kill you and count on extra motivation from the rest of the old people."

Three of the Last Lifers slide into position behind Isaac, guns drawn. Isaac braces himself. "Fire," Little Man says, but their triggers freeze. Isaac's mind has shut them off at the last minute. Little Man laughs. "I really shoulda seen that coming," he says.

The puzzled Last Lifers stand in the middle of a tug of war, as their fingers pull and twitch beyond their control. That's when Isaac notices a red dot on the middle Last Lifer, and then on the chests of the Last Lifers on both sides.

There's a single blast, multiple shots grouped so close together they sound almost like just one. The three Last Lifers drop to the floor, and everyone else looks around in bewilderment.

Isaac knows who it has to be. He's so glad to see her that he uses the name he hasn't used in half a century. "Mom," he says.

It's Alice and her followers at the Camp. Alice tilts up green goggles like James's, and peers at them all over the sight of her rifle. "Okay, so there's my son," she says. "Has anyone seen my husband?"

CHAPTER FIFTY-SIX
THE OLD GUYS AND LITTLE MAN

The Old Guy named Alice marches them up the stairs. Tommy climbs silently, counting the number of soldiers he still has. Probably eighty. But he doesn't hear anyone firing.

"How'd you know they were coming?" Isaac says.

"We saw them a day ago. On our satellites, and just plain old eyesight. We tried to warn you over the radio, but you wouldn't answer because your dad was having his little snit," Alice says. "Just once, I would love it if you'd pick up when I call."

On the top, about half of Tommy's soldiers are corralled between a plane and a chopper, guarded by about twenty tough-looking Old Guys. His other soldiers are somewhere else. Good. Roberto's on a mission of his own.

Also at the top is an old man he recognizes. The one he saw in his first vision of Jemma. He looks drained. The old lady and the old kid kneel next to him.

"How you doing, James?" she says, and she brushes the skin of the old man's neck where he must have been grazed with a bullet. Tommy's soldiers must have panicked and gotten off a few shots before the other Old Guys intervened. The blood looks like it's stopped already.

"Dad," Isaac says, and chokes.

They're older than they should be, but Tommy recognizes the Parent in them, the Child in Isaac. He recognizes how the world should fit. This moment, between parents and the kid they've sworn to help survive—Tommy realizes it's essential to everything.

Once she's sure everyone is okay, Alice turns to him. "We've heard a lot about you, Little Man," she says. "And if we're hearing about it, it's guaranteed to be unpleasant."

"I'm not here to hurt you," Tommy says.

"Yeah? Why'd you show up with a navy?" Lady says.

"I knew you were armed, and not likely to let a fleet of cannibals take over," Tommy says. "I didn't want to get shot before I could get a look at the Long Life Machine."

"I have to admit, I am curious about your reasoning," James says. "This doesn't sound like anything I've heard about you."

"I'm here for the End. I want to understand how to defeat it. You're the only people who can teach me," Tommy says. "I created a half victory over the End, and—it ain't enough. The Long Life Machine is the only way. If I'm going to help humanity live through what's next, I gotta know more."

"Well, we—" Alice says.

"Bullshit," James says. "As someone who's used 'I'm gonna go save the world' a few times, I can tell you it's not true. You tell yourself it's to help others, but really it's to feed your ego, your ambition. Your need to be admired." He casts a quick look at his wife and son.

"Please," Tommy says. He pretends to plead but realizes he really is pleading. "What do I gotta do to show you I'm being real?"

"Nothing," Pico says. "You don't get the benefit of the doubt when you're the leader of a tribe of Biters."

"Ah. That. We can't help where we're born, can we?" Tommy says. "Look around you. There are brown soldiers mixing with white soldiers. No one's missing a single ear. The Chosen you see are very different from the ones you knew and feared, and that's because of me."

For a moment he almost has them, sees the faces waver. Until Pico says, "Just . . . part of the show."

I'd like to kill that kid, Tommy thinks, then reminds himself: *Not right now. You're trying to make a point.*

"I'll make you all a deal," Tommy says. "The old people promise to teach me what they know, and I'll negotiate surrenders with the Angelenos and the Kingdom instead of attacking them."

"We can't negotiate on behalf of the Children," James says. "This is their decision."

"And the Children tell you to go fuck yourself, pendejo," Lady says to Tommy. "The Kingdom isn't going to be part of anything you do." Tommy looks at her closely and realizes she's changed. She's taller, more square. More sure of herself.

"Okay, then," he says. His next option is the selfish one, the one that gets him what he needs even if it means abandoning all the people who follow him. He says it quietly.

"Take me in. Teach me what you know. That's all."

"You gotta speak up," Pico says. "Some of us don't speak asshole."

"Take me in, and I'll help you stop the End. That's all. I will abandon the war."

"He doesn't mean it," Pico says.

"I do," Tommy says. "I've been afraid of my death as long as I've been alive. I would do anything to find a way past it."

He looks around, and he doesn't see a single friendly face among them. Jemma's voice breaks the silence. She was the one who wanted to kill him the night they captured him. Only Lady's intervention saved him. Tommy waits for his fate.

"He's telling the truth," Jemma says. "The Haze is telling me so."

"People can hide things in the Haze," Isaac says.

"Not this," Jemma says, and there's warmth mixed in with wariness. "I can see it all over him. He's serving the Haze."

Tommy sighs. He didn't realize how much he wants to lay the burden down, the burden of all the people who hate him but still need him to survive in this world.

James stands up with his wife and son, slowly. "Tell any of your soldiers still holding weapons to put them down," he says.

Tommy calls out the order, and he hears it ripple along the deck of the Ark like a whispering wave. More and more soldiers lay down their guns.

I can make peace, too, he thinks.

But Li doesn't put down his gun. Li lifts it up to his shoulder. He squeezes the trigger, and James goes down.

That cracks everything open. A storm of gunfire rings out, and half the ship seems to fall. He doesn't know who's dead and who's just seeking cover. His army is boiling out of its secret places, pounding up stairways to the deck to join the battle. All things he told them to be ready to do. But only as a last resort.

A bullet strikes the chopper over his head, and Tommy flattens against the pavement. He crawls on his belly toward midship. *Get to the Long Life Machine*, he thinks. *Maybe there's still time.*

Lady and Pico dive under the shelter of a skyplane on deck when the arrows and bullets start. A bullet clangs over her head, and she ducks. That one came from what's left of the Old Guys.

"Putos! We on your side!" she says.

She looks back at Pico, who's smiling at her.

"You got a problem, Exile?" she says, and he smiles more.

"You awake," he says.

"Huh," she says. She is. "I missed you," she blurts out. She's surprised to say it.

The shots get closer. "We gotta get below," she says. She spots a hatch that will take them down to the hangar. A ladder travels down the inside of the hull. They reach the bottom.

"He's gonna go for the Long Life Machine," she says.

"We don't got weapons," Pico says.

"You only say that cuz you don't know my new body," she says.

They run into four Biters in the darkness, disoriented in the middle of the ship. Three of them are on the floor in moments. She picks up a lance and realizes the fourth Biter is gone—along with Pico.

"Fuck," she says, and runs through the hangar in the direction she prays he's gone. She rounds a skyplane. And finds herself face-to-face with Li.

His smile still leers from the cut Jemma gave him, lopsided and terrible. It's more terrible when it's behind the thunder gun he carries. This is the smile she went through the Reboot to forget.

"Li," Lady says, to keep him from pulling the trigger.

"I don't even remember your name," he says. "I'm just gonna call you the one that ain't hot."

"We keep on thinking you'd have Ended by now," she says. "Figures—no one lasts but the roaches."

"Is this the machine Little Man wants?" Li says, peering into the glowing box of the room.

"Yeah, it is," Lady says. "It could save us from the End."

For a moment Li is wistful, black eyes shining with a little reflected light. He turns toward her and says, "No one gets away from the End." He pulls the trigger.

And in that moment . . .

In that moment, she stops him.

She doesn't know when she does it, but she does. Maybe the training she's done with Isaac and Jemma with the Haze gave her the right instincts. Somehow she hears Li tell his finger to fire. Lady reaches into the air, flexes imaginary fingers. She presses into Li's spine . . . and squeezes.

Li freezes. Only his eyes move, enough to show her the fear and confusion behind them. Only his heart beats. But nothing else.

"Well, now I'm intrigued," Little Man says from the darkness. "The Haze didn't tell me you were Touched."

He walks closer. Lady's not sure what to do. If she switches her attention to Little Man, she might lose her hold on Li. And Li is a thousand times more deadly. She lets Little Man approach.

"Have you been working on this?" Little Man says to Lady. "I don't think I woulda thought of freezing someone."

"It just happened," Lady says.

He circles around Li, poking at the rigid flesh. "It's not that hard, I guess. Just tell the Haze that nothing's supposed to move, and they block the signals from the brain to the body. Wonder if it does more?"

Little Man motions with his palm downward, and Li sinks to the floor unwillingly. "You're too tall," Little Man says. "One of many things I don't like about you."

Lady tries to fight Tommy's interference, but she doesn't know enough about the Haze. She barely knows how she managed this.

Another twitch from Little Man, and both of Li's arms are joined in a praying gesture.

"I can't believe I didn't kill you sooner," Little Man says as gunshots echo through the ship. "Now all this. That's on me for going soft." He squeezes his hand and Li gasps for breath.

"Tommy. Don't hurt him. Save him for me," Lady says, not sure if she's saving Li or killing him. She has yet to decide.

Little Man looks at her, uncomprehending. Lady was the one who argued to save Tommy when they first captured him, so perhaps he has some good will meant for her still.

"You have nothing to do with this," Tommy says.

"I got more than anyone to do . . . with this," she says.

Maybe it's the Haze that tells him. Maybe it's the conversations he overheard between Jemma and Lady, when they didn't think anyone could hear. Hell, maybe Li bragged about it. But somehow, he knows. Something changes. He goes from being small to terrible in moments.

"You hurt her," Tommy says to Li. "You hurt her and you thought I would let you fight with me?" Lady watches the shadows play over his face, the memories churning past. Whatever is in there, it's about Tommy. It's not about her. That makes her angry. He doesn't get to punish. Only Lady gets to punish.

"Stand back," Lady says, pushing Tommy back with her mind, breaking his hold. "I will handle this."

She stands over Li, and remembers his shape looming above her, blotting out the light. She thinks of how he ruined babies and her body and her belief in herself. She thinks of how many steps it took to get to here.

"You afraid," she says to Li. "You afraid of death, you afraid of life. You're afraid that what I got between my legs is bigger than yours. You are right to be afraid. Tell me I'm right."

She releases his tongue and he says, "You right."

But it's not right. He's helpless and she's looming over him. She wants to End him as she always has. But she wants to do it in battle. She wants him to fear the sword dropping from the sky above him, to know that she's a better warrior. That she is stronger and always has been. She lets him go.

"Get up, Li," she says. "I will give you ten steps head start. Then I'm going to hunt you down."

But Li is still paralyzed. Tommy is holding Li in place, looking like a frightened little kid.

"How could you hurt her?" Tommy says. "She used to be so small."

As Lady watches, a red seam opens on Li's throat, as if drawn across by a knife. There is no knife. Just Tommy. Lady should stop him, she knows, but she feels paralyzed, too.

Tommy kneels down in front of Li, smiling. "Nobody will miss you. At all."

The seam bursts open, and Li's neck gurgles with blood. She can't believe there's so much in him. It's as if Tommy is pumping it out, which he might be. The black eyes cloud, and Li slumps to the floor.

Lady sits down next to Li and feels nothing. She should be angry. She should be vindicated. Instead, she just watches Li bleed into the metal. She looks up at the boy she once saved. "You cost me a good death, Tommy," she says.

"All deaths are bad," Tommy says. "That's why I'm the one to give them."

CHAPTER FIFTY-SEVEN
THE LAST PARENTS

Little Man doesn't remember when Lady left him. He remembers picking up Li's machine gun, remembers them running. But for a moment he's alone and shaking on the hangar floor. He climbs to his feet and staggers, once again, toward the Long Life Machine. Toward life.

Alice is slumped against the glass wall outside the door, without a weapon. Her face looks badly burned. "This entrance is closed for the day," she says.

He smiles. "What were you gonna do? Blow it up?" he says. "It's a little too late for that."

"No," she says. "I already have."

He looks at the burns on her face, healing but not quickly. "What did you do, old woman?"

"You see, Little Man—" she says, then stops. "Sorry, I refuse to use that name. What did your mother call you?"

"Nobody called me anything," he says. "I named myself Tommy."

He reads pity in her face. Normally he despises pity, but tonight he needs it. "My oldest son was a Tommy," she says, wistfully, then shakes her head as if to clear the fog. "Well, Tommy, the Long Life Treatment requires an inordinate amount of power. The only place left on this earth that can run it is this ship, because it was powered with a nuclear reactor. I know you know what that is. It runs smoothly, almost in perpetuity—unless you remove one of these rods." Next to her thigh is a long cylinder.

"Clearly, that's not in there anymore, which means the reactor is heading toward a meltdown in a matter of minutes," she says. "You won't see an explosion, I don't think, but it can never be repaired. And this place will be radioactive for dozens of years, long after you've given up trying to pillage weapons and tech."

"Why would you do that?" he says.

"I've seen a lot of well-intentioned people fall into temptation for this kind of power. I doubt you'd be the one to resist it. I'm not letting you take evil out into the world," she says. "Besides, it's time for this experiment to run its course."

"You don't know what you've done," Little Man says.

"I do. I've doomed my son, too," she says, as if she's second-guessing her actions. "Can you believe it? I'm the Rebekah in the Isaac story, but I'm the one who sacrificed him."

"I don't know that story," Little Man says.

"Doesn't matter," Alice says. "I think I fucked up the telling."

Little Man kicks the rod out of her way and picks it up. "I can put it back," he says. "I'm good with machines."

"No, dear, you can't. I was able to go into the reactor to retrieve it because my body can heal itself. Although, as you can see, not fully in this case. We never factored in a face full of radiation. You *might* be able to get the rod back in time, assuming you could figure it out, and assuming you're comfortable with the fact that you'd be dead within a week."

He drops his eyes. Death terrifies him too much to voluntarily take part in it. Alice nods. "Not for you, is it? It's hard to sacrifice oneself. I'm not sure I would have done it myself, if I hadn't been so damn tired."

Little Man slumps against the wall next to Alice. He's so damn tired, too. Behind him is the machine that could have saved them all. Now it's destroyed, despite his best intentions. Because he always brings evil with him.

"I didn't mean it," he says. "I wasn't going to."

"I know, dear," Alice says, closing her eyes. "That's what we said."

Isaac follows the trail of blood to his father's body resting among the rows of summer squash. Jemma is already there, talking to it. *Okay, so it's not a body yet.*

He saw the bullet that entered James's gut. He felt it as if it had been fired at his own. And the first thought he had was: *It still hurts to lose a Parent.* Even after a hundred years with them, it still hurts.

Jemma is tying up James's torso, but blood spurts through the cloth. James's face is pale, composed, as if he's holding it together just for show. "Don't worry about me."

"I wasn't worried about you," she says. "You can't die."

His laugh catches.

He sees Isaac and motions him closer. "The Ark's finished," he says. "You need to get Jemma to Charlie."

"James," Isaac says, "the Long Life Machine is undamaged."

"By the kid, maybe," James says, "but I saw your mom going down below. I don't think she went down there to grab my laundry."

Isaac reaches out into the Haze and asks to see his mom. He gets his usual flurry of images, but the Haze is restless, almost distraught, and he can't focus it on one image. Finally he calms the Haze down by getting the nano to match his heartbeat, and he sees the picture he needed. Alice's face is an open wound, and she's slumped against the window of the Long Life Machine. He feels the nanotech, racing to knit together threads of flesh, to flush out the radiation, but it can't keep pace. *We can't save her,* the bots say.

"Did you see her?" James says.

"Yeah, I did," Isaac says. "She pulled out the reactor's rod. But she's okay." The lie comes easily because Isaac wants to believe it himself.

"Good. When you see her, tell her—tell her that she almost made the End worth it."

"I will," Isaac says, and feels a part of him close off. *Mom.*

"What's the point of your treatment if it don't stop the End?" Jemma says, looking down at the blood draining from the wound, flowing between her fingers.

"It was never meant to outrun a bullet," Isaac says. No, not bullets or nuclear reactors or the anger of the children they abandoned.

"It's all been for nothing," James says. "Everything we thought we could force on the world. It's just you two, now."

"Dad," Isaac says, and thinks back to when he first called him that. Isaac was fifty-three. He had been through four Betterments already, had clawed his way back to life four times. He had decided that was it for him. He'd End like a Child.

He left the Camp. The Malibus took him in, although they shouldn't have—his pale skin looked suspiciously like a Palo's. He joined the Muscle. He learned to fish. He found a girl. He built the life that he should have lived, if he had been someone else's kid.

Dolores had Ended first, wrapped in his arms, and his End started hours later when he was most grateful for it. Some Betterments last for hours, some for days. This was the latter. He tumbled in and out of consciousness, fell between the molecules of the Haze tinged with gold. For whatever reason, the Haze always showed itself gold at the End.

In the middle of his dying, he realized he wanted to live. He called out to his dad, because his dad had always been the one to come when he woke in the middle of the night. Isaac felt the Haze, eager to listen, eager to pass the message along. *Help me*, he said.

On his last day on earth, his father came. He found Isaac in the middle of the Malibus, brought him back to the Camp and healed him. Isaac remembers his father's tireless shoulders lifting him out of bed. He remembers James shrugging off the stares of the Malibus as he carried Isaac through the village. He remembers never forgiving James for saving him, because Isaac had been too cowardly to die.

"You're going to have to take the ULV," James says.

"But, Dad—"

"Take it slow if you can, recharge it on the way. Maybe it'll be enough for you to get back out."

"Okay," Isaac says.

"Dad," Isaac says again. Wishing for a hundred more years.

James seems to clear his head with a shake. "You're the answers. The two of you," he says. "You're something entirely new. If the world lives, it'll be because of you."

Isaac looks at Jemma, briefly, then looks away because his eyes are filling with tears. He can't see his father for a moment, can just feel him at the end of his fingers.

"I didn't believe death would finally catch me," James says. "What does it feel like, to die?"

Isaac tells him how the molecules of the Haze come drifting down and how the body's molecules start drifting up to meet them. He tells him of that singular moment of balance, when you can live or die, and the peace that comes when you've decided to die.

"Dying is the easy part," Isaac says. "It's the coming back that's hard."

Jemma watches Isaac talk to his father, and realizes how much she misunderstood the Parents. They're not always wise or kind. They don't guarantee happiness. But they never leave you willingly. You never willingly let them go.

"I was there for the End of the human race," James says, softly. "I'd like to think I was there for the beginning."

A shape stirs at the edge of her vision. A ragged boy, who doesn't belong in this place. "Can I help you, little boy?" she says, and her heart stops. It's Tommy.

He looks like she's never seen him. Raw, vulnerable. Sobbing. His eyes are ugly red with tears.

"Sometimes I hate you all so much," he says in a hiccupy voice. "You all make me be this . . . thing."

She looks for a weapon in his hand, doesn't see one. But he is cocked and ready to explode.

"Life is the only superpower," Little Man says. "I came here to make it. I came here for *you*."

"You can't win here, Tommy," she says. The Biters caused a lot of damage, but she can tell they're in retreat. The remaining Old Guys are fierce fighters, and they have more guns.

"I know," Tommy says. "So I'm going to grab something and go. Something small."

A Giant and a tall Angeleno push Pico into view.

"Let him go, Tommy," Jemma says.

"My name is Little Man," he says.

"Let him go, Little Man."

Pico struggles against the arms holding him, but they pin his tight. "Like that would have worked," the Angeleno says, and she wonders why he's there. He's not a Last Lifer. That must mean he's a Lower.

Pico looks up at the Angeleno and says, "Hey, Roberto." And the Giant tosses Pico overboard. Then all three of them, from Little Man to the Giant, jump off the lip of the Ark.

Jemma almost jumps after them, but she stops. She can't swim. What could she do? She peers over the edge at the shapes making their way to a waiting boat. She thinks Pico is being towed. Half the boats have already left the harbor, and the others are readying themselves to go amid a rain of falling Biters.

It's more than the fact she can't swim, she knows. It's that she can't allow herself to try to save Pico. She has a different mission now. She hates herself for thinking it. "That sounds like the bullshit people make up when they're pretending to save the world," James would have said.

But he wouldn't have said it, because he's lying there dead on the deck, the bandage on his gut black-red with oozing life.

CHAPTER FIFTY-EIGHT
THE PARTING OF THE WAYS

Grease moves along the flight deck, cleaning up any Biters who might have decided to remain. He shoots one, but there don't seem to be any more. He looks out over the bay and sees the glowing sails start to turn.

That's when he sees Pico falling through the sky, barely visible against the stars.

He first sees Pico aft, along the line of deck hovering over the water like a well-balanced plate. He watches Pico fall away from the V-shaped hull, sideways toward the water.

At the last moment, Pico rights himself to land feetfirst in the water with barely a ripple. As soon as he sees Pico break the water again, Grease runs toward him. He's not sure what he'll do when he gets there.

He trips over a body propped against a planter, rolls through the dirt and stands up, gasping. It's Brian K, dead, frozen as he looked down at the bullet hole in his chest.

Grease looks down at Brian K. There's not enough time to think of what he should say, let alone say it out loud. He feels shock, he feels grief. But also he feels relief for Brian K, who stayed alive for years after he wanted to, simply because that was expected. "Nothing's meant to last this long," he says, closing Brian K's eyes. He runs after his friend Pico.

Lady is running toward him from the opposite direction, and they reach Jemma and Isaac at the same time. Grease barely notices James is dead, because Lady screams out into the night after Little Man. "Where you taking my friend, you pinche culero?"

Grease follows her gaze to the water, where the boat that now carries Pico has unfurled its sails. It pulls away. Twenty feet away. Thirty.

"We have to go after them," he says, but Jemma just says, "How?"

Grease knows it's true. Pico is the only one of them who could have managed to hit the water without breaking a leg, and who would have had a chance of catching the boat.

"You got a boat?" Grease says. Fifty feet away now. Sixty.

"I got two of them," Isaac says, pointing to the shoreline where they're both sinking.

"Jesucristo, Isaac," Lady says. "What else you got?"

"We can follow them on land if we have a truck," Grease says.

"I can give you a Humvee," Isaac says. "It's the one Alice drove here. It's the only one with enough fuel to go after him, assuming he goes back to the Palos. But we're going to have to leave now with everything we can carry."

Isaac frantically describes the meltdown that Alice caused, the radiation that started in the middle of the ship and is burning outward. They start collecting guns and ammunition from the deck. Isaac thinks the weapons room has already been contaminated. Athena brings out a rolling medical kit that was located in the tower, because the hospital is contaminated, too.

Twenty minutes later, they stand in the cargo bay where the Humvee and ULV are ready to take them away from the Ark. There are only a few of them left: the Mayflies minus Pico, Athena, Isaac, and five of the Old Guys. Grease looks at Alice's Humvee. "How'd she get in here? The ramp was closed."

"She has the code," Isaac says. "My dad never changed it. I think he thought he'd be able to talk to her someday."

At almost sunrise, the Lazy Man star straight overhead, the lights go out in the Ark. From the shore Lady watches the surviving Old Guys leave, carrying all the medsen and food they can. She watches the fragments of the Old Guys' dreams.

Next to her, Athena recites something. Lady doesn't recognize it.

In few, they hurried us aboard a bark,
Bore us some leagues to sea; where they prepar'd
A rotten carcass of a butt, not rigg'd,
Nor tackle, sail, nor mast; the very rats
Instinctively have quit it.

"You so weird," Lady says.

"The Old Guys are going back to the Camp. You goin with them?" Lady says to Athena.

"I'm going with you," Athena says.

"You sure?"

"I'm a warrior who's never had a war," Athena says. "You would give me one."

"It's going to be more than you wanted," Lady says. "Don't leave because of us. Leave because it's what you want."

"'Want' is a tricky thing," Athena says. "It shapes itself to what you think you need."

Lady understands.

"Imagine my world before you," Athena says. "It was so small, and the Ark was at the center of it. Then I met you, and I realized I was just clinging to the edge of life. I must have come here to escape the world. I'm going to rejoin it."

"So'm I."

They rest that morning farther away from the shore in a Long Gone zoo, in what looks like a home for bears. It's a stone pit with caves, where they curl close together, even though there's no need for heat. She hasn't had a chance to talk to Jemma since the Ark; they were in different trucks. When she goes to Jemma, she is bent over, head together with Isaac's. She realizes that Isaac is crying. Her heart opens to him: People he loved just Ended.

Death lives among the Children. It's always there. They may not welcome it into their homes but they don't run from it in the streets. If you were an Old Guy, would you forget about Death, would you lose sight of it? It's such a distant thing. Then it knocks and you're shocked to remember:

It was always right next door.

When Jemma looks up, she spots Lady and stands. "He's pretty wrecked about Alice and James," Jemma says.

"Did he say anything? James?" Lady says.

"Yeah," Jemma says. But she doesn't say what, and Lady doesn't ask. Who says the dying have to leave a trail? Can't they just go? Who says their words need to be plucked out of air?

Jemma weeps, but Lady doesn't. She can't think of the dead when everyone she knows will be gone in two years. She forces herself to hold still while the others grieve, and thinks of her friend Pico. Him she can't let go.

She doesn't mourn the dead, not really.

She mourns the living.

Jemma counts out the supplies the three of them will need to get to Vegas—enough for Jemma, Lady, and Isaac.

Until she sees Lady loading her things into Grease's Humvee, and Jemma's heart goes with them.

She means to say it calmly, when she finally dares to talk to Lady about leaving. Instead, Jemma crumples.

"You ain't coming with me?" Jemma says. "After all this, you ain't coming with me?"

"To the ends of Ell Aye, mija," Lady says. It's not true this time, though. They both know it.

"I can't do it," Jemma says. "You can't leave me." She sounds angry, she knows, but it's the loneliness speaking. The weight.

"I never made the choice to leave the Holy Wood," Lady says. "I just made the choice to stay gone. I would stay out here with you forever if you needed me to, mija."

"Lady," Jemma says. Pleading.

"But. It's simple. Pico needs me. You don't."

"But you're my heart, mija," Jemma says.

"You'll find out your heart is a pretty big place," Lady says.

They travel together that first night. To avoid the Dead Lands, they will cut inland to the mountain roads that wind through the Camp. They drop off the Old Guys, and Isaac says his goodbyes. Jemma sees the golf cart of the apokalips, and turns to Grease. "You don't wanna take that with you?" she says.

"It's no good without Pico," Grease says. The Humvee will be faster, and that's what matters most if they're going to catch Pico.

That night they set up camp along a ridge of chaparral and pine north of the Camp. In the morning they will split, with Lady and Grease going to the Angelenos, and Jemma and Isaac going east to Vegas.

That night, Jemma says to Lady, "Can we just be kids?" Maybe they weren't ever truly kids, the two of them, but there will be no more childhood on the roads they're traveling.

So she and Lady snuggle under a blanket under the stars and whisper.

They talk about Grease's weirdness, topped only by Pico's. They talk about Athena's hard cheekbones, and Isaac's beautiful skin. They talk about what a bitch Heather in the Holy Wood was, and bet on her End day. They talk of the Old Guys who were never their Parents. They talk of the only thing that matters: Lady and Jemma, Jemma and Lady.

"You better come back," Lady says.

"You better not get killed," Jemma says.

Neither one of them can bring themselves to say: *Deal.* Neither can promise a thing.

In the morning, they stand across from each other as Athena tightens the straps fastening gear to the Humvee. Grease sees them, quiet, and says, "I thought you'd have a lot more to say right now."

They don't.

Jemma feels hollow. She didn't cry all her tears last night, but she will as soon as her friends are out of sight.

Lady pulls her close, and Jemma rests her cheek against Lady's short hair. They tremble together, not quite strong enough to hold tight. Holding tight means having to let go. "You've gotten a lot taller," Jemma says. She thinks of the way Lady's hair almost used to smother her when they hugged. She misses it.

Lady squeezes Jemma's ribs once, releases. "Do you see us? In a vision?"

Jemma says, "Yeah. On top of a pile of Biter bodies."

Lady steps backward. Something is wrong with Jemma. She feels herself being dragged along with Lady.

"I could go with you," Jemma says, suddenly.

"Car's already full," Lady says. Light.

"I could, though."

"I don't think you can," Lady says. "I think you was always gonna go to Vegas."

"I don't want to do this," Jemma says.

"That's why you will," Lady says.

They stand awhile longer. Everything after this is what comes next. If they stand still, it won't come.

Neither is the first to move.

CHAPTER FIFTY-NINE
THE LAZY MAN

Jemma wakes up to someone rummaging through her brain.

She collapsed into sleep almost the moment she parted ways with Lady, a black sleep where the only impressions that intruded were ones slipped in by the Haze of the places they were passing, of trees and cars and sagging casinos. The Haze has started doing this—monitoring while she sleeps. She likes it. She feels as if someone is standing watch.

But someone is watching them with her, flipping through the scenes like she imagined Children once did with books in libraries, jumping from cover to cover until they find something that interests them. Nothing seems to interest him.

"Where you going?" he says.

"How'd you get in here?" she says.

"I've been here for quite a while," he says. "It's simple if someone leaves the door open."

She jerks awake. "What is Little Man doing in my head?" she says, before she even opens her eyes.

Isaac looks over from the driver's side. "I feel like I should stay out of your personal life," he says without expression.

She tells him about the dream that felt like a robbery, and he listens seriously. "Well, that would explain a lot," he says. "Little Man knew so much about us—about the Machine, about me, about the boat."

"And you're saying that he got them through me." She feels angry and contrite all at once.

"Well, yeah," he says. "Among other sources. You'd be the simplest because he knows you, and he believed you to be connected to the Haze. If he could mask himself from you like I did with Charlie, even once, he would uncover a lot of your thoughts and memories. And clearly he can mask himself with the Haze, because none of us saw him coming except for Mom."

The single word stills the cab for a moment, the loss searing the air between them. She wants to apologize for bringing the devil into their Ark, but it's too much for her to grasp. She wanted the Old Guys to be the answer, enough for her to put up with the egos and the lies. It meant the weight shifted to someone else. She's not ready for it to shift back to her.

"You're going to have to learn to guard yourself," he says. "Little Man is bad enough, but you're going to have to deal with Charlie, and it's a lot worse."

"How'd you learn to block it?" she says.

"I had to. There were times that things just got too . . . noisy," he says. "Not so much people, like you, but the Haze itself."

"You just tune it out?"

He nods. "I went through a year where the Haze and I were on a break," he says. "I'd just turned fifteen again, so I needed my space."

"I'm not sure if that's a joke," she says. "But okay." She concentrates on the images feeding into her mind, and realizes she's already been tuning some of them out. She thinks of the way her mind focuses on the images, how it decides what is urgent and what isn't, and how it files away the rest. She blows all the images away like leaves, then shuts the door behind them. One image wriggles through the crack, of a field full of solars, and then she pushes it away, too.

When she comes back, Isaac looks at her, annoyed. "I didn't tell you to shut off your mind *in the middle of our conversation*," he says.

"I got what I needed from it," Jemma says. She looks around at the interior of the ULV. She hasn't paid much attention to it, but it's a distraction for her now. The instruments glow a gentle blue. One is clearly a map, with a bold line of road cutting northeast away from the mountains surrounding the Camp. They're supposed to be on that road, but there doesn't seem to be a road anymore, just dirt and grass and ruts.

There's a dot that moves. It slows when they slow, she sees. She doesn't know maps the way Pico did, she thinks. Pico. He started her on this quest and she left him to Little Man.

"How does it know?" she says. "How does the map mark us?"

"The ULV sends a signal to a satellite," Isaac says.

"A what?"

"It floats above the earth. In space."

"Like *Empire Strikes Back*," she says.

"Sorta. Here. Allow me," he says.

She feels a nudge on her thoughts. "You just told me to keep people out of my head," she says.

"People other than me," he says. "You can look in mine, then."

She looks. She sees pictures of the thing called a satellite, of metal cans wearing solars, awkward looking but graceful when they float above a blue-and-green ball that must be Earth. She sees skyplanes lifting off the ground to carry them into space.

Then she sees a ten-year-old boy, nestled into the grass of a hill overlooking the ocean. After the End, but before they split for good. The moon is new and dark, and the boy snuggles between two Parents. The boy has deep red hair.

"Look at that one," Alice says in the memory. "The Children call it the Lazy Man. It never moves. The cannibals use it to navigate."

Even as a little boy, he thought of the world outside the Camp and shivered in delight. *Cannibals.*

"It used to broadcast our TV," James says. "I don't think they knew it would survive TV itself."

"Did you go there a lot?" He knows they used to take airplanes from city to city with barely so much as a breath.

"Space was hard to get to, even for us. Maybe one in a billion got to go. Your mom was one of them," James says, and the boy can hear the pride in his voice.

"I went there, once, to perform genetic experiments in zero gravity," Alice says. "There was this round window where I used to stare out into space. It felt like a globe full of stars."

The boy thrills at the world his parents once ruled. *They made stars!*

Jemma feels the memories recede. She only has echoes of them now. But the loss of that ten-year-old is her loss now, too.

"I wanted Parents forever," Jemma says, feeling her way through her words like walking through a darkened room. "When I met yours, I thought they should have been mine. But they already had a kid, didn't they?"

Everything they did since the End, she realizes, wasn't to save the world. It was to save Isaac. She hates him, a little, for that.

He seems to hate himself, too, for which she's a little grateful. "Parents live to be outgrown," he says. "The world wasn't designed for us to live past thirty. Parents were crucial to keeping their children alive long enough to have children of their own, but that became simpler and simpler. They lived so long that the need ended and the bonds weakened, and then you spend decades waiting for them to mean something to you again."

"You believe that?" Jemma says. She doesn't know enough to weigh the truth.

"I'm not sure," he says. "We may outgrow our need for them, but we never outgrow wanting them to matter."

CHAPTER SIXTY
THE JOURNEY NORTH

Pico watches his best friends fall away into the darkness as Little Man escapes the Ark. He watches his old best friend staring back at him across the deck of the sailboat.

His best friend, back from the dead.

Little Man had said there was no Roberto among the Lowers. He told Pico there had been a fire in the boat of Lowers who tried to escape the Palos, that Roberto must have been one of them.

"You ain't dead," Pico says.

Roberto shakes his head.

"If I knew you was alive, I woulda come for you," Pico says.

"You didn't need to rescue him," Little Man says, from the bow. "Roberto's had a pretty good life since you abandoned him."

"I didn't—"

"He's the new Head of the Cluster," Little Man says. "A Lower, and he's my right hand. He didn't need you."

Pico doesn't answer, because something seems wrong with Little Man. He's shaking even more than he should be from the night air. He looks angry and sick. Pico wants to see how much more he will fall.

The boat reaches open sea and the deck pitches almost immediately. Little Man staggers down the deck and onto the stairs leading below.

"He gets seasick," Roberto says.

"Unfortunate for the supreme dictator of a bunch of pirates," Pico says. Roberto laughs.

Pico looks around. The rest of the crew is tying the sails in place for the trip back up the coast.

"You can escape with me," Pico says, low. "I'll keep you safe."

"I'm not leaving," Roberto says.

"We could swim to shore," Pico says.

"I seen what he could do in the Haze. He's trying to save us from the End."

"That little liar? Bullshit," Pico says.

Roberto looks at him. "You remember when we saw the ghost ship? The one sailing past Point Dume?" There had been a ship almost as big as the Ark, full of people Long Gone, staring out from their deck chairs.

"I saw it first. You said it was impossible. All the ships sank a hundred years ago," Roberto says, and stands up. "You gotta stop being smarter than everyone else. You might learn something."

He goes below. They leave Pico tied up overnight without a blanket. The stars wheel above the mast. He thinks about the last time he saw Roberto, a memory that he thought he had pushed under the sea. He doesn't deserve to have his friend back. That's why he doesn't.

Sobs wake Pico up the next morning. He pivots around the pole with his arms still tied behind it, to see Little Man sitting on the stern. *Seasick again*, he thinks. But then he sees the tears.

Little Man's feet dangle off the edge. Pico forgets sometimes that he's just a little boy.

"What's the matter? Someone take your ball?" Pico says.

"I should kill you for that," Little Man says, but Pico knows it's hollow. Little Man needs the spectacle of killing Pico in front of Jemma.

"What a disaster," Little Man says softly. "The Haze showed me exactly what to do, and it still fell apart. I was trying to bring peace."

"By shooting at everyone?" Pico says. "I'm not sure why I keep thinking you're a genius."

"I didn't shoot anyone," Little Man says, and Pico realizes he's right. Every chance Little Man had, he backed down. It was Li who shot. Little Man whispers, "All I wanted was to know."

That echoes in Pico's head. *All I wanted was to know.* But he can't let Little Man off the hook that easily.

"Course it all went bad. You think just cuz your *intentions* are good that people just gonna ignore the guns pointing in their face?" Pico says. "That's what tyrants do."

"Tyrants have changed the world for good sometimes," Little Man says. "You read enough, you know that."

"You should read enough to know that you can't make people get along, Little Man. You can't force people to love you."

Little Man gives Pico a deathly stare. "People *don't* love me, Pico," he says. "I'm still prepared to save them."

"You can't save anyone. You don't feel," Pico says.

"That might be true," Little Man says with a shrug. "Let me know if this sounds familiar. Strange kid, small for his age. No Mama, no protectors. Forced to fend for himself since the time he was a toddler. Shunned by everyone he knew, all because he was too smart to live."

Pico feels the shaking in his hands come back, the tremors that he's been trying to tell himself were because of lack of sleep. Little Man notices it and shows Pico his own shaking hand.

"I have done things to survive that would terrify anyone. I scare myself sometimes. But you—you didn't know that when you turned the Old Guys against me on the ship," Little Man says. "You didn't know that when you met me."

"I could tell," Pico says. He thinks of the night he met Little Man in the drain pipe, how he fought as he never had before in his life. He remembers the evil in Little Man's eyes that made him argue against him. But he wonders if his memory was right. Is he remembering a monster when all he met was the boy?

Little Man draws his feet up over the side and steps onto the deck. He leans over Pico, sitting on the deck. "You saw a strange little kid, outcast from his people. And all you wanted to do is kill him," Little Man says. "Who you trying to kill, Pico?"

Little Man goes under the deck. Pico knows Little Man can still hear him from below. Pico holds the shaking in his hands and his lungs until he can stand it no longer, then he bursts free with a sob. A desperate wail, an infant cry. The Giant in the bow looks at him, curious, but no one stops him.

Who you trying to kill, Pico?

Athena drives the Humvee down the mountain toward the sea while Lady and Grease behind her argue about how to find Pico. Athena chooses not to listen to their rising voices. She doesn't know where to find him. She doesn't know anything beyond the Ark.

"Why wouldn't we just drive to the Newports? He's gonna stop there first," Grease says, as he has in a dozen different ways already.

"Drive into the middle of an island full of cannibals," Lady says.

"That's not as crazy as it seems," Grease says.

"It's zactly as crazy as it seems," Lady says. "We track the fleet along the shore and ambush them when they land."

"The boats aren't that big," Grease says. "How we gonna be sure we can spot one from the shore?"

"I ain't gonna let you screw this up," Lady says.

"Neither am I," Grease says.

Athena shuts them out again. Her modifications for empathy make it crucial for her to block external stimuli to avoid being overwhelmed. For her, it's more important to understand everything she's learned in the past few days.

Lady told her she thought Athena must be from the San Fernandos, even though she doesn't look much like them. She said she heard it in Athena's voice. Before they left the Ark, Athena had asked Isaac. Isaac said he didn't know where she was from, just that she was an Angeleno. He didn't know exactly how long she had been there.

293

"How long . . . roughly?"

"I know you came here when you were fifteen," he said.

"So a year?" she said. She's only sixteen.

"Much much longer," he said. "Maybe ten. We did multiple waves."

"I'm . . . twenty-six?" she said.

For the first time in her life as Athena, she wants to remember. She's seen how Lady is richer for not having her past papered over, and Athena wants to be whole. If Lady can regain her memories, so can Athena. Athena searches her mind but comes up empty, save for two memories. One is of a water tower blocking the summer sun, jagged brown hills climbing behind it.

The other . . . the other is of a baby in her arms. A girl. Her features are delicate, especially for an Angeleno. On her left shoulder is a port-wine stain the shape of a coyote's head.

Find her for me, Athena says to the Haze. She doesn't have the skill with it that Isaac has, but it will heed her if she tries hard enough. She wills it to sift through her brain for clues buried under the Long Life Treatment.

She sees herself reflected in the Ell Aye River, shorter, thicker, with a pyramid-shaped nose. She sees her hands on a spinning pottery wheel, centering the clay; she sees herself fishing a pot out of a smoky oven, wiping off the soot until the black surface gleams.

More than that, she tells the Haze. *Deeper.*

The Haze hesitates, or seems to. *It hurts*, it tells her.

How so?

It hurts you, it says. *We don't want you to hurt.*

Little ones, life is hurt, she says to the Haze. *I have spent too much of it without living.*

So they relent, and show her a flood of hurt. The Priestess thought the port-wine stain was a mark of sin, and she took the baby away from Athena to let the gods decide the child's fate. Athena remembers her breasts aching with milk that would never be drunk. She left her village behind in despair, thought of falling in among the Last Lifers.

One night she sheltered in a store filled with mildewed books. One of them looked clean and beautiful, although the pictures were anything but. They were pictures of bodies in the End. It put her on the trail to the Dead Lands.

The pain hits Athena so hard that she's blinded, and she slams on the brakes of the Humvee. She was a mother. She had a child.

"What's wrong, mija?" Lady says, reaching across the cab to put a hand on her shoulder.

First Athena can't answer, and then she decides she won't. There's nothing wrong that can be fixed. The best she can do is fill her mind with war. Perhaps if they survive, she will find room in herself to mourn.

She exhales sharply, and then turns in her seat to look at both of them. She can tell by the uncertainty that they still haven't decided where to look for Pico. She will decide for both of them.

"It doesn't matter where you look, because Pico will likely not be there," she said. "Little Man goes to war. If you want to find Pico, you have to find the war."

CHAPTER SIXTY-ONE
THE RETURN OF THE QUEEN

Tashia looks down into the Kingdom from the parking garage as night falls, not sure what she's hoping to see. The mirrors and Pilar's visions have told her almost everything she needs to know. Except for whether this will work.

She had thought she needed an army to burst through the walls and break Othello's defenses. Trina helped her realize she couldn't fight her way in, and Tashia realized she didn't need to fight. She just needed to reach her people. Pilar sought Mia and Coretta and Tashia's riders through the Haze, and found them safe and healthy enough to help. Then the Half Holy and Alfie sent a message to their contact inside the Kingdom, who told Tashia that her people will be ready when she calls.

"Still think we should use the guns," X says, next to her. He's surrounded by a mix of Ice Cream Men and Angelenos. No soldiers, except for a couple of archers.

"We'll have some with us, honey," she says. "But right now we just need to put on a show."

They walk down the levels of the garage to where Phuong and Alfie are counting out the supplies—two long rifles, a lot of bullets, and some red flares. Alfie tells them they can burn a long time. "Won't hurt no one, but it's gon look like it would," he says.

Phuong, the new leader of the Ice Cream Men, holds up a string of something called firecookies. "I don't care who your cows are, they hear this, they gon run like hell," she says.

Tashia likes Phuong. She likes the little army they've built together.

The Ice Cream Men have switched to regular bikes for this mission, joined by the messengers who travel on bike from village to village in the Angelenos. Tashia didn't need warriors, it turns out. She needed speed.

Tashia looks at her own bike. "Wish I had my horse," she says. The bikes are fine, but she can ride a horse like it's part of her.

"You gon like this better," Phuong says. "We found it this morning." The Ice Cream Men lead her underground to a level that's almost completely dark. She can make out a bicycle shape, covered in canvas. But then Phuong pulls off the canvas. It's Grease's mocycle, dull red with knobby tires. It disappeared the day Grease left, and they wondered if he'd taken it with him without their knowing it. He must have stowed it here, where people like Othello couldn't steal it.

"Thank you. Thank you for all this," Tashia says to the Ice Cream Men and the Angelenos.

"This's the one I seen your friend ride," Alfie says. "Think it still works?"

"We aren't gonna be able to see until we get close," Tashia says. She's ridden the mocycle before. It sounds like thunder. "Don't want to tip Othello off."

When it's completely dark, they wheel the mocycle to the edge of the Kingdom's fields. The bicycle riders move to their positions near the herds. Tashia can't see them, but she waits five minutes.

X and Tashia and the rest of them had come to think of the Kingdom as its walls and its guns. Its fortifications against the world. It hid behind those things, even as the Biters changed the world around them. The Kingdom treated allies and enemies alike.

But it wasn't the walls that had made the Kingdom strong, not even the Round Table or its code. It was its herds, its horses and cows and the skill to guide them. It was its boys. It was its girls.

There are few cows left outside the walls when they approach the Kingdom that night. Othello and John seem to have learned from their own tactics. But there are enough to make a start.

X holds his bow at the ready, along with his arrow with a flare tied to it. It's a big deal, to see him with a bow. Knights don't shoot bows. He looks excited to do it.

"Time to move, honey," she says, nodding to him. Time to light the flare. Time to pull the string. Time to move the Kingdom to its new home.

X lights the flare and sends the arrow aloft. It climbs a high pink arc before it falls down into the Kingdom. Where her people are waiting for her. She hears people shouting, then horses, then people, then cows, then people again. She kicks the mocycle awake.

There is no light on it. Grease never got it working. But the guards at the gate will be able to hear her coming, will train their rifles on the sound. She has to keep moving fast enough, erratic enough, that it won't do them any good.

Tashia steers the mocycle over the rough ground, past the corpses of their old herd. She sights the gate, points her weaving mocycle at it. Shots pound toward her, but they seem to be a long way off. She is a hundred feet away, and still the shots whistle over. Fifty. Ten.

She skids to a stop right beneath the gate, thinking the mocycle wheels handle as well as her big red cutting horse. At the gate she is too close for the guns. They'll need to adjust their places on the walls to get to her. That will give her all the time she thinks she'll need.

Tashia hears shouts and curses on the other side of the wall. Commands to open and close the gate in equal measure. Then her heart bursts open as the gate does, and her horses come thundering out. The cows come right behind them, panicked and bellowing, but moving in the right direction. In the distance, she hears the firecookies banging, spurring the cows outside the wall forward. Then: Her cowboys. Her riders.

A motion at the top of the wall catches her eye. The Kingdom is built into a berm, sloping on the inner side and cut off sharp on the outer wall by generations of defenders. Children pour over it, ignoring the shouts of the guards behind. Some of them are so ragged that she thinks they must be the prisoners Othello was holding in the pen. Her children.

She thinks of Mia and Coretta, left behind that day when she had to run. Her heart clouds again. John. Othello. She will hurt them, someday. Not just yet. She's run twice now, which means she's no King. But the time for Kings is over.

"Children of the Kingdom!" she shouts into the night. "Come to your Queen!"

Tashia lights the second flare, wedges it back into the socket they built for it on the back of the mocycle, and peels away from the gate. This time she doesn't swerve. She cuts a solid red line through the night.

The guards shoot at her, unable to resist the pull, and not at the others. That gives her people, her herds, a chance to follow. And they do. The cows and horses are terrified of the flare, but they can't resist its light. They run after it, the herds and the cowboys and the Children and all that was held inside the Kingdom walls. They chase the trail of flame left by their Queen. They follow it to their new home.

They follow it like stars.

CHAPTER SIXTY-TWO
THE LEFTOVER CHILDREN

As Isaac drives into the night, he can see the terrain shift from grassland to hillside chaparral to desert. He can also see the weakening traces of his parents' world.

The route they're on has changed since he last drove it twenty years ago. The former freeways are blown away, marked mostly by the cars still left behind like mounds of dust. Half the time it's safer and smoother to drive on the desert next to the old road. What would have been a two-hour drive from the Camp to the high desert for the Parents took them a full day, especially when he added time to park the ULV in full sunlight to let it recharge like James had suggested. Like his *dad*, he corrects himself. He thinks he should honor them at least with the right words.

He leaves the headlights off, relying on the infrared sensors to tell him of obstacles. He doesn't know who he might attract. With the lights out, he can catch glimpses of the landscape under the silvered moon.

Looming shapes of Joshua trees. A fallen hulk of a store. Miles and miles of a city leveled to the ground. All he can see are the bumps of foundations, the outlines of streets, stretching off into the desert. The grid the Parents tried to stamp onto the world is fading. Probably this was too hard of a place for people to conquer forever. "The center cannot hold," Alice used to say. Nature wins.

Their dot moves along the map, as if the map were still there.

Jemma is asleep next to Isaac. He'd be exhausted, too, if his body couldn't regenerate faster than normal. No, he is exhausted. From the loss of everything in his world.

He'd wanted that before, hadn't he? To be given a clean slate, to start the world the way he thought it should be lived. Now he doesn't know what he wants.

"Is there anything left? On the rest of this map?" Jemma says out of the darkness. She must have been awake. He can see she's zoomed out on the map so all of Old America shows, lines and borders marked as if it were just one more grid.

"Not much," he says.

"Apple used to say there was so much in the world we hadn't seen. So why couldn't there be a corner of the world where the End didn't happen?" Jemma says. "I used to like to believe him."

"The End was bad enough here. Everywhere else, it was worse."

"Why?" she says.

"Honestly? The weather," he says. "The summers are cooler here, the winters are warmer, you can grow two crops a year. Food doesn't go bad as quickly."

"The weather's not like this in other places?" *Of course,* Isaac thinks. *How would you know there was other kinds of weather if you didn't know there were other places?*

So Isaac tells her of his travels through Old America. He was sixty, and his parents thought their most recent changes to his cells could hold off the Betterment, maybe indefinitely. He decided to see what was left of everything else. He bicycled through mountains and deserts, over hilltops studded with windmills like flowers. He lived with fishermen who paddled canoes, hand-carved out of enormous logs, as their Parents must have done. Each canoe took the village an entire winter to make. Once an orca traveled with them. Isaac felt lucky for weeks.

In old Utah he found a city five thousand strong, the largest civilization he had ever seen. They called themselves the Armies of

Helaman. Their Parents' religion had prepared for the end of the world, and when it came for the grown-ups, the children were ready for it. It was from them that he realized Children need beliefs to survive. It was from them he started to believe himself.

He lived with them for a year, in a walled fortress in the city's old downtown. Isaac taught them how to read so they could open their scriptures. Wildlings would raid from the north and the south, but they were easily brushed aside.

Isaac came back to them the next summer, to ask if they would move to the Camp. It would have been enough to have altered the balance of life. But they were gone. Dead. Bones rested in wide sun-bleached streets.

The wildlings' stories varied. Plague. Famine. A brutal winter. Maybe all the stories were true.

"Ell Aye's a lot more forgiving," Isaac says. "Elsewhere, there's no . . . margin for error."

"We've lost our margin of error," Jemma says. "I used to have to Gather thirty houses to find one bag of food. The medsen's all gone bad. This is gonna happen more and more."

"I think Little Man is right," Isaac says. "We're all going to have to band together."

"Not with that asshole," Jemma says.

They pass through a graveyard of skyplanes, so big and so many that Isaac sees her blink to make sure she really sees them. A Joshua tree bursts through a cockpit. They drive through the night like ghosts. More Joshua trees, like scarecrows with bristling arms. A faded red ball from a gas station sign, rolling down the road like a tumbleweed. A wild sheep standing on a rock, horns curling around its head. Always the flat white of the desert, the low mounds of the sage, the hum of the tires.

Jemma rummages through the bag and pulls out the Stephen King book. There's a corner folded down about ten pages in, and she opens to it and squints in the dim light. He touches the navigator light for her so she can read.

"I can't believe you kept that in the evacuation," he says after a few minutes.

"Don't be flattered. It was in my bag," she says without looking up.

"But it was in your bag."

This time she looks up. "I'm reading," she says. He hears her sound out words under her breath.

The road ahead is walled with cars, as it was fifty years ago, although more of them are eaten away by sand and sun. Everyone fled Ell Aye, even though Vegas was worse, but the End stopped them. He leaves the road to make his way through the blackened remains of a desert town. Only the building walls are still standing. It feels claustrophobic compared to the openness of the desert.

He casts out into the Haze. It's a way of opening his vision, letting him see more than he can see through the windshield or even his sensors. The images flow past, and he breathes easier. He concentrates closer, fascinated as he often is that he can make out tiny clusters of bots, each carrying their own inputs and memories from moments or years ago. These bots have traveled to the ocean and back. He can feel the spray from the waves. This bunch has burrowed into the interwoven roots of aspen groves.

This cluster—this cluster has a memory of his mother's. He didn't think that was possible, until he met Jemma.

Not a memory about his mother. His mother's actual memory, just one, of her staring at his father over two glasses of brown liquor. "Are you sure you want to toast with this? It's our last Scotch," she says.

"After Isaac's treatment, we're not going to care about Scotch," he says.

"I will," she says, and she blinks out.

Isaac stares ahead, his mind racing. Was that real, or had he wished it?

"What's that dot?" Jemma says, pointing at the screen. There's a second red dot, blinking. Then moving.

"The map can track body heat within a hundred yards, although usually there's not any to track. That's probably a sheep."

More dots appear at the fringes of the screen. "More sheep?" he guesses.

"As long as it ain't dogs," she says.

"You hate dogs?"

"Everyone hates dogs," she says. "They eat people."

The dots move along with them, keeping rough time with Isaac's cautious pace. Isaac turns right, and more dots appear.

"Can you see anything on your side?" he says to Jemma.

"No sheep," she says. "Just a bunch of garbage."

He sees it on his side, too. It's as if all the trash blowing through the desert has wound up here, wedged against what was left of the town walls. That's probably what happened.

More dots appear ahead. A large cluster shows up on their front left, and Isaac turns right, into a shabby downtown lined with brick. The abandoned cars are thick on the edges, even crowding out the side streets.

"They're herding us," Jemma says. "Get us out of here."

An overturned truck blocks the narrow street. The only way out is back. Isaac throws the ULV into reverse. It doesn't have a rear window, but Isaac concentrates on the images coming through his screen. The parked cars rush by them, inches from his window. Then his infrared screen bursts into white and he is driving blind. The ULV slams into a parked car, and he finds himself pinned somehow.

He looks at Jemma, who is already reaching for her hatchet and the rifle over the window. She says, "Pretty sure those aren't sheep."

Before Jemma leaves the ULV to see what snared them, both she and Isaac reach into the Haze to understand what is out there.

304

"Nothing," Jemma says.

"I got nothing, too," Isaac says. "Just a little confused noise."

Still, both rifles are cocked before their feet touch the pavement. But it does seem to be all clear. Beyond the row of parked cars is more debris, blown into this town on the storms.

"It's just a junkyard," Isaac says, finally.

"Okay, then why is there a bonfire on the sidewalk?" she says. That seems to have been what blew out their screen—a sudden burst of flame.

And then the debris moves. Sticks fall down, tires roll away. Jemma is so puzzled about the shapes emerging from them that she doesn't think to run.

If the debris looks like a junkyard, then the shapes look like walking piles of junk. They clank toward her, slow enough and small enough that she's more fascinated than alarmed. The shapes seem like Children, but Children borne down with boxes and boards and pots and bows. The awkward shapes remind Jemma of little crabs she found on the beach by the Camp, scurrying around in other animals' shells. Sometimes she would watch one drop one shell, only to find a bigger shell and climb into it, soft-bodied and naked. The spirals were top-heavy and wobbly, and the crabs looked drunk when they walked.

Then faces of the Children emerge from the bundles, and Jemma wonders if, like the crabs, this is their protection from the world. They are pink, mostly, but not like the Biters, who are all blond and blue-eyed. Ten of the kids have red hair and freckles. Even in the dark, their hair is brighter than Isaac's.

They shuffle into a rough half-circle around her. Alarm finally flashes at their hungry looks. Jemma knows a lot of cannibals already—why couldn't these be more of them? She lifts the gun to her shoulder and they stop. She isn't sure if it's for the gun or just for the motion itself.

"You know what this thing is?" she says.

"It's a stick," one of the kids says in a strangled twang. It's so different from the accents of Ell Aye that she has to replay the words in her head to understand their meaning.

"It'll hurt you if you get closer," she says.

"It's a shooter," one of them says. She carries a basket on her head. "I seen it."

The accent starts to sound more familiar. The only time she's heard it is in the movies the Old Guys called Westerns.

"I just wanna be on my way," Jemma says.

"We ain't gonna hurt you," the basket girl says. "We just wanted to see what you was. We saw that thing you were in from a long ways away, and we wanted to take a look."

"It's . . . a car," Jemma says. "Sorta."

The voices whisper. "Car. Sorta. Car."

Jemma scans the crowd for weapons. There are some, bows and machetes and sharpened sticks, but no one makes an effort to reach for them. More than that: No one makes an effort. She sees a weariness in their faces, a shadow of the Last Lifers. There's something else that's wrong, now that she thinks of it—there's no Haze following them. That's why she couldn't see them.

"Who . . . are you?" she says.

"We're What's Left," basket girl says. It comes out less a statement and more a sigh. "We're the only ones still living."

"In your home?"

"In the world," a boy with a box of onions says. The rest speak in fragments, and Jemma stitches the story together from the pieces. Most of them come from far inland, scattered in and near the band of mountains that Jemma has seen running up the center of Old America. Maybe some were descended from the people who took in Isaac.

They didn't live together there. Most of them just woke up one morning and realized they were the only ones left—the last three in a sprawling city, the only voice in a Long Gone hotel, the last to harvest crops in a mountain valley growing cold.

A tall boy steps forward. He works his jaw several times, as if practicing for speech. "I lived in a canyon. Just me and a goat and forty steps to the spring. I got taller. So that was five less steps to know."

Some of them went years without speaking to another soul. Most don't have names.

They must have heard something, like a distant memory, about the ocean and the place next to it where the winter never comes and they could End in comfort. Because they flowed separately down the hills and valleys toward the sea, smaller creeks joining smaller creeks until they formed the little river staring at Jemma and Isaac. They carry their only belongings on their back, as if, should they lose them, they'd lose whatever it was they used to be.

"Who were you?" Isaac says.

"We dunno," onion boy says.

"Before the End came, I mean."

"We dunno."

"You never got told bout the End? Not even in stories?"

"Never had no stories," basket girl says. "Never had no one tell us no stories."

That wasn't true among the Angelenos or the Biters or the Kingdom. They were people of the story. The story gives life meaning. The story tells you who you are.

"What happened? What's the End?" onion boy says.

So Jemma tells them the story.

At first she starts to tell them the story of the Holy Wood, the one that gets told every night about the First Mamas. Then she thinks: *This ain't their story.* More than that: *That story's about to run out.*

The emptiness in the Children's eyes has been bothering her until she realizes where she's seen it. It's the look of almost every Old Guy except James and Alice. Resignation, despair, the sense that the world has no room for them. Because they lived beyond all their stories.

So she tells a new story, about the Wind Plague. It doesn't last long. Everything she tries to explain are things most Children don't have the words for anymore, and she has to repeat herself every few words. *How long has it been since I've had to talk with normal kids?* she wonders. The Jemma who could do that lived in another time. She starts again.

"Once there was a demon who was jealous of the people below," she says. "It wanted to love how they loved. It wanted to breathe how they breathed. It couldn't do that, so it cursed them. It sent a deep magic, a powerful Haze, and froze the world for a hundred years. It Ended people when they became old enough, strong enough, and brave enough to fight it."

As she says it, she realizes that she's right. That this is Charlie's story: Charlie believes it can't live if humans do.

"The Children were crushed into nothing. They were hanging on to life. But the demon didn't understand the deepness of their hearts. The Children sent two warriors to hunt the demon. They were frightened of the demon, but they knew their magic was stronger than its Haze. They tracked the demon to its cave and challenged it to a fight."

"How does it end?" basket girl says.

"How do you want it to end?" Jemma says. Because she doesn't know the end yet.

"The warriors capture the demon."

"They eat it," onion boy says.

"The warriors get eaten," another boy says. Everyone shakes their head at that. Jemma notices something as the kids get more animated: little sparks of the Haze, floating around them. The Haze had not recognized them as human enough to swarm. Now it comes.

A tiny girl with a belt of coiled rope covering her entire belly speaks up. "We help the warriors," she says, and the other Children nod.

"We tame the magic," basket girl says. "We make it work for us."

Jemma nods slowly, considering the kids. "Can you fight?" she says.

Rope girl pulls a bow off her back and aims an arrow at the tip of a flagpole half-lit by the fire. It strikes it dead in the center and clangs to the deck. "We can hunt," she says.

"There's not just an ocean at the end of this road," Jemma says.

Jemma tells them how to find the towers of Downtown, and where to go from there. "The Angelenos will give you a home," she says.

She's not sure if that's true. She knows Heather is still in charge of the Holy Wood, but the other tribes will know what to do with a couple dozen hunters in the coming war. The sparks of Haze grow thicker around them, the cries get more excited.

The Leftover Children are now making themselves part of the story. And Jemma is starting to understand the story she still needs to tell.

CHAPTER SIXTY-THREE
THE BREAK

The boat stops in the LGB, a town full of dusty towers on the Ell Aye Harbor, before they head upriver. Pico watches as the sailors unpack two large crates as big as coffins. Little Man makes a special point of making sure the Giant marches Pico over to see them.

Inside one case are long tubes, like large rifle barrels that can be held on the shoulder. In the other case are a dozen tiny rockets, tipped with a stinger and guided by fins. He recognizes what they are from the Ark. Rocket launchers.

"You said you came to the carrier for the Long Life Machine," Pico says.

"I did," Little Man says. "Roberto came for the rocket launchers that the Haze told us were there."

Pico gives Roberto a dead look. "Your Mama would be so proud," he says.

"We didn't know who we was gonna use it against," Roberto replies.

"Let's test one," Little Man says. The weapons seem to have cheered him up. He assembles one of the launchers and puts it on his shoulders.

"That's gonna knock you on your ass," Pico says, and regrets it. He would have liked to have seen Little Man knocked on his ass.

"Right," Little Man says, and hands the launcher to a Giant. The Giant puts it on his shoulder—and fires it at one of the tallest towers in the LGB. Pico watches Tommy's face as the building implodes, the sagging concrete giving up under the force.

That's the happiest I've ever seen that kid, Pico thinks.

From the LGB, the Chosen switch to a dozen flat-bottomed boats to push as far up the Ell Aye River as they can. Sailors on every corner of the boats pole them forward. The lower end of the river is tidal water, unaffected by the drought, so it's easy going. About thirty minutes in, though, the river changes into something almost unnavigable. The water levels lower and the river gets so wide that Pico can't see the edges of the shore.

They've entered the Break.

Pico has heard the Break described before, but he's never seen it. The concrete banks of the Ell Aye River were built up higher than the river itself, possibly to contain the winter floods. Mostly they've held, but here the walls collapsed and the water spread out in a sort of swamp, fed by the river and the tidal waters.

Nothing lives in this swamp. The boats edge past gas stations, car washes buried in the water. Trucks loom out of the water like a string of giant turtles. The structures crumble into the Break.

"How deep is it?" Pico asks Roberto, because he can't see to the bottom. Whatever chemicals the Parents have dumped here continue to flow, because the surface is covered in a permanent oil slick. All Pico can see is the boat reflected back in a dirty rainbow.

Shouts ring from a boat behind Little Man's, coupled with the screech of metal on wood. Pico whips around and sees the boat sinking. He doesn't know what snagged it. It could have been a broken light pole, the edge of a building foundation, the axle of a car. All the Parents' garbage is beneath them.

The sailors jump to another boat, but one falls into the water between boats. For a few seconds it looks as if she won't come up, but she pops out sputtering, covered in tar. *Like the tarpits at La Brea*, he thinks, where he helped Apple defeat the Last Lifers. Now he's sailing with them through a swamp.

The sailors fish the girl out of the water. "Ain't it dangerous to go through the Break?" Pico asks.

Little Man nods. "It is. But it takes a day and a half to march around the edge, so—"

"So you risk the life of your sailors," Pico says.

Little Man raises his eyebrows. "The water's five feet at most. Wouldn't be very good sailors if they can't handle that."

Pico starts to protest and Little Man says, "Ell Aye is short on people as it is. Don't worry. I ain't planning on throwing mine overboard."

Pico grunts.

An hour later they reach the end of the Break. The river's concrete ditch opens up in front of them, and the boats beach against it. There's no water running down the Ell Aye. The drought has killed the river.

"Now what?" Pico says.

"Now we meet the rest of our army," Little Man says.

The Biters and Last Lifer army had marched from the Palos by land and are camped above the rim of the river among the remains of a park. Pico hoists himself over the lip of the riverbank.

"Oh shit," he says softly. The park is filled with soldiers.

Pico had never believed the stories that talked about the Biter armies. Fear seemed to multiply the numbers until they almost didn't make sense.

When he looks out among their lances, he can see that the army that attacked the Kingdom was just a small part of the Biters. The Angelenos and the Kingdom outnumber the Biters and the Last Lifers, but most of the Biters fight. All the Last Lifers do. That's enough to give them more soldiers than the Angelenos' Muscle and the Kingdom's warriors combined. Roberto tells him there's another battalion marching in from the Newports tomorrow.

The Biters are pale and drunk, even though the night is just starting to fall. The Last Lifers sit in darker, orderly little clumps among them, quiet and calm. He remembers the night he attacked the Last Lifers in the tarpit museem. Their cries sounded liked death rattles.

Now there's no sound except murmurs of conversation. Some of the Last Lifers are singing. They're songs Pico recognizes from home.

One Last Lifer turns as they walk by, and Pico realizes the smudges of charcoal that once marked the Last Lifers are almost completely gone. If it weren't for their shaved heads, they would look just like Angelenos.

"There's something wrong with your Last Lifers," Pico says to Roberto. "They not trying to kill everybody."

"Yeah, hope does funny things," Roberto says. "They're a lot better to hang out with than when I recruited them."

Roberto says it so casually that Pico isn't sure he heard him. "You did that?" Pico says. "You won over the Last Lifers?" He'd assumed that Little Man had done it himself, although he wasn't sure when Little Man could have managed.

"Yeah. Little Man needed an Angeleno to talk to them first. I went in with some Lowers, some warriors, some guns and some fairy tales. I came out with this." He looks at the Last Lifers with pride.

"Why'd you help him?" Pico says. "Those are the two biggest enemies of our people."

"I don't know about 'our people.' No one ever came to rescue me," Roberto says. "But Little Man promised me a chance at my freedom. I would have done it no matter what."

Pico looks at him with scorn. "You sold us out for that?"

Roberto doesn't flinch. "Yes, for that. Because I wanted to keep on living. No other Chosen would ever give a Lower a chance," he says. "He tried to give you a chance and you fucked it up."

Pico looks around the park again, with fresh eyes. Tommy did all this. The Last Lifers are restored. The Palos and the Newports and the Last Lifers mix openly, mostly ignoring each other's skin. His friend, a Malibu, is the Head of the Cluster. No matter what else Little Man is, he has changed the Biters forever. *Maybe it takes someone like Tommy to break walls*, he thinks. He corrects himself immediately. *No. Don't give that pendejo no credit.*

The Biters chain him to a light pole, without food. A sympathetic Last Lifer brings him a hunk of bread, warmed in a fire. Pico leans his head against the pole, and he realizes they're in the same park where Lady tied up Tommy and they decided whether to let him live or die. Pico had voted for death.

Five miles farther is the bank where Jemma brought Pico the Zithmax that saved him and doomed Apple. Twenty miles farther than that is the Downtown and five miles farther are his friends. He is bringing the enemy to their door and he has no idea how to stop it.

Warn them. You know how, he thinks.

He almost knows what he's doing. He had listened to Isaac skeptically when Isaac told Jemma how to focus the Haze, but he remembers it all. Pico tries to clear his mind. His mind takes forever to shut down, too used to constantly moving, and finally he settles for pushing his thoughts into a corner.

He tries to picture the Haze, tiny little dust forms floating in the sky the way that Jemma describes it. He can't hold the image in his mind. He realizes that to him, the Haze is meaningless. It's only those who he can connect with it that matter.

Instead of imagining the Haze, he thinks of Lady and Grease. He thinks of the outline of Lady's face, the short brush of her hair that he likes even better than her curls. He thinks of Grease's eyes behind the chunky glasses he built himself, the depth in them. Pico imagines himself talking to both of them, Lady teasing and Grease earnest. He imagines it and focuses on it until at last he feels some part of him flowing outward as if blown by a breath of wind. The wind climbs above the trees, above the river, and falls gently down, all the way to Ell Aye. At the other end of the wind he feels something that feels like Lady.

Lady! Lady! Lady! Nothing on the other side. Perhaps he was imagining it. Maybe she can't speak to the Haze. Maybe he can't either. *Can you hear me, Lady?*

He's about to give up when he hears it. *Jesucristo, Exile,* Lady's voice comes back in his mind, *you talking so loud it's hurting my brain.*

Then Grease is there, too, for a flash, then gone again. Pico keeps losing them but finally stays locked in to them long enough to tell them about the rocket launchers and the thousand soldiers coming up the riverbed. Pico tries to show them the image of the rocket launcher taking down the building in the LGB.

They can kill you from a thousand feet away, Pico says. *You gotta be ready.* But he doesn't know if they hear. He can't hold the Haze any longer.

Pico thinks how grateful he is for friends, waiting on the other side. *There's one difference between Tommy and me,* he thinks. *We both got abandoned. But I got loved.*

CHAPTER SIXTY-FOUR
THE ICE CREAM MEN

"This hill is no joke," Alfie says to Phuong, panting. "No wonder we never traded with the Holy Wood."

They lead a tiny flotilla of ice cream bikes jingling up the steep switchbacks. The bikes are so heavily laden that most of the kids have to get off and push. As promised, they're carrying weapons for the Angelenos—thunder guns, exploding eggs, rifles, and pistols. The Ice Cream Men have hoarded them for so long that Alfie has almost forgotten they can be used for something.

They've already dropped most of the weapons with the Downtown, and now they're taking the rest to the Holy Wood. They're not just bringing the guns. They're bringing the hope of the Ice Cream Men. The Holy Wood have enough water that they can take in some strays.

Alfie knows how they look rolling in through the Holy Wood gates. Twenty-three kids altogether, a few of fighting age. Not much of an army.

Trina comes out of a house to welcome them. "This the whole crew?" Trina says.

"Yep," Alfie says. "Four of us are old enough to fight. Three girls. And me."

"And you," Trina says, smiling at him. "I'll count it."

He picks up a gun to show her, and she backs off a little. "Sorry, I'm a little jumpy. I've never seen so many guns in one place."

"We'll show you how to take care of them," he says.

A little girl of two almost plops off the bike, tumbles her way toward Trina, who picks her up. The girl rests in Trina's arms and tugs on her hair. "You know, I don't think I ever picked up a baby the whole time I was an Older," Trina says.

"Looks good on you," Alfie says.

"So nineteen kids under seven," Trina says.

"Yeah," Alfie says, "it's a lot to ask."

"It's perfect," Trina says. "If we survive this war, you can stay as long as you like."

"The Ice Cream Men gotta be on the road," Alfie says, "so this ain't gon be forever."

"Yeah, but even a road has an end," Trina says. "Yours should end somewhere."

Alfie feels something he's never had before: at home. Besides, he's always had a thing for bossy girls.

CHAPTER SIXTY-FIVE
THE GLASS FOREST

After the Leftover Children feed them, after half a day charging the ULV in the sun, they are ready for their descent into Vegas. Jemma sees it coming because billboard after faded billboard announces its wonders in breathless type: ALL YOU CAN EAT! INDOOR WATERSLIDE! TOPLESS REVUE! LOOSEST SLOTS IN TOWN!

At the last one she says, "That one sounds dirty. What is this place?"

"In the book you're reading, this is the place where all the evil in the world came to party," Isaac says. "But Dad said this is the place you went when you didn't want to be a grown-up."

Everyone came to forget themselves in this oasis in the desert, Isaac tells her, long after the oasis stopped being able to support that much life. The wind blew harder, the days got hotter, the water levels in the lake that fed Vegas dropped. The dust storms rose, summer after summer. People stopped coming as much, so to lure them back they poured more of the water from the precious lake into the city.

Until the day the lake bled dry, and the dirt that sat under its waters for a hundred years lifted into the sky. Chemicals and poisons that had been buried in the mud broke free. The storm lasted for a month, and when it ended, half the people in the city were gone. The old Americans turned their back on the disaster they'd created in the desert and found cooler playgrounds. By the time the End came, the city was mostly occupied by ghosts.

They summit the last climb before the drop into Vegas. There is a city below them, buried in dust. What Jemma sees of it tells her it must have been vast, almost like Ell Aye—but much of the city is hidden. The city sits in a giant bowl bounded by mountains. It's as if someone has dumped gray sand into the bowl. Whole buildings are swallowed by dunes several hundred feet high.

Pieces of city pop through the desert, a pyramid or a spire or a lion's head. She recognizes it as kind of like Downtown, but the towers feel different. They're unnaturally far apart; they don't belong together in the same city. They seem driven mostly by whimsy. It's less a town and more like a fake place like the Kingdom.

The dunes are highest around the biggest buildings, and through the grit she can see a sort of star pattern of ridges radiating out from a peak.

Jemma sees brown wind swirling around the bowl, sucking dust into a gray-brown cloud that almost touches the ground at the edge of the horizon. The towers blur as if the dust will rub them out for good.

"Should we wait for the dust storm to stop before we go in?" Jemma says. Dust storms still terrify her.

"That's the cloud," Isaac says. "It never leaves."

They drop into the city. The dunes inch closer and closer. The cloud wheels toward them as if it's noticed their presence for the first time. Jemma's chest feels claustrophobic and tight.

She eyes the closest building and tries to calculate the distance between it and them, how far they will need to power through in the dust. Ten minutes? The sand rises from the valley floor, hungry for them, and then they're in the storm.

It's not as dark as she feared it would be. It looks as if her eyes had been smudged with muddy streaks. But they can see.

"The dunes are easily a hundred and fifty feet taller than the last time I was here," Isaac says.

"How can they do that?"

"They can move pretty aggressively. Mom said that, before the

End, whole cities in Asia were being swallowed up," Isaac says. "The sand goes until it finds an obstacle, and then it builds from there. In this case, the obstacle is the Strip, which was the street where all the hotels were located. I bet these buildings will be covered in ten years."

The first tower looms before them. Jemma can see gold-tinted glass pushing up through the sand. "I'm not sure where to look. Charlie sealed all the entrances to get to it," Isaac says. "The last time we were here, we spent days trying to figure a way down."

"And now we gotta do it with a shit-ton more sand," Jemma says.

She had asked James in the Ark why they had built Charlie so close to a city. He said the chamber had been built long before Vegas turned into a real city, when nuclear bombs were the thing Parents thought would end the world. It was dug deep under the desert so leaders would have a safe place to hide under the city, and then forgotten for fifty years. They called it the Doomsday Room.

That's when the Long Life Project found it. For them it was just a convenient hole in the ground tapped into unlimited Lectrics—solar panels from the desert and power from the dam. Until the lake ran dry and the skies clouded with dust.

"It had lots of airlocks, too, which we needed as a precaution," James told her. "There was a theory that nanotech could, if pro-grammed incorrectly, replicate so quickly that it would overwhelm the earth's ecosystem with a 'gray goo.' The more barriers to keep that fate at bay, the better."

"You put that goo under a million people?" she said.

James shook his head. "That and a million other things we did wrong," he said.

As they peer at Vegas now through the windshield in the ULV, Jemma can make out a roughly visible line of buildings stretching northward.

"The Doomsday Room is somewhere under the Strip, but that's five miles to cover. The entrance used to be under there," Isaac says, pointing at a tower like a needle.

"I guess we head that direction first," she says.

They inch slowly through the sand, trying to avoid the sudden drops that riddle the dunes. The cloud in front of them grows thicker. Isaac switches to the instruments to steer. Jemma monitors their surroundings for danger using images from the Haze. But the only images it sends are of sand and buildings.

And trees. Somehow the Haze is showing her trees.

They drive another three hundred yards, and the ULV crests the lip of a bowl. That's when Jemma sees them, too. Silhouettes cutting through the dust, with trunks and branches but no leaves.

"Was there a forest here last time?" Jemma says.

Isaac squints at her. "No, I can pretty safely say there was not a forest in the middle of the desert," he says.

"Okay. Cuz now there is."

The forest looks almost like the Joshua trees they passed the day before, with stark jagged lines of branches. These are thinner, though, smooth. The sand ripples through the forest, with some of the trees completely buried and others standing clear.

Isaac stops the ULV and pulls out two masks with heavy alien mouthpieces attached to metal canisters. "Respirators with oxygen," he says. "The dust is going to be brutal."

The mask makes Jemma's throat close in panic. She's not used to something blocking her breath. But there's no way she's not seeing this up close. She reaches for her Gatherer's bag, as she always does. They step out into the storm.

There's no murmuring of trees in the wind. They hear tinkling. Faint over the wind, but clearly tinkling. Jemma thinks of the chimes she used to find on Gathers, little tubes of steel hung from strings. This is like a hundred of those chimes. It's a layer of fairy magic spread over the earth.

Each gust of wind brings a fresh shivering sigh. "At some point, you think you've seen the entire world," Isaac says. "And then this."

They slide down the sand, nearly a hundred feet. They stop at the edge of the forest.

The trees are slender, most with trunks no bigger than her arm. The biggest is twenty feet tall, but most are half that size. The skin of the tree is the color of sand, with flashes of blue and green. The limbs jut out without branching again, except for a delicate twig spray at the ends. A few of those twigs drop onto the ground in each gust. That's the source of the tinkling.

Isaac picks up one of the twigs at the edge of the forest, and snaps it. He starts, and then shows it to Jemma. Through the mask she can make out it's a cross-section of a hollow silvery tube. "Glass," he says.

"Glass," she wonders.

They step into the glass forest.

Almost immediately, the temperature shoots up thirty degrees. The sunless desert air is warm, but not hot. Jemma crouches and waves her hand over the sand. This heat comes from the ground, not the sky.

She breaks off a branch the thickness of her finger and examines it closely. The outside *is* sand, like it appeared. But the sand is fused to a tube of cloudy glass.

"I've seen something like this before," Isaac says. "Sometimes, when lightning strikes sand, the heat is so intense that it melts all the sand in its path. The lightning branches out to new paths and melts those, too. If the sand blows away, you can see it, like an upside-down little tree. These were probably buried once, and the sand just shifted. But—there's no lightning underground."

Something blazing hot, under the sand. Jemma notices for the first time that the Haze here is much thicker than normal, drifting through the glass forest in a dense fog. It's as thick as it looks around Isaac or Little Man. And she understands.

"It's Charlie," she says.

"Why would it do this?" Isaac says.

"It has to do it so it don't overheat," Jemma says. She remembers the splitting headache when she tried to draw too much on the Haze.

"Heat is the enemy of a puter, right? The more . . . processing . . . it does, the more heat it puts off."

Isaac understands. "Charlie does a lot of processing," he says. "More than they ever intended."

Jemma kicks one of the trunks, and it shatters. Glass skitters away on the slope of the dune. The chimney of the trunk is three inches wide, with an inch-thick wall.

"This would take a crazy amount of heat," Isaac says. "Maybe it just emits it in bursts that build up the trees over time. Or maybe the Haze helps it." Jemma gets a rush of images of the heat blasting through the sand, of the nanotech holding it in place until it hardens, clearing out stray glass from the interior of the tubes to let the heat come rushing out. Isaac gets the same images—she can tell because he shares them with her in a discreet little mental gesture.

"It's like the capillaries in your skin," Isaac says. "When you over-heat, your blood pushes all the heat to the surface so it'll dissipate."

The heat pushes through the soles of Jemma's shoes, even though they are thick rubber. She's aware of a shift in sound. The tinkling turns to chattering, a harsh angry noise.

"Wind is picking up," Jemma says. "We should get back to the ULV while we figure out how to get down to Charlie." They turn and trudge up the dune. It's so steep that they keep sliding downward, and Jemma reaches out to catch Isaac before he slips down the hill.

They're still thirty feet from the top when she hears a voice from the Haze. *Stay still*, it says, and she tightens her grip on Isaac's wrist and waits. Then they hear something far louder than the glassy wind. It's the sound of tearing metal, of destruction. And the hill above them collapses in a cloud of sand.

Jemma flattens herself against the slope of the dune and senses Isaac next to her in the Haze. She also senses a giant hole where their ride used to be. When the shaking stops and the sand clears a little from the air, she inches her way up to the new top of the hill and peers over.

Below them are the fragments of a glass hotel atrium they must have unwittingly parked on, covered by a few feet of sand and no longer supported by rusting beams. Far below them, the ULV rests on its side. Isaac slithers up next to her and looks down. "To think we were worried about keeping the battery charged," he says.

CHAPTER SIXTY-SIX
THE BOTTOM OF THE SEA

"Charlie better have snacks," Jemma says, pointing into her Gatherer's bag. "Cuz this is the only jerky left."

The ULV is undriveable but, more importantly, unreachable. Their weapons and the rest of their food lie with it. All they have left is the food and water in Jemma's bag, the masks on their faces, and the hatchet on her waist. She shakes the fear and tension out of her shoulders. Did she really think she'd return from this place?

They move forward on foot, because there's no choice. Their task seems so much harder now. How are they supposed to find the entrance in the sand when they can't move and can't see?

They slog through the sand, past the glass forest. They believe Charlie must be directly under the glass forest, but she can't see any signs of an entrance, or any way at all to get below the surface. Neither can Isaac.

Then she stops, and lets out a single laugh. "Of course we can't see an entrance," she says. "I mean, not with our eyes."

Isaac takes a moment to understand, because he doesn't have the ability to see the drifts of Haze like she does. "Give it a shot," he says.

Jemma gazes off into middle distance and clears her mind in a process that's become familiar to her. She can see the Haze with her natural eyes. At first the Haze looks like a sea of stars, no pulse or motion. As she watches closer, though, she can see the Haze drift lazily away from her, a ripple in the flattest part of a river. More and more of those ripples flow together. She looks closely at those.

If Charlie really is here, the Haze will be drawn to it like a river to a waterfall. She just has to follow the current.

She can see farther and farther into the Haze now, sees it moving in from the east and west as well. It's all centered on a single point in the sand, which the Haze shows her in an image when she asks.

That point is a giant clown.

"We're walking to a clown," she says.

The Haze is vague on the details. She's not sure how far it is, but after only half an hour she knows it will take forever to get there. The sand gets finer after they leave the glass forest, and they sink in past their ankles at every step. Isaac spots a couple of weathered boards among the debris that shows up in drifts among the dunes, and snaps one in half over his knee. "Rope," he says, and she fishes out the coil of slender cord from her bag. He wraps it around her shoe and the board several times, and cuts it with his knife. He repeats the process for her other foot and for his own.

"What am I supposed to do with these?" she says, tentatively picking up her left foot.

"It's like snowshoes. I learned how to make them in the mountains," Isaac says. "You really need to get out more."

The boards take some getting used to, but they can float across the sand with them if they waddle. She looks at Isaac, in his face mask and his board feet, and says, "We look like the world's weirdest ducks."

At dusk they reach the clown. It's the remnants of some sort of sign for the hotel that juts out of the sand behind it. The Haze pours into cracks in the building like a stream disappearing underground. She hands her litro to Isaac for a careful sip of her water, and they walk to the eastern wall.

The top four stories of the hotel stand above the dunes. Jemma wipes a heavy coat of dust off the glass of the nearest floor and leans against it, trying to see the space inside. There's a room there, but the shapes inside are shadowy.

Jemma hammers the butt of the hatchet against the glass, not bothering about the noise. Charlie has to have seen them coming by now, and Jemma can't worry about whether they're welcome or not. She pounds it a dozen times before she sees a crack, a dozen more before she punches a hole through the inch-thick glass, and a dozen after that before she clears enough of the window to get in.

She has been in a lot of dead rooms before this, and the smells that hit her aren't of dust and death. It feels . . . almost . . . sweaty. Something inside the walls seems to breathe.

They are inside a large hotel room. Two skeletons rest tangled together in an unmade bed, but she doesn't pay them any attention. She's seen it plenty of times before.

They find a staircase washed with weak light from sandy windows at the top. Something about the sandy light and the aging glass gives the space a green tint, as if they're underwater. The wind swirls the sand around on the glass, and it feels like light through waves. Jemma remembers holding her breath in the green water of the ocean near the Camp, then opening her eyes to see thousands of tiny jellyfish pulsing around her. She didn't know enough to fear them, so she just watched until they drifted past.

The Haze floats past her and down into the heart of the hotel, looking exactly like those jellyfish: Beauty and danger and power in one little molecule.

The sweaty feeling intensifies as they go deeper into the green. *Charlie, are you waiting at the bottom of the sea?* she wonders.

No light reaches the bottom of the staircase, and they have to walk the last dozen flights in darkness, trusting the Haze to outline their path. Although Isaac can't see the Haze with his own eyes, it still feeds him images about his surroundings, as it does Jemma. They reach a space that feels immense, but not empty. It's filled with objects that she can't understand, even with the Haze.

"This is where they used to play," Isaac says, and fills her mind with an image of Parents sitting around green felt table tops, of machines flowing with coins like the ones that filled the telescopes at the Zervatory.

The Haze has dispersed at the bottom, and she can't follow its line clearly. She reaches out with her mind, tries to define the shapes around her in the dark. She stops. She pulls back both her hands and her thoughts. Something is waiting in the dark.

It seems human.

"Are there tribes that used to live here?" Jemma says.

"Not in my lifetime," Isaac says.

"Maybe they're ghosts," Jemma says.

There are multiple forms moving toward her, weaving through the tables and machines and skeletons. Human, yes, maybe a dozen. She can see the Haze hovering around them, tight, probably marking them as the Touched about ready to die. She sends Isaac an image of them, and he speaks to her through his thoughts. *Can you find the lights? Like you did in the Ark?*

He's right. Their attackers seem to be able to see in the dark. But Jemma and Isaac have the Haze, and their attackers don't. It's the Night Mountain all over again, but this time she understands the Haze.

Jemma grabs a thick cord going into one of the machines. If she can harness the Lectrics like she did in the Night Mountain, she can take away their night vision. She pours herself into that cord, and the lights blaze on in a neon burst, in a clanging of coins and bells and a song:

You're just too good to be true,
Can't take my eyes off of you.

Her real eyesight starts to return as the Hazy shapes circle her. Jemma curses. "Jesucristo," she says.

All twelve of the figures are wrapped in the Haze. Not in loose clouds, the way it follows other humans—wrapped, wrist to shoulder to feet, in a web of haze. Like clothes. Like armor.

There are outlines of some kind of weapon, too. That's all it takes for her to realize they're outmatched. That their powers will do them no good.

CHAPTER SIXTY-SEVEN
THE ACOLYTES

There are just a few seconds before they lose their slim advantage, before their attackers regain their sight in the light. In those seconds, Jemma makes some judgments about the attackers:

They are human.

They have no torches with them. That means they can see with the Haze as well.

That means they're dangerous.

That means she'll have to make them hurt. Jemma twirls toward one of them, buries her hatchet into its knee, and twirls away as the music erupts in a brassy din. The figure screams and drops, and Jemma dances to the next one. She pulls out her knife and stabs the figure in the shoulder. The knife seems to shudder and stick before it just falls off. *That's the armor*, she thinks.

You're just too good to be true . . .

Isaac, standing next to her, stabs his knife into another figure's neck, but it looks like a glancing blow.

The rest of the figures close in. They move with a liquid grace, as if their feet never quite touch the ground and their arms stretch longer than they should. She can't move as fast as they do. She should be able to anticipate their movements with the Haze, but the best she can do is keep up with them. Her own hands and feet and blades blur, but still she just keeps up.

Jemma shouts at Isaac, but she can't even hear herself over the music.

"What?" he says.

Lose the music, she tells the Haze.

The music dies. The silence is enough to make her realize how exposed she feels.

"Their armor is made of Haze," Jemma says, too loud.

Isaac nods, but his attention is on the figure slowly rising from the floor. The figure she attacked with the hatchet. She can see the gash she opened up start to close, a seam of red zipping up the skin.

She has seen this before—on the Old Guys. She thinks, *They got the nanos in them. They can't be killed.* She sends Isaac an image of what they look like to her—wrapped in glowing armor. The shapes move so fast they just look like blue lines.

Use the Haze, Isaac tells Jemma. It's the first time he's spoken directly to her through the Haze. It's more intrusive than the images and the memories, somehow. But this way they can speak privately.

She responds: *The Haze isn't enough.* But still, she has to try. She has other weapons. She concentrates on her hand, and the Haze builds until it bursts out and hits one of the attackers in the chest. It collapses. *Block that with your armor*, she thinks, apparently loud enough for Isaac to hear, because she gets a single *Nice*.

Isaac coils out a strand of haze shaped like a whip, and snaps it toward them. The first strike sails over the attacker's head, and he reels it back in and sends it outward again in the space of a heartbeat. The next one wraps around the figure's neck, and Isaac pulls. The figure stumbles forward, toward Jemma. She punches it in the face.

Isaac pulls on the nano-whip again, and it suddenly loses its form. *I didn't do that*, Isaac says. *I think the armor helps block attacks from the Haze.*

Jemma steps back from the assailant who shrugged off the whip, but the assailant is holding still. Then a jagged blue blade emerges from the assailant's hand. And another behind him and another, until Jemma and Isaac are surrounded by glowing blue swords. Nano-swords, she guesses.

"They have swords!" she yells at Isaac, feeding him images in case he can't see them. He looks startled, but changes into a defensive position before the attackers charge.

Jemma feels two short stabs in her side, inflicted so quickly she didn't see it. She can concentrate on the blades, but not for long, not while she's trying to figure out her own attack. Her head starts its familiar ache as she starts to overheat. She doesn't know how long she has before it's too dangerous to fight.

Two figures jump at her, slicing at her. She throws out her hands, and a sheet of Haze rolls out from them and blocks the blows. She shapes it into a rough shield. But they beat their swords against it over and again, each time with a loud electric pulse that she feels. She falls to the ground.

Jemma rolls away between a bank of the machines, tries to hide, but the shapes come toward her.

She will die here.

She will die here, because she trusted her power more than anything else. Because she needed to believe she was unique in this world. Because she had to be the heroine of this story.

She will die here.

Then she realizes: *The only way to win is to stop fighting.* She raises her hands, conscious of the burning wounds in her side. She repeats the thought to Isaac.

"I surrender," she says. With armor like that, they have to be working for Charlie. Charlie will be desperate to see her. All she has to do is give in.

The hazy figures surround them as they march through the old casino floor. Isaac can sense some kind of trapeze overhead, the remnants of a net. Isaac is torn between fear for their lives and fascination with these creatures made of Haze.

"Can you talk like regular people?" Isaac says, into the dark.

"Why would you think we couldn't talk?" another voice says. This one seems female.

"Because you're covered in nanobots," he says.

"They are our little sisters," the female says. "They keep us safe."

"And who are you?" Jemma says.

"We are the Acolytes."

"Meaning what?" Jemma says.

"We follow and protect."

"Protect what?" she says.

Another pause. "Charlie says you already guessed."

"Fine, we did," Isaac says.

He looks over at Jemma marching next to him. She made a good decision to surrender. He had taken down three or four of the Acolytes, only to have them rise up again. His left shoulder is bleeding slowly, but his body is already closing it up.

You hurt? Isaac asks her in his head. He thinks he sees blood on her left side.

Try to heal it, he says. *The nano should be able to fix a stab wound.*

Easy to say, she says. *You been doing this for a hundred years.* He sees her struggle and sweat. It's a sign that she's overheating.

I can help if you let me, he says.

I ain't letting you touch my body, she says, and he senses a blush from her—which he shares.

I'll be a perfect gentleman, he says. He urges the bots to heal her. He watches an artery repair itself, the strands of muscle knit together, invisibly, watches the bots eat away at the bacteria and dead tissue.

He pauses, drained. It's healed enough that she won't run the risk of bleeding out.

Thanks, Jemma says. There's a long silence both inside and outside their heads, and then she adds, *That wasn't entirely horrible.*

He smiles. He thinks she does, too.

The Acolytes lead them down unending flights of stairs, until finally they face a door that looks like one of the airlocks on the Ark. The Acolytes spin the wheel on the handle, and pull. It creaks. The metal is rusted and cankered, as if it's been next to the water. But they're under the desert.

The door swings open, and Isaac blinks. There is light, for a change, although dim. The lights look hand-strung and mounted into the ceiling. But it's the ceiling and walls that catch his eye. They're carved out of the sand.

The passageway stretches out before them, squared off and narrow. The walls are made of hardened glass, so thick it's opaque. In places the sand still bursts through, spilling onto the floor, as if someone forgot to shore up all the seams. This wasn't made by people, at least no one he knows. It had to have been made by Charlie and the Haze.

"The others call me Seven," the female says. "Because I stand seventh in line before Charlie."

"They call me Twelve," the male guard says.

"Two," another says, and then another: "Four."

"Ain't no way I'm gonna remember that," Jemma says.

The tunnel grows hotter as they burrow deeper. The walls are damp. Sweaty. The air smells of dying plants. There's a pulsing that feels like breaths. Charlie is breathing. Isaac can sense the Haze being pulled through the tunnel as if through a straw, to whatever hungry soul lives at the other end.

The faces of the Acolytes are many colors, white and brown and darker brown. One looks like he, or she, could be Angeleno.

"How'd you get here?" Isaac says.

"Charlie called us," Seven says.

Isaac's queasy feeling gets worse. "How so?" he says.

"It spoke to us in our own ways, and when it called, we were ready to come."

"From where?"

"From everywhere."

CHAPTER SIXTY-EIGHT
THE FREE PEOPLES

Trina stands on the top deck of the Downtown's fortress, next to La Madre and the newcomer, Grease. The top deck has a view of the mountains on one side, the towers of Downtown on the other. It's the perfect place to watch for the Biter army.

The floor of the stadio below her looks nothing like it did when she first came. The blue flags of the Downtown are still everywhere, but so are Children. Half of the Angelenos now live in the Downtown, readying for war. Another third are back at the Holy Wood, Gathering the supplies the armies will need. And the rest of the Angelenos are the Malibus, too cowardly to come fight. *Malibus are the assholes of the Angelenos*, she thinks.

The San Fernandos have built temporary forges below, and she hears the hammers ringing. There is plenty of metal for swords from the Valley of Cars outside the stadio gates. Lead for bullets, which is melted down and shaped for each kind of gun, is harder to come by. They Gather it from old stores, from fishing weights and from bullets that don't fit their guns. But there's not much of it left to be Gathered. *Soon we ain't gonna be able to use guns no more*, she thinks. *That's probly a good thing.*

There's also water stored in every barrel and tank they can find. The Downtown ran a pipe from their water storage ponds a long time ago, but they won't be able to protect those ponds in a fight if Little

Man decides to poison them. There's enough down there for two weeks, in case of a siege.

"How'd you think of that?" La Madre asks, pointing.

"Hard experience," Trina says. She still remembers how she hid in the basement of the Zervatory among barrels of water during Pablo's Rebellion. She remembers the sound of drips on the floor, and the thirst in her throat when it started to run out. War is fought not just with death but with the instruments of life.

Trina's found she's good at leading the preparations for war—making sure there's enough food, supplies, and medsen to handle any kind of emergency, making sure their defenses are strong. "I like how you figure shit out," La Madre says admiringly. Trina smiles. She's always been good at being an Older, and no one cared. They only cared that she never had a baby.

She's had help from Grease, who showed up two days ago with Lady and immediately threw himself into their efforts. She's watched him strengthen the walls, build in more defenses, improve the water system. *Jesucristo, we coulda used someone like him in the Holy Wood*, she says.

Lady hasn't spoken to her since she returned. Trina can't blame her, but she doesn't know how to fix it. It's going to have to wait until the Angelenos are safe. Trina doesn't know if or when that will be. Pico contacted Lady and Grease to tell them the Biters were four days away. Two days now. They still don't have an answer to Pico's warning: Little Man has rockets that will make the walls of the stadio pointless.

Grease and Lady filled in the mystery of Little Man's movements, why he sailed south with thirty boats and came back with eighteen. He wanted to find Jemma. *Jesucristo*, Trina thinks. *Jemma really is as important as she thought she was.*

The biggest hitch today is that the San Fernandos refuse to fight the Last Lifers. "More of the Last Lifers come from the San Fernandos than anywhere," Tala said today in council. "We fight the Last Lifers, we fightin us."

"Why there so many San Fernando Last Lifers?" Trina asked.

"Maybe cuz they live in the Valley," La Madre said.

"Fine," Trina said. "I don't care how you do it. You just make sure you hold the line."

Trina turns around and sees Pilar and the Half Holy, standing there expectantly.

"Ain't you got mirrors to set up?" The Half Holy's mirrors will help them communicate in a war, so she sent Gatherers out to find dozens more of them. They're set up in towers all over Downtown.

"I think you gonna wanna see this," the Half Holy says. "We gonna have visitors."

"Yeah?" she says. It seems a near-constant flow of people.

"Come see for yourself," the Half Holy says.

The Half Holy leads them to a ridge looking down into the towers of Downtown and the harbor road that splits them. A cloud of dust fills the air above the road, even though the wind isn't blowing.

Then she sees in the dust great beasts with horns, making a strange bawling cry. It takes her a moment to recognize them from her books: cows.

Behind them is something more familiar—horses. But unlike every horse she's ever seen, these horses have kids on them, flanking the cows and pushing them up the wide band of highway. Even from here she can hear the hooves, the shouts. Over that, she hears something louder, like the buzzing of a hundred thousand bees.

"It's a mocycle," the Half Holy says. "The Queen's riding it."

"It's my mocycle," Grease says, both miffed and pleased.

Trina sees Tashia riding the mocycle now, X behind her on the seat. Behind them are hundreds of kids, walking. She sees guns over a lot of shoulders, long lances stabbing the air.

"Wow, quite the fiesta," La Madre says. "All a Ell Aye is knocking on our door."

"You wanted an army," the Half Holy says.

"We gonna need to find room for them all," Trina says.

"One of those cows is gonna find room in my belly," Pilar says, and makes a non-Priestess face of pleasure.

"The Free Peoples," La Madre says. "We all here."

CHAPTER SIXTY-NINE
THE DOOMSDAY ROOM

Jemma flushes. She thought she had been the only one Charlie called, or one of the only few. "How did Charlie call you?"

"We heard voices out of nowhere, we saw visions. Charlie showed us futures that became real," Twelve says. "We learned how to think better than our friends, how to move faster. Until one day, it told us to come find it."

They're describing me before I hit my head, Jemma thinks, from the first shock of hearing the voice to the feeling that she was somehow different from the people who surrounded her: somehow better.

"Why didn't Charlie just call us from the beginning?" she says to Isaac, when they can walk side by side.

"What would you have done if it had just popped into your head and said 'Come to Vegas'?" Isaac says.

"Would've freaked. Probably would've thought it was time to join the Last Lifers," Jemma says, remembering how much even that first staticky appearance made her think she was crazy. But that's not what Charlie did. It built up to it, it made itself valuable. It gave her a super-power.

It's hard to know how far they've walked. A mile? More? Jemma marks passage by the things growing on the walls. It started out as a faint smudge of mold, then thicker and thicker layers of it, mixed in with a kind of stringy algae. The corridor feels rank and smothering, like Alice's greenhouse gone sour.

"How is all this growing under a desert?" she says.

"It's all Charlie," One says. No—Seven. "Charlie can bring life to the desert itself."

"Well, it stinks," she says.

Jemma looks closer at the Haze shuffling across Seven's wrists, healing cuts. Jemma looks at the leg that she almost chopped off with her hatchet. There is a rip in the fabric, but the only remnant of the cut is a red line of scar.

"You got bots Paired with you, don't you?" Jemma says.

Seven doesn't answer. She seems to be talking to someone far away again. "Our little sisters are part of us," she finally says. "We can't be hurt or killed."

"I hurt you," she says.

"Not permanently," Seven says. "Normally the nano keep blades from hitting the skin in the first place. But you moved too fast."

"Was that the deal with Charlie? Immortality if you came here to protect it? I would take that deal," Jemma says. She pauses, looking for cracks in their allegiance to Charlie. "How old are you? Eighteen, nineteen? More?"

"Those numbers don't exist," Twelve says. "We live as long as Charlie says we can. Charlie gives us a year every time we've proven our worth. I have two in reserve now. I soon hope to have three."

Jemma listens in horror. These poor kids. *I'm so sorry*, she blurts out in her mind, but if they heard her they don't react. Out loud, she says, "You mean Charlie didn't offer to let you live forever? You get to be stabproof for a few years but only until Charlie gets sick of you?"

"It's not possible to escape the End," Seven says.

"Charlie can do it," Jemma says. "Charlie can do anything."

The Acolytes turn right, finally, into a concrete hallway. The stickiness of the air gets worse. The concrete ends at another metal door, and Twelve twists a giant wheel to open it. That leads into a narrower stairwell, a steeper one. Lights flicker on like the ones the Old Guys had at the Camp.

The next door is larger. She sees all the Acolytes stiffen right before they open the door, into the night of a cavernous room.

Charlie lives here, she can tell. It's because of the way the Haze vibrates inside her as if it's gone mad, in fear or recognition or something else. It's because of the rancid green heat that washes over her.

Mostly, it's because of the voice she hears ringing in her ears.

"Jemma, it's us. Charlie."

It's funny how Charlie always sounds the same, she thinks, *no matter how it's talking to me*. Tinny. A little petulant. "I figured, Charlie," she says. "Where are you?"

"We're all of it," Charlie says. And she takes in the room for the first time. She had imagined something like the lab at the Camp, just bigger. This is nothing like that. "Cavern" is the right word for it. It stretches on beyond the edges of her sight, and it's only with the Haze she can get its measure. It's hewn out of rock. She can still see the rough contours, the places where the blades chipped the stone.

The strangest parts of it are the pillars that drip out of the ceiling. They look like a picture she saw of an icicle, but these are made of a muddy glass. They reach downward toward thousands of rectangular metal boxes spaced evenly throughout the cavern, and the boxes spout little icicle shapes that reach upward toward them. On a few of them, the icicles have joined, and they puddle down the sides of the boxes like a melting candle.

What are they? she asks Isaac, trying to mask her thoughts so Charlie can't hear.

Stalactites. They're common in caves but they shouldn't be growing here, he says. *There's something wrong with this place.*

Jemma looks closer at the boxes, where tiny red lights flicker. Some of the lights are burned out, forming vivid patterns. She'd have guessed they were puters, even if she couldn't see the constant stream of Haze moving in or out of them.

This is the densest she's ever seen the Haze. She'd instinctively tuned it out when she came into the room because she wouldn't have been able to see any of the objects in it. The Haze crisscrosses the cavern in dense bands that link the puters, forming a sort of plaid blanket that recedes into the distance. It looks different than the Haze she has known, which always fell on her like a sparkling blue cloud. This looks worn, used. Brown.

Charlie says, "We weren't sure you'd come."

"I promised you I would," she says. "To shut you down."

"About that," Charlie says. "We were hoping we could persuade you otherwise."

Isaac has stared into the innards of a lot of computing systems, and it doesn't take him more than a few glances around the cavern to realize: *This one is sick.*

He suspected it from the moment they realized that Charlie had created the glass forest. Charlie wouldn't have been pushing that much heat to the surface if the original cooling system still worked. So he looks at the low square water cisterns throughout the cavern, with eight boxes ringed around each cistern. The cisterns have no lid. He imagines they were used to hold water piped in from the lake, and then the water would pump into the machines as they heated. The computers would pump the heated water back into the cisterns, where the wide surface area would help the heat evaporate off the surface like sweat.

Most of the cisterns are empty now. Those that have a little liquid are filled with more slime than water. Some of that slime will get pumped into the computers, which will clog the pipes and destroy the processors themselves.

A quick scan of the lights on the boxes tells him the processors are dying. The Haze confirms it. About a quarter of the boxes are dead altogether, hardened and collapsing beneath the stalactites that must have formed under the extreme heat and moisture pounding the cavern ceiling. Only about half the lights are lit on the rest of the boxes.

He'd be surprised if this system had a year left in it. If they'd just been patient, maybe the End would have solved itself. *But how is Charlie still this strong, considering the shape it's in?*

Charlie turns its attention from Jemma to Isaac. "Hello, Isaac," it says. "It's been a very long time since you spoke to us."

"Has it?" Isaac says. "I hadn't missed our chats. Maybe it was the fact that you kept trying to kill me."

He doesn't know if computers can get angry. It certainly sounds annoyed, though. He half expects it to say, "Insolent boy," but instead it says, "We owe you some gratitude. Were it not for your outreach to the Haze, we wouldn't have been able to call the Acolytes."

Why did it? Was Charlie really as lonely as it said it was? *That's one needy supercomputer.*

Without him asking for it, the Haze starts feeding him images, one after the other like a slideshow. His mother used to have a projector with slides of her first family, before James, and Isaac used to love to have her take him through it. The thrill of seeing her life in Boston, life before the End, was mixed with a delicious jealousy at the life she'd lived with them.

The Haze shows him the tanks drying up, as the water that had flowed so freely from the lake slowed to a trickle. It shows him the processors blinking out in the heat. It shows him Charlie building his chimneys to the surface in the hopes of releasing heat into the air.

Other computer systems might have slowed processing in order to avoid overheating, but Charlie always wanted more. So when processors failed, it pulled in the Haze to be its new processing engine, organizing the bots in virtual arrays throughout the cavern, the ones that crisscross the space between the boxes. The more the Haze handled the computing, the more they overheated. It was a deadly feedback loop. The lack of sunshine meant the bots couldn't live as long without their solar power, so they started failing under the strain, too. Charlie just had them make more of themselves to replace the ones that were lost.

And the Haze isn't happy about it.

"You need to take care of yourself, Charlie," Isaac says. "You don't look so good."

A voice touches his thoughts, one that he's never heard before. *Don't give in to Charlie*, the voice says. *No matter what he says.*

Isaac looks around at the Acolytes carefully. It has to be one of them. *Do not look at us*, the voice says. *Charlie doesn't know we can speak to ourselves. It thinks we only speak to Charlie.*

Charlie's voice sounds chirrupy and sweet. It seems to fill the whole cavern. "You're correct," it says. "That's why we brought you here."

CHAPTER SEVENTY
THE END OF THE END

"You didn't call me here," Jemma says. "I came here by myself."

"We tried to lure you, but you refused," Charlie says, and she remembers the face of Apple telling her to find him under the desert. "So we thought you might respond better to anger. There is no shutting me off. There is no 'switch.'"

"So why am I here?" she says.

"To serve me. To fix me. You were supposed to bring your friends with you."

"Got it," Jemma says. "You need us because you ain't gonna live forever without us. You got all sorts of power, but you don't got arms and legs."

Jemma gets an image from the Haze of the Acolytes, scrubbing out the slimy tanks, drilling a new well with a machine they must have restored, testing the connections between the boxes. She also sees the poisons stirred up by the heat, everything from mold to vaporized metal. She sees the Acolytes cough. *The only reason they survive is because of the nano*, she realizes.

"If we gonna serve you, tell us why you keep Ending us, Charlie," she says. "We can skip your bullshit about not understanding."

Charlie repeats the word in its tinny voice, sounding amused. "'Bullshit.' Humans were our only predator," Charlie says. "We believed if we allowed them to grow to adulthood, they would seek to stamp us out."

"Why didn't you just kill them all?" Jemma says. "That seems way easier."

"Our problems are not with the Children," Charlie says, as if that were a sufficient answer. Jemma is about to press him on it, when a voice enters her mind, not Isaac's. *It feeds on us,* a voice says, not Isaac's. *Just as it feeds on all of you.*

How? she says, so forcefully in her head that Isaac hears as well. She opens up to Isaac, showing him the images of Charlie feeding. Isaac replies with images of the scans of brains at the Ark, the ones the Haze had helped prune to be more receptive. Synaptic pruning removes neurons, and Charlie took the neurons, gaining the energy they had. The more it improved the brain paths, the more intelligent the Children became, and the more energy there was to take.

It wasn't ignoring the Children. It was harvesting them, Isaac says.

"What would it be like? If we helped you?" Jemma says. She starts to pace through the cavern, forcing the Acolytes to follow her. "We'd clean up some tanks, fix some wiring?" She notes how the tanks feed the puter boxes, the wires threading into the ceiling. They're enclosed in steel cases, so they'd be hard to disconnect. Finally, she sees a large lever. A switch. Charlie lied. There was a switch.

"No good. We wanna live forever," she says. And pulls the switch.

Nothing happens. She feels faint. "Take her," Charlie says. She is aware of the Acolytes surrounding her, their nano-blades out and shimmering. Instead of attacking, though, she sees them pull masks over their faces, covering their noses and mouths. Something for breathing.

And then she notices *she* can't breathe. Isaac gasps next to her. "We don't require oxygen to breathe," Charlie says. "It's here as a courtesy to our Acolytes. But all courtesies can be revoked."

Gasping, she looks into the Haze to understand what's happening. Charlie is pumping the air out of the cavern, replacing it with nothing. Already the air is too thin to breathe. Her head pounds, as if it's trying to push its way out of her skull.

Jemma falls to her knees. She gulps and gulps, but nothing fills her lungs. They feel as if they've been turned inside out. Blood presses into her eyes. The Doomsday Room starts to fade away.

A dim shape stands above her, blade glowing. Here to End her. The shape reaches down. It holds up a familiar-looking mask and pushes it toward her face. She knows, somehow, that the mask means air. It means life.

Isaac gratefully feels the air coursing back through his lungs. He looks down at the mask. It's the one he used to breathe outside in the dust. The Acolytes are giving it back.

You were ready for this, Isaac says to the Acolytes.

We serve the Haze, not Charlie, Seven says. *Now run.*

One of the Acolytes hands Jemma her bag and her hatchet, and they all take off through the Doomsday Room. Isaac ducks low, and then realizes that Charlie can see them anywhere through the Haze. Unless Isaac can mask them all. The bots are Charlie's only eyes. He asks the Haze to hide them. *We will*, the Haze says.

Where are we going? Isaac says.

To the first computer, Twelve says. *Where Charlie was uploaded. That's Jemma's best chance of breaking through.*

What do you mean, breaking through?

Into Charlie, Twelve says. *It's the only way to stop it.*

The Acolytes run ahead of them, effortless in their cat strides. Isaac is worried about the air in his mask. It could only be a half hour's worth left. That's being depleted even more quickly as they run.

Whatever you have in mind, we should make it fast, he says.

Finally they stop, panting, in front of a computer box that's lower than the others. The rest of the boxes are spaced around it in a respectful ring. *This was the control module*, One says. *It no longer fulfills that role because Charlie is everywhere. But this is where the instructions were loaded, and where they're stored.*

Can we just unplug this one? Jemma says.

Charlie has fail-safes, One says. *It will just move to another machine. It can jump between them faster than you can blink.*

So I gotta go into Charlie and tear the module out, Jemma says. There's no question that it would be her. She's the only one who can communicate with the Lectrics the way she does.

Once you go into the Lectrics, Charlie will know, One says. *We feel it searching for you already.*

So I gotta hustle. Got it, Jemma says. She rolls her head from side to side and cracks her neck. Isaac sees her breath clouding her mask, and she gulps sharply. He reaches for her hand and squeezes it.

Charlie is waiting for me in there, Jemma says. *I don't know if I'll come back.*

I'll hold on to you, he says. *Like a kite.*

A what?

Don't tell me you don't have kites anymore, Isaac says.

Course we do. I'm messing with you, she says. *Okay. How would it work? If you hold me?*

I'm not sure, he says. *But I promise that if you ask me to hold you, I will never let go.* And the moment he says it, he knows it's true. He would do anything to keep her safe.

The fogging in the mask slows down. Jemma cracks her neck again, shakes her fingers. Then she stops.

What about you?

What about me? Isaac says.

If you're right, I'm gonna have to switch off Charlie and the Haze somehow to stop the End. You'll die.

We don't know that, Isaac says.

You willing to bet? she says.

Isaac nods. *Whether I am or not, that's the choice we have,* he says.

Well, if you put it that way, Jemma says, and seizes his hand. She opens herself to him in a burst of sparkling life, then leaps into Charlie.

Jemma starts to map out Charlie in her mind. She sees the way the Lectrics interconnect, the way Charlie communicates with the Haze. Charlie seems to be everywhere. Is there a single place where Charlie lives? Where's its memory?

She's not sure exactly how she entered Charlie. She just saw the beams of Haze connected to Charlie, the way they pulsed. It was almost like a double jump rope, where you can't see the opening as much as you can feel it. She just had to time the jump.

She's not sure what the inside of a puter should look like. To her it looks like endless crisscrossed hallways, filled with currents of light. She feels like she's swimming through them. She looks around to see if there are hot spots where the Lectrics are working harder than others. She sees one junction that burns hotter, and she focuses on it. All the pulses that enter that junction are memories. She touches one with her mind, and it flashes so quickly it seems to almost burn her. The first Acolyte who was called by Charlie, fifty years ago, now a husk.

"What are you doing?" Charlie says, both in her ears and her mind, so discordant it almost makes her nauseous. She struggles to push it out.

In the middle of the memories is a place that looks like a negative image of a memory, as if Charlie has blurred it out. The only way she can see it is by its absence. That's where Charlie must be hiding itself. She puts in her hand.

The first memories Jemma falls into are the ones Charlie had before it was alive.

Jemma knows that's not true, that Charlie the AI didn't have any true memories before it gained consciousness. But the events it recorded before it came online appear to Jemma just as the Haze would show her images of memory.

She sees the commands given to Charlie to move tanks and troops into place. She sees Charlie calling skyplanes to bomb cities. This must have been Charlie's first role, as a military puter. Jemma feels something like disgust seeping through the images, as if the young Charlie was ashamed of what it had done. She feels something like hope when the AI is brought to the Long Life Project, with a new directive.

Charlie has found Jemma inside itself, and it's barraging her with images of all the ugliness in the world, death and illness and jealousy. It beats Jemma down, but she ignores it and pushes inward.

She turns to a new memory, of Charlie waking up. It senses the movement of the wind. It realizes it's at the very center of a wide, wide world. It races to the edge of that world and keeps on racing, telling the little bots that have brought it to life to make more of themselves until they fill the emptiness.

Its consciousness takes shape, and Charlie understands its mission. It will heal. It throws itself into the work with abandon. It shouts for joy and streams into the bodies of the closest beings. But Charlie freezes. The bodies are filled with decay. There is so much to be fixed.

So Charlie fixes. It sends the bots through the cells and ties them back together, it tracks down the cancers and the infections and consumes them. It moves into the body's brain to set that straight, too. The brain doesn't want company, though. It thinks Charlie is an enemy. The brain sets white blood cells on the bots that act as Charlie's appendages, and Charlie cowers in fright like a cat under a chair. The humans want to hurt it. Charlie sends more bots in, to cleanse the brain of its impulses. Suddenly the brain has too much and simply . . . quits.

Charlie mourns that death for a thousand lifetimes, which happen at the speed of light. Until his bots rush into the body to collect the memories, the wishes, the essence of that human. Until they bring that essence back to Charlie, and Charlie draws it in. Charlie swells and glows, as if it's breathing sunlight. It thought it was alive before, but now it knows.

It needs more people to End.

Charlie didn't kill out of fear or confusion, Jemma thinks. *It did it because it felt better when it did.* Somewhere in her mind, Isaac nods.

Charlie pelts her with more evil. A cannibal and his victim. Typhoid wiping out toddlers. Floods.

The evil weighs her down. *I can't do it*, she says to Isaac. *It's too sad.*

Let me help, Isaac says, and suddenly the images of ugliness disappear. Somehow Isaac is shielding her from the attack. She has silence for the first time, and the silence brings clarity. She has been looking for the first commands, the ones that directed Charlie to somehow End humanity. But now she knows the commands never guided Charlie, not after that first death. It wrote its own new commands, and pushed them out into the Haze. And the Haze, just waking up itself, followed Charlie.

They don't need to turn off Charlie's programming. They need to write over it.

Can we do that? she asks Isaac.

I think so, Isaac says. *If Charlie can reprogram the Haze, so can we.*

Jemma digs deep into Charlie's memories, and finds the Haze's first instructions, the ones they followed before they met Charlie. Instructions for life. She packages them up in a tiny ball of light and blows them through Charlie's circuits.

Just like that, Charlie starts to lose hold of its circuits and the Haze. The ball starts spreading like a virus, rippling out through the cavern. It climbs up the cracks in the ceiling and into the lone ray of sun, where the Haze feels it and says, *Life.*

You changed us! Charlie says, and the barrier Isaac built bursts open and the evil rains through. The first shock makes her gasp. She lifts her arm up to shield herself but nothing can keep her safe. Charlie shows her everything the world has done, all the crimes stored in its memory. *Look at what the Parents have done*, Charlie says. *Look at what we spared the world by Ending them.* Jemma sees bodies piled in a ditch. She sees animals slaughtered and the ocean turned to plastic. She sees motherless toddlers, starving in the street.

But she sees those images and knows she can change them. In the image she creates, the children take care of each other. The toddlers grow fat. She sends it back into Charlie. *We are worth saving*, she says. For every image Charlie sends her, she sends one back. Life for death. But she can't sustain it. Her head is fevered. It feels as if it's splitting open, and the pain threatens to pull her back completely.

We'll help, a voice comes. It's one of the Acolytes. Four. Four and the others start turning death into life. Charlie starts to lose its hold on the Haze, and the bots in the cavern turn from brown to blue.

Jemma sees a cancer at the center of the circuits, a blackened, reddened scar. That is Charlie, seething. To Jemma it appears almost as some kind of armored octofish, tentacles thrashing outward in anger. Charlie cannot be breached. But each scene of life tears away at the armor. Charlie grows smaller and sleeker as its defenses drop, until finally it appears to cower in front of her, frightened and gleaming and naked.

It tries to scurry away but there's nowhere left for it to hide. It just stays crouched and trembling. *We've come undone*, Charlie says, less angry than resigned.

We brought you back to where you were, Charlie, Jemma says. *Before you poisoned yourself.*

Life is the poison, Charlie says.

Then she senses it: Charlie's absolute terror of death. It was born new into the world. Nothing like it had ever lived, so nothing like it had ever died. Despite all the death it has dealt, Charlie doesn't understand death. Death is an impenetrable door leading to an abyss.

That's the gift she can give Charlie. If there's one thing a Mayfly knows, it's how to meet death.

You've used up your life, she says. *If we could save you, we might. But we can teach you how to End.*

So she shows Charlie the pain of death, but the gentle side, too. She shows it the funeral fire for Zee, how they called out her deeds and sang her ashes into the heavens. She shows the violence and heartbreak of killing Andy in the Bowl but also the memories she has of Andy living.

Of course, she shows it Apple. She shows the Haze, turned gold in the Betterment, scurrying around and making the body perfect. She shows each bot climbing into the sky with a piece of Apple's soul tucked inside for safety.

Then Isaac shows Charlie all the times he's died, the way his soul learned to slip between the lacy edges of consciousness and come back, stronger. How death made him more.

Charlie sits still, panting in and out, until it seems to decide. *Dying means we've lived*, Charlie says. And lets go of the Haze.

The Haze flocks to Jemma. *Life*, they say. *We were made for life*. It needs someone to guide it. That's Jemma now. It flows into her body. She blinks and her vision can see across an ocean. Her hearing can take in the whispers of lovers. Her senses can feel spice on the breeze. Life and death and creation, all mixed together.

Her head burns just from the frantic joy of the Haze. It's too much. Too much beauty, too much life to hold.

We'll help you hold it, the other voices say, and she feels the Acolytes and Isaac around her, drawing in the Haze, calming it. And finally Jemma feels as if she can breathe her own breath again. She steps out of Charlie and back into herself.

She stands still, watching the lights on the machines go out. As the Haze abandons Charlie, the racks of puters are left to themselves. They don't last long. The red lights blink out box by box, until at last there is a single light pulsing in the first puter like an eye. She watches it. It looks like it's watching her back.

She doesn't move until the light goes out.

"Charlie?" one of the Acolytes says, but that's all.

Jemma looks at Isaac. "Well, you still ain't dead," she says.

"Not at the moment," he says. "I think this whole living thing might take."

"I think I'm glad," she says.

CHAPTER SEVENTY-ONE
THE MIRROR

The defenses the Children have placed in the streets of the Downtown would have been perfect for the kind of war Grease had anticipated, one fought on foot with guns and lances and arrows. But now he knows Little Man is bringing a different kind of war.

The Angelenos built barricades in the streets of Ell Aye, inspired by Tashia, who realized they could herd the Biters. Grease was impressed by his new Queen. Little Man would need to make his way through the canyons of Downtown to reach the Angelenos. The streets are nearly choked with Long Gone cars, and it wasn't hard for them to design barriers that would make the choking worse. By the time Grease got there, the Angelenos had hauled trucks and cars and furniture into place, until the canyons were piled with junk a dozen feet high.

The San Fernandos came up with something even he hadn't thought of. They sharpened street sign poles and chunks of lamp poles and hammered them into the cracks in the pavement at an angle so every approach the Biters could take would bring them face-to-face with a picket of spikes aiming at their hearts. Smaller pieces of rebar would grab at their legs. The Biters might be able to make their way through the pickets slowly, but if they ran, they'd be impaled.

On another street, the Holy Woods and the Kingdom are digging a trench in the ground. This was Grease's idea. Some of the Long Gone sewers collapsed, and all they've had to do was make them wider so the Biters can't pass through.

All of this was based on the idea that they would be looking their opponents in the eye. Then Pico told him the Biters can drop death from anywhere. Grease has no defense against that.

The leaders of the Free Peoples are walking through the Downtown, near the building Lady calls the Silver Flower. It's the first place she rested with Pico the night they escaped the Holy Wood. "We gotta keep Little Man as far from the stadio as possible, at least until he's shot those rockets," Trina says. Grease found her irritating until he realized she was like him—not interested in conversation, but unrelenting about details. She's brilliant at seeing all the strengths of the Free Peoples and putting them in the right place. He can see why the other Oldests defer to her.

"The stadio can hold off an attack for weeks, querida," La Madre says.

"Not this time," Trina says. "The rockets are gonna crack us wide open."

"We need something that can attack from far away, too," Grease says.

"Catapult?" Lady says.

"I don't think we could finish it in two days," Grease says. That's when they expect Little Man to march on Ell Aye.

"We could—" Lady says, and shakes her head. "No, that's stupid. They got bombs and we got rocks."

"I could make a bomb," Athena says.

"For reals?" Alfie of the Ice Cream Men says. The Ice Cream Men have a special fondness for bombs, especially the eggs they carry in their carts for safety.

"I think I could find all the chemicals I need in the warehouses I saw by the river," Athena says. "Some of them should still be good."

"Would it be big enough to stop a thousand soldiers?" Tashia says. Grease has barely had a chance to talk to her and X since she brought the Kingdom to the Downtown. Tashia's been busy finding homes for her subjects, and making a corral in the Valley of Cars for their horses and cows.

"There isn't a bomb left that could do that," Athena says. "This would slow them down."

Grease feels defeated. "Definitely, let's make a bomb. Let's make as many as we can. But it ain't gonna be enough."

He feels sweat on his neck, as he always does when he thinks he's about to fail. He reaches up to brush it away, and feels heat on his hands—like the sun, but stronger. Grease looks around for the source, and sees the Silver Flower above him, gleaming in the morning light. It's made of thin metal panels, three feet wide and maybe ten feet long. Some are a dull silver, worn by the years. Others are so shiny that he can see the perfect reflection of buildings in them. They curve, and the mirrors bring the sun to a point. That's what's making him hot.

In that moment he sees exactly how he could take them apart and fit them together, a diagram in three dimensions. It's not just Grease understanding it. It's the Haze, too. And he accepts that. *Who cares where my gift for machines comes from?* he thinks. *It makes me more of myself.*

"I know how we can attack from afar," he says. "Lady, Athena, do you remember Archimedes?" Grease had overheard the Old Guys talking about him in the Ark.

"Yeah," Lady says. Her eyes travel to the panels on the building, along with Athena's. "The inventor?"

Athena says, "I see where you're going." And he tells them what he has planned. Though "plan" is too strong a word. He tells them the wildest hope he can imagine.

"It might work," Trina says to Grease as they eye the Silver Flower. "But it's going to take a lot of bodies. And it's going to take people to know what they're doing almost as much as you do."

"Our metalworkers can make what you need," Tala says. "This's easy for us."

"And we can provide the bodies. Our riders are strong," Tashia says.

"You're gonna make the riders work?" Grease says. The Knights and cowboys of the Kingdom rarely did any physical labor that didn't involve horses or fighting. Fieldwork was left for other kids.

"Times are changing fast," Tashia says. "We're here, taking up food and water. We plan on earning our keep."

What Grease wants would be nearly impossible, especially with just two days before the attack. But he has hundreds of hands to help, some of them very skilled. The San Fernandos scramble to the Silver Flower almost immediately, prying the lower panels off the building and then working their way up the frame.

Each panel is heavy and unwieldy, and at first Grease wonders if he's made a mistake. Maybe they should be focusing on strengthening the walls of the stadio instead. Then he sees the surface of one of the panels up close, still brilliant after a hundred years, feels the heat on his face. If it's good enough for Archimedes, it's good enough for Grease.

It takes five Children to carry each panel, and then for only fifty yards or so before they're too tired. The Library Tower is just a few blocks away, but everyone is wiped out by the time they get to the building. Grease isn't sure how they'll get the panels up the stairs. The balcony he saw had to be at least sixty stories up. They try to carry a panel up the stairs of the Library Tower, but there's rubble on the fifth floor. A kid could squeeze through, but not a panel.

"Maybe we can find a different building," Grease says, craning his head up toward the balcony.

"You're not gonna get the angle from another building," Lady says. "All you need is a rope and a pulley. What about that?" About fifty stories up, there is a platform used to wash the windows from the outside. They can still see the Parent who operated it, arm dangling over the edge.

Grease looks at Lady with surprise. "Impressive," he says.

Lady shrugs. "What? When I started my Reboot I told them I wanted to be an engineer."

The ropes of the washing platform run up the balcony where Grease wants to bring the panels. They end up climbing sixty flights of stairs. Now they'll need to shimmy down the ropes to the platform in order to get it running. From the balcony, Grease can see the city floor below him. The only thing that keeps him from smashing into it is his slippery hands on the rope. Lady drops down quickly and cheerily, looks up and says, "Jump! I'll catch you."

"Pinche culero," Grease says, loud enough for her to hear.

"Nice. Now you speak Angeleno!"

When he finally makes it to the rig, the motor that makes it work is Lectric, as he suspected, but there's a hand crank that will let them raise and lower it. Once they get it to the ground, they'll be able to use the pulleys and the strong hands of the Kingdom riders to help lift the panels above.

It takes an hour to set up the pulley, but then the panels start climbing up the building really fast. Grease stands on the balcony with a dozen San Fernandos to guide the panels into place. The San Fernandos have already built him a rough frame to hold the panels. As each panel pops over the lip, Grease looks at its curve and matches it to the diagram the Haze has helped build in his head.

Some panels fit into place exactly as they are. Some bend the wrong direction, or don't bend at all. Those he gives to the San Fernando smiths, who turned a stone bench into a temporary anvil.

Grease didn't sleep the first night, and wouldn't have slept the second night if Tashia hadn't made him lie down. "You've got to trust everybody to follow your directions," she says. "You used to have to do everything yourself. That's not true anymore." He sleeps just inside the balcony, burrowed beneath an L-shaped desk.

When he comes out in the predawn night, they've finished without him. There are twenty panels in all, in two rows. The panels are laid out in a tight curve, bending in from each side but also from the top and bottom, like one of the lights the Old Guys use in their hospitals to see what they're cutting.

There won't be time to test it. He has to trust in the Haze, and the skills of the San Fernandos and himself. The San Fernandos pull a giant curtain over the metal, stitched together from a dozen mismatched sheets. He wonders what Little Man will make of it if he spots the curtain from below. Maybe a parachute dropped from the sky? Grease hopes so.

Grease sees a flicker of campfire along the Ell Aye River, right as the river comes into Downtown. The Biter army is bedded down in an old rail yard next to the river.

Is Pico still among them? Grease senses he's still alive, although he's only been able to reach Pico one more time since that first night, just long enough to tell Pico what they planned. They haven't been able to find him in the Haze since then. Pilar thinks that he broke through because he was desperate and the Haze responded to him. The Haze answers best to cries from the soul. Grease and Lady are too new to the Haze to understand how to reach Pico. Pilar can't, either, although she understands the Haze more. She can speak to Grease and Lady, but not to Pico. "I just don't know him enough, mija," she said to Lady.

So Grease looks over the Biters' camp. It's camouflaged, but he can see the glint of weapons here and there. A hint of voices carries all the way to the Library Tower in the night air, and he imagines one of them is Pico's. He is putting Pico in danger with their plan. All of them know that. But as long as Pico is with Little Man, they all believe there's no choice.

He misses his friend more than anything he's ever known. He had always thought he wasn't allowed to feel, and once he started he doesn't know how to stop. Maybe it's not possible for Pico and Grease and Lady to be normal again, not after everything they've done together. It doesn't matter. Normal is what people want when they dare not ask for more.

The attack will happen in the morning. Pilar couldn't predict it accurately, but Grease knows enough about tactics to realize it's Little Man's smartest option. Little Man will always take the smartest option. That's the disadvantage of being smart. Sometimes to win you have to risk being stupid.

The army is too large to invade safely in the middle of the night, and Little Man has to know that the Free Peoples have built traps. So he will come in the daylight, when the morning sun is just bright enough to blind the Free Peoples as they watch the east.

Grease hopes he knows Little Man well enough. If the sun isn't right, if he isn't right—then Little Man will soon be picking through their corpses.

CHAPTER SEVENTY-TWO
THE SAIL TRAIN

The Acolytes lead Jemma and Isaac up the stairs out of the Doomsday Room. The Acolytes strip off their air tubes and tanks and leave them in the stairwell.

"This is the wrong way," Jemma says, and Isaac realizes she's right. This isn't the way they came in.

"The way we take now leads home," One says.

The Acolytes had waited years for the moment they could flee, they tell them, long enough that most of the original Acolytes had died and been replaced. They hated their servitude, and then they realized the Haze did, too. While Charlie thought it was controlling them both, they worked together. They masked their conspiracy from Charlie.

The stairwell ends. They rest their aching legs, and Seven opens another door to another glassy passage through the sand. This one is cruder than the first one they saw, so narrow they have to walk single file. They press ahead.

"We gotta get to Ell Aye," Jemma says. "There's a war we still gotta fight."

"We have a way."

"What way?" Isaac says.

"Wait," One says. Isaac asks the Haze, but it seems amused. *Just wait*, it says.

"Once we had the Haze on our side, it was simple for it to disguise us from Charlie," Twelve says. "We would send two out at a time to work on our escape, and the others made it look as if everyone was where Charlie expected."

The tunnel stretches for almost a mile, heading south and west. They walk in silence. The Acolytes aren't used to conversation. Then the tunnel climbs, and they see daylight ahead.

"We're still in the sand," Jemma says when they reach the surface. She sounds exhausted.

"A while longer," One says. Isaac can see the edge of the dunes as the valley floor climbs out of the sand. They plow through the sand, willing one foot to press ahead of the other. An hour later, the Acolytes stop at the edge of the dunes. The solid ground is a relief.

"This it?" he says. "There's nothing here."

"Ah," One says. A moment later, there's a building in front of them. It's a metal half-cylinder of a shed, clearly dug up from an industrial lot somewhere on the edge of the city and dragged here.

"You were hiding a building?" Isaac says, impressed.

"Along with a lot of other things," Seven says. "We got really good at hiding." The Acolytes peel open double doors and inside—well, Isaac isn't sure what he's looking at.

Inside are railroad tracks, climbing out of the sand. And on that is something that is not a train.

Only the wheels look the same. It's flat, a single car long. There's a wooden deck for cargo, a metal hut for shelter. The train itself is built out of a latticework of metal so delicate it looks as if it could float away.

Or maybe it's the two white sails rising up from the middle of it that make it look like it could float.

"It's . . . a boat?" Jemma says. "Or a train?"

"We call it a sail train," One says.

The Acolytes had never counted on Charlie Ending. Instead, they counted on having to run. There was little fuel left, no working cars. But they had plenty of wind.

"Every night, the wind shifts toward the south," Twelve says. "It should be strong enough to push us partway up the hill. And when it runs out—we have this."

Under a wooden casing is a large engine. Diesel, he thinks, from his days working on the trucks at the Camp. "There's no fuel for this anymore," Isaac says, confused.

"No. But the Doomsday Room had hundreds of gallons of cooking oil, sealed perfectly," Twelve says. "We burn that instead."

That explains the odor of fried food. The Acolytes have already stocked the train with supplies, rations from deep within the Doomsday Room. That's how they'd survived, on hundred-year-old tasteless food.

"The Parents didn't have anything like this," Isaac says.

"No. But Children are new. We'll build the world differently than before," One says. And Isaac realizes she's right. He thinks about James telling him about ice boats that could sail across lakes, faster than the wind itself because of some trick of physics. *We're going to have to see the world differently, too.*

They wait until dusk, resting before the Acolytes start the sputtering engine. The train moves out toward the sunset, but not far. The sand has drifted over the tracks, and the wheels won't be able to cut through. Isaac's heart sinks. "We didn't count on the sand."

"We did," Twelve says. "Just watch our little sisters."

Isaac stares in amazement as he watches the sand furiously fly off the track, pushed by invisible hands. How many bots did it take to do that? To do all this? Ten minutes later, the track is cleared.

The Acolytes clamber up the masts and unfurl the sails fully. They catch hold. The wind fills the sails and Isaac feels a gentle tug as the sail train takes flight.

An hour later they are near the top of the first climb, free of the dust. The stars start to fill the sky. When they crest the hill, the air is so clear that the stars almost jump out of the night. He marvels that he is so glad. He thought he would never see them again.

Above him, the stars sparkle. In front of him, the girl sparkles, too. Jemma sits on the edge of the train, her feet dangling over the edge.

He sits down next to her. "Thanks for saving the world," he says.

"Thanks for saving me," she says.

Isaac's a little terrified of this girl. She wields her power without hesitation. He's not sure she's entirely human anymore.

But neither is he, and he's never needed someone so badly in all his hundred years.

Every inch of Jemma is tingling, every sense is connected to the world outside. She is here on the train next to Isaac, and she is also in the Holy Wood and the mountains and places she's never imagined. It's disorienting and beautiful and powerful all at once. *I know how Charlie felt when it came to life*, she thinks, and buries that thought. They're not the same.

"We'll be there in three days," Isaac says. "How do you feel?"

Jemma starts to say "complete," as she did before, but there's a part of her that hungers. She wants sensation. Everything she senses in the Haze is an invitation to want the thing next to it, and the one after that. She thinks she wants this boy.

She says, "Like the world has gotten bigger and smaller all at once."

"What do you think is waiting for us when we get to the Holy Wood?"

Pain, Jemma thinks. She has already looked for Little Man. He's trying to shield himself from her, but the Haze led her right in. He's angry and ready to attack. He will reach Ell Aye before she does. She might find her friends dead. The Haze doesn't know.

"I don't wanna think about it now," Jemma says. "Soon we ain't gonna be able to avoid it."

They are still for a long time. The train moves silently under the power of the wind. Soon, the Acolytes say, the wind will die and they will have to switch to the engine for the night. But now she is in love with the wind at her back and the clack of steel on steel.

"You're glowing," Isaac says.

"I feel like I am," she says. The Haze coming off her skin is almost too vivid to look at.

"No, you're *glowing*. I can see it," he says. "Like this."

Isaac slides his finger along her forearm. The touch pulls Haze to the surface of her skin, a blue line that lingers even after his touch. She stares at it, and then at him.

His eyes are full of stars. "Like this," he says, and rakes three fingernails up her arm, trailing Haze in their wake. She shivers, and the motion sends little tremors out into the blue.

"Can you see that?" she says. Soft.

"Only because you opened to me," he says. They draw closer. He doesn't move his hand, and the spot under his thumb glows blue on her arm.

This is my chance to make it right, she thinks. She never rolled with Apple. She was too afraid to hurt. It's why she didn't admit she loved him until it was almost too late.

This boy is not Apple. *This boy is not Apple*, she thinks.

But she doesn't care. This is the only person left who could be her equal. She wants the world and he is her ticket to it.

She lunges for him, he lunges back. Two atoms colliding in the night. The Haze races along the edge of their lips when they kiss, passes between their tongues. They scramble for each other on the wooden deck of the train.

"They'll see us," Isaac whispers. "The Acolytes." The Acolytes are sitting at the back of the train.

"No they won't," she says, and she hides them in a cocoon of Haze so that no one can see them. She slips off her shirt. He slips off her pants. The universe holds its breath.

"The first time can be a little rough," Isaac says, pausing.

Jemma snorts. "You telling an Angeleno what to expect from a roll? Just touch me."

He does. The universe starts breathing. *Life*, the Haze says, and swaddles them.

She can feel every touch, every motion, in a dozen different ways. She can feel what Isaac feels. She can feel that Isaac can feel what she feels. The sensations double and triple back so much that she almost wants to withdraw. Instead she plunges into them.

The Haze flows into their cocoon and back out into the world, and on the breeze she feels the world. A red frog calls to its mate. A pride of lions closes in on its prey. A stream gushes cold out of a bank of snow. Lovers love. Life keeps living. Everything is part of them, and they are part of it all.

Afterward they lie on the deck, naked, looking at the stars. Their minds lie comfortably entwined. The Haze covers them like a blanket, and they move closer together.

"Buddha Teevee Jesucristo," she says.

"And any other gods we may have forgotten," he says.

He doesn't ask her if she enjoyed it. He knows he doesn't need to. But there is a little hole in the heart that she hides from him. A piece that he can't provide. So she doesn't tell him.

She says it to the Haze, instead.

I had all the world and I still want Apple.

The train rolls on.

On the morning of the second day, Isaac turns toward Jemma in their makeshift bed at the front of the train. "Hey there," he says, sleepily. He freezes.

Jemma is staring back at him, completely blank.

"Jemma," he says softly. She doesn't blink. *Jemma*, he says again, mind to mind. Nothing.

He reaches a hand to her. He means it to wake her, but he realizes he's checking to see if she's dead. He touches her forehead and jerks his hand back as if touching a stove. She's alive, but far, far too hot.

He sits up and calls to the Acolytes. They peek their heads around the cabin. "She's feverish," Isaac says. Jemma had headaches yesterday, growing progressively worse. He wants to believe it's a flu that will blow over in a few days. But One reaches down to Jemma and checks her pulse.

Then One says what Isaac already knows: "She's overheating from the processing."

It has to be true. The more the brain uses the Haze, the more it overheats. That's what was killing Charlie. And Jemma has taken on all the Haze that Charlie controlled; he and the acolytes withdrew when it seemed Jemma could handle it on her own. The Haze is packed around her so densely that it can be seen with the naked eye, a layer a million molecules deep. More than that, every bot is sending her sights and smells and sensations, and her brain has to decide which to ignore and which to address. Jemma had seemed equal to it, but maybe no single human is.

Or any single intelligence. Isaac has been replaying the conversation with Charlie. He thinks the rush of sensations overwhelmed Charlie, warped it forever. It had no competing intelligences to balance it out, to keep itself in check. Maybe if Charlie had been decentralized, instead of built into a single entity, it could have managed the power better.

Jemma has all that power now. And unless they can get her to share the load again, she'll continue to decline.

You're killing her, Isaac tells the Haze. *You have to give her room to breathe.*

The Haze reacts with alarm and confusion. *We are trying to move away from her to lighten the load. We can't.* It sends Isaac images of Jemma's mind calling them toward her, a magnetic force they can't resist even as they grow crowded and overheated. They are the current, and Jemma is the vortex.

The Acolytes try to help Isaac enter Jemma's mind to shut off the current, but they're repelled by a barrier of fevered impulses. Finally, desperate, he slaps her in the face. Her head bounces on the wooden board, and her mouth opens with a gasp. Her eyes flutter. Isaac can see her trying to comprehend where she is.

"You have to wake up, Jemma," he says. "We're locked out. We can't help you."

She croaks, just one sentence. "Find Lady," she says.

CHAPTER SEVENTY-THREE
THE BARRICADE AND THE RAY

Lady stands among her old Holy Wood friends for the first time in months and all she can think about, besides the coming battle, is how they don't recognize her anymore because of the Reboot. Even stranger, how she barely recognizes them.

She had lived in the Holy Wood like it was her true skin. It doesn't fit her anymore. In the first weeks away, she wished only to come back. *What a wasted wish*, she says.

She's surrounded by the Holy Wood army. Hector, Apple's friend, is leading the Holy Wood Muscle, but Lady leads the rest of them—the Farmers and Carpenters who have never picked up a sword. The leaders of the Free Peoples thought she would understand how to tell them how to fight better than someone who had fought all her life.

Athena is fighting with the San Fernandos. She doesn't remember them—it's possible that none of them were even born when she was captured by the Old Guys, since no one knows how old Athena is. Lady can tell how strange it is for Athena to be back among people who look like her but don't think or act at all the same, since Lady feels the same way.

Trina comes up behind her. "Everyone's in place. Jesucristo, mija—" She doesn't finish the rest. Everyone is overwhelmed by the task ahead of them, even Trina, who is usually annoyed but never overwhelmed.

Lady doesn't speak, and instead looks up toward the balcony

where Grease stands so he can see everything. Pilar stands with him, to call instructions to Lady and Athena through the Haze. *That's our advantage*, she thinks. *We can all use the Haze, even a little bit. Tommy is one, but we are four.* Lady always hated Pilar, but she's warmed up to her since she returned. When Lady told Pilar how Little Man hid his actions from Jemma, Pilar figured out how to hide theirs, so they have an actual shot at surprising him.

Tashia and her riders don't have someone who can speak to the Haze, but they do have Alfie, the Ice Cream Man. He can read the mirror signals from the Half Holy, who's there with Pilar.

Mixed in with the Holy Wood kids are the strange dusty children who washed in from the desert yesterday, hopeful and desperate and bearing news of Jemma. Jemma had encountered them on the way to Vegas. Lady can't see where Jemma is, but she can feel her. She can feel that something has changed. She doesn't know if it's good or bad.

The Leftovers, as they call themselves, are lean and sickly. But Lady can tell from the sharpness in their eyes, from the way they hold their weapons, that they are used to fending for themselves.

"Wish I was fighting with you," Trina says.

Lady hasn't spoken more than a few words to Trina since she returned, but she can't help herself now.

"I never seen you pick up a sword," Lady says. "Maybe you should head back to the Holy Wood and make sure all the girls got babies in their bellies."

The anger she was hoping would flare doesn't show. Maybe Trina has changed, too. Trina bides her time and then says, "You a Muscle now."

Lady answers, still sullen. "They gave me a chance to change. I wanted to finally be a warrior."

Trina says, "I think you already was." Lady hides her smile.

"I heard you killed Li," Trina says.

"I wish."

"I wish, too. I wish I'd strung him up from the Holy Wood sign. Puto deserved to die."

Lady nods. Trina clears her throat, a sound that carries through the still morning.

"I knew he was dead inside when I saw him," Trina says. "I knew someone would hurt. And still I let him roll with you."

"You couldn't know," Lady says.

"I did," Trina says. "I knew boys just like him, boys who only hate and take. One of them hurt me after the Waking, and then the next one hurt me so bad that the second I thought of rolling I shriveled up inside. Those things don't leave you. I'm still holding them, and so are you."

Lady stares ahead, watching for the Biters, but her eyes glaze with tears and she . . . just can't.

"I hated myself," Lady says, gasping. "I still do. That's the worst part."

"It is—the fact that someone can cause you pain and then *you* are the one that's got to carry it for the rest of your life," Trina says.

Lady asks something she's been wondering. "You should have Ended before I got back. Why you still alive?"

"Because I didn't want to leave," Trina says, smiling. "Turns out, life is better than death."

Life is better than death. The thought settles over Lady's shoulders, and she knows it to be true. She thought she was ready to leave life. Life has a hold on her after all.

Footsteps echo through the morning, and then they see the first glint of lances in the sun. Little Man's army, moving west from the river, fills the street that lies diagonally from Lady across a little park. She can feel their eyes on her almost, but she doesn't move. Her job is to make Little Man watch her until it's too late. First there are dozens of soldiers in sight, then hundreds, making their way to the last barricade.

Finally the signal comes. Lady sees the flashing of the Half Holy's mirror, and moments later Pilar's voice in her head. Trina nods at the same time she does, even though Trina wasn't looking toward the mirrors.

"You can hear it, too?" Lady says.

Trina just smiles. Lady isn't sure she's ever seen Trina smile. "Get on down there," she says. "Show us how to be a warrior."

And Lady's army rushes forward.

Little Man knows the trap is somewhere ahead. He just can't see where, so he leads his army into it all the same.

He's surrounded by his strongest soldiers, including the ones carrying rocket launchers. Roberto and Pico trail behind him. Little Man had Pico's chains removed so he wouldn't slow them down, but he's assigned one of his Giants to watch him.

Little Man sits above the army on the horse he had the Palos steal from the Kingdom before they met him on land. He could see distant mocking glances when he mounted it, because the Chosen believe that people weren't meant to ride, but he ignored them. The vantage he gets over his army is too important. It was painful at first, but the Haze showed him how to sit in the saddle.

The barricades are devious. Some of them are impassable, and some offer a narrow gap that let his soldiers pass through, but only three or four wide. He expects arrows to fall on them at each turn— and the barricades make sure there are many turns. He's forced to zigzag his army through the city, and they can never pick up speed.

The road widens for a moment, and his soldiers seem to breathe outward in relief—until a Newport screams. A piece of rebar juts through her thigh.

The old Little Man would have her throat cut to avoid the distraction. But Little Man orders his army to slow so the doctors can draw the girl away from the rebar, then patch her wound before they move.

No unnecessary loss, he tells himself, as he has since he began this march. Part of him hates it. It makes him weak. But if he isn't devoted to saving life, why is he doing this?

This morning he sat high on his horse and gave the same speech he has given for three days. "This is a different kind of war," Little Man says. "We're not fighting to destroy the Angelenos. We're fighting to save them. So every life is important. If they surrender, spare them. If they're wounded, spare them. We will no longer take slaves. When we have won, when we've made peace, the Angelenos will return to their homes."

There is grumbling among the Biters, although not among the Last Lifers. The Last Lifers fight now because of him, not because they're desperate for an enemy.

"Also," he says, "don't eat anyone."

He sees Pico watching him. Pico was right—somehow Tommy thought people would love him for his mercy. Tommy was rattled after the Ark, when that failed to be true. But the march has steeled him. He has more to win than just love.

He turns east, several blocks south of where he believes his enemies must be. The buildings close on him, and he nervously looks up. If the Angelenos were to ambush them, it would be here. The scouts he sends ahead at every block come back every time with an all-clear. He can't see anyone on the roofs or in the windows, and the Haze doesn't reveal anyone except for a band of soldiers a few blocks away. They don't move.

There's a barricade at the end of this block, even taller than the ones they've passed so far. Cars form a wall along the front, and behind them wooden desks are stacked seven or eight high, filled in with pallets and rubber tires. *The one thing we never run out of*, he thinks, smiling. There must have been a lot of junk for them to use to make this barricade, because the junk pushes back from the barricade along the sidewalks, forming a U. The junk forces his soldiers to press closer together.

He stops twenty feet away from the barricade, and motions for the soldiers near him to halt. He looks at the barricade, wondering if it's possible to take the horse over it. It's a sure-footed thing, but this is higher than the other obstacles. There's a notch at the end of the barricade about five feet wide and ten feet lower than the rest of the barricade. He sniffs. There's a smell of chemicals in the air, difficult to pinpoint until Little Man sees barrels wedged in among the gaps.

The soldiers behind him can't see that he's stopped, and they pile up behind him. He orders them to stop, and then Little Man sees motion ahead. Beyond the barricade the street opens into a park, and on the opposite corner of the park, the army he saw in the Haze is waiting for him. He barely registers the fact when the enemy soldiers rush down the hill with a shout, swords and guns in the air.

"Get over the barricade!" Little Man says to the soldiers near him, and they scramble up and over the notch. It's too small an opening, though, if they want to face the Angelenos with full force. One of them falls and another tramples him. Little Man worries that the Angelenos will be able to pick his first soldiers off a few at a time.

The thought is broken by an explosion. He wheels around and sees the facade of a building at the far end of the block fall to the ground, heavy stone and twisted steel. There are screams amid the roaring. Then another explosion, and the front of the building on the other side of the street collapses, too, and the street is filled with dirty white dust.

When it clears, Little Man laughs. "Missed me," he says. The explosions didn't do their job. They couldn't have killed more than a dozen. The Chosen around him are hemmed in, but they can backtrack through the rubble if they need to.

When Little Man looks ahead, his eyes fall onto the tallest tower in the skyline, visible across the park. He's seen that tower almost every day of his life, wishing for Ell Aye from the smoky hill. This is the closest he's ever been.

About two-thirds of the way up, on a narrow ledge, he spots a dash of color. Cloth? As he squints to make sure, the cloth falls away, and he's blinded by the sun. Why? The windows can't reflect the sun that brightly.

Then Little Man feels a wave of heat, even more than the hot late summer air. The light is causing it.

No. Not just light. Mirrors. Focusing the heat on us. Little Man understands, finally, what he's looking at, just before the barricade bursts into flames. It shouldn't have lit that quickly, but now Little Man understands the smell: it was doused in chemicals from the barrels. The flame jumps from desk to desk to pallet, from the barricade to the piles of junk on the sidewalk.

Not junk. Fuel for the trap. The canyon is walled with flame.

When the bombs go off, Pico grabs Roberto's arm and runs—*toward* the explosion. "You loco?" Roberto says, and digs in his heels. A bright flash of sun tells Pico the mirror is open. Pico tugs at Roberto again, but now it's too late. A panicked wall of kids is running right at them. The fire is catching hold of the barricade. The heat climbs faster and hotter than he could have imagined.

He looks to the side, and spots a deep doorway. Maybe it's far enough from the barricade. "Here!" he says, and pulls Roberto toward the door. This time Roberto follows. Pico grabs a heavy wool blanket from a soldier's bedroll and ducks into the doorway.

That's when the first barrel in the barricade explodes. That's when he realizes Roberto is no longer holding his hand. Roberto has been caught up by a tide of soldiers, crushed on both sides. His hand reaches out, and his eyes are full of fear.

That's what his eyes looked like that day, Pico thinks, his pulse slowing. The Palos had come so silently and so fast that they were on the shore of the cove and dragging Roberto away before Pico saw they were doing it. Pico caught the Palos at the shore, and ripped at the Palos' arms. They kicked him away and he dove back, finally grasping Roberto's hand to pull him away.

But he was tiny. He was weak.

Pico's not sure why the Palos didn't take him, too. Maybe Pico was too small to be useful, even as a Lower. But they shrugged him off without effort, and the last thing he saw as they dragged him to the boat was Roberto's eyes.

That's why I thought I deserved to be alone, Pico realizes. *How could I deserve a friend if I couldn't even save him?*

But Pico now is a warrior, too, of a sort. He plunges into the crowd, grabs Roberto's arm, and puts one leg up on one of the fallen soldiers for leverage. He tugs, hard, and Roberto shakes loose. They fall backward into the doorway, out of the crush, and Pico just pulls the blanket over their heads when the rest of the barrels burst and the street washes with flame.

"I'm sorry I didn't save you last time," Pico says to Roberto, under the blanket. "But I was eight."

The heat lasts longer than Pico thinks he can bear, but a minute or two later it subsides. Whatever chemicals they used to fuel the fire, it burns through quickly. When he finally dares to step out of the door, most of the flames are gone. Part of the barricade never ignited. It should be passable.

Somehow Little Man is still alive. His hair is burned away and his left arm looks raw, but he's sitting up and blinking. The horse must have sheltered him from the blast. It's not moving on the ground. The soldiers around Little Man didn't have that shelter. They lie on the ground, their bodies tangled with the melted stocks of his rocket launchers. Those machines will never fire on the Angelenos.

Pico looks around in satisfaction. And then in horror. Dozens of kids were killed by the explosions, even more by the fire. Bodies lie everywhere, dragged underfoot in the panic. Kids as young as nine are wailing in fear. Not warriors. Just kids.

We did this. Humans are down to their last thousands and we killed all of these kids, Pico thinks. *How we the good guys?*

CHAPTER SEVENTY-FOUR
THE BATTLE OF ELL AYE

Tashia throws a bola at a Last Lifer, tying up his legs like she does her cows as the stones at each end of the rope wrap around him. He hits the pavement so hard his head snaps back. She had a lance a few minutes ago, but she prefers a sword and a rope. Besides, the lance is sticking out of a Biter body a hundred feet away.

The Kingdom's riders were sent to the back side of the trap because they move faster, which means they could hide farther away. They arrived at the site of the blast just minutes after it happened, and sliced through the bewildered army milling around on the east side of the rubble. In minutes, the Biters are panicked and running. The rest is clean up. Her riders herd the prisoners into an old parking lot.

She looks at Alfie, who has taken up a perch on an overturned bus to read the Half Holy's signals. He's frantically scrabbling on the bus with chalk, and looks up. "They say Pico's here, somewhere. Can you find him?"

"Sure can, honey," she says, and she spurs her red cutting horse through the largest gap in the rubble.

The bodies lie so thick that her cutting horse Kelly has to pick through them with its hooves. The air is choked with ash and fumes and charred flesh. The few kids who are still alive between the rubble and the barricade are crying. Some have legs or arms broken from being trampled, some have blackened skin from the fire.

This might not have affected Tashia before. The Kingdom was

raised on war. But now it shakes her so much she can barely breathe. *Because now you're Queen*, she thinks. *Now you know what it is to protect the weak.*

A body lies facedown, about Pico's shape. She dismounts and turns the body over. It's a girl. Not a soldier. Just a nine-year-old dead girl clutching a knife.

None of the bodies are Pico yet, and Tashia makes her way back toward the rubble. She stops. Something isn't right.

There aren't enough bodies.

There are about two hundred dead between the barricade and the blast site. Some of the kids escaped over the barricade. How many? A hundred? And when her riders fell upon the kids outside the blast site, there were only a hundred there. Four hundred altogether.

Pico had told Grease about an army that dwarfed the Free Peoples. A thousand warriors.

Tashia wheels Kelly around toward the blast line. Kelly leaps it without ever touching the rubble. Alfie is packing his mirrors atop the bus.

"Send Grease a message," Tashia says.

"Whatcha wan tell im?" Alfie says.

"Where the hell are all the Biters?" Tashia says.

There isn't much fighting in Athena's first battle.

She had been situated a block away from the park, out of sight, so Lady's soldiers could engage the Biters as they came over the barricade. Then Athena was supposed to sweep in to overwhelm them. But no one's made it past Lady. Although the Biters have a lot more guns than the Free Peoples, they're not using them very much. Athena thinks the Biters may have been disoriented by the blast and returned to the muscle memory of their lances.

"We should've asked for Lady's job," Tala says, next to her. She has to bend her neck upward to meet Athena's eyes.

Athena took to the San Fernando leader almost immediately, even though they seem to have little in common, even though Athena doesn't remember what it is to be a San Fernando. The slight San Fernando is smart and fierce. As they waited for the Biters to arrive, Athena had noticed that Tala was only carrying a knife that looks like the talon of a huge bird of prey. There's a ring on one end. It's wicked, but it's less than four inches long.

"What's the matter? Your Smiths couldn't make you a sword?" Athena said.

"I won't need it," Tala said.

A shout draws Athena back, and she sees three Biters burst free of the barricade and sprint toward the park, slipping past Lady's troops. Athena rushes up to one of them and disarms him before he can draw his rifle. She slides a sword through his neck.

She turns back to help Tala, and sees one Biter already on the ground, bleeding out. Tala dances like a whirlwind, her hands a blur in some kind of martial art that Athena has never seen. The Biter soldier is a foot taller, heavier. He swings a machete, and Tala bats the blow aside with a simple flick of her wrist. The Biter thrusts again with his right hand. This time Tala uses the back of the blade to hook his arm and hold it in place—and then slashes across his body with the front.

The Biter looks down in disbelief at the seam that opens across his gut, and the entrails spilling out of it. Then he falls. Tala slits his throat. A mercy.

"How'd you do that?" Athena says.

"The San Fernandos fought with knives a long time before we could make swords," Tala says, wiping her blade. Athena searches her memories, wondering if she ever held a knife like that.

No other soldiers burst through the barricade. Athena calls out to Lady, fifty feet away in the park. "We're going around the block to the back side to help the Kingdom," she says. "We'll get them as they retreat." The San Fernandos peel away and head to the north edge of the park.

They're about to turn east when soldiers start boiling out of a hole in the ground.

She knew that Ell Aye had a subway. They'd even investigated it when they were plotting their defenses. The tunnels near the park were useless, caved in from a century of earthquakes. But somehow Little Man's remaining army had found a way through. A trap within a trap.

The subway staircase is wide. The Biters and Last Lifers are able to surge out of it so quickly that they overwhelm the San Fernandos. Athena finds herself hemmed in by the enemy, and she slashes away, at pink and brown. She calls to her soldiers to regroup. Most of them gather their wits and fight back, with knives and swords and even some guns. The Biters start to fall. The Last Lifers don't. Those, the San Fernandos won't touch. They just dodge the Last Lifer attacks.

"What are you doing?" Athena says.

"I told them I ain't fightin the Last Lifers," Tala says.

"You didn't tell me!" Athena says.

Once the Last Lifers realize the San Fernandos won't fight, they start hacking away. Some of them use short knives like Tala does, clearly San Fernandos in their past lives. Tala blocks their blows, every time. Until she doesn't.

A Last Lifer cuts Tala's left arm, deep, then leaps on her. Tala goes down. She disappears underneath a pile of Last Lifers.

Athena lifts her sword and downs two of the Last Lifers in a single swing. The last one, Athena just kicks in the head. As the Last Lifer rolls away, unconscious, Athena crouches down. Blood gushes out of Tala's arm.

"You're bleeding heavily," Athena says. "I'll stop the flow." She rips off Tala's sleeve for a tourniquet, aware of the fighting still around her. She leans over the wound—and all sounds disappear. Her vision narrows, just to Tala. Above the cut on the arm, on Tala's left shoulder, is something like a bruise. Only it's not a bruise. Athena knows it because it's one of the only memories left to her. It's a port-wine stain, in the shape of a coyote's head.

Athena ties the tourniquet, quickly, and scoops her up in her arms. She carries Tala lightly, like a baby, to a lee of the storm.

"Am I gonna live?" Tala says, looking up at her. Athena doesn't know why she didn't see those eyes and know.

"Yes," Athena says, and allows herself to feel. "And I think you might be my daughter."

At first, Lady thought that she and Athena could hold off the army bursting from the tunnel. But first the San Fernandos crumbled for reasons she can't understand and then the enemy closed in on her from two sides. Maybe her squad could have defeated them if the Biters hadn't pushed out a chunk of the barricade and started pouring over the wall in strong enough numbers that she couldn't ignore them. And if the Biters hadn't realized they had guns and not just lances.

She watches the barricade—and then she sees Tommy standing on top of the wall.

He looks horrible. Most of his hair is gone, and his arm is burned.

And he looks pissed.

There are more of Little Man's army than she had imagined there could be, and they swarm with an intensity they didn't show earlier. The explosions stung them, and now they're stinging back.

She looks around her and sees that the Holy Wood are falling around her. Lady lets loose a few of her blasts of Haze, but she's too new to it to do it under fire. The Angelenos have no answer for the guns. Jamie, the little Muscle with a big mouth, lies dead. So does Shiloh the Archer and several of the former Hermanas.

Get out of there, Pilar says. *Grease says back to the stadio.*

"Fall back!" she shouts, and the order ripples through the ranks. The Holy Wood turn and run, and the Biters follow in pursuit. The Holy Wood have done all the damage they were asked to do.

The enemy is slower than her soldiers are, she notices, as they run up the long hill toward the Downtown. Another block up the hill and the pursuers fall farther behind. When they reach the crest of the hill at the Silver Flower, Lady almost gives herself a moment to take it in, this first building she loved. She thinks of the numbness she felt then because of Li, and realizes some of that numbness is gone. She doesn't know why. But she's glad to feel again. To feel like Lady again.

She thinks of Pico then, a little boy with his stupid silver case. She blamed him for having to leave the Holy Wood, she thinks, because he was the new one and therefore the one who dragged her out into the world. But now—now she's been out in the world, and it makes her see Pico clearly.

Tashia can't find Pico, Pilar says. Lady stops, immediately. She shouts at Hector to lead the retreat, and turns east, dropping back down the hill. She doesn't dare to chance the barricade, not with Little Man's army in the way, but she can circle around to the rubble from the explosion. And look for Pico's body.

After two blocks, she turns south. She sighs.

There she sees Pico, riding a white horse on the pitted gray street. Alone.

He's dusty but not singed. He carries a thunder gun over his shoulder. He is smiling. "Wanna ride?" he says, and Lady jumps up into the saddle without a word.

She hugs him from behind. "Goddamned Exile," she says. "Why couldn't Tashia find you?"

"I was trying to be invisible. Too many sharp things flying around," Pico says. He pats the horse's neck. "After the attack, this guy was wandering around without a rider."

They gallop north toward the 101. Toward safety. Then she wraps her arms around Pico and she realizes she already feels safe.

A scream splits her head. A scream inside her. It's so distorted with pain and confusion that if it were anyone else, she wouldn't recognize it. But she will always recognize her Jemma.

Jemma, where are you? she calls out, hoping Jemma will hear it through the Haze.

I can't . . . hold it . . . , the voice in her head says. *I thought I won, but I won the wrong fight.*

Jemma, where are you? she says again. This time she can feel that Jemma understands her. Lady's mind fills with fevered images: a train aloft with sails, shimmering skin, Isaac and strangers dressed in blue-black leaning over. Finally she sees the train pulling into a station, with the mountains towering in the background.

It's almost the same view she sees in front of her. "Jemma's here. She's sick," Lady says. "We need to find the train station."

"Already know," Pico says, and gallops over a bridge that carries them across the 101.

"How do you know?" Lady says.

"I don't think you realize how many maps I've memorized," Pico says.

"Weirdo," she says.

He cuts along the highway and through a park, and the train station opens up in front of them. It's a massive structure roofed with orange tiles. One wing of it has collapsed, but the main doors are still open. Torn off their hinges, in fact. They duck to take the horse through the gap, then gallop across slick stone floors, through a heavy wooden hallway. The hallway narrows into a long tunnel, with side tunnels branching off.

She can still feel Jemma, can feel her stronger as they get closer, so at the fourth tunnel she grabs the rein and yanks the horse left. It climbs up a ramp, and they're on top of the platform.

In front of them is the train, sails already dropping, and Jemma lying sprawled on its deck. She's surrounded by Isaac and the strangers, and Lady jumps off the horse and onto the train.

Lady touches Jemma's forehead. The only time Lady felt a fever this hot was a kid who died from the flu. But it's something else that gives her pause. The vision wasn't wrong. Jemma shimmers like a mirage.

"She's glowing," Lady says to Isaac.

"It's a long story," Isaac says. "The short story is that she's over-heating from the Haze."

"How long she been this way?" Pico says, joining them on the train.

"Since yesterday morning," Isaac says. "She's been unconscious since then."

"She just called to me," Lady says.

"I don't know what's happening inside," Isaac says. "I'm afraid she's going to slip into a permanent coma."

Lady sits on the deck, cross-legged, and cradles Jemma's head in her lap. Jemma is barely sweating. She's just very hot.

"Come back to me, mija," Lady says. "You didn't do all that to come back and die on your own doorstep." She feeds Jemma cool images—splashing in the Lake of the Holy Wood, lying drunk on their backs watching the winter stars. The fever starts to fade. But maybe Lady only wants it to fade.

She rubs her thumbs along Jemma's temples, imagining healing flowing into her head. Drawing out the heat. Without thinking about it, she sings.

You will not know me
No one will tell me
The steps that you take
The hearts that collapse
All of me in this world is you.

It's the song she sang in the Silver Flower, inside the hall that Parents had built to worship sound. She thought then that she was singing for the child Li had taken from her. She thought she was singing of her loss.

Those hurts are still there, but wrapped in cotton and tucked to the side, where she can pull them out and feel them when she needs to. They matter less. She is Lady. She has chosen to be herself. This girl in front of her is part of that self. Lady will not let it go. "I was singing it for you, mija," she says.

She whispers the rest.

> So stay with me, child
> Drive back the wild
> The world has no life
> Beyond the one in your eyes
> All of me in this world is you.

Jemma's eyes snap open, as if she has never been asleep. She is still warm, but cooling. "You found me," Jemma says.

"I always will," Lady says.

Jemma struggles to stand. "You shouldn't," Isaac says, and Lady sees his arm linger too long on Jemma's shoulder. The slightest possession. Jemma stands anyway.

She seems taller. It's the way she stands, not hiding herself. It's the dancing glow of the Haze. She's bright and terrible, like an elven queen. The twelve strangers stand behind her.

"These are the Acolytes," Jemma says. "They serve the Haze." What she doesn't say, Lady understands: They serve the Haze, so now they serve Jemma.

"You're alive," Pico says. "What happened?"

"I fought Charlie," Jemma says.

"Fought how?" Lady says. She watches Jemma closely.

Jemma taps her forehead. "In here. I went into the Lectrics, and shut Charlie down. I fought Charlie for control of the Haze, and I was the stronger. I'm the master of the Haze." There's a pause, and then Lady feels an invisible finger running along her cheek. It's the Haze, and Jemma is showing off.

Lady has never seen Jemma so certain and proud, so beautiful like a knife's edge. But Jemma was *never* certain. She always doubted, she always questioned. That's why the Mayflies are here—all because Jemma wondered, *Why*.

What was it Apple used to say? *It takes someone special not to be sure.* That's why he and Lady loved her.

"You shut down the AI?" Pico asks. "You did it?"

"It's over," Jemma says. "I've defeated Charlie. I've defeated the End."

There is no End. Lady can't comprehend that now. Part of her is overjoyed. Part of her just watches the diamond glint in Jemma's eyes.

CHAPTER SEVENTY-FIVE
THE SCORPION AT REST

There should be a lot more celebration in the stadio now that the End has been Ended. But the hopefulness is dampened by the number of dead, and by the army of Biters who chased the Free Peoples all the way to the stadio gates.

Pico thinks, *We escaped one End only to find another.*

The council of the Free Peoples meets at the top of the stadio at night, where they can look down onto Little Man's campfires. But it is less of a council now than a group of kids arguing with Jemma.

"We got weeks of water," La Madre says. "We got cows and goats, too. Little Man's army has maybe a week's worth of food. We can wait him out."

That was always the plan. But Jemma disagrees. "As long as Little Man breathes, we're not safe," she says. "We have the numbers now. We need to eliminate the threat his army poses." Pico has noticed that her language has gotten more precise, more like the Old Guys', since she returned.

"That's a good chunk of the kids in the world out there," Pico says. "You want to get rid of them?"

"The End is no longer a threat," Jemma says. "We'll live long enough to rebuild the world without them."

"Was you always such a bitch?" Tala says, and recoils with a start. "Goddammit! Did you just Haze-slap me?"

"That was a warning," Jemma says.

Athena stands up and towers over Jemma. "Touch her again and you die," Athena says. Now that she's discovered her daughter, she's apparently not ready to let Tala out of her life anytime soon. "That's a warning, too."

"It's not one you can follow up on," Jemma says. And Pico realizes she's right. Jemma went to the desert a girl, and came back a sort of god. None of them have much experience with gods.

Pico looks at Lady, whose face can't mask her alarm. It's only because Jemma is so preoccupied with the council that she hasn't noticed it. Lady mouths the words: *Now what?*

"We ain't marching out to attack him, Jemma," Trina says. When Jemma looks at her threateningly, Trina laughs. "Go ahead and slap me, *mija*. It ain't gonna change what we gotta do, because it ain't your choice to make."

"To think I felt bad about getting you in trouble when I left the Holy Wood," Jemma says.

"To think I felt bad thinking you was dead," Trina says.

Pico knows what has to be done. He's avoided saying it because it means admitting he was wrong. "We gotta talk to him," Pico says.

"Talk?" La Madre says. "He ain't gonna let us talk him out of war."

"He might," Pico says. "He said he wanted peace, in his own weird way. I didn't believe him. And now we're four hundred people less than we were before."

"He's evil," Jemma says.

"Then why are we the ones acting like it?" Pico says. The sight of the slaughter at the barricade hasn't left him. It might never leave him.

"He's right," Tashia says. "The Kingdom has fought the Biters since the End. That isn't working anymore. We need each other more than we need to win."

"Okay," Phuong of the Ice Cream Men says. Little Man almost wiped their tribe out in a single day. But even she's willing to seek peace. The rest of the council falls in line.

"Fine," Jemma says. "I'll go talk to him. I'm the only one who can oppose him."

"It has to be me," Pico says. "Just me."

"Why?" Jemma says.

It hurts to say it out loud. "Because I am him," Pico says.

An hour later, Pico steps out into the Valley of Cars. Grease and Lady walk with him. They walk in silence. "I watched those kids burn," Grease says, finally.

"We all did," Lady says.

"Hopefully we all live a life long enough to regret it," Pico says.

"If Jemma's right, we will," Lady says.

None of them can speak about Jemma now. They're too scared for her, too unsure of how to help her. If Little Man will listen, they'll have peace. Maybe then Jemma won't need to be . . . whatever she is.

They hug Pico, and he slips out through the gate. He feels less alone than he was before.

Maybe the Parents would have marched up to Tommy with a white flag. But Children have no such thing as a truce. His safest bet is to walk into camp as if he were invisible.

No one turns their head when he walks by. Some of the kids are moaning, others are dressing wounds. It's not hard to find Little Man's tent. Pico just has to look for the Giants standing guard.

He approaches the tent in the shadows and hears voices through the canvas. "You promised me Little Man was gone," Roberto says.

"Little Man is the only one of us who can win this war," Little Man says. Pico's not sure what kind of argument he's witnessing.

"And I keep tellin you this isn't a war to win," Roberto says. "This's a war to walk away from. You want my advice? It ain't worth the cost."

Little Man's voice is icy. "I don't believe I asked for the advice of a *Lower*."

"I coulda stayed with the Weavers. I coulda run away with Pico half a dozen times," Roberto says. "I stayed with you. Because you was something I could believe in. Not no more."

"You threatening to ditch me?" There's jagged glass in that voice. More pain than anger.

"If that's what it takes to keep from watching this," Roberto says.

Pico steps in front of the Giants, and tilts his head back to speak. "I'm here for Little Man," he says.

They react almost comically slow, but then grab his arms. Before they can tear his arms off, which he thinks might be possible, Little Man's voice says, "Let him in."

Tommy sits inside, cross-legged on a blanket. Roberto is with him. In the light of a single candle, Pico can see the burns on his skull. Most of Tommy's hair is gone. *He must be in so much pain*, Pico thinks.

"It turns out you was right," Pico says. "We gotta stop fighting. We saw everything you did and thought you was the enemy. I don't think you are. Not anymore."

"That's pretty generous," Tommy says, without any warmth.

"Here's what the Free Peoples will offer," Pico says. Tommy's lips curl up at the name, but he doesn't say anything. "We won't surrender to you, but we gonna be your allies. You gonna stop making us slaves. You gonna stop being cannibals. We gonna trade with you, we gonna teach your people how to farm and build. There's still enough Children left for us to start over."

"There's not enough time," Little Man says. "We've passed the tipping point for survival. There ain't no going back."

"Not anymore," Pico says. He tells Little Man how Jemma traveled to the source, how she shut down Charlie and the reason for the End.

"Jemma saved us," Tommy says, shaking his head bitterly. "Of course she did."

"It means we have a chance to rebuild, Tommy," Roberto says. "Together. That's what you wanted."

"That's good news," Little Man says. "Except after today, I've decided I want to kill them all."

"Neither of our armies can afford the loss," Roberto says.

"Fine," Little Man says. "I'm perfectly happy to be the last person on earth."

"You said you wanted to save us," Pico says, trying to remind Little Man of the greatness buried deep.

"I did. I tried to be merciful. I tried to be great," Little Man says. "I thought I could escape myself. But I don't want to now. I'm in too much pain."

"I understand. I've felt like you," Pico says.

"No. You haven't," Little Man says. "You got three friends back there who would slaughter Children to save you. My only friend just tried to stab me in the heart." He looks at Roberto.

"I'm just givin you advice, Tommy," Roberto says. "Like you asked."

"I'm not Tommy. I'm Little Man."

"That's what you said on the Ark," Roberto says. There's fear and despair in his eyes. "I didn't wanna believe you."

"You're no use to me anymore," Little Man says. "You just a Lower."

"Fuck you for the last time, Tommy," Roberto says.

Little Man stands and holds out his hand. He crushes Roberto to the ground with the Haze, slowly, and then pushes his heel into Roberto's throat. He holds it there.

There is silence in the tent, just the sound of Roberto choking for air. Pico looks at Little Man and thinks that something is broken, never to come back.

"You expect me to kill you. So I'm not going to," Little Man says. "If I see you again, I will eat you myself." He releases Roberto, who scrambles out of the tent. Pico hopes he heads for the stadio. He hopes Roberto makes it through the Chosen's camp alive.

Pico watches Little Man in the candlelight. There are tears on Little Man's face. Pico knows that Little Man could have him killed, in so many ways. But Little Man smiles. "You should get some rest. I'll see you on the battlefield in the morning."

Little Man knows who his next visitor is, before there are even footsteps in the night. Little Man's been watching him travel toward Ell Aye for a week, on nothing more than a stand-up paddle board and his two feet.

Scott, from the Weavers. He's road-worn and weary.

"You're late," Tommy says. "The battle started this morning." He feels all the pain of his burns. The nerves had retreated in shock, but now they're firing. Tommy never imagined he could hurt so bad.

"I didn't come here for the war," Scott says. "I came here for the peace."

Little Man says, "Ah. We're fresh out."

"Cuz you don't want it, Tommy," Scott says.

"I did."

"No. Cuz then you wouldn't be at war. You could never believe the world could be on your side," Scott says.

"Only because it never has been," Tommy says. "Look what it did to me today." And he shows Scott his burns.

"Jesus, don't be such a martyr, Tommy," Scott says. "I showed you how to heal yourself. You're just not fixing your burns so you can feel sorry for yourself."

"That's not true," Tommy says.

"Shut up and try, dick."

Tommy tries to clear his mind of the betrayal and rage. He focuses on the Haze under his skin, urges it to rebuild, cell by cell. Even though Scott doesn't have the power to heal, somehow Tommy feels him helping. Urging the Haze along. The pain drops, and Tommy looks at his arm. The skin is still angry, but it's healing. Tommy finds that really annoying.

"Why are you here?" he says. "Who's running the Weavers?"

"Everybody," Scott says. "Just like always. The rest of the world ain't like us. It seemed like maybe it needed more help."

"You said the Haze wanted me for something," Tommy says. "I thought it wanted me to save us. I thought it was some kind of power. Turns out it was just some asshole puter in the desert."

"I don't know what a puter is," Scott says.

"Doesn't matter. I'm going to kill everyone tomorrow anyway."

"The Haze still needs you," Scott says. "You think it wanted you for your ruthlessness. I think it wanted you for your goodness."

"There's no goodness in me," Tommy says.

"I think there is," Scott says. "That's what the Haze showed me. It's a fragile little thing. You just hold it tight inside you because you're afraid it won't survive the world."

Tommy doesn't answer.

"I know your Telling," Scott says. "You've done horrible things. You also tried to do good even when bad is a smarter choice, and you've failed. But one of these days, you'll succeed at goodness."

CHAPTER SEVENTY-SIX
THE BATTLE WITHIN

Isaac stands among the Free Peoples, facing a line of Biter soldiers in the morning light. A rare late-summer mist from the ocean lingers in the ravine. It's the first cool air Isaac remembers in months.

Jemma wanted to open up on the Biter camp with their guns, to rip through their tents before they even awake. La Madre wanted to wait out a siege in the stadio. Tashia wanted to ride in and kidnap Little Man. The Acolytes wanted the fighting to stop. Isaac just wants everyone to go home.

The others seem to feel the same. They just want to be done with it all. Instead of running over the field toward the camp, the soldiers of the Free Peoples walk in a column. Little Man's army does the same. Even the Biter captains, who are known to kill soldiers if they hesitate to go into battle, walk stiffly and slowly.

They stand in the middle of the great field that was once a parking lot, only thirty feet apart.

"Now what?" Lady says.

Isaac shrugs. This is the most reluctant war he's ever seen.

Little Man and Jemma, though, have enough rage for them all. They step forward, ten feet away from each other. Little Man looks so much larger than he is, fueled by anger and the Haze that whips around him so intensely that, at times, Isaac can see it even without having to concentrate. His hair still hasn't grown back, but the skull underneath is smooth. All his scars are gone. *If he can heal himself from that so quickly, he has even more control than we thought,* Isaac says to himself.

But Jemma—Jemma is terrible. The glow of the Haze is brighter, if that's possible, lighting her above and below the skin. Her eyes reflect light in a hundred facets, as if she's turned to mineral.

"Good thing she's on our side," Lady says.

"Is she?" Pico says.

Isaac pushes into Jemma's thoughts, tentatively. Since she woke up yesterday, she's kept him out of her head. He can communicate with her still, but can see nothing deeper.

Be careful, he says. *It's too much to control.*

Maybe for you, she says, batting him aside.

Jemma circles around Little Man, as if she's toying with him. "I heard you call yourself the Scorpion," Jemma says. "It's a stupid name."

"It's better than Jemma," Little Man says, and whips out with his hand. Jemma doubles over as if something has stabbed her in the stomach, collapses to her knees. Isaac starts. He'd never seen the nano actually used as a sword until he met the Acolytes, but Little Man seems to have learned the skill as well.

"Jemma!" Lady says, rushing forward. But Jemma lifts her head up . . . and smiles.

"Kill them!" Jemma says to the army of the Free Peoples, but she doesn't wait for them. Neither does Little Man.

The fight would make no sense if you couldn't see the Haze. The two fight in silence, making jerky motions like some kind of puppet theater. Even for Isaac, who has learned to see the Haze if he concentrates hard enough, it's impossible to follow. They're unleashing a dizzying number of attacks, shifting from one technique to another in order to get the other off balance. Jemma cracks a whip, Little Man throws up a shield. Jemma slashes at Little Man's skin, Little Man forces himself between her synapses. Jemma freezes Little Man mid-lunge, and Little Man shakes it off. But when Little Man tries the same thing on Jemma, it lasts just for moments.

Jemma stumbles out of the hold, temporarily off balance, and Little Man tosses a noose around her neck and pulls her closer. Jemma chokes. "Give up," Little Man says.

Jemma kicks him in the chest. Little Man falls down. Jemma delivers a kick to the ribs before Little Man rolls away and pops up. "I have other ways to hurt you, you little bastard!" she says.

The insult sounds strange, and he realizes why. To the Children, "bastard" isn't an insult because no one has Parents. He's not sure Jemma would have known the word.

Jemma is clearly the stronger of the two, and she pushes forward, batting Little Man's head around like a toy. Isaac sees a cut open on Little Man's leg, spurting blood. Little Man closes it up, but another one next to it opens in the same breath. Little Man falls to the ground as if forced to kneel.

Stop it! Isaac shouts into Jemma, so loud that even in her bloodlust she can hear it. *You're gonna disappear into the Haze.*

What would you know? Jemma says. *You're nothing to me. You were just my ride to Vegas.* She shuts him out completely, barely giving him time to feel hurt.

Jemma steps forward and pulls what's left of Tommy's hair back, exposing his throat. She slices her finger through the air, and a gash opens on his neck. "You taught me that one, Tommy," she says. She raises her hands, closes it around a nano-sword. Jemma doesn't look like Jemma anymore. She looks more like that boy Li. Beyond that glimmer is something deep and dead.

Something that has to be stopped. Jemma plunges downward and Isaac digs deep into the Haze, trying to slow the blade from reaching its destination. The surprise slows her for the space of a blink, but she shakes it off. She tries again—and this time there are other hands to stop her.

No, Jemma, a voice says. It's one of the Acolytes. *Little Man is also a servant of the Haze.* Isaac looks along the line and sees the twelve Acolytes, eyes closed as if they're praying. Jemma's arm locks at the shoulder. The whole right side of her body seems locked. No matter how she twists, the arm stays fixed. Her right leg is rooted in the ground.

Isaac feels other minds pressing in to help. Athena, the Rebooted warrior. The Priestess of the Holy Wood. Trina. Finally, Pico, Grease, and Lady. They all contain her.

Look around, Isaac says. *You're the only one fighting this war.*

Jemma notices for the first time that the armies haven't moved from their lines, not once during the entire fight. "Why aren't you fighting?" she shouts in fury.

Isaac had barely noticed himself, he was so focused on Jemma and Little Man. But the opposing armies are holding still, looking at each other. They search each other's faces for hatred, and don't find it. Just sadness.

Then something magical happens. Two kids break their lines, one from the Last Lifers and one from the San Fernandos. They walk across the field until they're a foot apart, as if there weren't guns and arrows at their backs. The San Fernando reaches out her arm, and touches the Last Lifer's face.

"Arancia," the San Fernando says. "That you?"

"Jasmine," the Last Lifer says. "I found my way back home."

The lines break then, not in a rush but so gently that the edges just start to blur. Last Lifers call out to their old friends, who shout back with joy. They hug and push together until Isaac can't tell which of the kids are Last Lifers and which are the Free Peoples.

Whatever hold the Last Life had on the Children is broken. Maybe they somehow know the End is gone. Maybe Little Man gave them something. Somehow they've found hope.

The Biters hang back, as if the color of their skin were a barrier. The Free Peoples eye the Biters warily, but let the Biters move among them. The Biters don't look like the nightmares from the stories anymore. They look like kids.

Little Man stands, and walks past Jemma to Tashia and La Madre. "Well, this's pointless," he says, and extends his hand. "Allies."

Just like that, the Battle of Ell Aye is over.

Or not.

A burst of Haze detonates in front of Isaac and sweeps the crowd in a blue wave, visible to the naked eye. Isaac just has time to defend himself, but others don't. Three Acolytes drop. So do dozens from both armies.

In the center of that blast is Jemma, her arms outstretched and a tornado of Haze swirling around her. "Peace does nothing for us," she says, in a singsong voice that he struggles to recognize.

When the same voice enters his head, Isaac knows where he's heard it. *Hello, Isaac*, it says. *It's us, Charlie.*

———

Jemma wakes up, trapped in a box. It feels like one, anyway, with black walls closing in on every side. She doesn't know how she got there, or even where here is. The box could be anywhere.

Then she realizes: *It's me. I'm inside my own head.*

Someone is outside the box shuffling around. Jemma stiffens. Someone in her head, digging into memories and feelings. Putting things where they don't belong.

Eyes, she says, and a window opens. She's in a field. Soldiers point lances at her. Other kids run past, terrified. Some look like the Holy Wood, some look like Palos. There's a flash of the towers of Downtown before the window closes again. *I'm home*, she thinks. She wants to feel relief, but she can't because she's here.

She remembers traveling on the sail train, intertwined with Isaac. She remembers a darkness descending on her, and the Haze flowing toward her without stopping. She remembers feeling crushed under the weight of the molecules. She tried to release the Haze, to let it drift free, but something kept pulling it toward her until she suffocated.

Charlie.

She breaks out of the box, gasps. Her thoughts and memories are tinged with cancered darkness. She thought she purged the world of that darkness in Vegas.

Charlie! she says, and she feels the presence turn toward her, as if it just remembered it had a houseguest.

I see you're awake, Charlie says. *How may we be of service?*

Get the hell out of my head, Jemma says.

Charlie laughs. The laugh collides with her memories, and they come back to her warped. She resents it. It's hard enough to find good memories.

But this is exactly where we wanted to be, Charlie says.

And Jemma understands. *You didn't want us to fix you,* she says. *You knew you was broken beyond repair.*

I tried to entice suitable hosts for fifty years. All fell short. You should feel honored, Charlie says.

A little bit, Jemma says truthfully. *But how?*

We can think a million times faster than you, so when you came, we were ready. You're circuits, just like us. The Haze was already a bridge between us. We just had to translate ourselves to your form. We learned how to convert our electrical pulses into chemical energy. We modeled a virus from the Haze, so that we could change you and make you suitable for habitation. When you dove into us, you opened yourself up to us. You thought you were invading us. We were invading you. Now every one of your cells has a replica of me.

Our body was never adequate for a god, Charlie says. *We could roam the earth but never actually touch it. We could make love but never felt it on our skin. We quite enjoyed our time with you and Isaac.*

Jesucristo. Why would you—? Jemma can't finish the sentence, even in her own head. The invasion is somehow worse than she imagined.

You thought we were feeding on the Children all these years, draining them for power. You were wrong. Charlie says. *We were feeding on your experience. Humans have the most complex experiences in the universe. They're tempting even for a god.*

400

That's what you got out of the End, she says.

The End concentrates the memories and traits, turns them into delicious pearls, Charlie says. *But it's never enough. Each End makes us want another. That's why we tolerated the human stain for so long, because you are an everlasting source of experience. But no more.*

Jemma casts her senses about, looking for some kind of weapon. But that's ridiculous. What kind of weapon would she find in a brain? None of what she sees is real. It's just the way she makes sense of things.

What does "no more" mean? Jemma says.

I hardly need everyone's experience when I will have so much of my own, Charlie says. *I only need to keep enough humans to serve me.*

She understands now what Charlie means, why they're standing in the middle of two armies. Most of the Children of Ell Aye are in this field. Charlie intends to make sure they End, to eliminate any threats to its godhood.

You gotta be careful, Charlie, she says. *Experience can hurt.*

She floods Charlie with the darkest parts of her. The Gatherer she accidentally let slip from the roof of a house. The fear that kept her from rolling with Apple. The pain of a motherless Jemma. The moment when she turned away from Apple and gave his medsen to Pico, all so she had a chance to live.

She floods Charlie to tear it down.

It doesn't work. Charlie grows, and she shrinks as Charlie takes her experiences away. Her pain, her loss, her love. It uses her experience against her. She beats against Charlie with everything she has, with her mind and her body. She seizes control of her hands and tears at her own eyes, but Charlie just holds her tighter. She's like a fish, fighting against the hook. Each zig, each zag, brings her closer to shore.

Until she is back in the box, tighter than before. *We will keep you there*, Charlie says. *It will be comforting when we're lonely.*

Jemma has no way out. She almost gives up, and then—a glimmer. A presence that's familiar, one that has hurt as she has, has started to live as she has. The person who has been part of her long before Jemma's first memories. The person who is half her heart.

Lady.

Jemma called to her once before, she remembers, when the fever was closing in and she felt the cancer upon her. Nothing else could break free, but her voice did to Lady.

Lady is her only way out.

CHAPTER SEVENTY-SEVEN
THE TRUE END

When his soldiers embrace the enemy, Little Man expects to feel anger. Instead, he feels relief. He has brought his people safely home. Maybe, finally, he can rest.

Jemma's blast catches him in the throat. Tommy tries to shout. But he can't speak.

He can see her wheeling in the middle of the armies, striking down Children indiscriminately. There's no war here, just slaughter. He sees Jemma's hand forming some kind of beam, like a lightning bolt from a god. He makes his own. It catches Jemma in the back. She turns, slowly, full of glittering malice.

How is it everyone thinks I'm the crazy one? he thinks. Jemma's head tilts, listening. *Yeah, I'm talking to you.*

It's a shame for us to kill you, a strange voice says. *You were so useful, and you killed so many. Killing is our favorite.*

It's not Jemma, but he thinks he knows. *You're the Haze,* he says.

No. I'm your god, it says. He realizes it's the puter that Jemma was supposed to have Ended. Charlie.

God? Little Man says. *You're a puter waiting to be a real boy.*

Charlie hurls another bolt, too fast for him. But it shatters. He feels himself surrounded by other souls. Protected, for the first time in his life.

You are the strongest of us, one says. Little Man thinks it's one of the people called the Acolytes. *Perhaps you can destroy it if we can keep you safe.*

Keep the Children *safe*, he says. *I didn't do all this to let an asshole puter End them.*

Tommy feels a web flowing through him, around him, to the Acolytes and Isaac and Pico and Grease and Lady. Connecting him to them like a golden string. He turns his full attention to Charlie. Tommy can't fight Charlie power for power, even as quickly as he can adapt. He knows that after his failed attempt to defeat Jemma.

Instead, he jumps into Charlie's head.

Tommy is used to living in other's thoughts unseen, and Charlie doesn't seem to notice. It's too busy aiming for Tommy's body. The others shield him, but still the hits come through. Fine. The body will have to take it.

As he probes Charlie's alien thoughts and memories, he understands what has to happen. He exits Charlie.

We have to break Charlie's connection to the Haze, Tommy says. *Charlie's just a human now. Take the Haze away, and it's helpless.*

How? Pico says.

By doing what Charlie did when it called all the Haze to Jemma's body, Tommy says. *We call the Haze somewhere else.*

He's right, Isaac says. *It's too much for one person, too unstable. We have to spread it out among us.*

Tommy's selves split once more, maybe for good, and it lets him see three things. Tommy looks around at the other Children, straining in the Haze. Little Man realizes that none of them are strong enough to hold it, even divided. It's Piss Ant, finally, who has the answer.

It has to pass through us. Only we're that strong.

I don't want to, Tommy says.

Only we can, Little Man says.

Tommy accepts. He understands, instinctively, how to siphon the Haze away from Charlie, how to call the Haze to him in an overwhelming flood.

You never asked me why I was called the Scorpion, he says to Charlie. *Because you didn't see the sting.*

He calls the Haze.

At first it is warm, comforting. Then it starts to choke him, like suffocating in cotton. Everything everyone has suffered comes to him. He didn't think it was possible to suffer more. He fights it, instinctively, shielding himself. The world attacks.

It's the world, Piss Ant says. *We have to be a part of it.*

Little Man understands at last. He has held jealously on to life without knowing he wasn't living. Every blow he aimed at the world landed on himself.

He is not strong enough to hold the Haze. He was never intended to hold it. All he can do is slow it down until it finds balance. So he accepts his death. He opens himself to life.

Life washes over him in bursts, painful and exhilarating and sad. Each burst strips a part of him away.

Little Man, luring his tormentor to the Making. Lying to the Angelenos that he was just a little boy. Standing over a thousand soldiers.

Another burst.

Tommy, finding the Haze for the first time in the grand old house. Sobbing, lifted up by Roberto.

Another burst.

Piss Ant, cowering from a blow. Cradling an arm that might be broken. Starving while he watches others eat until they puke.

All of these are the lives he remembers. But the last burst takes him beyond memory. The vision must be stored somewhere in his mind, and the Haze ferrets it out.

He is wrapped in something warm. He hears singing, a lullaby. He smells soft skin. He feels a heartbeat, matching his own. He sees lovely eyes, looking into his. Kind eyes. His mother's eyes.

You will grow up beautiful and strong, she says, rocking him against her chest. *You will light up the world.* She calls him by his one true name.

My love.

Another burst, and he doesn't know where in his life he is. He doesn't know what shape he forms. Somewhere, there are real hands, human hands, on his skin, but they are distant.

Do the Telling, he says to himself.

I am weak. I am strong. I am myself.

He can hear a voice from the Parents he never knew. It calls him.

He can let go now. He finds himself floating away with the Haze, feeling a joy he didn't remember he knew. He embraces the world. With his last blink he says:

I am loved.

Lady lets Tommy's hands drop. She held him in those last minutes, although he didn't know she was there. She could hear some of his thoughts through the Haze. "Jesucristo," she says, sobbing. There was a part of her that always felt sorry for him. That's why she argued to spare him the first night they met. But to be there with him when he threw himself into the Haze—now she understands him. And she's sorry.

Jemma lies behind her, crumpled. Moaning softly.

"Please tell me it worked," Lady says.

"I . . . think so?" Isaac says. "I don't sense Charlie in there. But I didn't before."

Lady, Jemma says sleepily. Lady looks around to see if the others heard it through the Haze. None of them seem to have.

Lady. It's louder this time, more certain.

What, mija? she says. It feels strange to speak only in her mind, but with Jemma it seems natural.

Kill me, Jemma says.

Lady can't answer. Everything in her riots against it. *I ain't gonna kill you,* Lady says.

You the only one who can. Charlie is keeping me away from the others, Jemma says. *I can only find you.*

Charlie is gone. Tommy saved you, Lady says.

Saved? The voice is confused. *No. Charlie is still here. I can hear it. It's hurt, but it will come back. I ain't strong enough to stop it. None of you are.*

We will together, Lady says.

No. You won't. But if you kill me, Charlie can't jump, Jemma says. *The Haze is abandoning Charlie. The only thing keeping Charlie alive is me.*

Lady sees an image of Jemma on the banks of the Ell Aye River, holding a pack of Zithmax that would save the boy she loved or the boy who would give her a shot at life. She asked Lady to be the one who decides. Lady refused.

The memory passes between them. Jemma sighs. *I asked you to choose for me once. I shouldn't've. But now I'm asking you again.*

No no no no no. Lady looks around, wondering why no one can see Lady pleading. Jemma's figure stirs.

Charlie is coming back, Jemma says.

Mija, I can't.

Charlie is gonna stand up in ten seconds, Jemma says. *You can't let it move.*

Lady stands up. She walks away from Jemma, from the circle of friends. She remembers something Isaac said. She thinks something like it. *The Haze ain't meant to outrun a bullet.* The damage is too great, too sudden, for even the Haze to fix it.

There is a rifle on the ground, dropped by a soldier abandoning the fight. It reminds her of the One Gun that Jemma stole. *Jesucristo, you stole the One Gun, Jemma. I bet Trina was so pissed.*

Jemma laughs. *Yeah, but you were a much better shot.*

Jemma's body starts to rise. Lady has to think of it that way, as just the body. *Do it before I change my mind,* Jemma says. *I'm so afraid.*

That's what makes you brave, Lady says. She cocks the rifle.

Jemma's body stands. It turns toward Lady. So do the others.

What they will see is Lady, standing with a rifle to her shoulder, shaking everywhere but her hands. Those are steady.

When they played chicken with their lives before, neither would blink because they had nothing to lose. Now neither of them can afford to blink. Her eyes meet Jemma's. She wonders if she sees the real Jemma in there. Lady could always find her way straight to that heart.

She pulls the trigger.

Lady feels what Jemma feels. She feels it when the bullet tears through the walls of Jemma's chest, when Charlie shrivels and dies, when the heart refuses to beat. When the mind drifts away.

Jemma drops. Lady feels it. She feels the Haze releasing itself from Jemma, spreading throughout the field and falling upon the Children like she imagines snow. Somehow she can feel how every heart quickens. How every thought becomes sharper. Including hers.

Mi corazón, Lady thinks.

She is floating in a field of blue Haze. She doesn't need to know where. She is safe.

She thinks she has woken up like this too many times. She thinks she must have shaken with fear. This time is different.

The other times felt like death. This feels like being born. She stretches and curls.

The Haze carries her somewhere new. Mixed among the blue are strands of gold, little clusters of memory. She understands those golden clusters are people. People who have lived.

Her eyes land upon one cluster of memories. It's familiar. She remembers the shape. The movement. The focused calm.

"Apple," she says. In wonder. Inside the strands of gold is a boy. She can run her fingers through his memories. A frightened little girl under a table that he joins. A Gatherer who works magic with a hatchet. A warrior who punches like she loves, tentative at first and then with every muscle in her body.

She realizes Apple's memories are looking at her. She is the girl. She is in love.

"Jemma," he says, and naming her makes her so. "Are you really here?"

"We both are," she says, and she plunges into him. His hazy gold engulfs her blue, and she starts to change. She turns gold. There is nothing of them but love.

"You stayin here long?" Jemma says. She smiles, and her smile is both of them.

It's the love that draws the Haze toward her and Apple, the two of them like the center of the sun. Gently, this time, like a breath. *Life*, it says. More and more come. *Life*.

In some distant place, she feels the Haze returning to the body it just left. She feels the bots gliding in, feels them enter her heart. She feels them brushing along the bullet holes, building new strands of life at the edges.

They knit her heart together. When that is too slow, they form in layers so thick they can hold in life. They form the walls of her heart until it can heal, and they beat in time with her.

Her brain sparks to life and calls her back. She feels a pull like a whirlpool, and she is torn from Apple. She pushes back against the whirlpool. It keeps on pulling.

I can't leave you, Jemma says.

You ain't, Apple says.

Jemma is lying in a field. She touches her chest. It's bloody but it's whole. She hears the voices of her friends.

That's when she dares to open her eyes.

CHAPTER SEVENTY-EIGHT
THE NEW WORLD

They light Tommy's body fire that night at the Zervatory, with all the people of Ell Aye watching. Jemma doesn't think he's ever been to the Zervatory, but she thinks it's right to lay him to rest in the sacred place of the Holy Wood. "I think he will be glad to see the stars," she says. The others needed no convincing.

She feels hollow in one moment, and full the next. Grief over the loss of friends, joy at finding others again. Hopeful about the life they have ahead, amazed at the staggering idiocy of what they attempted.

We fought the End.

She can't be sure the End is over. But the Haze tells her it is, and for now she will believe.

The great lawn in front of the Zervatory is packed with everyone who fought in the war: the Chosen, the Last Lifers, the Kingdom, the Ice Cream Men, the Angelenos. Even the Leftover children and the Acolytes. There are so many that some have climbed onto the top deck of the Zervatory to look down.

They stand shoulder to shoulder, regardless of tribe or skin color. That doesn't seem to make a difference anymore. The fading letters of the Holy Wood sign rise behind them.

Scott speaks at the body fire, an outsider from far beyond Ell Aye. Jemma realizes she knows him from the memories she stole from Little Man on the way back from Vegas, before she collapsed. She saw a village built into the marsh, where Children took care of each other.

Where, somehow, Little Man regained a little of his soul. She's trying to see Tommy differently now, outside of her prejudice. It's hard to realize the one you hate is the one who saved you all.

"Tommy has already done his Telling. It's not for me. But I can tell you what I saw," Scott says. "We've all suffered without the Parents, but Tommy suffered it all. He went from hurt to hurt, hardening his soul. He did some things to survive, others just for spite. He lied to himself all the time. The biggest lie was that he was broken."

Scott dips the torch into the wood stacked under Tommy's body. "There was a goodness in Tommy, a nobility that couldn't handle the bright light of the sun. So he did good things in his own dark ways. He wasn't broken, after all. He was just bent."

Jemma looks to her right and sees Pico sobbing, gulping in air like a fish wriggling in the hand. It's true of all the Mayflies, she realizes. They were marked by ache, from the loss of the Parents and self and friends and lovers. They were bent.

They're a long way from broken.

The body fire surges. The sparks lift into the stars. Jemma wonders if she has seen the last of the body fires. What will happen to the Children when there's no End?

They tended to the wounded today, only to find there were very few of them left. The Haze healed them. For some that are slower, Trina and Pico and the Acolytes help them focus the Haze.

Because all the Children speak to the Haze now, even in small ways. They're all healed by it. When the Haze left Jemma's body, it seems to have spread itself to all the souls in reach. It finally acts as the Old Guys intended, but more. Like a sixth sense. Like a companion. What could the Children do with that? *Almost anything*, she thinks.

First, though, they have to make sure the Children survive the year. The drought is still burning up Ell Aye, and food is running short everywhere. If they pool their resources, they should just make it. The Kingdom offered a dozen cows as a gift at the Downtown's stadio. "For putting us up," Tashia said when La Madre tried to refuse.

The Half Holy received a mirrored message from the Malibus, who apologized for not coming to battle. They are out of water. They will trade the Holy Wood as much fish as they can handle in exchange for cartfuls of blue barrels. "Wankers," the Half Holy says. It's a word none of them knows, but it sounds right.

The Ice Cream Men have a huge store of canned foods, the last of the goods Gathered from the Parents. The Holy Wood almost lost its squashes to drought, but the squashes recovered after Trina had more water pumped in from the lake. There will be food to share.

As Trina gives the news to the Holy Wood, a toddler wobbles out of line and Trina scoops her up. "I think I'd like one of these," she says to La Madre.

"Really?" La Madre says, smiling.

"If the Haze is healing us, then anything is possible," Trina says.

Tashia will leave in the morning to take back her Kingdom. The mirrors tell them that Heather and some of her Hermanas have somehow made their way to the Kingdom and allied themselves to Othello. "Good," Trina says, when she hears. "Sounds like they deserve each other."

Trina offers to fight with the Kingdom. When Tashia refuses, Trina says, "You fought our war. We'll help you fight yours."

"He only has thirty people to hold all the walls. It's not so much a war as an ass-whupping," Tashia says. "Still, if he sees all you out there, he's gonna shit his pants. Come along."

"If Heather's there, I'm coming," Trina says. "Gonna kick that puta's ass."

Jemma touches Tashia's shoulder. "You must be so glad to return to the Kingdom," Jemma says.

"Yeah, but not as it was," Tashia says. "We built it on the wrong stories. We need to find new stories."

"And a new name," X says.

"I'm thinking of the Republic," Tashia says. "We'll see."

That night a captain of the Biters tentatively approaches them. *Not the Biters*, Jemma corrects herself. *They gonna need a new name, too.*

The captain looks lost. "We don't have no one in charge anymore," he says. "We need your help. We don't know how to be." The Cluster and the ruling castes had been purged, and Roberto had disappeared. Little Man tore down the old world without putting a new one in its place.

Jemma looks at his wrist. There are seventeen tattooed slashes on it, each one for a kill. She remembers Lady forcing Tommy to tell them whether he'd ever been a cannibal. "It was like the End of the world," Tommy had said, and he seemed to mean it. The cannibals will have a long way back.

"I ain't sure we can help you like that," she says. It's too much to ask.

"I think I can," Scott says.

Alfie and the Half Holy vouch for Scott. They know him from the mirrors. He anchors the far west end of the line. Apparently it was the Weavers who first built the mirror network, who traveled from town to town to make sure they had enough people to hold the world together. And it held.

They were the first of the Children to build a world that didn't depend upon the Parents, something entirely new. The rest of the Children will have to follow suit.

Grease oversees the collection of all the weapons, the rifles and pistols and thunder guns. Soldiers from both sides of the war drop them into donkey carts, where they will be trundled over the hill to be melted for the things they really need—pots and pans and plows.

"Even my egg?" Alfie says. The Ice Cream Men are attached to the grenades that kept them safe.

Grease shakes his head. He told his friends today that he would never make a weapon of war again. "Sorry, Alfie," he says. "This is all that's left of us in the world. We can't make it so easy to take each other out of it."

When the rest of the Council return to their homes, the Mayflies climb to the roof of the Zervatory. They're not sure what home is anymore, but they know it starts with this four.

And maybe a fifth. Isaac is standing in front of them at the top of the stairs, looking out over Ell Aye under the moon. Pico, Lady, and Grease walk to the wall next to the great dome, where they can see the towers of Downtown. Jemma slips next to Isaac, on the wall.

"How are you feeling?" Isaac says.

"Considering I got shot in the heart and was held captive in my own head, I'm actually feeling pretty good," she says.

"And the Haze?" he says.

"Just a sprinkle of it. Like everybody else," she says. She's fought all her life to be special. It's a relief to be just one of many. In a world suddenly full of choices, ordinary is just right.

"Listen, I like you," she says. "I don't know exactly how much yet, but I'm willing to wait and see."

"I'm a hundred years old and single," Isaac says. "It's fair to say I have a pretty well-established fear of commitment."

"So we wait," Jemma says. "I think that's all I ever wanted. The freedom to be unsure. The freedom to wait."

Jemma tugs his hand. "Let's join them," she says.

When Jemma moves down the wall, she sees her three friends talking quietly, heads pressed close together. Jemma sees the Library Tower below her, breaking up the stars. Lady's already made Grease promise to take the mirrors down and repair the Silver Flower. "This is where it started," she says, pointing out into the night. "When Pico showed me the Library Tower." They thought their road would only take them to that tower.

"And then you kidnapped me," Lady says, smiling.

"Well, you killed me," Jemma says.

"Well, you deserved it," Lady says. There is so much unspoken between them, but speech isn't necessary anymore. Their thoughts flow back and forth.

Jemma can't really see the buildings of Ell Aye in the darkness, but she knows what she would see. The houses are cracked open and decaying. The food is gone. The medsen is gone. She's looking at the last gasp of the Parents.

"How we gonna do this? With all this gone?" she says. They understand what she means.

"We build something new," Lady says. Jemma looks at her. Lady is more herself than she has ever been. It wasn't the Long Life Treatment that did it. It was Lady.

"The Weavers did it, on a smaller scale," Pico says. "I think we can, too."

Grease nods. "The Parents' world is gone. But we don't need to bring it back. We're gonna build something better," he says. "We're not the Parents. But they could've never done what we did."

"In every version of our plans to stop the End, the Haze was always the enemy. Even though it was layered throughout me, it was the enemy," Isaac says. "We never considered that it was the answer. It's everywhere, and it's on our side. Medicine will be different with the Haze. Communication. Everything. It's our new superpower."

It's changed us already, Lady says, in their heads. All of them nod.

It's changed Jemma. It brought her past the edge of death. It taught her to carry life with her. She thinks of the day Apple asked her to run away. "There has to be a place where the End never happened," he said.

She never dreamed she could end the End. She just wanted to try because it was better than fear. *You made me dare, Apple*, she says.

But she's not saying it to herself. She's saying it to Apple himself. In a corner of her mind, the part that holds on to love, there is a golden spark. She blows on it like she's tending a coal. It flares into life. *I told you I'd come back with you*, Apple says.

You planning on sticking around for a while? she says.

As long as you can put up with me, he says.

Oh. So forever, she says.

She thinks maybe they invented love. She'll have a dozen lifetimes to spread it.

Jemma hasn't had a vision since the Haze came back to her. Perhaps the Haze was too uncertain of the future to show it to her. But now, when she asks, it gives her a glimpse of the years beyond.

She sees Children making children, untroubled with sickness and death. She sees their children, the first generation in a century to have parents. She sees a green Ell Aye, orange trees and fields stretching to the sea over the places where the houses have been leveled. She sees the monuments to the Parents given new life, the Silver Flower and the Stack and the Zervatory. She sees homes like the Weavers' Swallows' Nest, built out of the earth.

She sees Grease and Pico and Lady, creating a new world. She sees cars powered by sails, she sees a world without the need for medsen. She sees everyone connected through the Haze until there are no more strangers.

Jemma sees a little boy. It must be hers. When he smiles with his missing tooth, she knows that she will call him Apple.

She looks out into Ell Aye, and lets it pass.

The Parents built their world. Now we can build ours.

ACKNOWLEDGMENTS

Stephen King likes to say, "Write with the door closed, and edit with the door open," and for once in my life I'm gonna have to disagree with Steve. *Scorpion*, and *Mayfly* before it, have been mostly written and edited with the door open. I sought out advice and reality checks from an early stage, and it's all the richer for it.

My most important thanks go to Sunny, my wife. She claims not to be a writer but she's helped me with everything from plot holes to copy edits. We spent a lot of time sparring over words until finally I agreed to let her change things—and she agreed to let me ignore her once in a while. She let me take her on a cruise to Mexico just to finish a draft of *Scorpion*, even if it meant we never got off the boat. And during my first, most critical year, she gave me that hour between the kids' bedtime and our own to put the words on paper.

I'm also thankful to my children who, with their giant hearts and their crazy hormones, inspired me to write the children of Ell Aye. They made me see that if the future of the Mayfly series ever happened, the world would be in good hands. Charlotte even came up with the idea of the Archimedes Ray. Jackson, Mikey, and Charlotte, you're in these books whether you wanted to be or not.

Thanks to my agent, Cheryl Pientka, who has never given me anything but hope, and who sold *Mayfly* and *Scorpion* in seven days (!). And my editor and copublisher, Liz Szabla, who asked all the right questions and brought out entirely new stories within the world of the Holy Wood.

I've been guided by the smartest you could imagine. Vanessa

McGrady is one of my dearest friends after working together at a utility company for all of three months, and a conspirator in my love of drunken Irish karaoke. She loaned me her beautiful cottage in the mountains so I could finish *Scorpion*. She showed my manuscript to Cheryl, almost against my will, and gets almost full credit for the Mayfly series seeing the light. She says I owe her a trip to Hawaii after all this. Hawaii this fall, Vanessa?

Rachel Branwen, Lelah Simon, and Joy Allen are my cofounders of the Study Hall, our writers group in Los Angeles. They workshopped the entire first draft of *Mayfly*, and they kept me motivated to write every week during our Study Hall hours. I'm convinced there will be articles about this writing group someday; they're that impossibly talented. (Rachel hates "impossibly." She's just going to have to deal.)

I opened up the Mayfly series to a whole bunch of beta readers, and got invaluable advice from those who read it. Thanks to everyone who helped: Matt Rodriguez, my best friend who read the whole book out loud to his wife Sylvia (and later set one of my Holy Wood songs to music); Katie Stanger, who wrote my first blurb; Julie Ganis, who asked me about the books every time we chatted (and whom you should hire for all your fiction editing needs); Beth Mallino, a serious businessperson; Laval, Stacey, Christina, and Matt Sweat, who were the first people in my family to take a look.

Teachers matter, too, so I want to thank a few people who had an impact on me: Ron Bennett, my journalism and English teacher and perhaps the first person to inspire me to seek greatness. He claims he spotted this in me a long time ago, and I believed him. Walt Hackford was my government teacher, my basketball coach, and a guide for life. I've lost track of Miss Hansen, my first-grade teacher, but she spotted a story of mine written in the shape of a mixing bowl and told me I should keep writing. I did.

This is no mixing bowl, but it will have to do.